A Flash of Green

DAN, TO CATCH UP
GREAT TO CATCH UP
ON THE LAST 50 YEARS.
BEST WISHES!

Lew Kornek

A Flash of Green

A Novel
by: Lew Karrh

Copyright © 2017 Lew Karrh
Published by Gumbo Limbo Publishing

Designed by Vince Pannullo
Printed in the United States of America by RJ Communications.

ISBN: 978-0-578-19930-6

Dedicated to those who inspired this book and will never read it, to those who still might, and especially to John, Kelly, Rick and Babbie. Thank you for you for your patience and stamina.

GUMBO LIMBO PUBLISHING
THE QR SCANNER APP

Because I wanted to reference music in this story I began by adding the website locations to some of my favorite songs as played on YouTube, but I discovered it was hard to play them unless you were reading the book from a computer screen while on-line. This might become easier if an "E-book" option becomes available. I then became aware of the QR Code Scanner application. A free application which can be downloaded in seconds to your smart phone from the App Store. Once you acquire this application all you do is use it to scan the numerous QR Codes throughout this book. Within a few seconds the song will appear on your screen – available to play. I hope you will take advantage of this cool bit of technology. On the newest smartphones the QR Scanner app is already loaded.

I believe the addition of this music will enhance your enjoyment of the book, and you will discover songs that you will love, as well as re-discovering songs you already love.

Here is just one of the many sites you can find on Google:
https://www.scan.me/download/

I hope you enjoy reading and listening.
Also, please check out our website @:
http://www.gumbolimbopublishing.com

FOREWORD

Palm Beach proper is a sixteen-mile barrier island, and the eastern most city in Florida. Within its roughly ten square miles of land there are clustered an estimated ten percent of the richest 400 people in the United States.

Since its founding by railroad magnate, Henry Flagler, Palm Beach had grown accustomed to, and even bored with, the wildly famous and infamous. Presidents, tycoons, actors, and rock stars had all pretended to come there to get away from prying eyes and the supposed pressures of their mostly idle lives.

The Kennedys, America's closest thing to a royal family, had behaved badly enough to have their own chapters in the annuals of Palm Beach debauchery. In the decades since Papa Joe, about twenty minutes after prohibition was repealed, bought an eleven-bedroom hacienda in 1933, this modest casa with fifteen bathrooms, not counting the oft used Atlantic Ocean out the back door, eventually became the Winter White house on JFK's watch in the 60's. Shining a black light around the compound at 1095 North Ocean Boulevard, toward the northern end of the island, would demonstrate just how different are the rich.

In 1984, 28-year-old David Anthony Kennedy, son of previously dead presidential candidate Robert F. Kennedy, had turned up extremely dead at The Brazilian Court Hotel in accidental overdoses of Cocaine, Demerol (pinched from matriarch Rose's stash), and Mellaril. And less than a decade later the world had been held spellbound by the televised rape trial of William Kennedy Smith and the blue-dot concealed plaintiff – another not-so-great outing for a troupe of Kennedys led by the Lion of the Senate, Ted Kennedy and a bottle or two of his daddy's scotch whiskey.

Claus von Bülow, Roxanne Pulitzer, and the Fanjul sugar barons all sought their high-profile divorces in the courtrooms of West Palm Beach – just one drawbridge away. There is surely bad behavior in the colder climates of the north, as was displayed in another winter playground in Colorado, but when the temperature regularly drops below freezing, people tend to keep their clothes on in public, and do their laundry in the basement. After Claudine Longet got off with a $250 fine for shooting Spider Sabich to death in Aspen, she reportedly flew to convalesce, and to be consoled by Ethel Kennedy, who knew a little about recovering from the sudden death of loved ones. At the Palm Beach Kennedy compound, she was embraced in the understanding arms of the Palm Beach elite. There was something about the warm air and sea breezes of this island which seemed to bring Palm Beach sinners, and their sin-stained laundry, out to line-dry unashamedly behind the walls of their gated estates.

Head south past the homes of Rush Limbaugh and Rod Stewart to Mar-a-Lago at the southern end, the opulent Emily Post mansion, now occupied by extrovert Donald Trump, and you will unknowingly pass the domiciles of dozens of celebrities.

On one nothing-special Saturday afternoon, while strolling the half-mile stretch of world renowned Worth Avenue, one could encounter Jimmy Buffet strolling with his good friend Walter Cronkite. A hundred yards away, in different directions one might encounter Yoko Ono, Michael Caine, or Sophia Vergara. Mixed in among them within the small shopping enclaves, there were usually a dozen or so ordinary looking people who could buy and sell all those celebrities on a whim, and these transactions would appear as simple rounding errors on their balance sheets, that is except for frequent visitor Warren Buffet. It was just down the coast a few miles that Mitt Romney was caught on video among these same blue bloods scandalously denouncing 47% of the country for not being rich.

At the old-time favorite Palm Beach watering hole, O'Hara's, W.C. Fields, who reportedly still has three open checking accounts on the island, replied to someone who had used this line as an attempt to embarrass him into a more genteel demeanor, "You might be able to buy me my good man, but good luck when it comes time to sell."

As long as there were reasonable security provisions, wealth apparently liked to hang out with wealth, and, upon this rock-solid principle, the visionaries behind the Palm Beach Towers Condominiums built their non-denominational church. And the sales deacons of this ocean-side cathedral, while passing the collection plates, employed every variation of rationale to quickly sell the place out. Entreaties like these were used and believed, well, all but the last one, "What good is bread without butter?" "If you've got the scratch, I've got the itch." "You bring the green, I'll bring the bling." And the party-cooler of the group, "You can't take it with you." The rich, to a man, secretly took umbrage with this last truism, and they sincerely believed that when their time came, a loophole could be found, or an exception made, which would allow them to travel with silver spoons in place, to that golden place beyond the sea.

So, the greater and lessor of the upper class gathered their cash, securities, jewelry, and other valuables in the counting rooms and vault of The Palm Beach Towers, and dared someone to try and take it. **You know what? Someone did.**

The privately owned geostationary communications satellite designated Tango Gumbo Seven, or TG7, went about its business in utter silence 35,800 kilometers above the equatorial city of Quito, Ecuador. It was designed to receive and route communications traffic from both hemispheres to very specific land-based addresses at speeds approaching that of light. Sure, there was the intermittent and unavoidable delay of a few microseconds as the signal crossed mechanical relays, yet despite the gee whiz statistics of precision and the staggering speeds, one could still comfortably place TG7 in any metaphor concerning the proverbial watched pot. The blink of a hummingbird's eyelid was a crude equivalent to the speed at which the seventeen 512-bit packets of this encrypted message travelled to its three destinations. And while TG7 was not at all recalcitrant in its duty to communicate the news, or even mildly obstreperous at its post, two of the three recipients had been waiting for decades for this transmission and, having finally received it, travel plans were being made from Newark, New Jersey, and Buenos Aries, Argentina, to Palm Beach, Florida.

After thirty-one years the first news and clues of an unsolved multi-million-dollar, strong-arm robbery had surfaced, and despite enough elapsed time for the booty to have circled the globe many times, this first small trace was discovered exactly 1.29 miles from the site where the wait began. The legal statute of limitation for prosecution had expired more than twenty years ago, so other than curiosity, law enforcement organizations, from Interpol to the local constabulary, had no official interest, and as of yet, they were still unaware of the news. However, this brief blast of information also marked the resumption of mayhem and murder surrounding this brilliantly planned and prosecuted theft, which is known world-wide as **The Palm Beach Towers Robbery.**

If Johnny wanted to get in his "three laps at sundown" around the Palm Beach Gardens fitness course in December he needed to be running by 4:45. The course contained fourteen callisthenic and isometric exercise stations. Johnny only stopped at three of them as he ran the trail's one-mile length; 30 pushups at the first, 15 dips at the second, and 10 chin ups at the last. He figured that the running would take care of his wind and his legs, but he was a little self-conscious of what he considered, his skinny biceps. Whenever he got the chance his older, more muscular brother would tease him with his favorite jab, "Hey, you've got a string hanging from your sleeve. Oh, never mind, that's your arm."

He was not neurotic about achieving a personal best, but he did push himself and considered it a successful outing if he completed the three miles, and three sets of arm-work, in twenty-one minutes. After crossing the finish line, he would allow himself just a few seconds of hands on his knees panting before he walked to the oak tree where his towel and water bottle were stashed. He would ritualistically gulp two long pulls before making his way toward a picnic table where he recovered while enjoying the last fifteen minutes of the gloaming.

As he amused himself letting the sweat drops fall from the tip of his nose and flood out an ant hill between his New Balance cross trainers, a familiar voice fell upon him, "I purely love to watch you run."

Johnny Dendy's attention left the ant community to save itself, and he looked up to see Kathleen Rachel Callahan Montgomery, or more simply known to him as Katie. She was wearing running clothes, but she did not appear to be wet or winded, and he reasoned this encounter was not just a happy accident. She was here to see him, but he doubted it was to see him run. The last he had heard she was waiting out the last few months of the divorce process before she could return to the less contrived, and more convivial identity of Katie Callahan.

"It's not polite to make fun of your elders young Lady." He replied.

Katie joined him at the table and continued, "I'm not kidding. You look like a gazelle or an antelope, and you don't even notice all those guys you are passing out there who are trying so hard to get to the line before you lap them."

Johnny made a slight scoffing sound, took a sip from his canteen, and said, "OK Katie, first, a gazelle is an antelope, and second, you can put away the grease gun. What can I do for you?"

Katie could have protested and spent another hundred words defending her genuine admiration of the seemingly effortless way he covered the ground, but instead she just pulled her cupped hand from her windbreaker pocket, and extended it to him as if it contained something designed to surprise or amuse him. He reluctantly held out his open palm to accept whatever it was she was proffering.

Katie dropped a large diamond stud earring into his hand. Johnny held it aloft against the setting sun and looked at it for a moment and said, "You haven't gone back to rolling pirates again have you?"

Katie laughed and replied, "I wish. At least with a pirate you are pretty much guaranteed that their jewelry is real. I'm not sure the same can be said for my husband."

Johnny nodded and said, "So you're looking to liquidate a bauble or two?"

"Precisely."

Johnny said, "Why bring it to me? I'm all set when it comes to earrings, but if you've got a jewel encrusted dagger or a gold tooth, we might be able to do some business."

Katie explained her situation. One morning last week while laying out her options for fiscal independence, after a laughable attempt at updating her resume, Katie began taking inventory of her possessions and the items she could convert to untraceable and untaxable cash. Her first stop was her jewelry box. Most of its contents were either costume baubles or trendy pieces that were only worth their weight at the current spot price in the precious metals scrap market. After separating the few items which she truly treasured, such as several antique broaches, and an elegant cameo, from the things she never wore, she made a small pile of items to take to the jeweler. She then considered her engagement ring and matching earrings. She hoped these were valuable, but several points troubled her. Winston, her soon-to-be-former husband, had always taken care of the insurance, which presumably included a large jewelry rider under which the set would be carried. She had never seen an appraisal but had been repeatedly lectured about their value and her lack of responsibility, to the point she had stopped wearing them and had locked them in the wall safe of her closet. Since they were still squabbling over the financial details of their divorce, and she did not want to give Winston cause to further delay the final settlement, she felt with these pieces it would be best to go slow, but how? She had received unsolicited advice from several friends, but she felt these people, possibly fools, knew even less about how to proceed with this scheme than she did, and she had retired feeling confused and frustrated.

"I've got to figure out what I'm doing here."

However, an idea had arrived with the first rays of morning sunshine which she repeated to Johnny, "When I woke up this morning it hit me, I'll go see Johnny. I'll lay dollars to donuts he will know someone."

The sunlight was just about gone as Johnny handed her back the earring, stood and as the two of them walked back to the parking lot, Johnny said, "You might be in luck. I do know a guy over on the avenue we could go see."

"Do you think he is trustworthy?"

Johnny replied, "Not at all, but that's the sort of fellow you need in a situation like this. Don't worry, I'll watch him."

Katie giggled at the thought of getting some real cash and said, "Terrific. What would you think they are worth?"

"Let's not get too excited just yet." Johnny replied, "There are a lot of variables when it comes to diamonds."

Slightly offended, Katie replied, "I know about the four Cs."

"Yeah, but do you know what a pirate pays for his earrings?"

After a moment's consideration Katie had to admit she did not.

Johnny winked at her and said, "Buck an ear."

This silliness convulsed her a bit, and she staggered against him. He put his arm around her shoulder, and she slid her arm around his waist and as the last rays of that idyllic December day faded, they made plans to take a day trip to Palm Beach's famed Worth Avenue.

 Lake Street Dive – "What I'm doing here"
https://www.youtube.com/watch?v=lcUeothSPyc

Several days later Katie arrived at Johnny's modest office in West Palm Beach. While Johnny finished up a few phone calls, Katie busied herself with collecting the suit coats that were draped over file cabinets and chair backs around the cluttered, but clean, room. She found hangers and put them away in the small armoire upon which the too-big flat-screen perched.

As she nervously tidied Katie thought back over the years and her relationship with her lawyer. She had known Johnny Dendy all her life. He had lived just one block away in the old neighborhood. He was about ten years her senior and was a friend of her older brother. Her most memorable encounter with Johnny had happened when she was only eight years old and had crashed on her roller skates just outside Johnny parent's house. Aside from skinned knees and elbows, Katie had painfully sprained her right ankle.

Johnny had been coming out of the carport on his way to his job at the Food Pantry, but, to Katie, he seemed to appear from thin air. She was fighting back her tears as she surveyed the self-inflicted damage, but, as Johnny knelt beside her, the dam broke. Johnny smiled at her sympathetically, brushed a tear from her cheek, and said, "It'll be alright Sweetie."

After a quick triage, Johnny scooped Katie into his arms and carried her to the lawn chair on the front porch. Using the skate key she wore on a woven lanyard about her neck, he had gently removed her skates, secured an ice pack to her ankle with an ace bandage, and had cleaned up her scrapes with Unguentine spray. He helped her blow on the wounds to ease the sting, and by the time Katie's mother arrived in her Rambler station wagon, Johnny had Katie pretty well bandaged and laughing. As the years passed, and despite his neighborhood reputation as a tough guy, she clung to this gentle and caring image, and that one phrase.

Over the dozens of years that followed what Johnny mentally cata-
logued as the "I've got a brand-new pair of roller skates" incident, he had,
from a discreet distance, held a protective umbrella over Katie. One afternoon when Katie disembarked from her eighth-grade school bus Johnny
happened to see a middle-school bully intentionally knock her books from
her arms, and, when she attempted to fight back, the young Tommy Rotten
had laughingly, and repeatedly, pushed her down in the street. The next day
before school, Katie was perplexed by the same young hooligan's approach,
and contrite apology, which was accompanied by his sincere assurances
that, not only would this disrespect (a word he used liberally throughout
his brief, but sincerely remorseful speech) never be repeated, but no matter
what or who should assail her, he would, from this point forward, be her
steadfast champion.

Silently steaming with fury, Johnny had followed the little brigand home
from the bus stop, walked, without knocking, through the front door of his
house, grabbed a handful of the bully's curly locks, and dragged him out
the back door into his backyard. To get Tommy Rotten's attention, Johnny
had cuffed him soundly on his left ear, which set off a ringing in the boy's
head that lasted for several hours. He had pushed the hoodlum's face into
the sand, and repeatedly inquired, "Are you enjoying this as much as me?"

He then snatched the boy up by his collar, seated him forcefully in
a wicker chair, and insisted the two of them discuss, man to man, the
differences between gentlemen and ladies. Before ten minutes had passed
Johnny had explained that young ladies are sensitive and can be damaged
by a thoughtless act which a teenage boy might just shrug off. He had
calmly elucidated to the boy bully how an encounter with a beautiful young
girl like Katie should be considered the bright spot in his day, and that if
he had the sense god had given a goat, he should view just the sight of her
as a minor miracle, which at present he did not deserve. However, beginning with a brief, but sincere apology, he might be able to rise above a bad
start, and redeem himself in her eyes. After several rehearsals, Johnny felt,
that with continued practice, Tommy Rotten would be able to adequately
express his regret to her early the very next day. Before Johnny's departure,

the two shook hands, and, to re-enforce the points he had tried to make, Johnny delivered a single hard punch to the bully's shoulder as well as a steely-eyed glare, which implied both the threat and the promise of his continuing interest in the matter. Katie did not hear the back story for another three years.

Within a few minutes of her arrival they were in Johnny's 650 BMW headed east on Palm Beach Lakes Boulevard, and Katie asked about Johnny's friend the jeweler. "How long have you known this guy?"

"I would guess it's been twenty years since we played pick-up basketball on Sunday mornings behind Palm Beach Day School. He was just one of what the snooty members of the adjacent tennis club called "the unwashed horde"."

It was Johnny's turn to ask a few questions. "What do you know about these earrings? How long have you had them? Do they have any significant sentimental value?"

Not really knowing how to effectively make a long story short, Katie told Johnny the whole tale of how this jewelry came to her. Katie's failed marriage to a local real estate mogul had lasted some sixteen years on paper, but in reality, had withered before it had reached double digits. In the roughly fifteen months of courtship that had preceded her reluctant acceptance of Winston's proposal, she had been worn down by a steady stream of elaborate bouquets, expensive jewelry and nights on the town.

One night at Worth Avenue's ultra-exclusive La Petite Marmite, several shared bottles of Dom Perignon had created a warm and pliable mood. When she heard a slight clatter and murmur coming from the front of the French restaurant where they were seated, she turned to see a tuxedoed violinist making his way in her direction. The thought flashed through her mind, "Oh Goody, we are about to witness something special."

She turned to speculate with Winston as to what was going to happen and found him beside her chair on one knee. One second was all that was required for the circuits in her brain to complete the connections and force the realization upon her. Whatever was going to happen was going to happen to her.

Katie felt her face and neck begin to flush and as the violinist started to play La Vie en Rose, the music was slightly muffled by a soft but persistent voice in her head urging her to run away. In the years that followed, she consoled herself with the knowledge that her marriage was built upon this contrived series of atmospheric enhancements. Under the pressure from the suddenly silent dinner crowd who held their collective breath and the waiter who stood ready to fill her champagne flute - even the guy who had been hired to play the fiddle was urging her, with, what now she now considered, inappropriate and unprofessional nodding, to accept this thoroughly romantic man, she caved and nodded her consent. The restaurant went crazy.

 Laura & Anton - "La Vie En Rose"
https://www.youtube.com/watch?v=-NK9zdPj-os

Strangers embraced her and assured her she was the luckiest girl on the planet as they admired her new the flawless 4.89 caret Marquise-cut diamond ring. Several of Winston's buddies appeared with cigars for the men and roses for the ladies. Half a dozen corks popped as the wait staff charged everyone in the room's glasses. The violinist broke into, "Yes sir, that's my Baby," and the crowd sang along raucously. She had to hand it to him; Winston knew how to put on the dog. And as she had thought of it for the past decade or so, that was the night she was engaged to be buried.

Over the intervening years, whenever Katie heard either of these songs, she was transported to that point in her own yellow wood, before she made her choice of which road to take, and she always wondered if the other road was still available for her to travel. How did T.S. Eliot put it? *"Footfalls echo in the memory, down the passage we did not take, towards the door we never opened, into the rose garden."*

After a glamorous wedding, as a wedding gift for the bride, Winston handed over the massive diamond stud earrings which matched the engagement ring and tipped the scale at 3.25 carets each.

Those earrings marked a turning point in their relationship. Katie noticed the almost immediate reduction in Winston's attention level. He was spending the same amount of after-work time in the bars, but without her. Many of her home-cooked meals were eventually saran-wrapped and refrigerated and then reheated and served the following day as her solitary lunch. Surprisingly, the more time Katie spent alone, the more she preferred her own company. When she gave birth to her daughter, Fiona, her serenity and solitude were complete, and, as the beautiful little girl grew, so did the bond between mother and daughter. Fiona adored her father, but if there had ever come a need to choose between her parents, it was a lead pipe cinch that she would choose Katie.

Katie's husband was a good provider, and he spoiled Fiona with just about everything she might need or want: private schools, current fashions, elaborate dolls and their houses, ballet, piano, and gymnastics classes, braces – the list of things he provided went on and on. Upon discovering that Winston had provided Katie with a case of chlamydia, Katie provided him with a guest room accommodation, and herself with a new lock on her own bedroom door.

When Fiona turned sixteen she received an early admission to Sarah Lawrence College. On the tearful ride home from taking Fiona to the airport for her departure to the plush school in Westchester County, New York, Winston and Katie replayed milestone memories of the only thing they now had in common. Just before she slid out of the car in the garage back home, Katie handed Winston the business card of her divorce attorney and asked him to move out.

Fiona would never want for anything, but despite his deep pockets, from that day forward, as far as Katie was concerned, Winston had developed short arms. Fortunately, over the years Katie had been very inventive with the milk and egg money. The same year that Fiona left for school, Katie's secret Cayman Island M&E account passed the six-figure mile marker. She thought she would do okay financially in the uncontested divorce settlement but felt she still needed to be frugal.

As they parked on Worth Avenue, she summed up the story, "So that is what I know about them, and as for the sentimental value, the only sentiments I hold for them are unwanted memories."

"Plus, you are the one who is always saying, "God bless the child that's got her own."

 Blood, Sweat & Tears – God Bless the Child:
https://www.youtube.com/watch?v=04rClGsbWp4

Johnny steered Katie by the light grip of her elbow to the small shop in a charming Via off Worth Avenue. The neat gold lettering on the front window proclaimed Glenn Marietta – R.J., I.C.G.A. as well as the current Vice President of the Worth Avenue Merchant's Association. To Katie, the sign and the display cases bespoke the discreet reliability she sought, but Johnny knew Glenn had worked hard to suppress a series of nicknames he had acquired as a street-wise tough kid, and would have preferred just about any of these monikers to the one that stuck, this descriptive epithet given him by the Newark Arson Squad some twenty-five years earlier.

He had liked being known as the "Whiz Kid" for his ability to disable alarm systems, and did not mind a slight notoriety as the "Boy Bandit" during a brief spell as a second story man, but the one that stuck was far less flattering. He had been labeled for his supposed expertise with the proprietary wrench used to tighten, and in Gaspipe Glenn's case, to slightly loosen the high-pressure flanges of the New Jersey natural gas system. These minor manipulations were soon followed by a spark in the dark, a devastating explosion, three to five alarm fires, and large insurance settlements.

Johnny and Glenn exchanged a little small talk before getting down to Katie's secret business. All she wanted was a confidential appraisal of the quality and value of the earrings which she had brought along. Glenn softly whistled his appreciation of the stones as he inspected the studs through his jeweler's loupe, and then he suggested that they make a GemProof recording which would allow Glenn to better appraise the earrings.

Sensing her apprehension, Johnny asked Glenn to explain the process in layman's term, which he did. "You know that no two diamonds are exactly the same, right?"

Katie nodded, and Glenn continued, "Using a special three-dimensional camera, the GemProof precisely measures and records the size and cut of each stone and the style and composition of the mounting. It also detects any imperfections and occlusions. Using this data, and comparable stones from recent sales in its data base, well the process is automated to the point that the value almost falls off the end of the page. It's a secure, privately owned system, so it's confidential."

Within a few minutes the recording was completed and the earrings were returned to her with a promise to be in touch with Johnny within a few days. Noticing what seemed like a furtive glance between the two men, Katie thought they might know more about this, and each other, than they were disclosing to her. However, she comforted herself with her belief, without a doubt, that, with Johnny on her side; it would be alright.

Two days after his visit to the Palm Beach jeweler, at just after ten o'clock, the phone by Johnny's bed began to ring. He lifted the receiver before the second ring. A coarse whisper conveyed a note of immediacy and a sense of dread. The voice on the other end of the phone began, "Johnny, its Glenn. Some serious shit is going down – I suggest you make yourself scarce."

Johnny tried to clear the rum induced fog in his head as he stammered, "Glenn, Glenn who? What time is it?"

The voice increased in volume and in urgency, "It's Gaspipe, and it's time for you tell me what the hell you got me into."

"Meet me as soon as you can at the Pump House. Come alone and you might want to go serpentine to make sure you're not being followed." The phone line went dead.

As Johnny pulled on jeans and a dark blue sweatshirt, he thought back through his recollections of the pump house from his childhood memories. This structure which the Army Corps of Engineers used to keep the Palm Beach inlet free of silt by dredging the floor of the 400-yard opening to the Atlantic Ocean between Palm Beach and its northern neighbor in the barrier island chain, Singer Island, had been on line since the late 50's. A fine mixture of sand, rocks and seashells were pumped onto the Singer Island shore as part of the Corps' on-going beach replenishment.

The pump house and the adjacent beach had also served as a rallying point for the local surfer clique, which could be quite territorial. About half a mile up the beach The Amaryllis, a 441-foot Greek cargo ship was driven ashore by the winds of hurricane Betsy in 1965 and became an instant hit for surfers and tourists. The angle at which it had been beached created the most perfect wave conditions in the vicinity, but it was cleaned up and cut up before being towed off-shore about a mile and sunk to form an artificial reef three years later. The surf craze died out except for the hard-core shredders, and they returned to the dependable shore break of the pump house.

If you were not a known quantity to these over-tanned stoners, you needed an invitation, or a serious attitude. These often-bloody confrontations eventually prompted the Palm Beach Shores PD to declare the area within 300 yards of the pump house Private Property – No Trespassing! The signage posted, which contained threats of imprisonment and hefty fines persuaded everyone, but the surfers to find another beach. Since the goal of the police was to prevent gang-like turf wars, and the surfers were now the only gang that ignored the ordinance, a wise police chief reasoned if there was just one gang, there should be no fighting, plus he thought it was better to know where these delinquents were, than to disperse them, and not know what they were up to. As a nod to mutual tolerance the surfers maintained the area, kept the pump house clean of all graffiti, and the beach was pristine. Problem solved.

Johnny recalled many happy afternoons bobbing on his board or riding home-made plywood "apple boards" which were used to skim the shallow water along the beach on calm days. At nineteen he had eagerly relinquished his virgin status to a lovely wahine on that very beach under a grand harvest moon. That was a treasured memory, which he frequently revisited. However, returning to the present, tonight's rendezvous fairly crackled with the promise of unspecified danger.

Johnny parked on a side street about two blocks from the beach. He jogged the distance while trying to stay keenly aware of anything that might seem out of the ordinary. Unlike the balmy moonlit night when, after a liberal application of Herc's rum-based panty remover, Mandy Revere had surrendered herself to Johnny's inept advances, tonight was moonless, and the surf was rough, and the approach to the pump house was shrouded in shade. He found a dark corner near the levy from where he could observe the pump house cove while remaining unobserved himself. Within a few minutes a flame from a butane cigarette lighter illuminated the face of Gaspipe Glenn.

Johnny watched as Glenn inhaled and exhaled the smoke twice and flicked the largely unsmoked fag into the sea. Oddly enough, just that morning he had heard an article on NPR in which a study suggested that a smoker finds less enjoyment if he could not see the smoke as he exhaled and tended to smoke less in that sensory deprived atmosphere. "I'll be damned."

Apparently, Glenn had not heard about this study, and before he could shake out another coffin nail, Johnny grabbed his wrist and stopped him from lighting another butt. "What are you, a fucking chimney?"

Startled, Glenn recovered his poise quickly and nudged Johnny further into the shadow of the pump house, and up the ramp to the steel double doors. There he produced a pry bar and swiftly breeched the old lock. The salt of the sea spray had taken its toll on the bronze hinges, and they protested loudly at the fifteen-inch pivot of the door. The two stepped into the pitch dark of the control room, and Johnny commented nervously, "It's as black as the inside of mule in here."

Glenn clicked on a small Maglite flashlight, which illuminated the machinery and sent weird shadows dancing around the cylindrical poured concrete building. He cracked, "Better to light a candle, heh?"

Aside from lighting the dredge's machinery, the small light beam also revealed the bruises on Glenn's face. Actually, the bruises would not reach their apex of color for several more days, but even in this poor light it was apparent that Glenn's nose was off center and a mostly dry blood trail meandered from one nostril. Johnny noticed a nasty contusion upon his left cheek and the lobe of one ear was torn. "What's the other guy look like?"

Glenn tried to smile, but a grimace superseded and exposed the two broken crowns of his front teeth, which created a comic whistle as he whispered, "There were at least two maybe three. They got me down fast and started whipping my ass good."

"What were they after?" Johnny asked.

"Those fucking earrings you ask me to appraise!"

"I tried to explain that I didn't have them, but they made it clear with a switchblade," he said gesturing to his ear, "It was the earrings or blood."

"How did you get away?"

"Well, like I said, they had me down on the floor in my shop, and I looked up, and there was my .32 which I had placed under the display case in a quick release holster for just such an eventuality." I said to the ham hock on top of me "Okay, I'll talk."

The one who had the knife put it away, and the one called Rocco gets off me, and says to his partner, "I told you these jewelers are pussies. You knock out a couple of teeth, suddenly his memory gets better, and he's ready to spill his guts."

"Well I come off the floor blazing! I shot the guy with the knife twice in his leg – I was trying to shoot his balls off." Glenn chuckled, "Then the other guy throws a chair at me, before I can recover my balance to plug him, he drags his pal out the front door. I got off a couple more rounds, but that little gun ain't too accurate at more than ten or fifteen feet. I might have winged the other one – not sure."

Johnny's mouth was more than slightly agape, his lower jaw had dropped, and his eyes had never been so open, "Do you have any idea who they are, and how they found you so fast?"

Glenn whistled his reply through his broken teeth, "I have been giving that some thought, and it has to have some connection to that GemProof print I took of the earrings. As they were running away I heard one of them say L'il Augie ain't gonna like this."

"I thought that GemProof was a confidential inquiry." said Johnny, "and who the hell is L'il Augie?"

Glenn looked around the equipment room nervously as he fumbled with a stylishly compact gold lighter. It occurred to Johnny to comment to him that those gaspers were going to kill him, but in light of Gaspipe's past few hours, he suppressed that urge. Instead he calmly took the lighter from Glenn and held the flame to the end of a slightly crumped Lucky Strike.

Glenn inhaled deeply and let the smoke escape through his mouth and his single undamaged nostril, and then he thoughtfully replied. "GemProof is a private database housed in Edgemont, New Jersey, and it's supposedly secure, but I doubt it would be too hard to crack. The speed with which this search propelled these violent inquiries means somebody has those earrings flagged in the system, and I'm guessing that once the flag went up, L'il Augie was notified. Hell, I don't even have the results of the inquiry! I was expecting it in the morning mail."

Johnny reasoned a moniker like L'il Augie did not originate on the Princeton Lacrosse pitch or from the storied halls of the Vienna Boys Choir. No, and when you feed in the variables of New Jersey, thugs in black leather with fists the size of canned hams and semi-secret information, the conclusions one is forced to consider quickly arc toward a sinister minister of an organized crime family.

As this sequence of logic worked its way through the maze of rapidly firing synapse in Johnny's brain, a small spark of fear sputtered to life. He spun on his heel and blurted out the two salient questions, "What did you tell them? Do they know my name?"

Glenn flinched, but just a little, and replied, "We did not get that far in the conversation. I've been going over it in my head, and I'm certain I did not give you up, but…"

The fear spark in Johnny's brain had now grown to a flame about the size of a match head, "But?"

"Well the GemProof form has a spot for a reference ID, and I put in JD. I don't think they got into my files, but if they did, your card was paper-clipped to my hardcopy of the GemProof form."

"You didn't mention Angela, did you?" Johnny had added a little insulation by introducing Katie to Glenn with the single word nom de guerre of Angela.

Glenn was now taking an inventory of his tender ribs and facial bruises, and Johnny had to bring his focus back to his questions, so he grabbed his stained, and tattered cashmere sweater front, shook him a tad more violently than he had intended, and snarled into Glenn's battered face from a few inches away. "Did you mention Angela?"

Glenn demonstrated a distain born of past encounters with far more dangerous inquisitioners. He softly pried Johnny's fingers from his torn and blood-stained clothing, winked, and said, "Easy Boy. You're wrinkling my lucky sweater!"

Willis Laird and Johnny Dendy had been close friends since they were 10 years old, in a neighborhood where swarms of kids played tackle football with as many as 20 players on each side. They had both been small for their ages, but they were also athletic and wiry. At an age when testosterone and abundant energy compelled the almost daily physical confrontations which determined the neighborhood social hierarchy, they more than held their own.

Johnny Dendy was built like a young greyhound, but he had the heart of a full-grown wolverine. He could run you down and then kick your ass! Johnny knew all about double-jointed leverage – Now you've got him and suddenly now you don't! He could slip just about any hold and get behind you. Having Johnny behind you was the proverbial worst-case scenario. In fact, the fight was probably in its final throes.

Johnny had always been quiet and shy, lean and lanky. While he was comfortable in his own skin, his clothes did not seem to fit him. Like just about every kid in the neighborhood, he had an older brother whose hand-me-down clothes made up the bulk of Johnny's wardrobe.

Johnny's older brother was about five years his senior and named Hercules. Herc, as he was known, was indeed a physical specimen, with a broad muscular frame, dirty blonde hair, which was oiled and combed into a James Dean sort of ducktail. In fact, Hercules consciously imitated the motorcycle riding contrarian. He worked as a mechanic in a local garage and most of his income was poured into his work-in-progress '53 Studebaker Starliner. Undoubtedly, Herc had not just an image, but a vision splendid of how the shabby restoration would eventually emerge, but despite all the hours and skinned knuckles he invested, the car's appearance, to the casual observer, did not change. It was painted a flat black primer, the engine was loud and coughed clouds of smoke, which inexplicably varied in color from white through the entire grayscale spectrum to jet black. One afternoon he had whimsically hand lettered, in white, it's new, mystical name: Black Moriah.

Please pardon this digression, but Hercules was a formative influence on Johnny's fighting style and on his general philosophy of life. Johnny took poundings a plenty when Herc could catch and hold him, but more often than not, Johnny would pull a Houdini type of escape and run away. Just before his flee impulse took hold, he would deliver a very effective blow or two with his fist, elbow or knee. By the time Herc's vison had cleared, Johnny had become a quickly receding point on the horizon.

Most of the kids in the neighborhood knew that if you were chasing Johnny Dendy, you were probably the one in trouble. After a pursuit of 200 yards or so, you had fallen forty yards behind, so you gave up, or so you thought. Your hands found themselves gripping your thighs, lungs blowing like a Tin Lizzy, and as an after-thought you might yell weakly, something like, "That's right, run away you Chickenshit!" However, this was where it all changed. Johnny began a long arcing turn and before you could register what was happening, you looked up to see Johnny coming at you like a crazed mandrill. Johnny had never started a fight, and he sometimes turned and walked away from fights, but his high-speed retreat was simply the prelude to an ass whipping, and most of the guys only needed one to understand that Johnny Dendy was a guy with which you wanted to establish, if not an outright friendship, at least, detente.

Like himself, Willis knew it had been years since augments with Johnny had been resolved with fists. Johnathan Whitney Dendy, Esquire was a now a respected litigator and the widowed father of two girls, young women really. Danni (Danielle on her birth certificate) was a 25-year-old, former high school track star, and Melanie Dendy was 15 months older and still the holder of the Florida high school state record in girl's pole vaulting. They both lived in Nashville with their husbands and knew Willis as their father's law partner and as "Uncle Will".

When Johnny's wife Sheila was thrown from her horse, a high-spirited, high-stepping thoroughbred, she had bounced right up, and despite a nasty contusion near her right temple, she had caught the temperamental beast and remounted. She spurred the animal into a gallop that he held for three or four minutes, and then the winded horse acknowledged her supremacy, and Sheila could enjoy the last half of her ride through the winding trails of the Wellington Equestrian complex. It turned out to be not only the last enjoyable moments of her ride, but also the last moments of her life, period. Unknown to her, she had sustained a concussion which had led to a brain aneurism, and that event ended her life while she sat in her car in the parking lot looking through her purse for an aspirin.

Since his daughters were both riding scholastic scholarships at Vanderbilt at that time, Johnny was unable to face their empty house, and had put it up for sale and moved in with Willis. They spent the next three years, which they referred to as "The good Old Daze", reverting to their adolescence with every manner of game and contest they could contrive. In the half dozen years since Sheila's death they had been fixtures at local golf courses and pick-up basketball games, and the two-for-one happy hour buffets had accounted for a good thirty-five percent of their sustenance. Although Johnny eventually rented a nicely furnished apartment nearby, he still kept a small wardrobe in the guest room, and often spent the night.

Willis Stanton Laird, the namesake of his mother's favorite uncle, and the second oldest of five siblings, was scraping the last of the shaving cream and whisker mixture from his chin as the cloudless sunrise announced the official beginning of the new day. Years before he had built an outdoor shower which he loved for two reasons; it served his primal need to be naked outside, and it did not disturb whoever might be sleeping inside.

As on most days, he had longed for the dawn for several hours before it appeared. He had been a chronically poor sleeper since childhood and since it was all he knew, he had made accommodations to his insomnolence. When he awoke, usually after just a few hours of unsatisfying sleep, he would walk out to the backyard pool, swim a few laps, and sit with a diet coke on the steps in the shallow end. Over the years, he had slowly become proficient at naming the constellations of the northern hemisphere, and he knew the schedules of the annual meteor showers and moon phases.

From the pool Willis' pre-dawn circuit took him to his garage workshop where he would apply the next coat of primer or varnish to whatever project might be in the hopper. Over the years his neighbors and occasional roommates had persuaded him to avoid using the noisier power tools which interrupted their eight hours of peaceful slumber, at least until the sun was casting shadows and the newspapers had been delivered. So, Willis quietly played about with tooled leather and wood burning projects during his early hour ramblings. When accused of being nocturnal by nature he awkwardly nodded his nolo contendere to the charge, but to him the word nocturnal meant alone, and often it meant lonely. He had long ago adopted the first stanza of the 1970 Brewer and Shipley protest song "Seems like a long time" as his pre-dawn anthem:

Nighttime is only the other side of daytime
but if you've ever waited for the sun
you know what it's like to wish daytime would come
And don't it seem like a long time
seem like a long time, seem like a long, long time…

He had witnessed many a sunrise while softly singing these lyrics to himself. Willis had a nice signing voice, but like his skillful use of power tools in the hazy predawn light, no matter how melodic or lyrical, if it fell upon sleepy ears, it came as an intrusion, and, thus, was unwelcome.

 Brewer & Shipley – Seems like a long time
https://www.youtube.com/watch?v=cdCKjfVwfzc

His ruminations on the song's meanings were interrupted by an amused, if hushed, voice, "Please cover that stuff up. No one wants to see that first thing in the morning."

He turned to see Johnny's grinning face craned around the lanai enclosure and replied, "No shit! That's why I shower out here – no mirrors. I can go weeks without having to see it myself."

Johnny uncharacteristically abandoned this vein of humor and said, "Get dressed. I need to talk to you."

Willis finished rinsing himself of the suds, turned off the shower, and quickly toweled himself mostly dry. He pulled on shorts and a tee shirt, and found his friend in the garage. Johnny was busily covering his 650 BMW with the canvas which usually covered Willis' partially restored 1970 El Camino 396 SS. The El Camino was standing in the driveway. Johnny said in his typically matter of fact, minimalist way, "I need a fresh ride. Someone may be watching for my car."

Willis nodded his consent. As he seated himself on one of the rolling hydraulic stools nearby, he asked, "By somebody, do you mean somebody's husband? How goes the search anyway?"

"The Search" was their term for Johnny's dating pattern. Johnny possessed all the attributes of an eligible bachelor except one; he could not suppress his need to compare every woman he met to his long-lost love, Sheila. Within a few dates Johnny would, more, but usually less, gracefully, withdraw from further contact. He would use some sparse variation of "very busy at work, got a lot on my plate right now, it's not you - it's me", and then just disappear.

Johnny responded in his slow and easy way, "It's nothing like that, plus, as far as that stuff goes, you know," Willis laughingly joined him in completing the sentence, "I'm just trying to avoid the heartaches that can plague a man."

Johnny continued to transfer the electronics of modern life and their accoutrements from his car to the El Camino, whose designers, while artistically and mechanically progressive, and possibly even futuristic, had not even briefly glimpsed a need for satellite guidance, global positioning, prepaid turnpike transducers, or Blue tooth cellular connectivity. Johnny selected a variety of cables, splitters, adapters, and transformers from the glove box, "I hate to admit it, but I need all this crap to get me through my day."

Willis inquired, "What sort of day have you got planned?"

The final items Johnny slipped into the black canvas satchel were his Glock 26, a sleek 9mm semi-automatic pistol and two ten-round magazines. He saw Willis' raised eyebrows and replied, "Listen up. Let me catch you up on a couple of things."

He said very quietly, "I've stumbled into something dangerous, and I have no idea how it's going to end."

Johnny continued, "Several days ago a friend asked me to help her discreetly find out the value of some jewelry her husband had given her. I made a few calls and then took her to see Gaspipe Glenn who took some photos and for comparable sales value, he made a routine inquiry to an international database called GemProof. Ever heard of it?"

Willis shook his head and Johnny continued, "Well before you can say Bob's your uncle, the town gets thick with Brooklynites wanting these particular earrings. Let me tell you, they were not abiding by the Marquis of Queensbury rules. Glenn got the snot beat out of him before he managed to get ahold of a gun and shoot his way out."

Willis, who in the past had done a little business with Glenn, commented, "Trouble follows that guy around like an old dog. Whatcha gonna do now?"

"Good question," said Johnny. "I've been waiting for the sun to come up so I can check out the scene of the crime. I hate walking into blind alleys in the dark. That's the reason for the car swap and the artillery. Glenn has a way of leaving out important details which can get a fella shot full o' holes."

Like the dawn air, Willis was warming to the adventure, "Don't forget the .45 under the seat and the sling shots behind the passenger seat. I keep two jars of bolts and nuts with it. Those 3/8" nuts fly pretty true, and will raise a lump on whatever they hit. There are also some larger odds and ends that really pack a punch"

As 14-year old kids they had discovered the almost silent devastation which could be wrought with a relatively inexpensive slingshot which was set up for hunting. The regulation ball bearing ammo was too expensive to waste on stop signs and street lights so they used the drawers of spare hardware from their garages. Both of their fathers were depression kid packrats, and each knew the value of hardware, so they could not throw away the pounds of screws, bolts, nails and nuts they had accumulated. Between the two garages one would be hard pressed to name a fastener that they could not eventually produce.

One slow Sunday afternoon in autumn, they had ridden Johnny's Honda 50 out to the west end of 45th Street where older boys went to race their cars. There they found what they thought to be an abandoned '56 Ford. In the space of ten minutes the two of them had launched over fifty projectiles each into and sometimes through the car, breaking every window, headlight, and tail light on the vehicle. They agreed that had they been armed with Thompson submachine guns, they could have scarcely done more damage. Then, realizing they should clear out, they mounted up and headed for home.

The next day in school Willis had overheard two seniors talking about a car which had split a radiator hose while racing at "The strip". They had gone back into town to get a part, and when they returned thirty minutes later, the car had been "shot to shit". There must have been $2,000 worth of damage. The conclusion drawn by the car owner was that those punks from Northshore High had been spoiling for a fight, and by god, they were going to get a lot more than they wanted after school that very day.

Johnny and Willis agreed that this was a secret they would take to their graves. On the rare occasion when they did refer to the incident, they used the one word reply General Anthony McAuliffe made to a German demand for American surrender in the Ardennes – "Nuts!" But rather than the heroic refusal to surrender in what seemed a hopeless situation, they were referring to the 1/2 and 5/8-inch steel nuts they had used with their slingshots to decimate a car and ignite a gang war.

Johnny looked over his collection of gear and dropped the sack of goodies on the passenger bucket seat. He checked the glove compartment of the El Camino and found a pair of binoculars, an old racing form and a package of animal crackers. He considered the odd collection for a moment, returned it to the box, shut the door and spoke to Willis, "See what you can turn up on a mob guy named L'il Augie. He might be from New Jersey, but tread softly, it looks like he's plugged into the web, and if you catch his attention it comes with a whole lot of hell."

Almost as an afterthought Johnny pulled open a drawer of the work bench and extracted several Florida "Horseless Carriage" license plates. He and Willis had stumbled across a small loophole in the Florida's vehicle registration bureaucracy; once a vehicle has reached the age of twenty-five years, the owner was eligible for a tax-free tag from that point forward. As a result of no revenue being associated with these tag renewals, there was no real effort at reconciliation and even the tags of wrecks could be renewed under the name of the last owner of record, even if that last owner was deceased. They had bought a couple of these wrecks for spare parts and had renewed the registrations which gave them several tags for 1970 El Caminos, and each had a different home address in the official vehicle registry. Johnny selected the one with a Lantana address and quickly changed the rear plate, "I probably am being too paranoid, but I don't want a bunch of mouth-breathers showing up here."

Willis replied, "Good thinking. What is your plan?"

"It's a three-point plan. One: do a walk by of Glenn's shop. Two: if possible recover the GemProof form. Three: Pick up Glenn's mail to see if the report came back on the earrings.

Willis suggested a fourth step, "And get away clean."

As he pulled away from Willis, his mind kept circling those last four words, "and get away clean." There was a germ of an idea there – would it be the worst thing if he were to pick up a tail? See who's mixed up in this?

Corina Virginia Dare awoke one Saturday morning with a fuzzy sensation there was something different about the day. She resisted the urge to dress for the gym and elected to go for an easy run instead. All her life Corina had been fit, but when she was younger her physical condition had been a side benefit of her passion, and her passion had been surfing. From an early age, she had been regarded as a local Phenom, a goofy-footed, toe-headed jockette who could practically samba on a surfboard. At the age of seventeen, she had traveled to Costa Rico to compete in a three-day international women's surfing competition. She had performed as advertised in the first two days and had qualified for the semi-finals, but, on the final day, the wind turned from a moderate on-shore breeze which produced beautiful six to eight-foot waves that were eminently rideable to a strong off-shore gale which produced huge, surly rollers of twenty-five feet or more. Corina had been tentative on the first few rides on the final day and found herself in fourth position out of the four semi-finalists. She knew she would have to be more assertive in the afternoon sets if she hoped to reach the finals, and, after lunch on the beach, she paddled out with that mindset.

She dropped in on the largest wave she had ever seen, much less ridden, and, in less than two seconds, began a vicious wipeout. During the initial fall, her left arm had become tangled in her board's tether and her elbow hyper-extended, tearing a bicep tendon, and then dislocating her shoulder. She had somehow avoided the jagged coral out-cropping of the shallow reef, but the force and volume of the wave had forced her underwater and held her there. After being submerged for more than ninety seconds she was able to fight off the loss of consciousness and battle her way to the surface. There, her surfboard was thrown into the air by the turbulent wave action, and, when it returned to the surf, it struck her skull, dealing her a nasty cut and rendering her unconscious. Fortunately, a pair of alert life guards on a powerful jet ski saw she was in trouble, and charged into the froth to scoop her up and get her to the medics on the shore.

Corina's recollections of her rescue were muddled. If a theme could be woven from the coarse threads of flickering imagery, the mental weavings she could summon lacked substance and dimension; the colors of the incomplete tableau were the crimson of an ebbing life force splashed with garish flashes of the sudden and searing white of heat and pain interspersed with inexplicable sky-blue panels of flight and the perplexing yellows of urgency and all contained the charcoal stitching of terror. The last panels of this iridescent tapestry were colored in the pink and green of life and hope and love.

Her next reliable image was of her mother's tear-streaked face and the antiseptic aroma of her bed in Hospital Clinica Santa Rita in Costa Rica's capital city of San Jose. Over the next few days her mom gently reminded her of the accident and the surgeries required to repair her torn rotator cuff, ruptured long-head bicep tendon, and that her head felt funny because of the deep laceration her scalp had sustained. She repeatedly filled in the gaps until the anesthesia and morphine laced fog cleared in Corina's mind.

Corina's shaved head eventually sprouted hair enough to conceal the fifty-five-stich scar about two inches above her right ear. Another two years of thrice-weekly physical therapy sessions were required to regain the full strength and mobility of her left arm, but by then she had lost her nerve, and, without that, her world ranking was also gone for good. As she had learned in counselling, she had eventually made peace with the past, and her focus had become building hope for the future.

Since her recovery Corina found comfort in the routine of her workout, but she retained a phobia of drowning, so among her exercise rituals she hid, perhaps even from herself, an isometric component of breath holding which might extend her life underwater by as much as two full minutes. Nowadays as a strong swimmer and free diver, she felt comfortable skimming the coral reefs just off Palm Beach at sixty feet below the sea's surface, and Corina could, and usually did, linger, but as a safeguard, she stopped short of conspicuously loitering.

Her wrist watch captured and recorded each step of her morning run, her blood pressure, as well as her astoundingly low pulse. After a little more than a mile her heart purred along at eighty-five beats to the measure. As she ran that morning, she considered the advice both Lacy and Katie had proffered, "If you don't slow down some, how are you going to hear what your heart has to say?" A good question, and in recent years, it had been the one question and conversation she had intentionally avoided. It had become its own protest song with a poignant alto line, along the style of the Slim Whitman version of The Prisoner's Song "If I had the wings of an Angel, over these prison walls I would fly. Straight to the arms of my mother, and there I would willingly die."

Corina's mother had fallen prey to some foul cancerous wasting disease, and as the youngest of five sisters, it fell to Corina to help her beloved mom make the final crossing. During her mother's last six weeks Corina had hardly left the bedside; as often as not, at some point during the night she would curl in close on the hospital bed to comfort them both. The thought that her dearest friend should have to die while alone in that sterile place made her discard the usual "outside the bedrails" protocol observed by everyone else and allowed her to hear her mother's whispered memories and to whisper memories of her own.

Corina somehow countered inconsolable with pick yourself up and survived the funeral service and wake. She was continually rocked over the next few days as she sorted through her mother's lifetime of accumulated memories and mementos. Each drawer of several file cabinets contained not only her mother's generation of well-ordered documentation, but there was also copious representation of her antecedents and descendants with the periodic post-it note in her mother's wonderfully precise cursive, which concisely explained or mused upon on a folder's content and import. It was some consolation, and Corina felt her mother's calming hand upon her shoulder, but whatever consolation she found was sad consolation indeed.

Slim Wittman – The Prisoner's Song:
https://www.youtube.com/watch?v=ym_sYjjw4bM

On this peculiar morning, just two weeks since the funeral, as she ran the cart paths of a local country club, a persistent feeling came over her - It's time to start enjoying the time she had left, which meant it was time to discard some things. The list started with just a few items: one stoner boyfriend, two dogs which had been casually foisted upon her by her daughter who was passing through town on her way to the Keys, three minor friends who had become squatters in her apartment, and the four months of back rent they owed her. Upon her return to the cluttered flat, she roused all the lazy dogs and had a quick meeting. Ignoring the sleepy protests, she announced her plan, "I'm driving down to the Keys today to see Jenny and I'm taking the doggies, so say goodbye to them because Islamorada will be their new home."

She paused a few seconds to let the opening statement register and then continued, "While I'm gone, figure out how to pay me the rent, grocery and utility bills you owe, and clean up this pig pen. When I get back, I expect to be able to see the carpet and have $4,200 on the counter."

She packed a cooler and all the chew toys, flea treatments, heart worm medication, and leashes and whistled up the two Labradors saying, "You want to go to the beach?" Out the door they went despite the protests of the apartment's other occupants.

She felt a little weary, but as she hit the on-ramp to I-95 the radio accommodated her need for energy with Grace Potter and her sultry "Goodbye Kiss" which confirmed Corina's belief in the charms of music to soothe the savage breast. Her spirits lifted like a weather balloon and within a few minutes she felt she could see past her troubles and over the horizon to a brighter future, and a fresh start where her problems were separate from other people's problems. "What would be wrong with just looking out for me for a while?" she wondered aloud.

Grace Potter & the Nocturnals – Goodbye Kiss:
https://www.youtube.com/watch?v=MkLjw6j_9BQ

She thoroughly enjoyed the visit with 20-year-old Jenny and her 23-year-old boyfriend. She helped prepare a blackened hog snapper with mango salsa as a late lunch, and, about two hours before sundown, she announced that it was getting late, and she should get ready to go. As she expected, the two young lovers went to collect the dogs playing on the beach. She waited just long enough for the sliding door in the rear of the house to close before she rose and exited through the front door. She made a neat stack of doggie possessions on the porch and got into her car. Corina had parked with a quick getaway in mind and within ten seconds of stepping from the front porch she was driving back toward the mainland sans dogs. Within another 45 seconds her cell phone began to vibrate and did not stop until she reached the JW Marriott in Miami. She spent a couple of days enjoying the spa, room service and the stainless steel lined pool on the 7th floor.

While sun bathing and swimming she tried to unclutter her mind. What did she want? For the most part, she thought of herself as content spending time alone, but she also knew that she did not want to spend her life alone. After several strolls through local green markets, several massages and several meals alone, she began to separate the activities of solitude from the ones in which she wanted a singular companion. If she had had a clipboard, a series of questions would have been jotted upon it.

Was there a person lurking beyond her vision of tomorrow? Did she already know this individual, or did some particular corner await where a comically accidental collision would thrust her into the arms of that certain someone? Was there any move she might make to speed her to this intersection? She came away from these days of introspection with two resolutions. The first was to avoid her usual haste in settling for Mr. Right-now while she sought Mr. Right. The second was to take a hand in the pursuit of her own happiness; she was going to look up, and hopefully finally hook up with, Willis Laird.

To her surprise and delight she found the apartment cleaned and empty of people with $3800 on the kitchen counter. A better result than she had hoped although her temper spiked a bit as she read the IOU for the missing $400 from Charlie. She knew she was more likely to see the return of Haley's Comet before that money, but hopefully that minor debt would have him avoiding her. She kept her momentum and quickly packed everything she owned into eighteen 18-inch cardboard boxes. She then persuaded her older brother to store the perfect 54-inch by 36-inch rectangle under a tarp in his garage. She did not yet have a fully fleshed out plan, but, before the week was out she would, and her life would not include much from her current situation.

When she did look at her phone she found 37 voice mails, 21 texts and an even dozen emails. All but one of these communications were from the group of demons she was looking to exercise. The one call she returned was to Katie, who had written a very thoughtful note expressing her sympathy and extending an invitation to join her for a night of revelry under a single ground rule. After the first five minutes, tears would not be tolerated.

It was during this wonderfully cathartic night of wine and brownies, she learned of Katie's divorce scheme, and the two secretly hatched their cohabitation conspiracy.

Corina was the only co-conspirator Katie had. The weekend after Winston moved out Corina had moved in. Over the preceding years of Winston's exile to the guest room, he had upgraded everything. He had expanded the space to double its original size, added extensive/expensive bathroom fixtures which included a large walk-in shower with half a dozen shower heads which could be individually aimed as well as a remote-controlled steam unit. The two women spent the entire first day scrubbing the "Winston stink" from the suite, and as they finished Corina's spirit sagged a little and she said, "Well, here I go again, starting over again."

Katie knew exactly the way Corina felt and offered a tired and tattered platitude, "Give it time."

Corina bristled a little recalling similar advice, given at low points throughout her life, and quoted a lyric from a Brandi Carlile tune they both loved. "Someone told me a lie. Someone looked me in the eye and said time would ease my pain."

 Brandi Carlile – Cannonball:
https://www.youtube.com/watch?v=tBYOECquvl0

"Sit tight. Maybe we can give time a nudge," Katie said and hurried out of the room. When she returned, wrapped in a new white terrycloth towel, she brought an ice bucket containing a pricey bottle of Bordeaux lifted from several cases of Winston's collection and tossed a matching white towel to Corina. Katie then turned her attention to the steam shower control, setting it for thirty minutes, she discarded her towel and carried the ice-bucket to the tile bench inside the glass shower enclosure. She looked over her bare shoulder at Corina and giggled, "Let's get this party started!"

Corina was naked and at her side before Katie could get the cork out of the bottle. She took a long slug directly from the bottle, leaned back against the cool ceramic tile, whistled and said, "Good stuff".

Katie was constantly amazed at her friend's jock moves and nonchalance. "It's a good job that you are pretty." She shook her head in mock distain and took a pass at the bottle herself. "Winston would probably say you should let that breathe."

Corina replied, "To hell with that, it's finally your turn to breathe!"

The two girls laughed their way through soaping each other's backs and discussing the things to which they were looking forward in this exciting next phase of their lives. They took an oath not to settle just for the sake of company. They would go slow, and the next men they would kiss must, at a minimum, have style, smarts, as well as looks.

"One thing I'm going to do first thing tomorrow," Corina volunteered, "I'm gonna get ahold of Willis Laird and invite him to meet me for a drink. I've always liked the way that boy looks, and he's been on mind lately."

 Over the Rhine – Entertaining Thoughts:
https://www.youtube.com/watch?v=VZGZS0Qly80

Katie thought for a moment, took another slug from the bottle, and replied, "I don't know him very well, but he is good looking, and he's certainly smart enough. Do you think he's a good kisser?"

Corina nodded her agreement, "I hope so. He's kind of quiet, and I think he might be deep."

They both had lists of things they were happy to be rid of, as well as lists of things they had missed. Katie volunteered, "I miss kissing. Not a peck on the cheek or lips, but full contact making-out."

Corina agreed readily, and bolstered by the wine, Katie said, "Let me show you how I like to kiss." She started tentatively with a light kiss, and a flick of her tongue. She followed these with kisses containing slightly more urgency. Corina, never one for half measures, enthusiastically escalated the action to the point that not only were their mouths fully engaged, their soapy bodies also slid, frictionless, against each other.

This was the first time since college that either of the women had experimented within same sex affection. If asked, both would deny that this harmless release was lesbian-desire driven, or that they were now on the road to a same sex marriage. At this point in their reentry into the world, men, as their hard-earned degrees from the school of hard knocks had taught them, are mostly pigs, and had to be approached carefully. They were both washing away decades of mistrust to discover layers of longing for what they defined when they awoke from a short nap, "There is just no substitute for intimacy."

Willis was pleasantly surprised at the urgent message a courier had delivered around noon that day. Once he opened the courier company envelope, he found a folded note card. The front was comprised of two words engraved in gold lettering; An Invitation. The inside of the card was somewhat less formal, in fact it was printed in crayon with several misspelled words and a couple of backward letters. After reading it several times and pausing to laughingly wipe the tears from his eyes, he picked up the phone, and citing a sudden family crisis, he asked his secretary to reschedule his last appointment of the day.

My deer Willie,

Pleeze meat me at about sun-down @ the Honey Comb Hideout today.

I need zum legal advice!

Come alone if ya no whut's good fer ya.

Yur pal
Corina

Willis arrived at the proposed rendezvous. A sunset meeting at an open-air bar/restaurant, which flourished despite the warm beer and cold food, had been agreed upon. There was a cluster of large electrical cable reels which were topped by crude thatched umbrellas; there were also several fire pits, which were encircled by light-weight stackable plastic chairs, which fit the mood of the place. The parking lot, the restrooms, and the large thatched roof building which housed the main bar were attached, more symbolically than physically, by a boardwalk of weathered planks. It meandered through the beach sand and palm trees to approach the seaside structure, which to Willis, resembled a traditional Hawaiian long house. The timber frame construction was quaint, functional, and cheap. If the whole place blew away, which as a result of the recent storms had been more than a threat, it could be replaced in a matter of days and back on station, serving the public. The Honeycomb Hideout, as this latest rendition called itself, saw its primary role in the serving of said public, as the last opportunity for a libation before one encountered the vast Atlantic Ocean.

On the horizon, he could make out the silhouettes of several cruise ships under steam toward the Bahamas. From the speakers, positioned atop several tall poles among the tables, poured the liquid gold voice of Lani Hall singing "Sundown Lady".

 Lani Hall – Sundown Lady:
https://www.youtube.com/watch?v=FStTzPAOn5g

As Willis scanned the seaside, a cool, but paradoxically sultry voice inquired from behind him, "If you had to choose, would you rather have a cold beer or a hot chick?"

Willis paused a moment before turning to find Corina leaning against one of the reel tables. The sinking sun backlit her silhouette and displayed her athletic figure through her gauzy white halter dress. She was holding two bottles of beer and her expression said she was waiting for an answer.

He smiled at the sight and replied, "That's a tough one. You can't always get a cold beer."

Corina feigned shock, laughed, and closed the ten feet of distance between them. She handed Willis one of the beers, slid her empty hand around his waist, and planted a lingering kiss right on his mouth.

Willis savored the kiss for a moment and said quietly, "So you've already abandoned detached and aloof?" He took a long pull from the Corona which hit him hard and his eyes began to tear. An involuntary shutter coursed his body. When he could speak, all he could muster was, "What the hell?"

Corina giggled a little and confessed that she had added a lime-flavored vodka floater to the beer and warned him, "A man of your advancing years should be a careful with hard liquor in the bright sun."

"Don't I know it!"

With surprising strength, she used the one arm she still had at his waist and leverage like that used in judo; she nudged and guided him to a pair of stools by the table as she playfully slapped him on the back, as if to help him resume breathing. She got him positioned on the stool which also had the effect of bringing their eyes to approximately the same level. She stood between his legs, apparently comfortable with the dozen inches that separated his slightly bewildered brown eyes from hers, which twinkled a mischievous green. "Glad you decided to post," she said.

Willis smiled and replied, "How could I not? Your invitation was both elegant and compelling – it read like a sonnet."

Corina laughed and said, "Good, cause that's what I was going for."

Willis added, "Plus as an officer of the court, I am duty-bound to help bring the law to every corner of this country, or at least this county. Just what is this legal opinion you seek?"

Corina demurred slightly, but just slightly, and said, "Well, it's a question that has been on my mind for quite a while. All my friends tell me you are brilliant, and that you are the one to ask, so here goes. Can you think of any reason we shouldn't get to know each better?"

He should have expected this sort of candor from Corina, but it still caught Willis off guard, and despite the strength of his vodka enhanced beer, he took another sip to give himself time to formulate a response. At last he asked, "Intriguing. How much better were you thinking? After all I am considerably older than you. Do you think it would be appropriate?"

Corina's face flushed a bit and replied, "When we first met, it might have been a problem, but I was eight and you were eighteen. In my opinion, that's not nearly the problem it might have been thirty years ago. I mean you can tell from the invite that I'm done with my schoolin' n book learnin' now. Whatdaya say?"

Willis produced the invitation from his suit pocket, looked it over one more time and said, "You've got me there. Why don't we discuss this over dinner?"

It was true that as the decades since they met had slipped past, Willis had watched from a safe distance and cheered as Corina had developed into a world class surfer, and a beautiful woman. Perhaps those ten years of difference in age had lessened the starkly inappropriate contrast, and had moved Willis from a cradle robbing sophisticate with a fixation on a young athlete, to a dignified ARRPie with a crush on a Milf.

Despite his care at keeping his distance, the observant could see a constant, wistful, longing and a slight flush in his face when they shared the very occasional chance meeting. There was always a spark, which had to be concealed, or camouflaged in whatever the group dynamic. They had never been alone in just each other's company, until now. Still Willis felt certain this age difference would eventually decide everything.

 Leo Kottke – Corina, Corina:
https://www.youtube.com/watch?v=VCg2VMtTF9c

Alight knock at the door interrupted Corina's perusal of a two-page questionnaire which Willis had concocted while she had slept. It was neatly lettered in pencil and contained at least a dozen questions. She was lying on her side and was wearing panties and a tight tank top. She removed her reading glasses and watched as the door opened slowly. Katie craned her head through the crack and said, "Oh good, you're awake."

Corina moved a little further across the king-sized bed and motioned for her friend to join her in the warmth under the covers. Katie slid into a spooning position at her friend's back. She moved Corina's hair aside so that she might read over her shoulder and as an after-thought, kissed her lightly on the neck.

"Glad you made it home. That was some storm we had last night."

"It rained most of the night at the Honey Comb Hideout", Corina agreed, returning to the task at hand.

"What are you reading?" Katie said as she continued to snuggle in closer.

"It's this compatibility questionnaire Willis came up with – he worries physicality is not enough."

Just before their own physicality moved them from solid to semi – liquid, they heard the cacophony coming from the rear of the house that signaled their recent and hopefully, temporary roommate Lacy, was fighting her way toward consciousness. This noise had a rich blend of random minor crashes of medicine cabinet contents mixed with an intermittent splash or curse.

Lacy Walden possessed an odd dichotomy of passions. Her day job was assistant manager to a local bail bondsman, and her specialty was "skip tracer", which required her to find and follow the bonded-out felons who knew their case to be hopeless, so they did their best to disappear. The finding and following was performed from an office downtown via computer and telephone. These guys usually made the same bonehead mistakes with credit cards and relatives in distant cities and were caught within hours of her involvement, but despite her aptitude for the work, it held little interest for her.

The long hold times associated with collecting data over the phone allowed her to discover her gift as an artist. Her pencil doodling soon developed into full-fledged art, and she was suddenly in demand as a portraitist. She accepted a few commissions from friends but quickly discovered she was selling pieces of her soul, and that she preferred to keep this talent to herself.

Her other passion, which indirectly led to the vacating of her own home, came to her when she sought an interesting exercise to control her weight, and upon a friend's suggestion, joined an evening self-defense, mixed martial arts fighting class. While she had little interest in fighting or sparring with live humans, she found almost immediately that she love, love, loved punching and kicking the heavy bag. Her hands were quick and her kicks, propelled from what her class mates referred to as her hockey butt, were devastating, and they all agreed she belonged on the first list, of which there were only two. It was a simple list, and called the A list, of the toughest people you knew, and encountered in daily life, stack ranked as to those you would lease like to fight. The second list, B, was made up of those you wouldn't mind facing in combat. Lacy consistently ranked in the upper half of the A list.

She had recently caught her husband in an affair with a new arrival to the neighborhood. Lacy had stopped to pick up some Chinese food, and had then come home from work, rather than attending her usual evening workout. She had walked into the house and followed the obviously amorous sound emanating from the guest bedroom where she found them entangled in an elaborate Karma Sutra Dancing Cranes position. The suddenly interrupted lovers quickly abandoned this intricate arrangement shortly after Lacy announced her arrival by firing the steaming container of moo GU gai pan into the headboard, covering everything, and everyone with mono-sodium-glutamate-free stir fry with duck sauce.

Lacy's husband Dave had then mistakenly tried to approach and placate her. He walked into a flurry of haymakers culminating with an uppercut that caught him flush on the chin. His eyes rolled back, and he sagged, blood mixed with curry seeping between his fingers, and he groped to contain the vivid pain in his jaw. He had slumped into a neutral corner, and had assumed the less erotic, but infinitely more defensive armadillo position.

Even with the passage of time it seemed unlikely that reconciliation could ever occur after this withering corporal onslaught, but as severe as the physical beating had been, Lacy's verbal assault was even more violent, and promised a scorn reminiscent of Death Valley.

"I might be able to get past some of this rage if she were she some young, hot, thing, but she is a pig. She's a fucking pig, and you're a fucking dirt bag!"

In a bit of rational thinking, she fled the domicile before the cops responded to the panicked 911 call she heard being placed behind the locked bathroom door, by the new neighbor. She felt, with some justification that Lacy might turn her wickedly fierce onslaught to her. But that was three days and 26 martinis ago, and while she still simmered and sputtered toxins, Lacy was starting to re-open the curtains of gloom to let other people, and their light, into her life.

As they heard Lacy coming down the hall Corina pulled away from Katie's embrace and her own disappointment. She retrieved her glasses, and returned her attention to the compatibility questionnaire, "Who is David Clayton Thomas?"

Lacy staggered into the room and ricocheted from the dresser to the dressing table and fell backward onto the bed and rolled to a stop on the other side of Corina. Corina pulled back the comforter to let Lacy clamber in beside her friends. Laughing almost hysterically, Lacy offered, "Wasn't he a civil rights leader in the 50s and 60s in New York? Why?"

Katie hit the high points of the compatibility quiz and they exchanged furtive glances filled with incredulity. After a few seconds Lacy asked, "What happens if you fail?"

"I get sent to bed, without desert, to pretend I'm asleep." Corina said, smiling enigmatically.

The El Camino was kind of blue collar looking, with a couple of quarter panels which sported some bondo and red primer. It gave the impression that this might be a work in progress, and, perhaps, a carpenter's daily driver. However, over the past three years, Johnny and Willis had poured a small fortune into this restoration. Their last find had been a used set of sixteen-inch mag wheels which had come with competition Pirelli radials already mounted. These had been salvaged from a totaled Porsche 928, but once the boys at Let's Roll Used Tires on Tamarind Avenue had polished them up and performed a high-speed balancing, they looked as clean as new money, and the El Camino cornered like a cheetah in track shoes. To the header system, Willis, who detested loud cars, had added an extra set of Glas-Pak mufflers, which may have robbed a few horse power from the 396 Super Sport engine, but they made the exhaust almost silent, at least until the tach crossed 3700 RPM and the four-barrel Holly carburetor kicked in. Johnny reasoned that once that happened, no one would have to listen to the roar for long, because the car would soon pass one hundred miles an hour, and not only be out of earshot, but also out of sight.

The license plate it now displayed had come from a similar El Camino whose driver's number had, for whatever reason, been up one sunny morning about eighteen months ago. Benny Bigalow had entered the world on the second day of 1934; the second son and third child to Oklahoma corn farmers. It would have been hard to imagine a tougher time or place to start out. Most people must read John Steinbeck to get a sense of the terrible plight of the refugees of the Dust Bowl. Not Benny. His older siblings had succumbed to respiratory failure, commonly referred to as "dust pneumonia". He came up tough, but alone; he invented his relatives and claimed he was first cousin to drought, his uncle was blight, and that, as a child, the gritty dust devils were his only playmates.

His family joined the tattered masses on the road to California's lush valleys, but when they reached the coast they took a hard right and eventually found their way to Canada. After a few false starts, they broke into the fur business, where they flourished.

Benny had been a pretty wild guy in his younger years and, by his own admission, had chased it hard. He was still recognized in his late seventies as a man to be reckoned with, but to anyone who knew him well, it was apparent that he had at last found contentment in his fifth wife Consuelo.

The last morning of his life had begun with a breakfast of shredded wheat, strawberries, and black coffee. He was planning to meet a couple of guys to explore a new venture, sending container loads of used clothing and five-gallon jugs of cooking oil to the Bahamas. Alas he never made it to that appointment. He had always parked behind his small farm house, and this morning was no different, but for one small exception. After a laughing kiss and grope with his wife, he took his coffee and started to circle the house and then out onto the two-lane Lantana Road to drive east under the turnpike overpass. Consuelo noticed that he had forgotten his wallet and hurried out the front of the house, just in time to stop him, hand over the billfold, and tease him about how forgetful he was becoming. This slight delay had put him in fate's cross hairs, for driving west on Lantana Road that day was a two-ton flatbed truck, which was towing a trailer carrying a backhoe. As was later discovered in the police investigation, the driver of this truck and trailer had just left the Inlet Bar after a couple of "eye opener bloody Marys". He had not noticed that the boom of the backhoe was raised to the point it would not clear the bottom of the overpass bridge. Speeding to recover a few minutes of bar time, the bucket hit the bridge at almost seventy miles per hour miles and toppled the entire machine off the trailer. Benny happened to be under that same bridge and the offending arm of the backhoe sheared the roof cleanly from the rest of his vehicle.

Thanks to the love he had found late in life, Benny's head was filled with happy thoughts and a young man's plans when it was severed from his body by the tumbling farm equipment. Consuelo, however, could not forgive herself for delaying him those few seconds, which, as she saw it, had cost him his life, and had cost her all her past and future happiness.

Johnny had learned some of this story while buying the ruined wreckage of Benny's El Camino from the insurance company and then, he made a point of introducing himself to Consuelo to make certain she had proper legal representation in this egregious example of wrongful death. Once he dug just a little below the surface of this tragedy, the insurance companies of the large highway construction company, and the equipment rental company who owned the offending backhoe were quickly brought to heel. Johnny learned Benny was the third such victim of Lantana Road's killer bridge, which was almost a foot lower than required, and lacked proper signage to warn of this deficiency. He still represented the Bigalow family in an ongoing law suit versus Palm Beach County and the State of Florida which promised to bring additional punitive damages, and very expensive alterations to correct this deadly, and previously identified deathtrap.

Following a grand funeral which was very well attended, Consuelo planned to return to Guadalajara after sprinkling Benny's ashes around the twenty-acre farm they had both loved. The farm still sat vacant, although Johnny had helped her establish a trust from the proceeds of the large settlement to care for the small house and grounds surrounding it. Despite the graphic gore associated which Benny's exit from this cruel orb, upon the reflection of the "never knew what hit him" suddenness of his ending, Johnny thought, "All in all, not a bad way to go."

Johnny made a point of being in the neighborhood at least once a week, and he would stop in to check for vandalism, clean out the mail box, and refill the automatic barnyard fowl feeder. Most of the farm animals had been given to neighbors, but a few chickens and ducks had gone feral, and he felt a duty to see they did not starve. In particular, there were three white ducks which had remained and still inhabited the small half-acre lake behind the farmhouse. Consuelo had given him keys and encouraged him to make whatever use he could of the quaint little ranch style house. She had left all their furniture and appliances in the hope that time, would indeed heal her fractured heart and she might one day return.

Johnny had stocked the bar with a fine Mexican rum, and the freezer with Blue Bell vanilla ice cream cups and State Fair corndogs. He tried to time his visits to coincide with sundown, when he would sit with a rum drink on the back-porch swing and consider the issues, large and small, that were on his mind.

 Tim O'Brien – Late in the Day
https://www.youtube.com/watch?v=RtfWq_ev3RE

After half a dozen such visits the white ducks began to lose their fear of him and would approach to within a few yards of the porch. Although he, or no one else could tell them apart, he whimsically named them Huey, Lewy and Ed Smith after two of Disney's ducks, and the third he named after the captain of the ill-fated Titanic.

He felt comfortable and content there. He had occasionally spent the night, and, each time he did, he had been awakened by what he could only describe as a warm and benevolent presence, and at precisely twelve thirty-four a.m. – 12:34 on the bedside digital clock, which, at first had bothered him, but after he had calculated that this was the numerical representation of Benny Bigalow's birthdate, a secret he kept to himself, and now he viewed this as a welcome intrusion and a lucky omen.

J ohnny thought his reconnoiter of Glenn's shop should take a graduated approach. He cruised nonchalantly down posh Worth Ave affecting the persona of a sleepy craftsman on his way to the job. He was again on alert for anything out of place. He took a casual glance down Glenn's via and could detect no anomaly, so he made the block and parked on an adjacent street to return on foot. On this pass he a slung a small backpack over one shoulder which he hoped would give the appearance of a man with a purpose. He reached the smashed front door of the shop and observed a dried blood trail on the cobblestones and several smears on the pink stucco walls. Johnny noticed the tempered glass of the front door was in ten thousand pieces on the ground, but the door was locked, and thought, "How odd." Keenly suspicious and on guard, he slipped through the door frame and went directly to Glenn's small desk where he found, almost immediately, the GemProof form and his card which was still attached. He pocketed the form and then perused the stack of mail and, sure enough, there was an unopened window envelope from GemProof. Mission accomplished; now to get away clean.

As he drove across the Royal Palm bridge back to the mainland, he believed he had, indeed, picked up a tail. The sparse early morning traffic did not allow much cover and Johnny noticed a steel-grey sedan about three hundred yards back. Aside from the souped-up El Camino, he had several other advantages over those who followed him. Chief among these advantages was his intimate knowledge of the local streets and alleys of West Palm Beach. As soon as he cleared the bridge he turned right, and as soon as the corner of the building hid him, he goosed the accelerator, turned immediately into an alley, and parked behind a delivery truck. The sedan sped past with two passengers who seemed to have their heads on swivels as they scanned the streets. Johnny waited a few seconds and repositioned his car for a hasty exit, and then he concealed himself behind a large green trash dumpster. As he had suspected, the grey car was soon creeping down the alley. When it came almost abreast of the dumpster, Johnny released the manual wheel brake and shoved hard. The twenty-five hundred-pound, garbage-filled steel box quickly gained speed on its downhill run and slammed into the side of the villains' automobile. The force of the impact caved in the driver's side door and pinned the car to the building on the passenger's side. While it had not been his preference, Johnny had been prepared to do battle with the men he took to be gangsters, they were at least temporarily trapped in their car, so he hastily made a new plan.

Using his cell phone, Johnny took a photo of the license plate and quickly put in a call to the WPB PD drive-by shooting hot-line and reported multiple gunshots and several citizens down. He then scampered to his car, and still unseen by his pursuers, got away clean.

Inside the steel-grey sedan pinned between a dumpster and a building in a West Palm Beach alley Rocco and The Mic tried to gather their senses and sort out what had just happened. Although they had not seen the thin man in the El Camino, this series of events seemed too bizarre to be random. After a second or two Rocco tried to force his door open, but to no avail, the dumpster was solidly in place, so he tried reverse until smoke billowed from the spinning tires. He then slammed the car into low gear and stomped the accelerator. The fenders ground in the pinch, but the car made no real progress - the men were trapped with unregistered firearms and had to find a way to quickly get rid of them. Rocco was able to lower his window enough to allow him to toss their guns into the dumpster. With any luck the cops would not discover them. About the same time as L'il Augie answered his phone, the alley exploded into lights and sirens. Rocco and The Mic had just enough time to say they would call him from jail, L'il Augie said, "Don't bother. I'll send someone. Just keep your mouths shut."

As he disconnected, he muttered to himself, "How hard could it be to tail a guy and get his license plate number? I've got to upgrade my known associates file."

Johnny had watched the drama play out through the binoculars from the third floor of a parking garage about two hundred yards from the crash site. While he watched, he nonchalantly ate the small bag of animal crackers that had been in the glove compartment. Within three minutes, the boys in blue had arrived, and, within twenty minutes, they had extracted the two stranded men and had put them in the rear of separate cruisers and departed. Presumably they would get to answer additional questions at the precinct HQ.

Barely ten minutes later, Johnny was driving north on 1-95 with the two handguns he had retrieved from the alley. He had also used a little double speak and misdirection on the tow truck operator and had fished the rental agreement from the console. While he had no precise plan for their use, three things had occurred to him. First: Willis could probably make some hay with the rental agreement, second: the gangsters would have to rearm themselves, and third: he now had weapons with the finger prints and possibly the DNA of his enemies in a plastic bag behind the seat – they might come in handy.

On the way north, Johnny hit number 111 on his speed dial, "Wil my boy, I think I may have poked a hornet's nest!"

Willis did not doubt it for a second, and he replied, "You don't know the half of it. Meet me at the library on Military Trail and Northlake."

Willis had attempted to check out L'il Augie via Google, but before he could refine his search criteria his firewall detected an attempted breech. He shut it down quickly and whistled, "This guy really likes his privacy!"

About the same time that Johnny and Willis were reading the GemProof research document at the public library, L'il Augie was accessing the West Palm Beach Traffic Surveillance Network. He was searching for information on the mystery man who had made fools of the fools he had sent to Palm Beach to recover what he had come to regard as his property.

As Johnny and Willis read the report they discovered the earrings were among the vast treasure of jewelry which had been stolen in the Palm Beach Towers heist of 1977. They were reported along with a 4.89 caret diamond ring as having been taken from the plush condominium's private fault of safe deposit boxes in a carefully planned, and still unsolved, robbery. Aside from Katie's jewelry, which was very nice and, according to the report, had been for insured for $40,000, there was another seven million dollars of property taken.

A quick Googling of the Palm Beach Towers robbery yielded the basic facts of the case. Apparently three men dressed as security guards had entered and overpowered the solitary and aged Palm Beach Towers guard around midnight and spent the next five hours forcing open eighty-five of the one hundred forty-four safe deposit boxes within the vault. The robbers probably would have breached the rest of the boxes but for an alert newspaper delivery man, who noticed the locked front doors and the vacant lobby. They saw him hurry away and assumed he was off to blow the whistle, which he was.

By the time a Palm Beach Police cruiser arrived to investigate, the merry band of heist men had fled, leaving the switchboard operator bound hand and foot in the ransacked vault. Her only companion was an old man who had signed up for seven graveyard security shifts a month, because his wife had applied for, and had been granted, every credit card that the US Mail took the trouble and time to deliver. She had then maxed out each of them in support of a particularly egregious TV evangelist. The combined unsecured debt totaled an astounding $74,450. He was able to settle this debt for $8,300 cash, ruined credit, and a compulsory program of compulsive behavior therapy. His wife left him for the lucrative business of the Second Coming money laundry. Golden years, my ass.

After a thorough investigation, in which the Palm Beach PD declined help from the FBI, no substantial leads were developed or pursued. Insiders spread rumors that the actual total of stolen property was more than five times the reported seven million dollars. The missing millions went unreported supposedly because much of this wealth did not officially exist. Eventually the seven-year statute of limitations expired without a whiff of a lead, and was now a case on par with the Great Train Robbery or the Lufthansa heist, but since there was no chance of prosecution, it no longer held any interest for law enforcement.

Johnny and Willis were genuinely perplexed as to what should be their next move. Despite the use of a library computer, they were concerned about sending out a beacon on the internet on which L'il Augie might be able to home. Willis had checked with a friend who earned his keep as a private investigator. After disclosing their fears about being digitally tracked from New Jersey or closer, the P. I. suggested using a ricochet – bouncing the inquiry through a series of servers around the globe - that should buy them fifteen minutes to an hour of search time before they could be traced. For a nominal fee ($150) he provided a URL and login credentials.

As they logged in, Willis started the stop watch on his phone. They would not stay connected for more than ten minutes, and, as an extra precaution, as soon as they logged out, they would be prepared to skedaddle. Willis typed in L'il Augie New York/New Jersey and depressed the enter key. After a few seconds Google listed some 743 hits. Willis set about printing the results while Johnny skimmed the first few articles for pertinent information. It seemed L'il Augie, age 47, was the eldest son of Augustine Amato, a crime family honcho out of Newark, who had been the victim of an attempted coup d'état which had consigned him to a wheelchair, the lower half of his body paralyzed when a bullet creased his spine. After a short, but very bloody, reprisal, the insurgents were discovered and eliminated. Apparently, Augie the younger had a real aptitude for vengeance, and, with the help of a small, but vicious, group of psychopaths who were tagged AA Newark, he made it known that going forward, he was in charge, and those who crossed him would do so at their own peril.

"Why is a Newark gangster tracking three pieces of jewelry from an unsolved robbery that happened more than twenty-five years ago?" asked Johnny. "It seems like a lot of effort even if they are worth the hundred-grand mentioned in the appraisal."

Willis was packing up their notes and printouts, but paused as something important clicked into place. "His old man must have had some link to that crime. If he had planned it, he would probably know where the loot is, but if he were among those who were robbed, he might be holding a grudge." He thought another minute and continued, "What if Katie's rocks were the best clue to solving the crime?"

Johnny jumped right into this line of thinking, "What if they were the first clue?"

Willis took it another step, "He is not after Katie's jewelry. He wants to know where she got them."

They looked at each other and, in unison, blurted out, "Winston!"

That December morning, Winston sat in his underwear, reading the sports section of the Palm Beach Post, at the kitchen counter of his large, and, apparently expensively furnished apartment in West Palm Beach. He did not often disclose the second-hand nature of his accoutrement, but he knew the fickle attitude of the wealthy and had placed himself adjacent to the stream of quality, if slightly last season's retinue. Italian leather with goose down cushions from a Manalapan charitable thrift shop cost him a tenth of its value, and what he actually paid became a tax deduction. Ninety-year-old Art Deco case pieces by Ruhlmann and Leon Bakst were tripling the annual appreciation of his best performing index funds, plus he needed something on which his 70" flat-screen might perch. The art on the walls and the sculpture in the corners began, for him, as tax shelters, but he now knew, and appreciated, the ahead-of-their-time, Pollack and Chagall. When he thought of it, which he rarely did, he chuckled because he knew they appreciated him right back, possibly 25% per annum.

His attention was focused on the point spreads of the Hawaiian Holiday Basketball Tournament, which would kick off that afternoon. He liked Duke giving nine and a half points to Iowa. He marked the line with a yellow high lighter, folded the paper, and then began stuffing it, and several changes of clothes, $5,000 in twenties, and his shaving kit into a small carry-on bag for this trip to the Bahamas, where, among other errands, he planned several days of deep sea fishing. Thirty years ago, Winston's circumstances had been significantly different.

Winston Montgomery had grown up as a slightly spoiled, slightly smart kid in Palm Beach. His parents were on the tail end of a family inheritance which, if they watched after it carefully, would get them comfortably into their coffins. While Winston was clothed by the Prep Shop, Worth Avenue's haberdashery to all things adolescent, he earned his spending money as an assistant tennis pro during the season, and he had worked a number of construction jobs during the summers. He had served as the low man in the labor pecking order on such physically demanding jobs as a concrete finisher for the long and winding driveways that sometimes ran hundreds of feet and consumed truck load after back-breaking truck load, of high strength concrete ready mix.

Perhaps the dirtiest and most physically demanding job he ever mastered was swimming pool construction. During these twelve-week breaks from Palm Beach Private, a snooty prep school where most of his class mates summered with golf in Ireland, or skiing in Peru, Winston worked alongside Mexicans who supported large families with a meager $7.45 hourly wage. He had formed lasting friendships with young men, only a few years his senior, whose education had stopped before they had earned a high school diploma, and he became keenly aware of the wealth gaps all over the island. He actually enjoyed the jobs for the practical knowledge of construction he acquired, as well as the impact the work had on his view of the world; this was no way for a grown man to earn a living, and when he rejoined his class each September, his tanned and muscled body supported the "how I spent my summer vacation" claims of rock-climbing in the high desert of Utah, or smoke jumping in Yosemite. By the time he had acquired a basic understanding of most of the trades, he had also achieved his law school's scholastic ranking of 138th out of 276 of his classmates; precisely the fiftieth percentile, and he had also developed several lucrative sidelines which nicely dove tailed with his Juris Doctoral education. After passing the bar exam in Florida on the third attempt, he had added the traditional, if somewhat snooty enhancement of Esquire to his stationery to please his mother.

Winston had formed a closely-knit triumvirate with Chelsey Koch, number 206, and Bradford Hennessey, number 267. What these three lacked in scholastic accomplishment they more than compensated for in wily street smarts. What do you call a law school graduate who finished in the bottom ten percent of his graduating class? After several slurs concerning

his poor scholastic achievement, and a few questions regarding his understanding of the tenants of jurisprudence, one is forced to concede; his title
is Councilor.

One area of the law which appealed to him was that of helping his
n'er-do-well friends, and eventually, their friends and acquaintances, pain-
lessly into chapter 13 bankruptcy. He counseled his clients around a six
to ten step program, depending upon each one's theological vent, which
could not only discharge tens of thousands of dollars of credit card debt,
but also allow them to keep all their personal property, and after they had
paid Winston's healthy fees, come away with a pocket full of cash. His standard reply to questions about ruined credit, "If you can walk away from $1
million in debt, maybe you can do without credit for a couple of months.

There were also spin-off cash flows which he and his associates worked
like looms. These generally involved a tapestry woven from multiple misrep-
resentations concerning the appraised value of the defendant's assets and,
depending on the situation, could be high or low. High if the asset were
wholly owned and over-priced, or, if it had value and could be turned into
vague sums of cash, donated to questionable philanthropic enterprises for
tax advantages, or claimed for top dollar, under mysterious disappearance
insurance clauses. Low if there was another party whose equity would have
to be acknowledged and paid off. Winston could see the angles.

The late 70s and early 80s small town banking customarily still had the
local bank on the line if a piece of real property, upon which a loan officer
had bet depositors' money, and in which the bank had handled the transfer,
self-insured the title policy and aside from "expenditures associated with
escrow and filings" were also due a seven percent commission, should that
investment come up snake eyes. These potentially embarrassing miscalcu-
lations were quietly shunted off to the insiders of the local boys' club, who
picked up prime property cheap, using unsecured swing loans from any
of a number of local banks in a collaboration to keep the money moving
until a better deal, including another round of all the afore mentioned fees,
could be struck at a profit for all.

Many of these shady deals were assembled within a foursome on the greens, fairways and at the 19th hole bars of the private, and exclusive, Palm Beach country clubs. A lawyer, an insurance agent, the connected banker, and a rotating money man, all members of the bank's board, created, cooked and then carved up these deals on the back burner, while a game of golf bubbled happily away up front. The bank, its president and its loan officers were insulated from the appearance of incompetence by its very own board of directors, who placed themselves within this circular cash flow and did a brisk, if not entirely legal, business.

Over the course of his first several summers after passing the Florida Bar, the banks tended to clean out the dead wood of their folios during the slow months, the months in which the days were long and the real money boys were in the northern climes of Kennebunkport, Narragansett, and Newport; Winston had accumulated a small, but select, assortment of slightly rundown apartment buildings, small industrial warehouses, and vacant seaside houses. Most of these temporarily-held titles could generate their own little whirlwinds of tax advantages, lurid weekend bacchanalia, and untraceable cash.

This circus of activity required a ringmaster who excelled in the misdirection of the establishment's attention to one of the smaller side-ring acts during the switching of the flip. Winston was such a ringmaster; he could squeeze sounds, both riotous and soothing from this calliope without any stinkin' sheet music, and to say he merely enjoyed the show, would fall well short of the mirth and merriment, giggles and guffaws, and outright glee he and his larcenous cohorts drew from their semi-secret, hydra-headed endeavors.

It was after such a sun-washed day on the links that Winston had wandered into the Taboo Lounge on Worth Avenue. He sipped his Glen Livet as he checked his messages from the phone at the bar. One of these messages confirmed a meeting Chelsey Koch had arranged with an out-of-town German business man seeking a quiet sanctuary with a view of the Palm Beach Inlet. Winston tentatively and temporarily possessed such a retreat, and was only too happy to accommodate Heir Steinmetz's two-month rental requirement in exchange for the neat stack of Deutschmarks, which Winston would profitably convert to American greenbacks at a friendly bank the following morning. It was another fun-day Sunday for a man who had found his true calling.

Winston got a big boost up the financial and social ladder a couple of days after Heir Steinmetz's and his guests were due to either vacate the house, or hand over another stack of cash. He had called to check on the rental status with the invented story of another prospective tenant eager to inspect the accommodations. Heir Steinmetz answered the phone after several tries with an apology and a request, as he was not feeling well, could Mr. Montgomery please stop by the house for a quick visit to discuss some business. Winston could almost smell the opportunity to cash in. This guy wanted a long-term lease, or perhaps he wanted to buy. Either way he would figure a way to ring it up.

Winston returned his office phone to its cradle, grabbed his car keys, and headed for what would turn out to be a rendezvous with destiny. Following one of the axioms of southern etiquette, "Never show up as a visitor to someone's home empty handed", he made a quick stop at Hamburger Heaven, a local eatery and landmark on Palm Beach's main drag of South County Road. After a few minutes, he emerged carrying a white paper sack containing a quart of their famous chicken soup and several packets of soda crackers. He smiled and thought, "The perfect gift for a guy under the weather."

As he approached the fichus hedge-wrapped estate, he paused to appreciate the large modern mansion under construction on the adjacent three intercostal waterway lots. It was the latest extravagant architectural statement rising from the sand and coral. Its roof mimicked the shape of a tortoise shell, a very large tortoise shell of white concrete supported by massive columns which held the structure thirty-six feet above the ground. This height exceeded the local deed restrictions by twelve inches and had brought the construction to a halt, as the interested parties debated the costs versus the esthetic value those twelve inches would impart. Winston knew that, as always on this little island, the debate would wind down, a variance would be won, and the mansion would be completed. He estimated a shorthand six and five – to resolve this conflict; it would take six weeks and would cost the owner an additional five hundred thousand dollars. An architectural variance would be grudgingly granted, and construction would probably resume within a few days. Money always got its way.

When no one responded to the repeated ringing of the front door chimes or the conspicuously loud knocks, Winston decided to try the back of the house. They were probably by the pool and could not hear the sounds coming from the front of the house. He stood on tip-toes to look over the six-foot wooden privacy fence and, as he had suspected, saw the back of the tall thin German sitting in a chaise lounge soaking in the sun of this fine Monday morning. He approached saying, "Good idea. Relax and catch some rays – always makes a guy feel better."

Taking in the Chamber of Commerce view he seated himself on the chaise adjacent to the one occupied by Steinmetz, but when he turned to offer the soup as a remedy for all things to do with cold or fever he saw that the German was slumped awkwardly to the right, and his hand held a rather large gun.

Winston's sensory awareness switched immediately to high alert. He stood and took the weapon by the trigger guard and placed it on a small cocktail table, and then he gave his tenant a closer look. By laying two fingers on the carotid artery of his neck Winston could detect a faint but rapid pulse. He scanned the pool deck and then the path to the rear of the house but could see nothing out of the ordinary. He tried to rouse Steinmetz by shaking him, gently at first and then more violently. The German slurred what Winston heard as "The bitch poisoned us – mushrooms!"

Steinmetz then slipped into unconsciousness. With nerves tingling like an electric fence, Winston headed slowly up the back walkway, and, about twenty feet from the patio doors, he saw the body of a woman, who, judging from the powder burns on her blouse, had apparently absorbed at least two bullets in her chest at very close range. He felt no need to check for a pulse; flies had begun to gather. "The cops are going to go crazy over this." He thought.

He continued into the house and, at the kitchen counter, he encountered two more stiffs in the beginning stages of rigor mortis. On the stove there was a cold pan containing what appeared to be Beef Stroganoff with mushrooms. There were several empty wine bottles nearby. As he looked around, a saying, and a practice his mother had used over the years to conceal her poor culinary skills, skipped lightly through his mind, "Get 'em drunk and they'll eat anything."

"This was going to be bad" was the thought that kept insinuating itself into his consciousness at increasing frequency and volume. The investigation would uncover the shady claim he had on this property, the bad bank loans, and the deflated property appraisal and then, inevitably, other properties with similarly contrived bona fides would come to light. No matter which track he traveled in his mind, the ultimate result would be that he would have to take up smoking in prison. He had just recently, and with considerable effort, quit cigarettes, but the smoking that he saw in his future would be the forced smoking of the large penis of his even larger prison cellmate.

Winston explored further into the house, and when he reached the master suite, he could scarcely believe his eyes. On the bed and on the floor, were half a dozen large duffle bags, and out of them spilled bundles of cash, jewelry, gold coins and what appeared to him to be piles of bearer bonds, which he suspected were as good as cash, maybe better. Had he wandered into Ali Babba's secret treasure cave?

He had to think this through. He opened the front door and glanced around to make certain there were no other bodies lying about. While there, he collected the mail and picked up the morning newspaper. He relocked the door and took the small pile of letters, magazines, and the paper back to the pool deck. He once again checked the German for a heartbeat. The pulse had ceased and consequently, the German had expired. Winston adjusted the body to a more relaxed and natural-looking position on the chaise lounge and covered his quickly graying face with a towel.

He sat at a nearby table and fanned out the mail which consisted primarily of fliers and current occupant addressed advertisements. There was one letter bearing international postage and addressed to a Barry

Greunaurer. Winston glanced over at the corpse next to him and said out loud, "I didn't really buy that Heir Steinmetz bullshit." But when dealing in cash, aliases were just part of the program, and he bore the recently departed no ill will. He opened the letter, which turned out to be a little less than two pages of hand-written German; he set it aside for later consideration.

Even before discovering the loot in the bedroom, he had been considering a cover up to avoid all the nasty consequences he would surely face if the police became involved, but now it was as if he was being offered the chance to be handsomely paid to pull his own fat out of the fire. Absent mindedly, he opened the container of chicken soup and took a sip. When he realized what he was doing, he snorted a quiet laugh, and said aloud, in case the spirit of the recently departed still lingered nearby, "Boy that's good for what ails you. You don't know what you're missing."

After another sip or two of soup, Winston reached for the newspaper, and once again could scarcely believe what he saw. The front-page headline almost yelled at him: PALM BEACH TOWERS ROBBED!

How in the world had he been unaware of this giant crime? He quickly read the several articles associated with the headline. He was taken aback when the unofficial estimate of the bandits' take was reported at $6.81 million. He felt certain that this total would have to be revised, because in the few moments he had viewed the mounds of booty, he calculated he had seen about three million in bearer bonds alone, and he had not delved beyond the loot which was clearly visible. But then he considered the contents of his own safe deposit box, and quickly realized that should a similar robbery befall him, its' contents could never be reported to the authorities because of the questions such a claim would generate.

It was now approaching one in the afternoon, and any plan he might concoct would be best executed after dark. He felt he had enough time to consider all the angles and to hatch a scheme in which he could dispose of the bodies and rat-hole the swag. While the law enforcement community ran in circles, he could plan the best way to cash in.

After a few minutes cogitation, a word he had picked up from Gerry

Correll, his favorite law school professor, and from whom Winston had learned the value of deliberation and reflection, it became obvious that his first task would be to dispose of the bodies. It seemed likely to him that the knowledge of the robbery was limited to, and contained within, the gang in this house, a gang that had been killed by one of its own members and through bad planning or poor execution had also fallen victim to Steinmetz, or whatever his name was, just before he snuffed it. Apparently, no one had reported the gunshots – it had been pretty windy for the last few days, and there were always unexplained noises bouncing around the wide expanse of Lake Worth.

It also seemed logical to him that these people were about to clear out and there would be no one to inquire as to their whereabouts – if he could get them permanently out of sight, he reasoned they might go permanently out of mind. Now what would be the best way to sever any links between these bodies, the Palm Beach Towers heist, and himself? The inlet was less than a mile from here and the deep blue ocean just beyond, but that meant coming up with a boat and risking a random safety inspection by any number of the different agencies that scrutinized the goings and comings of boat traffic through the inlet. The Coast Guard, the DEA, and the Border Patrol were chief among his worries, but there were at least half a dozen smaller jurisdictions represented in the waters he would have to transverse. The same wind that may have concealed the sound of gunfire had also whipped the sea into a proper froth – lots of risk – what else you got?

He briefly considered chopping the bodies into manageable hunks and stuffing them into the garage freezer, but aside from the amount of hacking required, and the too little available freezer space, he did not feel he had the constitution for that grisly a procedure. Burying that big a crowd in the back yard had the potential to go wrong; a hole that size would require a big effort, and would always prey on his mind – one day in the future they might be discovered. Then an idea of such simplicity and genius broke over him like a rogue wave and he was willingly carried along.

He saw that the perfect place to permanently conceal the bodies was on the other side of the chain link construction fence just fifty feet away. He loosened the two bolts that anchored the six-foot galvanized chain link section to the two-inch fence post at the seawall, and then he went through the opening to explore the red-tagged property of the Turtle House. There were a number of excellent choices for potential burial sites available, but when he saw how close the large pool complex was to completion, he knew just what to do.

Winston considered calling in some help, but he knew, in the center of his being, that a secret as ghastly, one that held the almost certain ruin that this one held, could never be shared. So, for the next three hours Winston occupied himself digging a trench about two feet deep and twelve feet in length across the shallow end of the pool. While he worked he fought occasional bouts of guilt with reason; he had not killed these people and exposing himself to arrest and prison could not bring them back. At least two of them had been murderers and all of them were strong-arm robbers, and had probably done many other crimes, and while this was certainly a harsh sentence for the crime, it was just their turn to do the time. As his surging paranoia compelled him, he would periodically climb the concrete forms of the soon to be poured pool steps to survey the grounds, only to find he was as alone as any grave digger could wish. He had to untie a few rebar connections, but all the tools he needed were conveniently nearby, and as the sun began to set he was ready to haul the bodies from where they had fallen to their final resting place.

Using a wheel barrow, he made four trips between the two estates and with surprising ease he was able to transport the four bodies, and deposit them, two abreast, in the trench. With a little pressure, the bodies conformed to the shape of the shallow grave. Before covering them with the addition of half a dozen bags of ready-mix concrete, Winston took a moment to consider the stages these bodies would go through it the next few days. They would eventually decompose, but, before that happened, their bellies would swell from the trapped methane gases and they would bloat, possibly to the point of ruining his handiwork and drawing attention to their unmarked graves.

He climbed out of the pool and went next door to the kitchen and returned with a large butcher's knife. With care, he plunged the blade into the abdomen of each of the corpses to vent the gases. He then wiped the knife clean and laid it next to the bodies. He topped off the trench with a foot of sand and tamped the pool bottom flat. He had a momentary spell of panic when he tried to retie the rebar joints with bailing wire. The daylight was nearly gone and to perform this last task he would need to see what he was doing. He knew that using a flash light was a bad idea, but an even worse idea was to do a sloppy job on the rebar connections. Winston sat down and rested for the first time in eight hours. He was just about "give out" as the old rednecks from his summer construction crews had said at the end of a hard day, but he reckoned he still had the adrenaline boost he would need to finish the job; if he could just find some innocuous light source.

He sat on the first step of the formed-up stairs in the shallow end of the pool to consciously calm himself while he considered his options. As he sat trying to relax the muscles of his neck and back he looked up at the precise time that a flock of green parrots did a noisy fly-by. He recognized this particular flock, not that there were any other flocks of this unique collection of South American Amazon green cheek parrots anywhere else east of California. This flock that called the old-growth Casuarina stand along the original entrance to the Breakers Hotel home. These commonly named Australian pine trees, which had been planted more than one hundred years earlier, were the only trees on the island that provided the correct sized, naturally occurring cavities within their trunks in which these birds could establish successful nests. Sunset in these parts were key-noted by a lap, or two, around the two-mile circuit which included the Breakers, the Palm Beach Towers and the Turtle House before they settled back in their aviary for the night. These clever birds had survived since the 1940s, and the non-profit institution that fought to protect them was one of the few charities to which Winston made meager annual donations. He felt a kindred connection with these immigrants that flourished despite the raccoons, iguanas and sea gulls that threatened to drive them to extinction.

He did not really belong on the island either but, he, like they, hung on like grim death. In the twilight he silently vowed, that should he pull off this secret funeral, he would find a way to anonymously fund the Palm Beach Parrots Foundation into the next century.

As the Amazon greens headed home Winston was about ready to try candle light, but as he went next door for what he hoped would be his last trip of the evening, another amazing sight greeted him. A full moon was just rising out of the ocean. Within the hour, he would have the light he needed to complete the fifteen or so connections at the bottom of the pool, and he would be able to brush away his tracks, replace the two bolts to secure the chain link section to the fence pole, and slip silently away.

Over the next few days, Winston cleaned away the evidence of the violent ending the notorious Towers Robbery gang had met. As a test before he disposed of the toadstool-poisoned stroganoff, he deposited a teaspoon's worth in the small aquarium on the kitchen counter. The hungry fish attacked it with gusto and, as the dying German had alleged, the poison soon had the fish floating belly up.

Winston even secured a Luminal kit from a pawn shop on the mainland. He sprayed the chemical around the flower bed where he had found the body of the female gangster, and, to his surprise, the special light illuminated very little blood splatter. He scrubbed the deck, removed the tainted soil and foliage, and soon felt he had done all he could to erase every trace of his former tenants. Winston felt certain it would take a stronger forensic investigation than the Palm Beach PD could muster to follow this increasingly cold trail back to him.

He kept an eye on the project next door, and, within two days, a large gunite truck accompanied by a pumping crane arrived to spray the Pebbletech surface of the pool. By noon the grave was further concealed by eight inches of hardening concrete sprayed over the steel reinforced shell. Within a few more days, the pool would be filled with fifty thousand gallons of water and the deck be would scrubbed with an acidic solution, which would further obliterate any remaining evidence. Winston thought,

"Mission accomplished. Those guys might as well be at the bottom of a volcano."

He could now turn his attention to the duffle bags, and the as yet, untold wealth they contained. He carried each of the bags to the trunk of his car, and, transporting just one bag at a time, which he further disguised within a black plastic garbage bag, he relocated the loot to his apartment on the West Palm Beach side of the water. He had feared the cops might establish road blocks, bridge closures, and vehicle searches, but over the course of six trips, he was never stopped, and three days after stumbling into this bizarre scene, his tracks were covered and all the loot was safely in his apartment. Now, in a blackout curtained environment, he could examine and inventory this glut of ill-gotten goodies.

With a legal pad in hand he began to explore the duffle bags. He separated the cash, coins, jewelry, from the stock certificates and other securities. Although the securities ranged from fifty-dollar US Savings bonds to shares of IBM and General Electric, he was particularly impressed by the mounting number of $10,000 bearer bonds, which at the final count, totaled more than $19,000,000.

The cash came in a variety of dominations, and from a number of different countries, but the large majority was US currency. Of this, Winston separated the circulated and randomly numbered bills from the ones that were brand new, uncirculated, and sequentially numbered. One nicely, plastic wrapped package contained $750,000 worth of new one hundred-dollar bills with sequential serial numbers. Winston would have to do some research, but he reasoned that these bills might be on some official agency's watch list. The cash alone totaled more than the roughly seven million stated as the officially reported loss for the entire score.

The twelve hundred and forty gold coins amounted to about $400,000 at the spot price of $325 per ounce, and Winston was certain that many of these coins had much more intrinsic and historical value than just their weight in gold - more research. Then Winston began to categorize and value the jewelry. There were thirty-seven strings of pearls, sixteen diamond necklaces, twenty-three bracelets containing pounds of diamonds, emeralds, and sapphires. There were scores of rings, pendants and earrings, of which Winston was clueless as to their value. But of all the glimmering bobbles, bangles and assorted ornaments there was one which caught and held his attention; within an ornate and ancient velvet and leather pouch, which was tooled with what appeared to be Scottish runes, an emerald the size of a doorknob. He put on the white cotton gloves he found in the old pouch and examined it under his desk lamp using a jeweler's loupe he found in the bottom of one bag and could see no flaw or even the tiniest of imperfections. He then tried, without any success, to make sense of the markings on the bag. He then looked more closely at the museum style gloves he wore. Winston had relatively large hands and these gloves fit him pretty well, and the right-handed one bore a stylized monogram **"AA"**. After fifteen minutes or so he reached this conclusion, "This stone has to have a name." And, as an afterthought, he mused, "And probably a curse."

There was also a substantial pile of miscellanea, which contained several pairs of silk panties, a pair of bronzed baby shoes, several dozen war medals, a couple of ounces of pot, and a kilogram or so of cocaine. There were cigar boxes, not only containing illicit Cuban cigars, but others filled with love letters. There were marriage certificates and divorce settlements, lurid photographs, and tintypes of long-dead relatives, several diamond studded dog collars, four hand guns, and perhaps the sweetest item of all _____. Seemingly, the only missing example of things long hidden- away, there were no Japanese soldiers for whom WWII was still raging, despite decades of incommunicado. Domo Arigato Mr. Roboto.

Author's note: In an effort to make this experience interactive, please offer an opinion as to what the "sweetest thing" mentioned in the list of safe deposit plunder might be.

Winston struggled to conservatively estimate the total value, and after several attempts and several days of chewing it over, he finally spit out an astounding number of $28,000,000. From this number, he had withheld the huge emerald, which he guessed might be worth another five to ten million bucks and possibly a pox.

L'il Augie sent a bail bondsman to the county jail located on Gun Club Road, adjacent to the ultra-exclusive Trump International Golf Club. He was perpetually astounded by the city planning which allowed a nine-floor prison within such proximity to wealth, but this musing was just a diversion while he continued to scour the hard drives of the closed-circuit traffic cams from West Palm Beach's network purchased with post 9/11 Homeland Security dollars. He paid $500 a month to a technician within a Bayonne data center, and once a month he received an executive level password, which gave him unfettered access to any system tied into the national grid. He surprised himself with the number of times this investment multiplied itself. He had his own high-speed extranet, and he had quickly discovered how to set the search parameters to find all kinds of valuable information, but his abiding obsession was the hunt for the proceeds of the Palm Beach Towers Robbery.

He had inherited this obsession from his old man. Big Augie, who as a younger man, had been driven by a wide selection of interests and enthusiasms including a love of the sun, baseball's spring training, and the pursuit of record breaking billfish. He was a three-time member of the "World Granders Fishing Fraternity," whose membership, as the name implies, had only one requirement. The angler who hooked, fought, and landed a marlin, black or blue, with a gross weight of over one thousand pounds, was automatically in.

After his first encounter with billfish, a seven foot, ninety-six-pound sailfish he had boated during the 1965 Silver Sailfish Tournament, he was (please pardon the pun) hooked. He had been enticed by associates to spend a week among the fleet of large, fast, and elaborately equipped, sport fishing vessels harbored behind a smallish motel and restaurant compound on the shore of the Atlantic Ocean: The Sailfish Center. He soon found himself the owner of a brand-new condominium in the Palm Beach Towers located a scant three nautical miles from the Palm Beach Inlet and about the same distance to the tiny Palm Beach International Airport, international because of its service to the Bahamas, just 45 miles to the east.

Whenever his busy crime syndicate boss work schedule permitted, he would depart the dreary Newark International Airport upon a direct Eastern Airlines flight, and two and a half hours later he could have his bare feet in the sand, or betting on young Basque Jai-Lai players at the local Fronton. Augustine Amato was a suntanned, well dressed don of leisure long before John Gotti's ears were dry. Shortly after becoming a Florida resident, he made two visits to the local authorities. He told the same tale to both. He was in the area strictly for pleasure. Neither the Palm Beach Police nor the Miami mafia bosses of the Carafano family had any reason to view him as a threat, and if he could use his contacts or influence to assist either, just give him a call.

And so it went for the next dozen years. Big Augie would spend long weekends fishing and gambling, eating and drinking, swimming and screwing, until the day he got word of the Palm Beach Towers heist. The robbery had happened on a Friday night and Augie was in his first-class airline seat on Saturday morning. By noon on Sunday he had again made two visits to the same authorities. This time his offers of assistance had a more menacing quality, which warned, and even threatened, both sides of the law; should it come to light, or to his attention, which was not always the same thing, that his local friends had aided in the theft, or abetted in the disposal of the loot, there would be consequences. He stood ready to pursue any and every lead, but for months and then years, there were no leads. None of the swag came onto the black market through the normal network of fences, and despite the enormous value of any information, none of the normal snitches or stooges offered a hint or a whisper as to who had perpetrated this clever crime.

Augie was out about one point five million in cash and securities - about fifty of the bearer bonds had been his - several first editions by Steinbeck and Lewis, some coded ledgers, and one enormous emerald.

Winston had been right about the jewel; it did have a name, and now it had at least two curses and some foreboding prophesy attached to it. The emerald had sported a variety of names over the four centuries since its discovery in the tomb of a minor pharaoh along the banks of the Nile. It had resided for roughly a century in the Edinburgh Castle as part of the Crown Jewels of Scotland and had been liberated from the English by no less a thief than Bonnie Prince Charlie himself in the failed siege of 1745. The gem had made rare appearances over the next one hundred and fifty years, with the last reported sighting being made in 1906 by a young Louis Mountbatten, who, under the influence of the Jules Verne novel "Le Rayon Vert" (the Green Ray), accidentally referred to it as The Green Flash, and the moniker persisted. It was again the target of sneak thieves not long after and around 1960 was offered to Augie if he would take pity, and display the quality of mercy upon a vanquished interloper. Augie accepted the stone and Davey "Longball" Escudo was allowed to move back to Argentina with his life and eight of his ten fingers; Augie kept both of his little fingers as a sort of pinky swear that Davey would never come north of the equator again.

Jules Verne's description of the rarely seen mystical green flash is actually a description of the prismatic diffusion of light produced by the final rays of the sun at day's end, as it disappears into the sea, or over a crystal clear horizon, and had nothing to do with jewels, but to Augie it perfectly described the 714 carat stone: "A green which no artist could ever obtain on his palette, a green of which neither the varied tints of vegetation nor the shades of the most limpid sea could ever produce the like! If there is a green in Paradise, it cannot be but of this shade, which most surely is the true green of Hope."

While the main protagonists of the Green Ray, Oliver and Helena, never see the legendary sight because these lovers are gazing into each other's eyes, the rest of the party does witness the "Green Flash", which makes the whole ordeal worthwhile. Widely regarded as "not Verne's best work" the elusive nature of the sight has persisted, and is often among the bucket list objectives of the nautically inclined.

Aside from this description, Augie Amato read all he could about emeralds, and had he done this amount of research under the banner of some institute of academic erudition, he would be well on the way toward a certification as a Bachelor of Lithology. Titles did not hold the fascination in his perspective that pure knowledge represented, and the more he studied, the deeper he was drawn into the cult the stone generated. He gathered the lore and myths of emeralds the way a philatelist collected stamps. Among his favorites were: "All the green of nature is concentrated within the Emerald." and "The emerald is a seeker of love and a revealer of truth." To say that Augustine Amato, Senior was besotted at his first glimpse of the Green Flash was understating it by several levels of magnitude, and just like all of those who came before and after him, this obsession was destined to grow.

In the following years Augie came to attribute his robust good health, as well as much of his virility and wealth, to the fact that he held this green rock, and he also believed it gave him an advantage as he tried to plan for the future; he really thought he had genuine glimpses of what was to come, and he made bold decisions based on this belief.

To confound thieves and interlopers, Augie Sr. had once contracted with an old jewelry master with New York underworld ties to make an exact copy of the massive emerald, but after several tries, with disappointing results, he canceled the order and confiscated all the flawed replicas with streaked color and obvious physical occlusions. However, his order to destroy the plaster mold of the gem via sledge hammer, was carried out by an apprentice, the jeweler's youngest son, against the mold of a more common place crystal chandelier pendant. The only, and unknown, mold of the Green Flash secretly remained with the ambitious, but still learning, young gemologist, one Glenn Marietta Jr.

Over the years Glenn had approached the replication of this stone not only as the masterpiece and treatise of his apprenticeship, but also as the standard for his life-long pursuit of perfection. During the ensuing years, he had made about six sets of replicas, none of which could pass muster, but with each effort his process grew in sophistication, and the outcomes were becoming more authentic. He had educated himself on the science associated with specific densities, harmonic frequencies, and spectral diffusion. To the point, in more recent years, this process, aided by specialized lab equipment, computer assisted design software, centrifuges, vacuum chambers, and miniature propane fueled kilns, which not only reached the fantastic temperatures required to work molten glass, but also controlled the slow cool necessary to avoid the imperfections of earlier tries, had brought him closer and closer to his goal of an identical replica. During these decades of trial and error, Glenn had developed several plausible cover stories to explain his particular curiosities, and he had cultivated several useful acquaintances which gave him access to specialized equipment and explicit information in the field of replication. He slowly amassed a knowledge of the science and had become a paragon of the lore of the great treasures of antiquity. To be able to identify his own creation, he affixed an all but invisible jeweler's mark to one of the facets of the fake emerald's underside. This mark was cunningly designed and, using a computer controlled laser he had engraved **gg**, but lest some curious future investor discover Gaspipe Glenn's mark, he had made it incredibly small. This identifier was only seventeen hundred atoms wide, twenty-six hundred atoms long, and three hundred atoms deep. If this seems like too ghastly a gouge to intentionally inflict upon one's masterpiece, let's put this dimension in perspective. An average human hair is approximately three hundred thousand atoms wide. His technique had improved to the point his latest set of replicas would defy detection by anyone without an electron microscope, and a molecular gas chromatograph, and these tools were not around every corner and tended to be anything but portable.

Glenn had no specific plans for these fakes, but he felt confident there was a nice payday waiting in the wings, that is, if he should ever encounter that very specific buyer. A long shot, but he felt that this pursuit, this expertise, and this intense effort would not go unrewarded. And, while he still held them in a secret stash, almost as cleverly conceived, and concealed as the gems, what, for all intents, could be described as the perfect copy of "The Green Flash", his efforts had not gone completely unrewarded. He had used this expertise to fashion other replicas of other lesser gems to be substituted for the originals which were sold or bartered abroad. Ole Gaspipe Glenn, by just about anyone's definition, was a rascal. In very infrequent lapses of self-recrimination over his shallow morality, usually brought on by the recognition of years speeding by, or the occasional left-handed compliment concerning his talents and why he had not achieved more, Glenn dug his way out with the help of a Willie Nelson lyric: "I could cry for the time I've wasted, but that's a waste of time and tears."

 Willie Nelson – There's nothing I can do about it now: https://www.yuoutube.com/watch?v=vAS5sbt-8yE

True to Big Augie's fears and fantasies, within a few months' time of losing possession of the giant emerald, no longer protected by its benevolent green glow, he had been gunned down in the vaunted gangster idiom; a hail of hot lead, and consigned for the remainder of his days to a wheelchair, a colostomy, and an unfulfilled longing to bathe in the pale light of the accursed jewel.

Since coming into power after his father had been unceremoniously retired, L'il Augie had been on the lookout for any trace of the huge emerald he called The Green Flash – a mythic stone on par with the Hope diamond. His father, under the most excellent oath of secrecy he could devise, had once shown him the emerald, and it had made quite an impression. Big Augie had told him what he knew of the stone's history and how it was rumored to have mystic powers of healing and prescience for "the holder", and a mostly benign curse, only achieved, so usually achieved, through greed. He tried to put into words the powers that could be absorbed from one's proximity to it, and that this stone would never be for sale, as it was not only the cornerstone of their family fortune, but it was also the family's shield and its sword.

The prophesy this giant emerald had most recently acquired had been declared by Augustine Amato the day after it was liberated from him "Whoever stole this from me is a dead man." At roughly the same instant he had uttered this sentence; this latest prophecy had been fulfilled. Heir Steinmetz had left the here and now and had joined his three co-conspirators, as well as Augie the elder, Mountbatten, Bonnie Prince Charlie, and all the pharaohs in the hereafter.

B ack in Willis' garage, he and Johnny considered their options. They agreed that it was too early to go to the police, whose resume in crime solving probably did not include taking on a shadow-dwelling psychopath, or use of the subtlety this investigation would surely require. Add to that their shared dislike and distrust of the boys in blue, the donut munchers, as they referred to the local constabulary, and they crossed Coptown off the places they might go for help.

Gaspipe Glenn had disappeared, probably burrowing further underground than the Chilean gold miners who were trapped some two-thousand feet under the Atacama Desert. They would hear from Glenn when, and only when, Glenn felt it was safe to surface. Too bad, because they were sure, that unlike the local cops, who the boys believed could offer nothing but greater exposure, Glenn's street smarts and survival skills, a curious, but useful mixture of charlatan and shaman, would be invaluable in what they now, in standard pulp fiction gumshoe lingo, repetitively referred to as "cracking this case."

At length, the two finally reached the obvious next step. They should do a deep dive on Winston Montgomery's background. Where and when had this guy run into the good fortune that seemed to surround him? So, they returned to the Google search engine to look for a jumping off place.

There they found many recent appearances in the pages of the Palm Beach Daily – The Shiny Sheet. The society daily newspaper that catered to the socialites of the charitable donor class who posed in aged mink stoles and bad come-overs as mega donors within the gala events, which began at six-thirty exactly and ran as late as anyone cared to stay, which was never after ten. These sorts of hit went back a little over twenty years and included the occasional picture of not only Winston, but periodically, there was Katie on his arm. Now that the two super sleuths knew what to look for they were able to spot Katie in several photographs wearing the diamond earrings and opulent wedding ring set.

They uncovered a few references to Winston's real estate holdings, but no real information which would prop up his holdings as compared to his relatively small opportunity to earn major income.

He was a second-tier bankruptcy attorney in a small professional association of under achievers, and yet his current ride was an Aston Martin DB9. Not the most expensive sports car in Palm Beach, but they were not giving them away, and especially to someone who might earn the $200K sticker price every two years, and that was before taxes. He did not seem to work. Between his vacations, his rounds of golf, and his late nights, when did he have time to see the clients who could not afford to pay even their own bills, much less Winston's.

They checked out his parents, who had died a few years back, and found a very modest probate affidavit which stated that the parents had no assets to speak of. Other than a twelve hundred square foot apartment on Brazilian Avenue, which was paid off in the late 80's, and vintage Cadillac with 38,451 original miles, the two had nothing. The end of their money dove-tailed precisely with the end of their lives. Winston was not a trust fund baby.

Willis suggested they go poke around the courthouse records to find out just what Winston owned and perhaps how he paid for it. Katie could probably give them some help with a few account numbers, his Social Security number, mother's maiden name, first pet, favorite movie, and other obscure facts which might be helpful in breeching the first protective layer of his financial identity's armor. They could extract a couple of favors from the ladies who worked in the title plant of Flagler Title Insurance, a branch of a state-wide company, who just happened to occupy the second floor of the office building where Willis had the offices of his small legal practice.

Johnny pulled the El Camino back into the garage, and as they threw the canvas cover over it they shared a laugh about how this was the poor man's Black Beauty – Crime fighter and do-gooder Green Hornet's heavily armored Chrysler Imperial, which fairly bristled with heavy ordinance and sophisticated electronics. "Let's keep this dog out of sight, until it's time to answer the call for justice, and crack the case!"

Before he left, he handed Willis the rental agreement he had snatched from the steel grey sedan he had ambushed in a West Palm Beach alley that very morning. He asked, "See what you can turn up on the goons who rented this car. I'm going to see Katie and see what she knows. I guess we should tell her everything that's going on and maybe get her to lie low."

Willis replied, "I don't think that is going to go over too well, she's four days away from that gala benefit at the Breakers. She's the chairperson."

Five years ago, Katie had become involved with several wealthy ladies who wanted to sponsor a refuge for the victims of domestic violence on the island of Palm Beach. Occasionally the shelter actually rescued a woman from a dodgy situation at home, but mostly it catered to rich drunks who wanted to embarrass their bored husbands out of their private clubs and less private vices, and into loving them again. This was her last year on the committee and it was her turn to say a few words by way of thank you for coming, and you don't know what your support means to this community.

Johnny chuckled, "Oh yeah, The Tempura House, a sanctuary for lightly battered women."

Over the next few days Katie was planning to do anything and everything except lie low. There were hundreds of nagging details associated with the gala on Saturday night, which was scarcely more than eighty hours hence. Manicure and pedicure, an appointment with Philippe, PHD (Professional Hair Designer), for a fresh cut and blow dry, had been scheduled a month ago. Openings at this diva's salon were rare. In fact, there was a wait-list to be on the list of those waiting for a cancellation. She kicked herself for her procrastination in getting her green silk gown out of cold storage; she knew it would require pressing and perhaps an alteration or two to compensate for the seven pounds she had involuntarily shed in the past few months. There were the sterling bobbles she had ordered at Tiffany's as tokens of esteem for her fellow committee members, which had to be collected and gift wrapped. No, check that, she would have that done by the store. But to say the least, Katie was planning to be out and about.

One of the cakes she had assigned herself to bake was only about three quarters cooked. A little bit tricky, she had to finish convincing Corina to join her for the night of beef Tournedos or Chilean Sea bass, which would be washed down with fine Champagne, and between gourmet shellfish courses, and the intricately decorated canopies, there would be flutes of palette-cleansing sorbet. She smiled inwardly, thinking how pleased her mom would be to see her only daughter taste the good life she had only read about, and, as a nod to her blue collar, wisecracking father, "You know, sorta elegant like."

Johnny's warning had alarmed her, but not to the level he would have liked. She felt certain he was exaggerating the danger. How much trouble could she get into at a very public outing, which would be swathed in

security and tightly laced with unobtrusive, but highly professional protection? Plus, she planned to be virtually unrecognizable with her plunging
neckline, green eel skin stilettos and new do. It was time to get out and strut
a little. Instead of her normal routine of dowdy teas and warmed-over
crumpet, she wanted to interject a little harlequin tease and some sizzling
strumpet. She wanted, make that needed, to believe she could still be out
there turning heads in the street.

Johnny had said these mobsters might be on the lookout for her car.
He seemed unsure as to how they might find out that information, but
Johnny did not spook easily, so there must be something note-worthy to
his concern. Alright, she would just use another car. She knew Winston
would still be in the Bahamas, and since she still had a set of keys to his
Aston Martin, problem solved. She would get Corina to take her to his
apartment on Friday morning, jack his ride, take it to the Breakers the
next night and have it back the following day, with no one any the wiser.
She had better make a little time in her schedule to run it through the car
wash for air freshener and disinfectant – there was no telling what sort
of skank residue might need to be scrubbed, sanded, scalded, or in some
other industrially sanitary fashion, removed.

With that small hurdle mentally cleared, she turned her attention to the
other items on her list, such as finding the dress that would clinch the sale
with Corina. Since Winston had vacated the house, Katie had confiscated
much of his closet space for the storage of her own large closet's overflow.
This is where she would find the fine frock for her fetching friend. The
section that contained the little black dresses was at the far end of the
large walk-in where there were a few older suits and coats which Winston
had yet to retrieve. It occurred to Katie to check the pockets of these
garments. In years past, aside from crumpled business cards, some with
smudged phone numbers of floozies or drunks, although she supposed
the two categories did not have to be mutually exclusive, she had found the
occasional folded fifty.

Katie was having no luck until in the final garment, an old trench coat,
and judging from the archaic cut and fabric, it must had been hanging

unworn for decades. Within an inside breast pocket, she found an old envelope which bore a European post mark dated 1979, about the time of
the PB towers heist. She extracted the two-page letter and examined it
closely. The stationery was a high-quality bond with some sort of crest or
emblem as its watermark. "Expensive", she thought. On closer inspection
of the envelope's post mark, she determined the letter's origin had been
Berchtesgaden, Austria.

She could not read German per se, but she recognized a few words.
She could make no real sense of the content, but it was interspersed with
exclamation marks and double underscores. The valediction read, "Jetzt
muss ich gehen, Viel Glück!" I must go now, Good Luck! - Johnny would
definitely want to see this.

Back to the dresses, she selected several little numbers, and Corina
could choose which gown she wanted to wear. The seamstress, who was
coming by to work some magic on her own dress, could nip and tuck it
to suit her at the same time. It occurred to Katie that Corina should wear
something sleeveless. She thought, "show off those guns" she works on so
hard. They had done the math one morning after Corina's trip to the gym.
When you calculated the amount of weigh times the number of reps, it
worked out that during the course of every work out, she lifted the equivalent of a Greyhound bus. No sir, Corina did not dog it at the gym. And, yes
Ma 'm, definitely something sleeveless.

Corina did not really want to attend another ball. What Corina wanted was to just show up at Willis' house and see what happened. She could provide herself some light cover under the guise that she had a question or two about the compatibility quiz. Hell, she reasoned a friend ought to be able to drop by around cocktail hour with a pan of homemade banana bread and be received.

Alright, she would do it. After making the decision she spent a couple of hours selecting her wardrobe, bathing, and configuring herself for her opening line, "I was baking, and while I was at it, I made an extra loaf for you." She pre-heated the oven and ran out to pick up something already baked from the local bakery which would fit her bread pan. Corina was a fine cook, and could have done the "from scratch thing". But who had the time? She had been using this trick for years, just heat it up and scrape it off the pan. You don't find talent like that on every corner.

She had planned to knock on the front door ladened with the hot bread which she would handle with an oven mitt. He would have to invite her in so she could put it down. However, when she reached the end of his long driveway, there he was in his garage messing about with what appeared to be an oddly shaped birdhouse. He wore gym shorts and running shoes. Other than these meager garments, the only other thing he had on was the radio. When he saw her, and although it did not bother Corina even a little bit, he seemed embarrassed at his semi-nudity.

He did invite her in before he disappeared to "clean himself up a little", but she was not certain if the invitation extended past the garage. She laid the pan on his work bench, and, as she began to explore his wood shop, she thought she heard splashing from the pool. She walked into the house just in time to catch a glimpse of his bare white butt as he dashed into his bedroom. Within forty-five seconds, he was standing in front of her in clean jeans and a white tee fresh from his dresser drawer, the creases from the folds still apparent, and a few droplets of water from his combed wet hair had fallen on his shoulders. Corina was about to get into her bread line when she noticed his Christmas tree. It was a potted Norfolk pine about three feet tall with one string of lights and ten small ornaments. Her eyes darted from the tree to Willis, and back to the tree, around the living room's sky-high ceiling, modern marble hearth, and then to the bread in her hands, and finally she said, "Get a sweater and some shoes. We are going to get you a real tree."

Willis' protests were over-ridden with rolled eyes and the clucking, clicking sounds with which she propelled her point of view, and soon enough Willis was shoed and sweatered, and with red Solo cups they were in his El Camino, rumored to be completely unknown to the local constabulary as a vessel in which one might transport hooch. They had a bottle of Moet White Star on ice, cruising the Christmas tree lots of northern Palm Beach County.

If Corina had any shame when it came having the young men, some only mature boys, unwrap (cut the cords which kept the tree compact and intact) large Frasier or Douglas firs, it was not at all apparent. From there she would use her charms to have the fellows spin the trees to inspect for patches of sparse foliage, and "hop" them to encourage the limbs to "fall". She and Willis also made several stops at several local rathskellers to vanquish the chill with a shared mug of hot buttered rum complete with stirs made of peppermint-dipped cinnamon sticks. Before the cock could crow thrice, they had an eleven-foot Blue spruce installed, well at least balanced in a plastic bucket filled with water, and leaning against the wall in the corner of Willis' living room. From their perspective, a grand time was had by all, and this all to which they referred, applied exclusively to just the two of them. After a leisurely libidinous interlude before the dwindling fire, they settled in for a long winter's nap.

So wrapped up in their own merriment had they been, that they did not notice sliding through an intersection a full half second after the traffic signal had gone red. There had been no danger of a collision with another vehicle, as they were the only people within half a mile, but this slight tardiness across a painted white line had set in motion a very short sequence of events. The newly installed traffic cam recognized the violation and snapped two surprisingly clear photographs, one profile of the mostly black 1970 El Camino and its occupants, the other of the license plate of the same vehicle as it passed through the intersection against the light. Once captured on digital media, the Palm Beach Online Surveillance & Intervention System, Proboscis to its supporters and its detractors alike because of the system's propensity to, too often, get it wrong. There were problems with the camera's timing, as well as the interface to the Optical Recognition Software that cross-referenced the tag number with vehicle registration records, and then automatically mailed a $162.00 citation to the owner of record. The system generated an enormous cash flow, and even though as many as twenty-five percent of the fines were based on bad data, the county commissioners were slow to take it down for troubleshooting and problem resolution – correct or not, they wanted the money. Like the little wooden boy who nose would grow with every untruth, the affect upon Proboscis was much the same.

However, this time the system got it right, with one minor exception (not its fault). The address it sought and found was that of a small farm in rural Lantana, and the name it retrieved was that of poor, headless Benny Bigalow. The mail containing the citation and the eerie pictures of what appeared to be Benny's restored car, license plate and all, speeding through an intersection while hauling an oversized Christmas tree would be forwarded to Guadalajara. Eventually, weeks or possibly even months later, Consuelo would have her senses tossed about by the irreconcilable evidence, as well as the memories of her dead husband. This electronic process consumed a mere seven milliseconds of central processor computing time, and because of L'il Augie's request for all activity pertaining to 1970 El Caminos in Palm Beach County, it spent another eleven milliseconds notifying a laptop computer with a New Jersey IP address of the incident. At last L'il Augie had a lead. To be precise; L'il Augie had a bad lead, on the spectral Chevy.

Katie had been partially right about Winston and the Bahamas, but he had taken a little time away from the fishing tournament he and his cohorts were enjoying to visit a banker he had come to know well over the past twenty-seven years. Michael Gaines of The Royal Bahamian Bank and Trust had been instrumental in helping Winston understand the value of his Palm Beach Towers windfall. He had assured Winston of the bank's fierce commitment to client privacy, and he had explained how a confidential numbered account arrangement would confound those agencies and individuals seeking information about his holdings and financial transactions in the island nation. He was eager to accept millions in bearer bonds without any requirements other than the numbered account into which Winston would like the funds deposited, and that account's current password. For every $10,000 bond he transferred, the honorable Mr. Gaines would receive a $199 commission, plus the one percent annual management fee on all of Winston's considerable off-shore financial assets. Apparently, bankers operated under the same guiding principle all over the world: "Get that money." This mutually advantageous relationship had flourished, and both parties had thrived.

As the chase for the Palm Beach Towers robbers had quietly gone nowhere, Winston had carefully constructed and concealed a vault in the closet of his West Palm Beach apartment. His summer construction experience had given him the basics required to weld in enough steel to prevent a breech through the adjacent apartment's firewall. The custom rosewood cabinetry cloaked a hinged section that swung silently away from the closet wall to reveal a three-inch-thick vault door of case hardened stainless steel with a four-number tumbler combination, which was known only to himself. Within this vault he stored the proceeds of the heist as he developed a plan to cash it in. To quiet the misgivings he harbored about the neighbors, he purchased that adjacent apartment, at slightly above the market price a few months later. With his booty securely camouflaged, he punched through the party wall between his two apartments and doubled the 1350 square foot space. Not really wanting to wander too far from his hoard, he used about half of the new space as his law office, and there he had, without any fanfare, hung out his shingle; Winston P. Montgomery, Attorney at Law. Since then, there were precious few trips abroad that were not preceded by a visit to his secret stash, and thus began the slow migration of his treasure to his secret accounts off shore.

Like Augustine Amato, the elder, Winston Montgomery had begun to believe the huge emerald sequestered in his safe was at least partially responsible for his growing, if secret, net worth. Whenever he felt the pressure of all the secrets he now carried, he would repair to his castle's keep to spend a few moments alone with The Green Flash. His close proximity to the stone had the effect of calming him, and though he stopped short of prayer, at times he did find himself chanting a little. The result was always inspirational, and he was always able to see another slant or tilt and was always able to conjure up fresher and juicier schemes to camouflage and grow his fortune.

Today's meeting included tea, cucumber sandwiches, and a review of the open items which Michael was currently pursuing at Winston's behest. He had been able to find a Russian buyer, living in Cuba, who was willing to exchange 1,500,000 rubles (just over $37,000) for a stunning diamond pendant, and he felt that the price of gold had reached its zenith, so it might be a good time to convert gold coins to cash, say $25,000 or so. Michael also presented several opportunities to bankroll local real estate development projects with Bahamian partners, and while Winston listened politely, he knew this would draw unwanted attention to the wealth he was trying to hide. He would have to politely decline.

Aside from the privacy accorded the depositor, the beauty of off-shore banking was the institution's total disregard for, not only, the amounts deposited, but, also which nation's currency was being deposited. It all went through the same slot and within a few hours, no matter the amount or origin, would become just another credit in US dollars on a ledger within a secretly numbered account. Of course, Mr. Gaines would receive his nominal fee. God bless those nominal fees from all parties. As the final piece of business Mr. Gaines also reminded Winston that the St. Thomas passport of his carefully constructed alter ego, James St. Cyr, was due for renewal. Winston's paranoia had driven him to establish a run-out powder capability. Should his deceptions come to light he could simply disappear.

Like Blackbeard, Henry Morgan, and Captain Jack Sparrow, Winston had become a pirate of the Caribbean.

While Corina slept in, well to be fair, Willis awakened around three-thirty a.m. anyway, Willis retrieved the growing folder of leads/clues/suppositions surrounding the PB Towers caper. He thought, "Winston is connected to this by the earrings and ring he had given Katie almost twenty years ago. Katie's pieces of jewelry are the only artifacts from the Towers which had surfaced since the vault was cracked – as far as we know. Winston got rich about thirty years ago and the Towers were robbed thirty-one years ago. Could a thief be that confident in his cover – pull a job this big in his own home town, and stay there just thumbing his nose at the authorities from behind his mask of old Palm Beach respect-ability? It had always been thought that the heist had the flavor of an inside job – pin-point timing, clean getaway, and no good descriptions of the robbers. How the hell did a Jersey wise guy get in the middle of this? – Could he have been a Towers resident?"

That was his next step. When the sun came up he would spend a little time in the Flagler Title plant, let's see who owned those condos in the early 80s. That was still three or four hours away, so Willis returned to his bedroom to find that Corina, apparently in a subconscious search for his warmth or his scent, had inched across the mattress and had captured his side of the bed and his pricey, hypoallergenic, goose down pillow, the only pillow he felt could correctly cradle his active head to allow at least the chance of slumber. He smiled at her through the dark, and took the side she had vacated. By the time he had arranged himself under the bed linen he felt her begin the to move in his direction, and within another thirty seconds Corina had located him, thrown a bare leg over his leg, and her head was on his shoulder. With a sigh of resignation, he accepted the situation. Willis thought, "If life is as brief as everybody says, how come the night is so long?" It was alright, he had plenty to think about, and he consoled himself with the simple win of reclaiming his pillow.

When the earth's rotation did eventually reveal the sun in the east, Willis was chomping at the bit to get going. He placed a rose from his garden, and a note to Corina on the bathroom vanity, saddled up his horse, an ancient Triumph 650 motorcycle, and hit the dusty trail.

He had several stops planned before he was to meet Angel Delano, a very pretty friend, and the manager of Flagler Title's proprietary title plant. Among these quick stops was The Tulipan, a Cuban bakery, where he picked up several guava-filled pastalitos as a treat for Angel's early morning assistance. Angel had agreed to give Willis access to the various real estate search systems and all the records which were the heart of the title insurance business. Unlike most insurance which protects its policy holders from the risk associated with future events, which are largely unpredictable, and therefore subject to the whim and whimsy of weather, criminals, and bad personal decisions, the risk from which title policies protects its purchasers could be limited. A thorough investigation of the real property records, usually conducted in the county hall of records, could produce a continuous chain of ownership for a piece of property, which showed all owners, mortgages, liens, taxes, and satisfactions of all liens associated with any property. You show me any legal description of a deeded property, and with enough research, I'll show you every item ever recorded against it. Most of Florida's title chains can be traced back to the Gomez Grant, the 1699 document conveying ownership of vast tracts of Florida to one Vicente Gomez in payment for services to the Spanish crown. One must wonder whether old Vicente was being paid or punished. He may have been the first rube, after he presented his bill to Charles II, King of Spain, to bite on the line, "I'm a little short on doubloons right now, but I can give you a deal on some beautiful waterfront property in Florida."

Willis would only be going as far back as the 1960s, and the only questions he had were associated with who had owned the three hundred-sixty luxury waterfront apartments of the Palm Beach Towers at the time of the robbery.

Within thirty minutes, he had found what he wanted, and Angel, operating under their standing agreement, which granted her one dinner and perhaps a sleepover in the future with Willis, produced a printout of all records associated with unit F-19. The twelve-page report summarized the three-owner chain of title; The Palm Beach Towers Real Estate Corporation had sold, for cash, the sixth-floor corner penthouse apartment to one Augustine Emmanuel Amato, a married man, and a New Jersey resident, and, twenty-two years later, his estate had transferred the ownership in exchange for cash (one dollar) and other good and valuable consideration to one Augustine Emmanuel Amato Jr. A cold shiver coursed Willis's spine. That thug was not in New Jersey, he was just across the bridge.

Corina surfaced from her lights out, run silent, run deep, plunge into the blurry realm of slumber just as the sun reached the 15th degree azimuth to the horizon… …approximately 9:30 Eastern Standard Time. She felt content and reassured. Nothing calmed her down like a vigorous tumble with a guy who could surprise her. It seemed to her that the occurrences of last night might have surprised them both. Perhaps there are good guys out there with whom one might contemplate a future, but then she realized she was alone in her contemplation. "That rat bastard!"

The only thing worse than awaking unexpectedly alone at home is awaking unexpectedly alone in a strange bed, bedroom, and house. She wanted to grant Willis concessions for early morning plans around meditation or exercise, but when she found the note and rose telling her what she interpreted as, "Thanks for everything, gotta run." She could not help but notice and mark the trend. That's twice he was there when I went to sleep in the wet spot, and twice he wasn't there when I woke up.

She showered and dressed quickly, thinking as she gave herself a once-over in the full-length mirror, that jeans and cashmere has legs, paused for a romp through his pantry and frig, helped herself to a diet coke and a blueberry muffin top, and a tangerine for the road, and all the while she told herself that whatever this was, this was not a walk of shame, and she slinked to her car.

Still, she thought for a few seconds, "What a beautiful morning," but then the power of the positive switched poles. Her car would not start. No matter how she reassembled the stream of profanity, or how she repeatedly offered, at maximum volume, to give it a thorough thrashing, it could not, it would not go. As she considered her options, she sent a karmic forearm shiver in Willis' direction but then tamped her temper down. My car not starting is not his fault. It has been acting up for days, but then countered immediately, "But if he hadn't snuck out, he could and should fix my problem. He leaves me a note! I'll leave him a note." She went back into the house and, with her Strawberry Seduction lipstick, scrawled across the dressing room mirror, "My car won't start – took yours", and signed with a heart. She left her keys where the rose had been, piled herself and her stuff into the El Camino, adjusted the seat and mirrors, and headed for the front gate.

 Grace Potter and Daryl Hall "The Things I Never Needed"
https://www.youtube.com/watch?v=ypwcitHSEQo

When Katie awoke on Friday morning she thought, "At last this gala was finally going to happen and she could gracefully withdraw from the wealthy widows' club. She had done her turn in the barrel, and now it was time to hand the reins to her successor." Corina had disappeared right after her fitting with the seamstress yesterday, but not before they had agreed on shoes, jewelry, and hair. The Ramy Brook one shoulder black dress she had chosen really showcased her toned and tanned body, and, she looked in a word, sensational.

Corina was supposed to pick her up, and the two of them would then travel to the brand new, high tech, nail emporium owned by a Vietnamese family done well. This was one of seven shops where, daily, scores and scores of women were made comfortable as they chose from the simple to the extreme in nail couture. The average fifty dollars that each of these women handed over for their ninety minutes in the over-stuffed salon chairs equated to roughly one million Vietnamese dong and, had the Chin family remained in Indochina, would have represented one quarter of their annual income. It seems that Momma and Poppa Chin had made the correct decision when they had exchanged the palm tree lined shores of the Phan Rang for the palm tree-lined shores of Florida, and traded in their seventy-year-old wooden junk for a fleet of new Lexuses.

When Corina finally arrived mid-morning back home, she and Katie exchanged the obligatory, "Oh, don't you look nice. Is that new?", and from there went on to discuss the previous night's revelry. Corina told Katie about their joy riding and Christmas tree wrangling with all the gusto of a high school girl who had unexpectedly been crowned homecoming queen, but when Katie asked about the cold light of dawn, Corina just blurted out, "When I woke up that rat bastard was gone. He left me a rose and a note I don't understand." she pulled the folded note from the back pocket of her jeans.

Katie examined the few neatly lettered lines:

"Shall I compare thee to a summer's day?

Thou art more lovely and more temperate:

So long as men can breathe or eyes can see,
So long lives this, and this gives life to thee.

Katie's heart fluttered a little and she asked, "This is what has you upset?"

Corina replied, "Well yeah, is he giving me the ole`?"

Katie patted her friend's hand and tolerantly explained, "This comes from one of Shakespeare's most famous sonnets. He is basically saying that not only are you as pretty and fresh as a summer morning, but that in his opinion, you will always be this way. And he counts himself fortunate to know you."

Corina pouted, "I guess that's pretty romantic, but I wanted to have breakfast and afterglow. He keeps leaving me these tests. Is he trying to convince himself that I'm smart enough or me that I'm not?"

They continued to try to bust the code of what men meant with their gestures, and by their confusing behavior, as Corina drove them across the Royal Poinciana Bridge into Palm Beach for their morning of pampered repose. Katie had noticed the El Camino but never spotted the dangerous picture that emerged from the connected dots.

Katie finally said the thing which made it alright, "I think you should cut Willis a little slack. Johnny says he doesn't sleep at all and that his mind spins like a gyroscope all the time. He probably just had some stuff to do and didn't want to disturb your slumber. You know how hard you can go down."

Corina pulled up outside the Love You Long nail salon, tossed the keys to the valet, who watched the two of them as they wiggled and giggled their way inside. After some study, Katie selected Zoya Pepper from the elaborate lacquer color wheel and following several brief flirtations, Corina finally chose, as much for the name as the color, Hanky Panky Blue.

When they emerged from the salon, Katie had another forty-five minutes to spend just down the block with Philippe, so Corina took the car and pulled into the Saks parking garage, where the parking attendants fell upon her in a small hoard. One opened her car door; another extended a hand to assist her from the car, and a third held open the door into the plush department store. She smiled demurely at them and said, "You fellas sure know how to treat a lady."

Rocco and the Mic had been given very specific instructions concerning their second attempt at tailing the El Camino. They were to watch the traffic coming over what the locals referred to as the northern two bridges on to Palm Beach. This implies the existence of at least one more southerly bridge, which is true and, coincidentally is named the Southern Boulevard Bridge. It abuts the southern edge of Donald Trump's Mar-a-Lago. L'il Augie felt posting a lookout with a criminal record in proximity to a sitting president had only one way to go – Bad!

They had been at it in separate cars for about two hours when Rocco spotted the car and the girls. He called the Mic and advised him that they were headed his way, and quite adroitly, the Mic had slipped in behind Corina and Katie just as they reached the nail salon. He proceeded a half block ahead and then took a parking place from where he could see the El Camino and the entrance, adjusted his mirror, and sent a text to L'il Augie.

"Just keep a discreet distance and follow that car. Keep me posted on where it goes." were his instructions. Knowing that they were already on shaky ground with the boss, they both sensed the importance of not messing up this assignment.

When the blonde moved the car to Saks, Rocco joined him, and together they waited the thirty minutes she had spent Christmas shopping. At least this time they had been able to record the license plate number, and they had no trouble noticing the El Camino exiting the garage because Blondie lined it up for about twenty yards as she laughingly left the valet stand in a white cloud of burning rubber. They followed and from about a block back they witnessed the brunette slide into the passenger seat and with another two burnouts, they started across the Royal Park Bridge.

The girls made one stop at an apartment building just across the water.

The brunette had jumped out of the El Camino and into a dark blue European sports car, but once again the Jersey boys' limited knowledge of the local traffic patterns, that and the "I'll beat you to the interstate" street race which suddenly broke out, allowed both women and their vehicles to slip away.

Although L'il Augie turned the air a little blue with a torrid streak of profanity at their ineptitude, he could be, and had been, a patient man. Now, especially because he knew he was making progress on identifying several people he felt certain could help him in his decade's long effort to meet the thieves that pulled the Towers heist. He told the brothers dim to return to the parking lot of the apartment building where the ladies had collected their latest ride, record the names on the mail boxes, and see if they could deduce any correlation to the reserved parking spaces. He turned to his computer monitor and began the process of determining whose apartment was linked to that sports car.

Angel wouldn't have minded a go in one of the conference rooms, or a repeat of the copier escapade from a few months back, but she accepted the rain check, and a chaste kiss on the cheek, from Willis as he descended the stairs to his office.

Willis sat at his desk to make a few calls. First, he tried his own home phone hoping to wake Corina, but it rang on through to voice mail. He then tried her cell phone, again same story. He supposed there were many possible explanations, but he also felt a touch of dread creep into the back of his mind. Next, he called Johnny, who reassuringly answered on the second ring, with a cheery Crocodile Dundee "Gooday Mate," and, without much in the way of pleasantries, Willis started in on the results of his morning's investigations.

"Riddle me this. Who owned a penthouse apartment in the Towers back in the day?"

Before Johnny could respond Willis continued. "That's right, L'il Augie's old man! And guess who owns that same apartment today?"

Again, he answered the question himself, "Right again, L'il Augie hisself."

He explained his research further and when Johnny finally spoke, he asked, "How's Angel?"

"She was particularly friendly this morning. You know, for a pretty girl, she doesn't seem to be getting what she needs at home. I owe her one."

Johnny said that he had driven by Willis' house not long ago, but since Corina's car was parked in the driveway, he just kept going. This news gave Willis a little boost, and he signed off with Johnny, to hurry the five miles back home. Sure enough, as he coasted up the drive, there was Corina's fire-engine red Mazda Miata, but, before a wave of measured relief could even wet his feet, he saw that the El Camino was gone, and the spot of dread doubled in size and moved to the front lobe of his brain.

He rushed inside, noticed a few muffin crumbs on the kitchen counter, and eventually found the message she had written in Strawberry Seduction on his bathroom mirror. A fly on the wall might have registered the slight sag in his face in the mirror as he read the scrawl. He quickly tried her cell phone again, but rather than Corina's voice, he heard the trumpet of The Call to Post ring tone. It was somewhere in his bedroom. He found it under a pillow on the floor and, as he sat down to consider his next move, he wondered out loud, "Is it my imagination, or does this chick require twice the work?"

He called Johnny back to report, and, at the end, Johnny replied, "I'm sure those goons are still around. Boy, this could really go bad." He continued, "I stopped by Katie's place to pick up this old letter, which you ought to see. Her car was in the garage, but she was gone. They are probably together."

After a pause, they returned their attention to the letter Katie had found in Winston's old raincoat. "Don't worry, they'll turn up. Let's go see Herc about this letter, he reads and speaks German. Meet me there."

Back in the early seventies, Johnny's older brother Herc had been drafted into the army, but rather than just getting in line to slog through jungles and rice paddies where Charlie would do his best to kill him, Herc had talked to a couple o' guys he knew at Fort Bennington, Georgia. At their suggestion, he marked on his enlistment form that he spoke German, and, over the six weeks of basic training, he taught himself about two dozen common German phrases. Just enough to be of value to the US Army in Frankfurt, rather than joining the rest of his platoon in Da Nang. While enjoying not being shot at, he worked in the motor pool, and he became familiar with Germany's beautiful girls and excellent beers, and he also became almost fluent in their language.

Willis and Johnny reached the old neighborhood about the same time, and both thought that not much had changed in the past twenty years. The same houses that had been well kept years ago were still so, as well as the unkempt houses of days gone by being still shabby and overgrown.

Herc, perpetually dressed in coveralls, was stowing his diving gear. He had been out with some buddies that morning pursuing one of his few ecological endeavors; helping to clear the local coral reefs of Lion fish, a beautiful but toxic invader which was wreaking havoc with the natural balance of marine life. Voracious eaters with no natural predators Lion fish were slow swimmers and easy prey for this group of expert free divers, but the dozen spines which grew along the dorsal fins contained a potent venom, which in sufficient strength, could cause a variety of reactions, including extreme pain, nausea, fever, convulsions, chest pains, breathing difficulties, and could even cause death. The reefs he and his friends were working that morning were less than fifty feet below the ocean's surface and thus easy sport for this group of men who shunned the clumsy underwater breathing apparatus and could remain submerged for up to three minutes on a single breath. Today he and his pals had eliminated more than eighty of the interlopers. Despite their toxicity, once the spines were removed Lion fish made an excellent meal, and there were several of the little blighters on ice in the kitchen sink awaiting Herc's filet knife.

Johnny and Willis entered the house through the kitchen and it felt as though they were stepping through a time portal into the past. Herc had lovingly cared for their childhood home and it looked the same as it had the day Johnny left for law school.

Herc offered his form of hospitality, "Too early for a brew, councilors?"

Johnny declined, but Willis felt that he had been up long enough to warrant a cold libation "Now you're talking. My liver is beginning to think somebody cut my throat. You got a Pilsner Urquell around here?"

"Just out," replied Herc, "but I think you will find this Kronenberg an adequate substitute – a hardy old-world Pilsner." Willis and Herc loved their obscure brews.

Johnny waited while the brouhaha-house etiquette was observed. Then after the tasting and the critiques, Johnny turned the conversation toward their immediate interest "Herc, dust off your German – what does this say?"

Herc produced a set of cheaters from one of the many pockets of his coveralls and studied the envelop first, and then the letter "When did you get this?"

Johnny replied, "I got it from Katie this morning."

Herc murmured, "You talk about your dead letters."

"Well," Herc began, "First, this is post marked from Hitler's mountain retreat – The Eagle's Nest. Second, it warns Barry, the addressee, to be careful, no make that methodical, and to stick to the time-table."

Willis and Johnny exchanged quizzical looks.

"Turdly," Herc continued with a slight smile, "There is a short list of valuables that Barry should try to find, but, as Franz puts it, in box 619, there should be an emerald the size of a Prinzregententorte, like a fruitcake," Herc surmised, "called the Green Ray, or maybe that should be

Green Flash. Several other box numbers with cash and securities estimates, and a phone number in Buenos Aries for David Escudo, who is eager to be reunited with La Rayo Verde. Ask for Pinky."

Herc looked over at the two lawyers and finished his translation "Gotta run now, wishing you the best in hunting fortunes."

Willis dissected the safe deposit numbering protocol, "F is the sixth letter for the sixth floor, and nineteen is the apartment. 619 equals F-19, Amato's unit. No wonder L'il Augie is tracking this – that jewel has got to be worth $10 million."

Herc asked, "What have you shit birds gotten into now?"

Within a few minutes, Willis and Johnny had brought Herc up to speed, at least to the speed they had achieved, and, as they had expected, Herc saw about a dozen ways this deal could turn south.

"What do you know about these Krauts? Anything on the Argentine? Berchtesgaden and Buenos Aries smacks of Nazis to me. La Rayo Verde - The Green Ray, I guess that's what they call the emerald - what do you know about it – that kind of rock attracts trouble and probably has a bloody history."

After an hour's discussion, they all agreed that Winston Montgomery was at the bottom of this thing, and that this thing was coming home to roost, and it was not coming alone. It appeared the wolf had the scent, and it was just a matter of time before he sniffed and snuffled his way back to Winston, and, from there, it seemed like a good bet the big bad wolf might huff and puff and blow the man down, and, by association, Katie might be swept away in the gale.

Now that L'il Augie had some facts to analyze, he employed his rather impressive command of the internet to first connect the address, the blue Aston Martin, and the owner of both; one Winston Phineas Montgomery, Esquire. "Phineas," he mused, "mom must have been a John Knowles fan. English majors, whatcha gonna do wid 'em?"

When you have the resources and the skills, the passwords and permissions, it's astounding how quickly answers can be found for the formerly unanswerable. It turns out that Montgomery had worked on the Island at the time of the heist. He then went from a nobody to somebody, got married, has a kid in college up north, getting a divorce, owns several houses, including the one his soon-to-be ex occupies.

A little more fishing yielded pictures of the councilor and his wife, in what appeared to be happier days, and what's this? Kathleen Montgomery was the Chairperson and hostess at a charity ball at the Breaker's this weekend. He showed the pictures to Rocco and The Mic, and they confirmed that the brunette they had seen drive away in the European sports car was the same chick as in the pictures.

The Augies, both junior and senior, had for years, chanted the same mantra when it came to their pursuit of the Palm Beach Towers robbers, "One day they are going to slip up, and when that happens, there will be hell to pay!" That day had apparently arrived and the sinister minister was about to present the bill.

He cross-referenced the El Camino's license plate with the one the traffic cam had picked up last night, and bingo, they were the same. He quickly jumped over to Google Earth and found the address to be a small farm in western Lantana. The satellite image showed an isolated twenty-acre tract of land about fifteen minutes south of Palm Beach. Almost immediately L'il Augie's mind attached itself to an idea like the tenacious jaws of a fresh water snapping turtle, "Nice spot for an ambush."

With a few more key strokes L'il Augie accessed the U.S. Customs and Immigration data base to determine that Winston had left the country a few days earlier, so he would have to wait, but in the meantime, it could only strengthen L'il Augie's position if he could put some pressure on the people Winston might care about.

L'il Augie called New York and spoke to a long-time associate legally named William Potomas, but within the mob he had several other monikers which were based upon his professional skills, Billy the blade, Bad Billy, and for some unknown reason, Sweet William.

"Billy me boy," Augie began, "there's a college kid up at Sarah Lawrence I want you snatch for me. I'll send you her picture and her class schedule. I don't care if you have a little fun with her, but nothing too drastic, I will need her in good health to use as leverage against her old man."

Good henchmen for the mob tended to be on the psychopathic end of the spectrum. They very often had penchants for inflicting psychological as well as physical pain. Bad Billy was an over-achiever in this realm and his running companion, Boston Blackie Bartkowski, Black Bart, or just Blackie, was, depending on one's perspective, even worse, or maybe better. If they had you and you had a secret, very soon they would have your secret, and you would be down a handful of teeth, maybe a fingernail or two, and for certain, a couple of pints of blood. They were well paid, but in certain circles it was believed that these two liked their work so much that they actually hoped somebody would try to stiff them on their fee, so they could come around and collect.

L'il Augie reasoned that once little Fiona Montgomery was in their clutches, Winston would sing like James Brown. The crime boss was privy to some very graphic crime scene photographs, and critical reviews of these two sadists previous performances, and he could provide copies to Winston Montgomery should Daddy Warbucks' cooperation require a little lubricant.

His next call was to summon Rocco and The Mic. These two

heavy-handed thugs were part of the crime empire L'il Augie inherited when his old man let down his guard. They were several technical upgrades behind the new guard, but despite the heartlessness which was supposed to permeate organized crime, these guys had taken more than one beating and several bullets for the family, and they had also had amassed impressive arrest records without turning stool pigeon, and since the mob had no 401Ks or Roth IRAs, L'il Augie continued to employee them as his eyes and ears, but mostly his muscle.

Rocco was two hundred percent Sicilian and, if either of the Augies willed it, would wade through a shark-infested rip tide to get at you, and if he ever got ahold of you, you were a goner. He had been known to maintain a death grip upon a victim until reinforcements arrived, despite having absorbed several slugs and a loss of consciousness. Rocco's partner had so many aliases that even he could not keep track of them all, and because of his once blazing red hair and Irish heritage, plus the rumor that he had seven hits under his belt in the Bronx alone, he was simply referred to as The Mic.

Rocco and The Mic always stood when in L'il Augie's presence. In fact, it was a very self-confident gangster who seated himself, without an invitation, in either of the Amatos' company. There was never any confusion about who was the boss, and a big part of the appeal these two thugs held was their understanding of the chain of command. They took the orders others gave.

"Guys, you know the pretty brunette that got away from you today?" They nodded. "Well she is some sort of socialite and is gonna be down the street at the Breakers Saturday night at some fancy schmancy charity ball. I want you to grab her without making too much ruckus. And, since planning is not your strong suit, here is how you're gonna do it."

After having met with Johnny at the pump house Gaspipe Glenn had determined he had taken his last meeting in Florida for the foreseeable future. He had witnessed Johnny's drive-by, and a few minutes later he saw Johnny approach his small shop on foot, and upon his departure he had seen the two goons who had beat him bloody tail Johnny as he left a minute and a half later. He had witnessed all of this through the Bahama shutters of an elderly client's third floor apartment just across Worth Avenue. Seizing the opportunity to approach his own shop unobserved, Glenn entered the shop, opened his safe and selected the things he might need for beating a hasty retreat. Twenty-five grand in unmarked bills, his rolodex, several vintage Rolex watches, a small leather pouch containing a nice selection of loose gemstones and natural pearls, and his passport. He also collected all the paperwork from his desk and the few odd pieces of jewelry still in the display cases and placed them inside the safe. He made quick work of retrieving the steel hurricane shutters, and, with a battery powered drill, he sealed the opening where the, now shattered, glass doors had been the night before. He had hastily swept up the thousands of shards of tempered glass, and he paused to take a little pride in the blood trail from the wounded thugs on the cobblestones "Who's the pussy now?"

The entire list of chores had been accomplished in less than ten minutes, and his last task was to tape a neatly lettered sign to the panels "Closed due to a Death in the Family.' He then grabbed the small bag he had packed earlier, caught a cab across the bridge to the train depot, and took the Tri-Rail to the Fort Lauderdale International Airport. There he paid cash for a coach ticket to Seattle. When it came time to change planes in San Francisco, he didn't. From San Fran, he took a wine tour bus to the Sonoma Valley and checked in as one of several Johnsons, who were discreetly registered at the Mission Inn there. Reasoning that the chances of receiving bad news far outweighed those for good news, he had switched his cell phone to the off position when he boarded the plane and had opted to not turn it back on since.

Gaspipe had chosen the Inn in Sonoma for two reasons. First, it was twenty-six hundred miles from Palm Beach, and, second, he had a friend with connections there who owed him a favor. Several years before, he had arranged for exact copies of some very pricey jewelry to be made and had assisted in the low-profile sale of the authentic articles, just before his friend was served with divorce papers. He had carefully taken plaster casts of the diamonds and sapphires and replaced the gems in the original settings. The Ex got the glass replicas, the friend collected about a quarter million, and Glenn pocketed a nice cash commission from both sides of the transaction, and this favor to be named later.

It only took a day at the spa for the on-staff plastic surgeon to repair the damage to his face and ear, and early his second morning on Pacific Standard Time, a local cosmetic dentist corrected his snaggletooth smile. The bruises would take weeks to recede, but the Inn was set up for just this sort of R and R. The afternoon of his second day there, he decided to get massage. After a Scandinavian amazon used her strong hands carefully around and among the nasty contusions on his torso to expertly loosen his knotted muscles, he poured half a bottle of an excellent local chardonnay into a large plastic wine glass and began a stroll about the grounds to investigate what other amenities were available.

Dressed in a plush hotel robe and swim trunks he meandered about the lush terrain until a very pretty girl dressed in a short and sexy, off one shoulder toga, approached him to ask, "Hello, my name in Helene, would you care to take part in our Roman bathing ritual?

His decision was immediate and his response concise, "Yes please."

As he waited for his personal wellness counselor to guide him through the eleven baths, pools, steams and showers, he felt it might be time to check his personal communication device for news from the east coast, and Glenn reluctantly powered up his smart phone.

He had missed a total of twenty-three calls from four distinct numbers. Each of these four callers had left precisely one message. The first three of these messages Glenn had expected, and they had originated twenty-six hundred miles away, from the place he had left in hurried autonomy just a few days before. The other had traveled about two and one-half times that distance. Of the four, all had further rattled his jangled nerves, but the last one was not only unexpected and unnerving, but it also put a nostalgic half smile on his freshly repaired face and beaconed to him from the shimmering shore of days long past. Caller number four had spoken perfect English, but in a delightful Latin accent, and had hinted at an intriguing proposition.

Glenn had done a little consulting in years not long past for Anna-Sophia Escudo, and they had shared poignant parts of a wild fortnight in Fort Lauderdale; the world capital of conspicuous consumption.

The "consulting" he had performed for her was the repair of an antique pin, a largish ruby surrounded by clustered diamonds and pearls. The piece belonged to her mother and had sustained some minor damage in some unspecified accident. In the first few seconds of their meeting, with the glass display cases of his shop forming a translucent, if not transparent barrier between them, Glenn had delicately, but professionally, informed her that the center-piece ruby was not original to the pin and was, in fact, paste. He had developed a set routine when it came to breaking this sort of unexpected bad news to clients concerning the absence of value of long-treasured family heirlooms. State it quickly, point out the evidence before the piece ever left their sight, and determine the next step. In this manner, he avoided any chance of the fake coming back on him.

To his mind Anna-Sophia took the news without much alarm and with no theatrics, "My mother would be devastated to learn this, but I suspected as much. She has a birthday in about a month and she won't wear it because it might come apart. Can you repair the crack in the setting and clean it?"

They agreed on a price and time for completion, and after a little paperwork, Glenn thought of the movement of an expensive seventeen jewel Swiss timepiece as he watched her walk away.

He repaired the pin ahead of schedule and notified her it was ready for pick-up. Anna-Sophia arranged an appointment late the following day. Upon inspecting the impeccable repair, she offered to double the fee, and even to Glenn's astonishment, he declined and counter-offered, "It's quitting time. I'll let you buy me a drink at Taboo. Besides, I have a small surprise I want to show you."

She agreed and waited while Glenn quickly performed the closing procedures, and, over large martinis he pulled an envelope from his suit jacket. "I wanted to give you something to add a little luster to your mother's birthday."

Intrigued, she opened the parchment packet and a smile leaped into her eyes, "It is perfect, and you are wonderful to think of it. This will make her so happy."

The small surprise to which she had reacted so well was an official looking set of appraisal documents on his Worth Avenue letterhead. It specified and enumerated the weights, colors, and counts of the stones contained in the piece and guaranteed its authenticity. Glenn had observed several gender based laws in his life behind the display case, and this axiom, while not as well-known as the route to a man's heart travelling through his stomach, was in his view, equally as iron clad "A gal has only one mother!" The appraisal estimated the pin's value in today's market at $167,000.

This acquired knowledge of what women want, cunningly expressed in these parchment sheets, had propelled their evening leisurely through dinner, dessert and a dance or two, back for a nightcap, and a rhythmic, sometimes frenetic, horizontal mambo between the scented bed sheets in her hotel suite at the Brazilian Court.

It was during this two-week furlough that they stumbled across their shared secret obsession, the pursuit of a flawless replica of The Green Flash. Neither of them had developed any specific plan of how to use such a fake, and up until they comingled their knowledge of the emerald's history, there had been no framework on which to affix a con of this avocado color. Acting in their own self-interest, and at admittedly, and significantly less than an arms-length proximity, they concocted slippery schemes in which an identical decoy was deployed either as an obvious fake, or diametrically, employed as the genuine article. A game with such stakes would have to be so cunning you could shave with it. It would have to be planned so secretly in greyscale as to be invisible except in the light of a particular bandwidth, and so pin-pointedly executed that no image could be detected, even on high speed film, but for a cloudy mirage-like image in a background mirror, and only then in the negative. It would also require circumstances so inconceivably clandestine, and so quite naturally, to them these improbable scenarios were not only great fun to develop and discuss, but they also proved to be a powerful aphrodisiac.

Glenn had enjoyed her company, her mind, and her amazing body but could never break through the Argentine's first few superficial layers to establish a deeper connection. He did not spend much time blaming himself or seeking to identify and correct his shortcomings. Their mostly physical relationship was okay with him, but the barrier which kept him at a distance did not fall into the category of: "It's not you, it's me." No, it was exactly the opposite.

Glenn, having returned to the present in California, knew whatever scheme she was hatching in that pretty little head required his particular skillset, and she had the ways and means to persuade him. Her message was brief and concise, "I have an urgent need to borrow or buy your bright green light. We have both dreamed of this setup. Please call me to discuss the terms. Don't wait too long my darling."

Perhaps he would return her call after lunch, but for now, there was the Roman bathing ritual.

Just then Helene returned with Jasmine and Ginger. One was a spice used in the upcoming water sacrament, the other a sultry, red-haired, bikini clad guide to the sensual proclivities of the Roman bathing ritual. He willed the phone messages to recede to the lower levels of his cognizance, shook the hand of his wellness counselor, and using a technique he had developed as a far more interesting version of his collegiate friends' clumsy inquiries as to one's Zodiac sign, and said, "Such a pleasure to meet you Ginger. Do you happen to know your birthstone?"

The girl at his side responded, "No I don't, but I was born in September. Beyoncé and I share the same birthday."

Glenn was still very sore from the tune-up he had received at the hands of Rocco and The Mic. He still had the lingering effects of the general anesthesia the plastic surgeons had used, and, as Ginger helped him out of his robe at the first station on the Roman bathing circuit, she took a quick visual inventory of his lacerations and contusions. Despite his impressive assortment of bruises, he was on the mend and would soon recover, but she noticed his embarrassment when he saw her mild grimace at his condition. She felt her heart open slightly at his self-effacing shyness and good humor. When she asked how he had been injured, his response had been, "Got soap in my eyes, and slipped in the shower. Whatever happened to that No more tears Shampoo?"

As they moved from one station to the next, Ginger instructed Glenn on the benefits of each, and professionally recommended a list of herbs and ointments, espousing the healing qualities of each. Ginger drew a twenty-seven percent commission on every product she convinced clients they needed, and Glenn knew he was racking up quite a bill, but did not resist her charming sales pitch in the least. In fact, when she suggested a particularly pricey therapeutic cream to reduce the bruising and relieve his discomfort, he said, "Hell, something that expensive must be important. Better give me two."

The two laughed frequently and for the first time in a long while Glenn's countenance began to surge upward, but the accumulation of pain-killers, both proscribed as well as those Glenn had privately procured, the local wine, and jet-lag had combined with his anesthesia hangover to predictably turn him a little loopy. After about forty-five minutes, he was half way through the eleven stages of the bathing ritual and his energy had begun to fade. He turned an even whiter shade of pale and slurred, "I may need some help getting out of this mineral water bath, and, to be truthful, I don't know how much more exfoliation I can take."

Ginger came into the shallow pool and carefully helped him to his feet and then up the three steps to the pool deck, where she used a luxuriously soft towel to dry him. She retrieved his robe and when he was once he again ensconced within his terry-cloth cocoon she walked him to the spa's exit. She produced a list of spa products which he initialed, and as Glenn turned to thank her a sudden quiver of pain caused him to sag against the door. Ginger was immediately at his side to support him and laughingly said, "Given your condition and your history of bathroom trauma, why don't I help you back to your suite?"

She then seated him in a wheelchair, threw a light cover-up on herself, and pushed him down the path to the guest rooms. When they reached his room, she used a passkey, and helped ease him through the door. Once inside, she dried and combed his short hair, reached under his robe, and deftly removed his swim trunks. She turned down his bed, fluffed his pillows, removed his robe and gently rolled him between the sheets. Glenn smiled weakly and put something into her palm and curled her fingers closed. "Maybe you could come back later and we could share some room service?"

Ginger replied, "The Inn has a policy of no fraternization, but I guess I could check on you in a few hours when I get off."

The way she softly and rhythmically patted his back reminded him of his childhood and his mother's comforting touch. Ginger let herself out after Glenn had dozed off, and, once outside, she opened her hand to find an exquisite dark blue sapphire and immediately thought, "It's more of a guideline than a strict policy."

G lenn moved slowly, and in stages, from deep and dreamless REM
sleep, to a more fitful semi-consciousness fraught with ill-formed,
flickering images of sensual pleasures laced with vague threats of fearsome
reprisal. He wanted the show to slip into a better focused and more cleanly
defined plot, but every time he was about to be nestled in fragrant braids
of long hair, and wrapped in even longer legs, an unwanted and unwelcome image of Rocco or L'il Augie would leer from his peripheries, which
proved an irreconcilable distraction. He repeatedly turned away from these
disruptive intrusions, trying to regain a temporal grip of his fantasy and
settle into a rhythm of lurid indulgence. Slowly he established a foothold in
this favored hedonistic scenario. As he caressed smooth tanned skin, soft,
pliant lips parted, and his urgency was met and returned. Glenn was a big
fan of the mythological dreamscape in which a female demon, a succubus,
would emerge, demand and extract the essence from a tragically flawed
hero, and this sequence was the best his subconscious had ever contrived.
As he moved to take a more active role in what was soon to be a nocturnal
emission, a stab of real pain forced a slight groan, and a soothing voice
replied, "Go easy baby."

He opened his eyes to find within his embrace, instead of a king size
pillow wrapped in 1200 thread-count Egyptian cotton, Ginger, who wore
nothing but a smile. He started to raise the questions of when and how
but agreed and acquiesced to her common-sense statement, "We can talk
after."

With no need to protect a fragile projection of fantasy, he gave in to
Ginger whose legs encircled him seeking some purchase on his frayed body
which would not cause him pain, and eventually she locked in like a circus
bare-back rider with her calves pressing hard against the back of his thighs

for leverage. The two moved together like a precision drill team, and at times even emitted the same cadence calls, of "Oh yes," and, "So good!"

At last they collapsed together in a slippery tangle. Ginger's mouth was a quarter of an inch from Glenn's tattered ear, so her barely audible exultation came through clearly as she whispered, "That was wonderful."

Despite an understandably light chop on the fluid of his inner ear, the three tiny bones had vibrated an accurate transmission of her words, and Glenn's wobbly brain had inaccurately, but correctly transposed the sonic to its root meaning, identical to Alexander Graham Bell's first telephonic words to Mr. Watson, "I need you."

Or was the literal meaning more along the line of Bob Dylan's "I want you"?

 Over the Rhine – I want you to be my love: https://www.youtube.com/watch?v=xNX1NAbZKW8

It was a beautiful Indian Summer afternoon in Westchester County as Fiona shouldered her backpack with just one of its straps and began her long walk all the way back across the sprawling Sarah Lawrence campus. She had just finished the last of her Wednesday classes, a Chemistry lab. Today's exercise dealt with determining the composition of a numbered specimen which had been randomly assigned, using specific gravity. She ran through the problem in her mind and felt confident that her answer of cadmium would be correct.

She wore argyle knee socks with navy blue Bermuda shorts, a white cotton blouse, a Navy-blue school blazer, and saddle oxfords. Her auburn hair was pulled into a pony tail and bound with a white lace ribbon. To a time traveler observing her, it would have been difficult to determine if he were watching a current scene or one from the 1950s or the 1980s. While many of her class mates opted to draw attention to themselves through trendier fashions which included artificially tattered jeans, black finger nail polish, and blue or pink tinted hair, she opted to blend.

Fiona had been given several pieces of fashion advice a few years back which, and while somewhat crudely phrased, were composed of what seemed to her, bedrock truth, "Show me a chick chasing trends, and I'll show you a chick with holes in her confidence, who might as well be screaming, Somebody please notice me! Find an understated classic look and wear it – there are few things in this life more appealing than a naturally pretty girl."

As she moved quickly down the winding brick path a day-glow orange flying disc skidded to a stop near her and a gruff voice shouted, "Hey Fiona, little help."

She picked up the disc and turned to see two rather burly men dressed in mostly black approaching her with wide smiles. She tried to size up the situation as she had been taught by her mentor – "Pay attention to detail – there needs to be a reason for something out of place."

She asked, "Do I know you?"

The two men tried to smile warmly, but their sincerity was called into question as they said nothing, and they continued to approach. One of them angled away, in what appeared to Fiona, an effort to restrict her options for flight. She glanced around and determined that aside from herself and the two strangers, there were no other people within a hundred yards. When the closer of the two, who tried to conceal the white cloth in his right hand, was about ten feet from her she fired the Frisbee which she still held, backhand, and caught the man in the excruciatingly tender place just below the nose and above the mouth. As his eyes began to well up with tears the other man made a grab for her which she easily avoided. She charged between the two goons like a forward on the field hockey pitch and took to her heels. She was particularly thankful at that moment she had paid attention to another of the fashion tips which she had been given. It had immediately appealed to the tomboy lurking just below her preppy surface and bore the stamp of common sense, which she had possessed in spades from an early age, "Please avoid silly shoes. You never know when you might want to run." The two mouth-breathers started to give chase, but realized the futility almost immediately. Now that the element of surprise had evaporated, the two goons had about as much chance of catching the girl on foot as did two giant Galapagos tortoises of running down a frigate bird in flight – precisely none.

Fiona, now covering ground rapidly, glanced over her shoulder and, seeing that she was not being pursued, ducked into a grove of maple trees and peered back down the path. The two men, one holding a crimson-spotted handkerchief to his face, conferred briefly and then turned and walked back in the direction from which they had come. She followed them from a distance, making herself small, and keeping to the shadows.

She fished her cell phone from her backpack and hit the second name on its favorites list. As she waited for the circuitry to complete the call, it occurred to her just how physically far New York was from Palm Beach. She had strained at the controls her parents insisted upon for her own good and had deliberately chosen a school thousands of miles away in search of freedom. Now she would gladly trade that liberty for security. The connection completed and a male voice answered after just one ring, "What's up baby?"

Despite the separation of hundreds of feet between Fiona and the strange men, she whispered hoarsely into her phone, "Herc, two men, gangster types, just tried to grab me. I ran away and now I'm following them."

You, the reader, might wonder why and how a seventeen-year-old girl would choose to place a slightly seedy, middle-aged, weight-lifter, grease monkey just below her mother on her speed dial. You would assume correctly that her mother's was the number she dialed most frequently, but for number two, you would quickly raise the more obvious possibilities of roommate, student advisor, why not her father for Pete's sake? You deserve an explanation; however, it will not be quick, nor will it be simple.

The Dendy family was composed of four rather unique individuals. Mr. Guy Dendy owned a small paint manufacturing business which required eighty hours of his life each week. The business earned them a comfortable middle-class lifestyle but left little time for him to explore his myriad interests, which included Renaissance painters, operatic music and ancient mythology. So, in his few spare hours he read obsessively. This also accounted for the naming of his eldest son Hercules.

Mrs. Beatrice Dendy was a house wife, but she was also a student of the arts, and she and Guy were drawn to each other through these common interests while they awaited the slowly moving machinery of the US Army to honorably discharge them at the conclusion of World War II. There was not much to keep the victorious soldiers and WACs busy at Fort Dix, so Guy and Bea would sneak away to ride the train into Manhattan and soak up the culture that was, after five years' wartime interruption, now returning to the Mid-town museums and the theaters of the White Way. There was another common interest between them. They both loved the Friday fights at Madison Square Garden. In fact, Guy had fought in the New England Golden Gloves Tournament of Champions in 1942 and was making good progress until his unit was deployed to the European Theatre. One of his coaches had been the legendary fighter Sam Langford who had showed him some of the nuances of pugilism. He had been a good student. A middle weight who could hit hard with either hand and a technique of quickly following a landed blow with at least one more from the other side. He truly grasped and internalized Langford's primary mandate, "Whatever the other man wants to do, don't let him."

Guy knew that boxing was a pastime, not a career, and like just about everything he tried on, he approached the sport with exacting discipline in the ring, but when away from it he treated the game with almost pure insouciance. He was unsung and the quiet man no one wanted to face, and had quietly acquired a nickname which bespoke his strong, silent style: "That Guy."

During a 1946 Fort Dix boxing tournament, which was designed to foster both discipline and moral, Guy had won the three bouts in his weight class required to be Battalion champ, and in the last of those fights, Bea had been in his corner as his second and "cut man".

By the time they were "processed out" they had fallen in love and were married. They soon moved from the cold they both despised to sunny Florida and began raising their family.

"What's that you say reader? Could I please move this train a little further down the track?" Fair enough.

Guy and Bea begat Hercules and John (Bea refused to have a second son named after a Greek hero) and raised them to be thoughtful, self-reliant young men. Just when their labors should have been paying off and paving the roads they longed to travel, tragedy struck. Guy was killed when a high-pressure fitting at his paint plant gave way, leaving Bea to mourn him for the rest of her life.

Although all the pews were filled and many stood at the rear, there were just three large wing-back chairs, and one grand piano on the raised dais of the Trinity Methodist church at Mr. Dendy's funeral. Johnny and Hercules occupied two of them and Willis the third. As the sanctuary slowly filled, Bea had sat alone at the piano playing a variety of tunes from memory: Chopin, Bach, Porter, and Berlin. When she rose, the entire congregation also rose, and only re-seated itself after she had taken her place on the front row. Johnny spoke of happier times and mentioned, with a muted laugh coming from the crowd, Guy's oft used catch phrase, "Shake the hand that shook the hand of Jack Dempsey." Willis talked about Guy's love of his family and his love of color and his belief that at the end of construction, it is the painter's job to make it all come out right.

When Willis finished his part of the eulogy, he looked over his shoulder, and the two sons stood. Herc went to the piano and Johnny joined Willis at the podium. Johnny said, "Dad was a musical man; he whistled, hummed and sang all the live-long day. Just recently he had been very fond of this new song "Hallelujah" by Leonard Cohen."

Herc began playing with just heavy rolling lower scale chords and he took the opening stanza in his gruff bass voice. At its completion, he opened up a little with a technically difficult interlude and key change, then Willis sang the second verse in his strong baritone. Johnny took the third verse and chorus in a clear melodic tenor, and, at the bridge between the third chorus and final verse, Herc improvised several keyboard riffs, and then the three sang the last verse together. When the chorus came upon them Johnny asked the assembly to join them, and "say something nice to your neighbor, they might not always be around."

The congregation did just that, and the chorus of Hallelujah filled the place, and was reprised and repeated for the next ten minutes. The over-whelming opinion of those in attendance as they filed out could be summed up in just two words – "Nice sendoff."

 Nilsen, Lind, Holm, Fuentes – Hallelujah
https://www.youtube.com/watch?v=AdyTXBT5CQE

And because I could not choose between the many:

Pentatonix – Hallelujah
https://www.youtube.com/watch?v=LRP8d7hhpoQ

After His father's unexpected demise, rather than pursue his own dreams of going racing, Hercules, stayed home to care for his forlornly sad mother. In an effort to occupy her time Johnny and Herc bought her a baby grand Steinway and used their contacts in the community to recruit aspiring piano prodigies who could come to their home for weekly lessons. Johnny suggested this program to Katie and before you could beat a rug, Fiona was among Bea's first students. Like just about everything Fiona tried, the piano came easily to her, which was handy, because BD, as Fiona had dubbed Mrs. Dendy, was subject to bouts of depression. When these spells came upon her, she gave little instruction other than "Please practice your chromatic scales."

One day Herc, who was working on his old car in the carport, came in for a beer to find Fiona repeatedly running the exercise while his mother dosed in her Barco lounger. He said to her, "I think you've got that one." With his hip he nudged her over, sat down next to her on the bench, and said, "Let's try something a little more fun."

He cracked his knuckles for effect and placed his hands on the home keys, closed his eyes, and to Fiona's surprise, played a softly hypnotic version of the civil war tune Ashokan Farewell. Before the eleven-year old could comment, be broke into the same tune, but now in ragtime.

 Fiddle Fever – Ashokan Farewell:
https://www.youtube.com/watch?v=oDkQ4FeooLA

That's the plain truth of how Herc had acquired such status on Fiona's cell phone speed dial. Instead of once a week, Fiona came more often to the Dendy house. When BD was up to it, she learned classical piano; when BD was not up to it, and she learned Boogie-Woogie from Herc.

Fiona had once asked Bea what she had done during the war, and her answer confirmed Fiona's thinking that we are all the collection of traits, talents and predilections which are handed down from our predecessors. Her answer, "Oh I had some medical training and could manage minor cuts and bruises, and wasn't squeamish around blood, so I was the medic in the motor pool. Mostly I would work on Army vehicles, but when anyone got hurt I would patch them up."

One day, upon her arrival, Herc opened the front door, and put his index finger to his lips indicating the need for quiet. His mother had a headache. Fiona turned to go, thinking today's lesson would have to be cancelled. Herc touched her shoulder and motioned her to follow him to the carport. He tossed her a pair of coveralls, size small, and that was the day Fiona learned to weld. No one could say for sure when automobile repair replaced the piano, but soon Fiona had more interest in timing lights than metronomes and had learned that she preferred the muscular strains of a Hurst four on the floor to the delicate chords of Strauss waltzes in three quarter time. Herc used her as an extra set of hands and feet, teaching her not only the intricacies of internal combustion, but also shaping and sharpening her opinions on politics, fashion and life in general. Fiona soaked all of it up like a sponge and, as a secondary reward, she pocketed the piano lesson money and became the last member of Winston's clan to start a secret slush fund.

Reader, I could go on about this distinctly odd partnership, and still may, but now, as you have politely, but repeatedly requested, let's get back up the Hudson to Sarah Lawrence.

Hercules' thoughts came out in a flurry of questions and instructions, which may have seemed random, but to him, were actually arranged in descending order of importance, "Are you okay? Where are they now? Fiona, look around carefully, are you safe? Can you take a picture of them? Do you have transportation?"

Reassured by her calm responses he asked her to replay the encounter, and note anything unusual. He chuckled softly, and proudly purred, "Good girl" as she told him about how she had created a little space for herself with the Frisbee; she paused and said, "Herc, they knew my name."

Herc thought for a moment and replied, "This has got something to do with your old man."

He silenced Fiona's protective protests over Herc's barely concealed distrust of her father, "They knew where to find you, so they have your class schedule and probably know where your dorm is. My guess is they will hang around and try again. Don't go back to your room. Turn off your phone; they might be using it to track you. Get to the train station and head for Manhattan – I'll see you at the Oyster bar in Grand Central in about four hours. Keep your head covered and become as close to invisible as you can – you know like we've talked about – Blend."

Within twenty minutes of disconnecting from Fiona, Herc was shaved and showered, dressed, had collected the items he thought he might want, and was headed to PBI – Palm Beach International Airport. While en route he tried to reach Johnny, but got his voice mail, so he left a message, "Listen Baby Bro, some of that shit we were talking about earlier today is happening. I'm headed to New York – call me."

He was able, just barely, to catch a non-stop to JFK. Just as the door was closing, Herc tried Katie's cell and once again went to voice mail, "Katie, it's Hercules Dendy, get ahold of Johnny pronto!" Why doesn't anybody answer his or her phone?

While he impatiently waited out the two-and-a-half-hour flight, he surreptitiously prepared several text messages to be ready to go as soon as he regained a signal, made a few notes on the cover of the Sky Mall catalog, and began to draw together the threads of a plan.

It had been a while since he had gone up against any formidable foe. His last skirmish had occurred a few months ago as he left the poker room of the Palm Beach Dog Track. He had filled a flush on his single card draw and collected a $7500 pot, which when added to his other winnings, totaled a shade over ten grand. Apparently, the game contained some sore losers, or perhaps the payout at the cashier's cage had caught the attention of the two unsavory types who would try to take his money in the parking lot. These guys were big, but slow and Herc surmised were used to getting their way through ambush and intimidation. He suspected it had been a while since either of them had had to do anything more demanding than to hit someone from behind to get paid.

"Pay attention," was the phrase he had tried to convey to Fiona, and it was the way he lived his life. He had spotted the two miscreants when he stopped for a nightcap at the lobby bar, and he saw their shadows as they lurked in the parking structure, waiting to waylay him and abscond with his winnings.

While still inside, Herc had noticed one of them had a slight limp, which probably meant a bad knee or hip, and the other wore dark rimmed glasses with coke bottle-thick lenses. He had turned these observations into an attack plan. When, in a dark section of the parking structure near the greyhound kennels, they had tried to pounce on him, it was this dim-witted quinella that finished dead last.

When they stepped out of the shadows to confront him, Herc, without hesitation, slapped the glasses off Mr. Peepers, and then spun to deliver a bone crushing round-house kick which dislocated the already damaged knee of Gimpy. He then returned to the first thug, who was on his hands and knees in search of his bifocals, and from behind, kicked him hard in the balls. He relieved them of their wallets, threw a set of keys into the shrubbery and left them writhing on the garage floor. His final insult was to step on the glasses, smashing the lenses to powder. Walking away he said loud enough for the hoodlums to hear, "Now let's see, have I got every-thing?" and patted his pockets. "Cash, keys, spectacles, testicles. Yep, ready to roll."

This entire encounter had not lasted thirty seconds, and he had not even bruised his knuckles. As he ambled toward his car, he thumbed through their billfolds to discover he had just made another $1800. He would give their IDs to a cop friend in the morning. Yeah, that was a good night.

Herc did not mind inserting himself into a dicey situation because he had been in plenty of them over the years. He knew there were several key elements required if one was going to come out alive and on top. At a young age, his parents had exposed him to organized religion in the form of a small Methodist church that they sometimes attended. Herc had decided early in the going it was more harmful than helpful, but he also found there were some beautiful concepts and he was moved by the New

Testament passage, "And now abideth faith, hope, and love, even these three: but the greatest of these is love."

Over the years he had mulled this verse over in his mind until he had distilled it down, filtered the precipitant, and made it fit his truth. He used this structure in stating his beliefs, however he substituted calm, resolve, and initiative, but the greatest of these was initiative. Take the fricking initiative. True and tried, this was the plan he took with him to New York. He had no problem with the plan containing components of silent surveillance, appropriate transportation and ordinance, or teamwork, but the core of his plan was to find the hoods that were threatening Fiona, come at them hard, and whip their asses to such an extent that they would abandon their ill-conceived behavior and just quit.

As soon as the wheels touched the runway at JFK, Herc hit the send key on his pre-loaded texts. The first was to Francisco Gonzalez, an old army buddy from the motor pool in Germany, a real freak when it came to souped-up cars, both building them and driving them. Since going fast was his primary obsession, and his heritage was Puerto Rican, he could not avoid, and so he embraced his inevitable nickname, Speedy. Herc felt certain that when in New York, and in need of wheels, he would be hard pressed to do better than Speedy Gonzalez.

The second text went to another army buddy who, until just recently, had been employed by the NYPD. Jimmy Gregg had put in his retirement papers last March after thirty years on the job, the last eight in the Organized Crime and Rackets Bureau, which had been particularly aggressive in prosecuting higher-level organized criminals under the Organized Crime Control Act (OCCA), the New York State counterpart of the federal Racketeer-Influenced and Corrupt Organizations (RICO) statute, which permits law enforcement to deal with groups on an enterprise-wide basis rather than just the pursuit of isolated instances of criminal conduct.

Herc forwarded the picture of the duo who had attempted to put the snatch on Fiona. His text read, "Jimmy, I just hit town. Do youknow where to find these goons? This afternoon they tried to grab a good friend of mine. Herc."

Before he could make it from the plane, through the terminal, and down to the subway which would take him to Grand Central Station, he had received a call from Speedy. Herc gave him an abbreviated version of what was going on and asked to borrow a car, something non-descript and innocuous, but it should also have some guts. Speedy said he had one in mind and they agreed to meet up in Manhattan around ten o'clock. He also asked Speedy if he could bring along a small cooler with some ice, to which Speedy replied. "Does a bear wear a funny hat in the woods?"

While Herc was waiting on the train, Jimmy Gregg called him, and without any fanfare began his side of the conversation, "Those guys you are looking for are really bad men. They're known up here as Black Bart and Billy the Blade. They've killed off more people than David O. Selznick."

"I suspected as much," replied Herc, "Do you know where you can put your hands on them?"

Herc then gave Jimmy a similar version of what he had related to Speedy, and he then told him that it was his intention to put these two out of business. That was all Jimmy needed to hear. He wanted in.

Johnny and Willis returned to Willis' house to find Corina's car was still in the driveway, but the El Camino was back in the garage. Willis tried her phone but remembered that he still had it when it rang in his pocket. Johnny tried Katie again – straight to voice mail. She was avoiding his calls.

Out of frustration and a need to do something, they turned their attention to Corina's Miata. Willis said as they pushed the little red convertible into the relative warmth of the garage, "She says she's been having trouble starting this rice burner for a while, but once it starts, it runs fine."

Johnny seated himself behind the wheel and turned the key. The tiny car made a valiant attempt, but try as the starter might, the engine would not catch. He released the hood latch and Willis raised the hood, and in an almost believable English accent he clowned, "Let's have a peek under the bonnet. Shall we governor?"

They jiggled the distributor cap and the spark plug wires, but these seemed correct. They checked the tension of the alternator fan belt - still good. Willis asked Johnny to try it again, and, while he watched, Johnny turned it over again. There was the problem. He drew two fingers across his throat to signal Johnny to stop cranking the motor. He leaned over the engine compartment, and, with only his fingers, he bent the end of a stainless-steel hose clamp about a quarter of an inch, and said, "Try it again."

The engine roared to life and Willis dropped the hood and went to the garage refrigerator and grabbed two beers. Johnny looked at him quizzically, and after a long pull on his Becks, he quipped, "The hose clamp was retarding the spark. Saw it right off."

They sat and enjoyed the beer and the late afternoon sun, setting aside for the moment, the concerns about the gangster and what seemed to be a gathering of storm clouds. Then Johnny said what they were both thinking,

"Why don't we run this little sled over to Katie and Corina's joint and see if we can talk some sense to them?"

And so, the two lawyers washed up a little, and then Johnny suggested that they might be well served if they were to build in a little time cushion between their arrivals. He would go first in the Miata and cruise the streets of Katie's neighborhood just to see if he could spot any lurking trouble in the form of seedy mobsters watching and waiting for an opportunity to swoop. Willis would follow a few moments later in the El Camino, or get waved off via cell phone if the girls seemed to have acquired watchers. Their thinking was based upon the vague notion that these goons had not yet seen Corina's car, but for all they knew, this might be flawed logic.

Johnny scanned the shadows and cul-de-sacs for anything or anyone he sensed might be sinister as he crept through the oak tree lined streets of Katie's community, and then he spotted the same couple o' guys. They had acquired a new automobile, but still wore the same dull expressions as they sat and smoked, just around the corner from the girls' place. From the small pile of cigarette butts on the ground near the driver's door he did not think they had been there very long. Rather than alert them to a new vehicle, he just rolled on by and called Willis to advise him of the two broke-nosed loiterers.

They agreed to meet at a small park just up the road to discuss the options. Willis thought it might be time to call the cops in. Johnny agreed, but the question that took them a moment to reconcile was how best to stay off the police blotter themselves. They decided on a simple plan. They would go together in the Mazda and park a block or so away, from there they would use Corina's phone to call the Village of North Palm Beach police department to report two suspicious characters lurking near a community playground. This is just the sort of call which would roll a couple squad cars containing a couple of bored cops, but to make things a little more interesting for all concerned they broke out their trusty slingshots.

Once they were in an elevated and concealed hiding place with a view of the thugs and their car, Willis placed the call. He hoped that by not using the 911 number the police switchboard would not automatically record the source of the call, he whispered into the phone to hide his gender and to suggest to the police operator, a citizen who might be in trouble, and he kept the call short, "There are two scary men who have been parked in a white sedan outside my house on Coventry Lane for more than thirty minutes. I think they are watching the kids at the playground, it's kind of spooky and I'm afraid. Oh, God I think they just saw me!" and disconnected.

From their vantage point, they could see the entrance to the community, so, just as the patrol cars entered, Johnny let fly with two slightly rusted 3/8-inch coarse thread steel nuts which struck the windscreen of the hoods' car and made the two snap to attention and draw their fire arms. The cops arrived a few seconds later to find these two gun-wielding guys in a car which appeared to have fresh bullet holes in the windshield. Johnny chuckled to Willis, "This ought to be worth a trip downtown to see what the boys at lab can make of it."

Sure enough, the cops fell on them like a pack of hungry redbone hound dogs. Three police cars screeched to a stop, and before the men in the car could choose between winding their watches and shitting a ring around themselves, there were several pump-action Browning 12-gauge shot guns leveled at them. A loud speaker commanded them to drop their weapons and keep their hands in sight. Johnny and Willis snuck back to the Miata and cut out laughing, "That should keep those cats busy for a few hours."

Herc followed the signs two floors downstairs to the Sutphin Boulevard subway station. He purchased a one-time use Metro Card and proceeded to the train platform. After several transfers, he rode the Number 7 train into Grand Central Terminal. The throng of passengers made it easy to be inconspicuous, but still he stayed close to the walls and kept his dark brown felt fedora pulled low, allowing just a small gap between the collar of his black leather jacket and the brim to view his progress.

Once he had the Oyster Bar in sight he slid to the side and studied the entrance to the iconic restaurant with its vaulted tile ceiling, and then he spied Fiona in her school blazer and a New York Yankees ball cap. She stood at the far end of the arc and just the sight of her safe and apparently sane brought a slight smile to his face. He felt certain he could have told her to meet him at the Dili Bazaar in Kathmandu, Nepal, at the top of the world, and she would have confidently found her way there.

He noticed she happened to be standing in the whispering gallery and decided to have a little fun. A whispering gallery is most simply constructed in the form of a circular wall and allows whispered communication from any part of the internal side of the circumference, in this case the arc of the ceiling, to any other part. The sound is carried by waves that travel around the circumference clinging to the walls. He sidled to the other end of the entrance, and, with his head turned away from her, he whispered, "Fiona, can you hear me."

Fiona's head jerked and she looked around at the people near her. Herc smiled and repeated the question, "Fiona, can you hear me?"

Despite her confusion at not being able to find him, she nodded. Herc, again whispered, "Fiona, if you can hear me, bend down as if to tie your shoe lace and make an X on the floor with your finger." She did as she was told and then he said, "Good girl, now touch your nose and pull your left ear lobe twice."

About half way through this series of instructions, Fiona recognized the sequence as the counter-sign Herc had used when coaching her softball team to mean the hit and run play was on, and suddenly the perplexed look gave way and was replaced by a relieved smile. As Herc approached her, she broke her cover, ran flat out, and jumped into his open arms. After a few seconds' embrace in which Fiona's feet were a foot from the floor, he put her down, took her hand, and walked toward the exit and the cab stand. He said simply, with a flinty resolve she did not recognize, "Now let's go put the hit and run on Billy and Blackie."

Like most successful gangsters, L'il Augie controlled and segmented the information concerning the different sectors of his criminal empire. He did not want the left hands knowing what the right hands were doing and vice versa. When in residence in Palm Beach his back was protected by one Diego Lazette. Unlike the old school thugs, Diego Lazette did not have a string of braggadocios monikers, or even a known associate's file. He had no impressive arrest record splattered and streaked with convictions and jail time stretching back decades, and in fact Diego had never been arrested or convicted of any crime. His entire interaction with law enforcement could be easily summarized in three words: he was clean.

At the age of thirty-one Diego held Bachelor of Science degrees in Accounting and Finance from Rutgers University, and a MBA from the elite Wharton School of Business in Philadelphia. He was the under-publicized prototype of the changing face of organized crime. Like the FBI, Wall Street, and the Final Four (the remains of the Big Eight international accounting firms), the mob was quietly competing for America's best and brightest, and the package of perks and bennies they could proffer made their very select offers almost impossible to refuse. Aside from the handsome tax-free cash signing bonus (just an expression, almost no records were kept, and no signatures were ever affixed to any documentation), there was little emphasis on the oppressive certifications, and ongoing education required if one wanted to swim in the largest legitimate ponds. Local wise guys were becoming global smart guys who could see and play the odds and angles without all the paperwork camouflage requisite at Goldman Sachs or Credit Suisse.

Fleecing the sheep now entailed far more artistry than ardor, and the need was for more binary code and Boolean logic, and considerably less call for the sociopath and his dim witted younger brother, the psychopath. Technology and stealth had all but replaced brick bats and blow torches. The really big money was no longer in prostitution, small-time numbers racquets or big rig hi-jacking, but instead a very profitable enterprise could be quickly built with a few very bright associates operating in the shadows and could be disassembled and disappeared in half the time. L'il Augie loved a powerful reverse gear, "I want to be able to get out of trouble twice as fast as I got in."

Piles of money could be found within the vagaries of the international monetary system, and rather than the past generations use of intimidation and brute force, the modern mover knew the best crimes were insider crimes of guile, which would never be detected, and were usually committed from half a world away.

The days of the no-neck, broke-nose thug were waning – waning but not extinct. Diego Lazette, despite his impressive academic achievements, was not all theory and no application, and he also had no neck and a broke nose. He had been a serious contender at the NCAA regional track and field meets for three consecutive years in the discus and hammer throw, and was undefeated in 109 light heavy-weight bouts as a collegiate wrestler. He had either evolved or devolved to the place that he actually enjoyed pain and had discovered it was the switch to his overdrive. In one match after receiving an accidental elbow which deviated his septum, he not only came back to win the bout with a pin, he had dislocated his opponent's shoulder and cauliflowered his ear.

He was a quiet and unassuming fellow whose exterior calm was bolstered by confidence born of competence and hardened in the crucible of the arena. Behind his passive blue eyes resided an imposing intellect, and if necessary, he could draw upon remarkable physical gifts. If he were ever inclined to put the squeeze on someone, he knew the pressure points, and he had the hand strength of an iron worker, and, rest assured, someone would quickly cry Uncle!

He lived in a mob-financed six room apartment next door to L'il Augie in the Palm Beach Towers, and mostly Diego spent his day scanning and skimming the financial back waters of the internet in search of poorly protected securities, or capitalizing on unstable third world currency futures. Amato backed Diego's plays with accredited funds or, if preferred, untraceable cash, and should a disruptive labor strike, or industrial accident, be needed to disappoint Wall Street analysts a few days before a targeted company's quarterly earnings statement, L'il Augie would work the correct underworld levers. Diego applied discretion and the proper financial instruments to profit on both the inevitable fall, and the predictable rise of that company's common stock. Diego was as close to a friend as L'il Augie ever got, which was a real anomaly, and the gang paid attention. He respected the young man's abilities, and he liked his style, and Diego scored additional points of endearment in his commitment that should any hostile force come at L'il Augie Amato while he was in Florida, that force would first have to get past Mr. Lazette.

Former NYPD Detective Jimmy Gregg and Bronx chop shop owner Francisco Gonzalez waited in front of Grand Central Terminal at the cab stand on 42nd Street. While they waited on Herc and his mysterious "friend," just a flash of his gold shield was all the Yellow Cab dispatcher needed to leave them undisturbed in Speedy's rather plain looking dark gray four door Chevrolet Caprice. While the Caprice looked non-descript, it was anything but. Speedy had replaced the 4.3-liter V6 power plant with a fuel injected Corvette 427 cubic inch engine, which alone doubled the original 245 horse power. He and his pals replaced the four-speed automatic transmission with an electronic six-speed, paddle shift, which converted the fantastic horse power into massive torque to the low-profile rear wheels, and a gear change could be performed in less than one quarter of a second. This car had a top end of 170 miles per hour, but the truly impressive stats were tied to its hole-shot. It could go from a standing start to sixty in just under four seconds, and, if you stood on it, the car would rocket past 100 in less than six seconds.

"Very cool," replied Jimmy, "Sounds like a lot of hard work"

Speedy replied, "It was as easy as falling off a piece of cake."

He shared the story of the car's transformation with Jimmy, who was also a gearhead and appreciated the details. Jimmy sighed and used the endearment Francisco's children used, "Popi loves mambo."

The two had been friends in the army and, for the most part, had retained their friendship, but, to avoid potential conflicts of interest, their relationship had been maintained from a hailing distance, with plenty of notice given should Jimmy want to drop by for a cup o' Joe.

Neither of the men really knew what to expect, but, from their past experiences with Herc, they felt certain whatever he had planned would jump off quickly. Hercules Dendy liked the direct approach.

Even though they had kept an eye on the exit of the station, and the crowd of commuters was relatively thin, neither of them noticed Herc's approach and were startled by his tap on the passenger side window. They recovered their composure quickly and started to climb out to welcome him, but Herc gestured for them to stay put as, first, what appeared to be a young woman and then Herc slid across the rear bench seat. Without any fanfare, he said to Speedy "Let's get moving."

It was obvious that Herc was concerned about being observed, but, since two of his best friends could scarcely recognize him at close range, Jimmy turned his trained observation skills upon the girl, who had by now removed her ball cap and turned down the collar of a school blazer. Once they had "moved" about fifty yards from the cab stand, Herc made spare introductions, but not in the Emily Post approved style of "Mr. Jimmy Gregg and Mr. Francisco Gonzalez, please say hello to Miss Fiona Montgomery." It was done more in the style of a park ranger pointing out the curiosities of a natural vignette, "One of the guys in the front seat is a cop and the other's a criminal, I'll let you decide which."

After a brief look of confusion had cleared from her face, Fiona extended her hand, first to Jimmy and then to Speedy, "You'll have to excuse my friend here; he does not get into the city very often. I'm Fiona."

A quick glance passed between the two men in the front seat, which even to the untrained and unfamiliar, could be read as a clearly as a large rubber stamp across an application: Approved.

Herc interrupted the pleasantries of Fiona's more socially correct form of introduction, "Jimmy do you have a handle on where to find these two jailbirds?"

Jimmy responded without turning to face him, "A nephew of mine is on them. They left Sarah Lawrence about two hours ago and had supper at some Guido joint down in Brooklyn. Bad Billy seems to have a fat lip."

In the rear-view mirror, Speedy noticed Herc flash a smile of pride,

"Good, it probably matches his fat head. That memento is from our girl here, and I suspect it will make them try a little harder next time."

The words "next time" sent a chain reaction shiver through the car, and Speedy said what the others were thinking, "Next time. I thought we would just stash our girl here somewhere safe, like my mom's house in the Bronx and go deal with these guys from a distance. You know, one shot, one kill."

Herc's calm response made Fiona realize there were very deep pools in his past of which she was completely unaware, "Not this time. These guys did not just wake up this morning and say to themselves, let's take a run up the Hudson and snatch us a girl." He had their attention, "No sir, they are on somebody's payroll, and, should they disappear, others will get the nod."

Jimmy nodded in agreement, "Better the devil you know, than the one you don't."

Herc began peering into the small piece of luggage he had brought and asked Speedy for the cooler he had requested he bring along. Speedy handed back a plastic six pack cooler and said, "I put a few Red Stripes on ice."

Herc accepted the cooler, cracked open a beer and, offered a sip to Fiona who declined with a quick shake of her head, but she was very curious about what he was pulling from his bag. She reached out to pull open the top and Herc intercepted her hand with starling speed and force using a phrase he only used when he wanted to remind her that she did not yet know everything. He said, "Careful little girl!"

He placed a brown paper wrapped package about the size of a meatball hoagie on top of the icy beers and put the cooler on the floor between his feet.

"What say we go get a look at these guys?" asked Herc.

Speedy replied, "I suspected you might want to get right into it. We are rolling in that direction."

"Then let's kick this pig!"

Speedy, eager to show off a little, knocked the paddle shifter down a couple of gears and punched the accelerator. The Caprice roared across the Williamsburg Bridge and onto the Brooklyn Queens Expressway.

Former NYPD detective Gregg checked with his nephew Stevie Fontaine via cell phone as to the whereabouts of the two goons he had been asked to tail. Blackie was on his forth beer and Billy had switched over to scotch. Reportedly, if Billy had wanted to get the warm brown liquid down any faster, he would have needed a funnel and a stevedore. Stevie thought they would probably be headed home soon.

Herc's plan was simple and very direct. They would relieve Stevie and send Jimmy home with him. As the only real representative of law enforcement on the team, the men agreed that Jimmy should be in some other part of the city, with plenty of witnesses to establish his alibi. Speedy called a young nephew to bring him another car which would allow him to watch one of the men when they eventually split up to go to their separate homes in Brooklyn. And that's how it went down.

When the two drunken gangsters staggered out of the restaurant and to their car, Herc and Fiona tailed them from a distance in the souped-up Caprice, and Speedy and his nephew Manolo tagged along a few blocks back. There was no need for close surveillance since Jimmy had provided the home addresses where Billy and Blackie were probably headed, and sure enough, Blackie pulled up in front of a small and surprisingly well-groomed cottage on Alder Avenue. Billy sloshed out. Apparently, Blackie would forego a goodnight kiss, and he drove away without waiting to see that his date safely reached the front door. Herc coasted to a stop at the curb with the head lights off several houses away, pulled on a pair of black leather gloves, and silently exited the car. Fiona slipped behind the steering wheel and adjusted the seat and mirror to better fit her diminutive stature. She would wait for Herc's whistle to signal her to bring the car closer.

The Speedy squad followed Blackie on down that long dark road. He was headed to a similar home on Dixon six blocks away.

Billy the Blade had had a tough day, and it was about to get immeasurably worse. After putting away the best part of a fifth of Dewar's, his swollen lip only pained him when he accidentally brushed or bumped it, which he did about once every five minutes, and each incident would elicit a short burst of graphic profanity. When he dropped his keys after unlocking the front door Herc was on him like an irate gorilla. He grabbed the back of his shirt with one hand and his belt with the other and slammed Billy's head into the solid oak front door. This propelled Billy onto the carpeted floor of his home's entry hall. As Billy rolled over to face his attacker he reached for the nine-millimeter pistol at his waist, but before he could draw it from his belt, Herc delivered what Guy Dendy, Herc's father, had called the invisible Marciano knockout punch. This punch only traveled about fifteen inches, and if you blinked, as Billy did, you might not see it at all. This punch had the same effect on Billy as it had had on Jersey Joe Walcott when it was delivered by the Hard Rock from Brockton. Bad Billy went out.

Fiona was astounded at the speed with which Herc's whistle reached her, and she slipped the car into drive and zoomed up to the curb in front of Billy's house. When she reached the front porch, she saw Herc tying the hands of an unconscious Billy behind his back with an extension cord to one of the decorative columns which separated the dining room from the parlor. Herc motioned for Fiona to come in and close the door. As she did, Herc withdrew the gun from Billy's belt and slid it across the floor to her and said, "Hand me that cooler."

Fiona scooped up the gun feeling the heft of it, and let a snort of laughter escape as she handed over the small igloo cooler, "Is this the best time for a beer?"

Herc flashed a grin and replied, "It's never a bad time."

He removed the remaining Red Stripe, popped the cap and took a short pull from the bottle and savored the flavor for a few seconds. He then poured the rest of the beer over Billy the Blade's head, which brought him sputtering back to a fuzzy and confused consciousness, and as he began to writhe and struggle against his bonds, he slurred, "What the hell, who the fuck are you?"

Herc tossed aside the empty beer bottle and replied, "I'm the guy who is about to rip your lips off and feed 'em to my turtle if you don't answer some questions."

Before Billy could finish his standard reply to such requests for information, "I'm not telling you shit," the cell phone in his pocket played a ringtone which would have surprised all but a small group of men – In the Navy by The Village People. Herc retrieved the phone from his jacket despite the protests and attempts by Billy to kick and bite him. On the cell phone's small display there was a picture of Blackie wearing a lopsided grin. He allowed the phone to ring on through to voice mail, and said over his shoulder to Fiona who had been watching the exchange with a mixture of horror and curiosity, "You'd be surprised how many of these wise guys like the Fandango."

This jab at Billy sexual orientation further incensed him and he screamed, "When I get loose I'm gonna teach you to dance." Herc had read that Billy was fiercely homophobic in a copy of the police file which Jimmy Gregg had given to him and remembered that Billy and Blackie had begun their criminal association some thirty years back hi-jacking truckloads of cigarettes while serving in the US Navy. He got their joke but continued to taunt his prisoner with gay epithets, "Sweet William, if you ever want to get back to smooching with your girlfriend here," Herc gestured to the phone, "you are going to have to come clean. Why is L'il Augie after this girl?"

As Fiona stepped into his field of view, Billy saw for the first time that Herc was not alone, and he recognized the Sarah Lawrence coed who had split his lip earlier that day. With this realization, he started another profane rant. Before three syllables had cleared his mouth Herc landed a quick left with this gloved fist to his nose which silenced Billy, "Language, Billy, you are in the presence of your betters."

Herc tossed the phone to Fiona and then turned his attention to the

cooler, "See what you can find on this moron's phone. I'm going to introduce him to my little friend."

Herc gave the front of Billy's shirt a vicious tug and the buttons
flew about the room like a broken box of chicklets, exposing his scarred
white underbelly. Herc retrieved the package from the cooler and, while
still wearing his gloves, he carefully unwrapped what had appeared to be
a submarine sandwich. Keeping his eyes on Billy's eyes, he asked Fiona,
"What do you know about Lionfish?"

Fiona, who stood several feet away still holding Billy's gun in one hand,
and his phone in the other, looked up to find Herc holding the brightly-
colored fish that he had speared on the reef a few miles off Palm Beach,
just twelve hours earlier and replied, "Well, they are really beautiful, and
they taste great with a peach and mango salsa."

Herc held the fish by the tail, and without warning, suddenly slapped
it down hard across the right side of Billy's belly, and calmly persisted with
his questions of Fiona, "That's right. What else?"

"They are really becoming a problem on the reefs because they eat
everything and have no real predators."

To Billy's astonishment, he began to writhe in reaction to the pain,
and he begun to feel the effects of the toxins which were released by the
Lionfish's dorsal spines. Several of them had broken off and were lodged
in his side. The look in his eyes had almost instantly transformed from
seething contempt to confused fear. Herc quietly asked, "And if they make
such fine eating, how come they don't have any predators?"

"Oh yeah," replied Fiona who was picking up her queues like a pro,
"They are poisonous."

Herc eyed Billy's growing panic and replied, "Close. Actually, they are
venomous. Poison implies a substance which must be ingested to cause
damage. These little guys carry a venom which only requires a puncture of
the skin as the method of delivery. Do you remember what the effects are
on the unlucky bastard with a little prick?"

"Let's see, first, intense pain and reddening in the affected area."

Herc peered closely at the welts beginning to radiate from the small wounds next to an old jagged scar on Billy's side. "I think our boy here is experiencing those symptoms, but judging from some of these scars, a little pain doesn't mean anything to him." Without warning Herc dealt another Billy another vicious smack across Billy's other side, "What else?"

"Usually the pain is just the beginning. Depending on the victim's conditioning, the venom can cause nausea, vomiting, respiratory problems, convulsions, heartburn and diarrhea."

Herc nudged Billy's leg with his foot, leaned in close to his battered face, and said, "Pretty and smart, huh, but I'm afraid she might be sugar-coating the truth just a bit. What she is describing is a casual, accidental puncture of a hand or leg from a fish that's just trying to get away. You know, an extremity. What we have here is deliberate injections to the torso in the vicinity of the heart and kidneys. Pretty soon those organs will react to the toxin by slowly shutting down. Believe me Bill," said Herc as he pressed on one of the broken quills lodged in his side, "It is no way to go out."

By now Billy was sweating profusely, and the pain had reached a searing level and was indeed affecting his breathing. Herc turned away from the thug and said to Fiona, "Anything interesting on this scumbag's phone?"

"Well aside from Blackie, there is a number from a Palm Beach County area code in the recent calls."

Herc said to Billy, "My guess is that's L'il Augie's number. How about it Billy, or do you want to see how good the good doctors around here are at isolating an obscure venom from the Caribbean while your kidney's turn to goo? Oh yeah, did I mention I have a whole cooler full of this guy's relatives? You might not make it to Belleview in time, but I understand they have a fine morgue."

At last Billy broke, "Alright, you win. Augie just wanted us to grab the girl and hold her. We are supposed to text him when we have her."

Herc again persisted with his questioning, "Is that goon down in Palm Beach?"

Billy hesitated as he considered the consequences of ratting out the boss, but, as Herc inspected the Lionfish still in his gloved hand for undamaged quills, Billy quickly saw the wisdom of crossing that bridge when and if he ever came to it. He started to nod his head when Herc noticed Billy's eyes break contact with his own and dart toward the front of the house. Just then the door burst open and Blackie rushed in holding a silenced pistol which he planned to use to silence whoever it was that was hurting his friend.

Thanks to Billy's tell, Herc was already a moving target when Blackie opened up. The first two shots were clean misses, but the third grazed Herc's left shoulder, and, before he could get off a fourth, he was surprised by a vivid pain in his own shoulder. That pain was short lived, as the second bullet Fiona fired from Billy's nine-millimeter passed through his throat and spine, dropping him to his knees, and giving him about eight seconds of consciousness to see and recognize the coed who had eluded him and Billy that morning holding the proverbial smoking gun.

Blackie then tumbled forward on to his face, his dead eyes fixed and dilated. Fiona dropped the pistol and ran to the open front door, glanced quickly outside for anyone who might be coming as a second wave, and, seeing no one, she closed and locked the door. She then rushed to Herc who was kneeling on the floor inspecting the wound in his shoulder. The bullet had passed cleanly through without much bleeding, or any major damage to bone or tendon, but it still hurt like hell. Tears began to well up in Fiona's eyes at the sight of the man she regarded as indestructible grimacing on the blood splattered floor. When Herc saw her reaction he quickly composed himself, winked at her, and spoke quietly, "Not too bad. See if you can find a clean dish cloth to plug this hole."

Fiona dashed into the kitchen and returned quickly with several white linen cocktail napkins and a bottle of cold water. She helped him remove his arm from his black leather jacket, pulled apart the already torn fabric of his grey tee shirt, and began delicately dabbing at the wound. Herc took a long draw from the bottle of water and sloshed a little onto the bullet hole to facilitate the triage. It was at this point he realized that, aside from his shoulder and shirt, the bullet had also left two small holes in the leather jacket he treasured. Fiona knew there was about to be a scene as Herc roared, "Billy, you sonofabitch, somebody is going to pay for this!"

But as he turned toward Billy, who was still tied to the column, Herc knew immediately that Billy was beyond any revenge he might seek. Apparently, Blackie's first two misses were anything but clean. The first had struck Billy in the abdomen just below the sternum, and the second had entered his skull just above the right eye. The two dead gangsters now seemed to be looking at one another from across the room with identical blank stares. Whatever remained of them would have to face the Styx River boatman without the customary coins thought necessary for passage through the underworld.

Fiona's eyes scanned the bloody mess and then looked to Hercules for guidance. As ever, his mind was a step or two further down the path to what next, but his wound slowed his physical movement. Much like working on a car in the small carport in Lake Park, Herc used her as an extra, undamaged set of arms and legs, "We need to erase our presence from this place. Get a couple of garbage bags from the kitchen. Look in the cabinet under the sink."

As he sat in a straight-back chair, he peeled off his gloves and gave them to the girl who slipped them onto her delicate hands, and then she followed his instructions to rearrange the crime scene. "With a little luck, the cops won't discover this for a day or two, and when they do they'll think these guys got into a ruckus and shot each other. It might also buy us some time before L'il Augie calls in reinforcements."

First, using a roll of paper towels, she wiped up, as best she could, the relatively small about of blood that had leaked from Herc's shoulder. She then removed the extension cord which bound Billy's hands, and, after wiping Billy's gun clean of her prints, she placed it in his right hand. She then found the two shell casings that had been ejected from the gun and tossed them closer to Billy. Carefully avoiding the widening puddles of blood, she retrieved the Lionfish and empty beer bottle and returned them to the cooler. Herc was now up and moving. He fished the wallets of Blackie and Billy from their stiffening bodies as well as Blackie's cell, and reminded Fiona to collect Billy's phone from the parlor floor. He found the thermostat and moved the indicator from heat to off and instructed Fiona to open several of the casement windows which could not be seen from the street. His brief explanation registered with Fiona as a prudent move, "These guys are going to get ripe pretty quick unless we put them in the deep freeze. It's getting cold outside – let's let it inside."

Almost immediately the temperature began to drop in the small parlor and Herc noticed Fiona, still dressed in her school duds, was trembling with the chill. He tossed her an obviously hand crocheted afghan which was folded neatly on the back of the fifties style divan, saying, "Well what do you know? Even Billy the Badass had a mom."

There was never any discussion between the two about how this crime should be handled as far as the police or the NYC District Attorney's perspective. A friend will help you move – a good friend will help you move a body. Fiona's and Herc's friendship fit easily within the latter category. After one last inspection, Herc, with Fiona's tender assistance, put his leather jacket on, and pushing the button on the front door lock, the oddly matched pair of night fighters stole away.

Herc was torn between embarrassment, that because of his wound the girl would have to drive, and the pride he felt over her unquestioned ability to pilot this rocket as well as any man. Fiona was struggling to encapsulate and segment her feelings concerning the grizzly scene they were fleeing. Had she really just killed a man? She had no choice. Right? It was us or them. And a rationale from childhood – They started it. There would be plenty of time for her to reexamine her reactions and her actions of the past few minutes if they survived the next few but, for now, there was just no time for recrimination.

She would explore these another time, and, without any conscious recognition that she was using Scarlet O'Hara's tactic, she thought, "I can't worry about this now. I'll think about it tomorrow."

Once Herc was secured in the passenger seat, Fiona hurried around the car, jumped in behind the wheel, and looked over at her passenger who was slumped, in obvious pain, against the door. He smiled through his grimace and said, "Let's go find out why we didn't get any warning from Manolo." He said as an important after thought, "Baby, you have done great tonight, but it's not over by a long shot."

Fighting back a tear, she turned the key in the ignition, lightly slapped his knee, and replied, "Where to Boss?"

To Herc, the plan had seemed clear. While Speedy took Jimmy Gregg home, Manolo was to follow Blackie to 1621 Dixon Street and watch to make certain he stayed there. If he should stir, Manolo was to call Herc's cell and apprise him. On the short drive from Billy's blood bath, Herc checked his cell phone to confirm that he had no messages. He then compared the phones of the dead guys and saw the call Blackie had made to Billy had happened within a few minutes of when they had split up. He had left no message and Herc estimated that Blackie had burst through Billy's door about fifteen minutes after the call. How did he get past Speedy's nineteen-year-old nephew?

Manolo Gonzalez was Speedy's younger brother's oldest son. When he was introduced to Herc and Fiona Speedy whispered, "A good kid, but still a little green behind the ears."

Manny worked around the garage and given any say in the matter, would have chased the opportunity to play his old Martin guitar in the after-hours jazz clubs of the village. He could really pick it, but any time the subject of a musical occupation arose, the jokes would begin. "What's the difference between a musician and a park bench? A park bench can support a family of four."

Over his objections, the entire family insisted he attend NYC University. As Speedy had repeatedly told him, "You might end up a garbage man, but you are going to be a garbage man with a college degree. Maybe you will see the value in a degree working here and sweating like a bullet."

He was a handsome kid with a brilliant smile and Herc had noticed Fiona's usually outgoing personality had been more reserved, and he saw that she could not seem to draw her eyes away from his face. Herc knew some kid would eventually catch her eye, but he had thought it would be some preppy at school, or maybe a surfer, but as he witnessed her attraction to Manny he thought, "She could do much worse."

Herc instructed Fiona to slowly cruise past the car where the boy sat, apparently asleep a few houses away from Blackie's place. They made the block and seeing nothing stirring, they pulled the Caprice in behind his car and Herc started to get out and wake the kid, but Fiona stopped his labored effort with, "Stay put – I'll go."

Fiona shrugged the afghan from her shoulders, exited the car, crept forward and tapped lightly on the driver's side window. The sleeping boy did not move, so she tried the door which opened easily, but as it did the dome light came on, and a crimson streak on the boy's shirt front became evident. From the Caprice, Herc noticed the change in her face as shock seemed to engulf her. Despite his injury, Herc was quickly at the girl's side. Together they discovered the reason they had received no call. The boy had a sizable contusion on his left temple and a small rivulet of dried blood seemed to flow from his ear to his chest – he was not asleep, he was unconscious.

Blackie had apparently spotted him either as he drove or when Manny parked. When Billy failed to answer, he had slipped out of the back door and surprised the kid when he suddenly jerked open the car door and clocked him soundly with his gun barrel. From there Blackie had quickly made his way to his appointment with the reaper.

The pressures of the day had finally caught up with Fiona, and tears began rolling down her pale cheeks, "Is he dead?"

Herc replied. "No, but he's gonna have one hell of a headache when he comes to. Help me get him into our car."

Ordinarily Herc could have snatched the 160-pound boy from the driver's seat and put him in the back seat of the Caprice with one hand, but tonight he would need Fiona's help. She took Manolo's head and shoulders while Herc used his good arm to grab the tattered cuffs of the boy's jeans. He was pleased to see the concern in Fiona's eyes as she did her best to gently cradle his head. Within thirty seconds the transfer had been made, and Herc returned to Manny's car to move it a few blocks away just in case the cops should become involved.

When he climbed back into the Caprice, he saw that the afghan Billy's mom had so lovingly knitted, God knows how many years before, was folded to form a pillow for Manolo's battered noggin. He glanced over at the girl who said defensively, "What? We've got a heater in the car."

Herc called Speedy and quickly explained their need for a doctor. Speedy told him he would arrange everything and to head for his garage. After a few quick turns to make certain they were not being followed, Herc helped Fiona find a ramp onto Interstate 678 North and Garmin's Go Home setting supplied the other directions. Herc returned his attention to the cell phone he had taken from Billy the Blade. "Let's let L'il Augie think his boys got the job done. Here, put this towel in your mouth and act like it's a gag."

Herc fumbled with the phone until he found the camera and said, "Look wide-eyed and scared. This one is going to the goon who started all of this crap."

Fiona lightly tied the hand towel around her neck and put on her timid and terrified face for the picture. Herc texted the photo and just four words to Billy's boss, "We have the girl."

It took only two minutes for a response, "Good job. Throw her in the trunk and start heading this way. Don't hurt her."

Herc glanced over at Fiona who was now using the linen hand towel they had liberated from Billy's kitchen to wipe her eyes and blow her nose. She smiled weakly. Herc said to his young friend, "Come on. Let's get a move on – we've got places to be!"

This was just the remedy Fiona needed. A slightly twisted smile slowly spread across her face, she went a little snake-eyed, tapped the paddle shifter, and as the needle on the tach jumped, the car's acceleration pushed them deeper into their seats and she replied, "Drop a gear and disappear."

The Garmin GPS in Speedy's Grey Caprice predicted an arrival time of 1:22 A.M. but with no traffic to speak of, and only one very quick stop; a fifteen second pause at a Bronx dumpster to deposit the debris from Billy's place, they arrived at 12:59. To merely say they made good time did not pay the proper respect to how quickly they had covered the distance. At one point Fiona felt a bit of panic as she blew past a black and white parked in the breakdown lane of the interstate at 125 miles per hour, but either the cop was asleep, or the more likely scenario was that a veteran policeman this close to the end of his shift did not want to engage in a chase, and the mountain of paperwork which would be required, especially considering this pursuit had a foregone conclusion. There would be no catching this lightning bolt, so why start a big commotion over what might have been a mirage?

Manolo was still unconscious, but his breathing was deep and regular. She figured that he would be okay, but she harbored real concern for Herc, who had also down shifted and was conserving his energy. He did not speak and he stared dully at the dash board. At one point, it occurred to Fiona to lay two fingers on the inside of his wrist to check his pulse, which barely elicited a response from her weary and wounded passenger. His pulse was strong and steady, but she playfully taunted him with a threat upon which she knew she could never make good, "Listen up old man, the minute you turn corpse I'm going to get myself a real mentor," her voice trailed off, and softened, and she felt a catch in her throat, "and you know how hard you were to train, so please don't go."

 The Band "It Makes No Difference"
https://www.youtube.com/watch?v=uSHzODm-Ik8

S peedy rolled up the steel garage door and motioned for Fiona to pull into the spacious bay. He opened the passenger door and attempted to help Herc from the car. Herc brushed away the offer with a glare that said, "Do I look like a woman?"

Speedy grinned and introduced a bespectacled gentleman carrying what appeared to be a physician's satchel, "Say hello to my oldest brother Gomez. We all call him Doc."

The brief rest in the car while en route to Speedy Gonzalez's garage, and the hot bowl of chili Speedy handed him upon their arrival, had a remarkable effect on Herc. He insisted that the doctor, another member of the Gonzalez clan, take care of the still unconscious boy first.

The doctor agreed with Herc's assessment, "He's been out for quite a while. Maybe there is something going on inside his head."

Dealing with his concern in the usual tough guy way, Speedy said, "If there is, it will the first time."

Speedy and Doc carefully moved the boy from the car's rear seat and up the stairs with Fiona close behind. She had been worried that a garage, while fine for repairing automotive maladies, might not be an appropriate setting for patching problems with the human condition, but she need not have been concerned. The plain door at the top of stairs concealed a rather spacious and spotlessly clean apartment complete with plush carpeting, grand entertainment center, and a kitchen which gleamed with modern stainless-steel appliances. The solid oak kitchen table had been cleared and covered with a clean bed sheet, and that is where they laid Manny.

Fiona jockeyed for position to keep watch as Doc began his examination. But within a few seconds Speedy's wife Marie, appeared at her side, and noticing the specks of blood and brains on Fiona's clothing she said, "These guys can handle this. Let's get you cleaned up a little."

Marie guided her through the bedroom door and into the tastefully decorated bathroom, and made conversation to distract the girl's attention and lessen her concern, "Don't worry. The head is one place this whole family has repeatedly shown they can take a punch."

Fiona tried to nonchalantly extract some information about the injured boy, "Shouldn't we call someone about him? His mom or his girlfriend?"

Marie immediately saw through this less than subtle probe, but rather than bust her, she smiled and replied, "His mother knows, and he doesn't have a steady girl. There are plenty who would love to be with him, but the right one has not yet appeared. Love is a capricious fellow you know, and timing is everything."

Marie turned on the shower, helped her out of her soiled clothes, and handed her a towel saying, "We've got a cousin who owns a dry-cleaning business just around the corner. We'll get these cleaned and pressed and back to you in no time."

"But it's so late. Won't you wake him?"

Marie replied, "As many times as he has called Francisco in the middle of the night, broke down and drunk, I hope I do wake him – don't you worry. Until then, I have some underwear that will fit you and you can wear these."

From Fiona's reaction, an uninformed observer, which Marie was, would have thought the girl had been given cashmere and calfskin, but the neatly folded garment she had been handed, the cause of Fiona's wide smile, was a worn, but clean, pair of white coveralls, size small.

Winston Montgomery's cell phone began to vibrate on the night stand next to the digital clock/radio which read 5:05. Ordinarily he would have just rolled over and ignored it, but what his mind, subconsciously or not, registered from the dimly lit clock face was not so much the time but the alternate and urgent message: **SOS**.

His danger sensors were tingling as he accepted the call, and a familiar voice Winston could not initially match with a face began, "Mr. Montgomery, this is Hercules Dendy, do you know who I am?"

Winston lost all pretense of playing it cool, "Fiona's softball coach. How did you get this number?"

The voice on the other end replied, "Not important, and as time is the thing, please listen. I have just a few minutes to tell you some things that, should you survive the next couple of days, are going to change your life."

Whatever remained of Winston's lethargy vanished and, like Ross Perot, he was all ears as he said simply, "Go."

Over the next seven minutes Herc rolled out the events of the past thirty-six hours. His reconstruction describing the structure and content of the impending peril facing his daughter had the precisely truthful ring of a tuning fork, and his conclusions focused a homing pointer upon Winston's past sins, which had finally, despite his long-running habitual denial, come home to roost.

"We have a small window of opportunity," Herc concluded "I suspect you will be getting a call from Mr. Big making some outrageous demands, which will no doubt, include the surrender of The Green Flash." Herc paused to give Winston a swing at plausible deniability, and, as none was forthcoming, continued, "Reluctantly agree to any exchange point he suggests, but insist the swap be arranged for daylight hours in a public place, and demand to see Fiona before you give up anything."

Herc concluded his view of the opening skirmishes with, "Fiona and I have been playing an away game, but we are natural born homers, so get on the blower and arrange an executive jet to get us back to the home-field advantage. Call me back."

Winston was not accustomed to being told what to do. For over two dozen years, he had been the one calling the shots, but everything Dendy had said made sense, especially when Winston conceded that he had no plan at all. Would he make the arrangements that had been suggested, or was that demanded? He bridled a bit at the choice of verbs, but finally settled on a compromise; he would make the arrangements that been requested. His next move would be to activate some of the doom's day defense plans he had carefully constructed.

By the time the clock/radio read 6:35, he had methodically worked the speed dial of his smart phone like a bookie on Derby Day. He called Herc back to report his progress, "Mr. Dendy, there will be an eight passenger Cessna 560 Citation jet waiting for you at Farmington General Aviation Airport on Long Island by eight o'clock this morning. The pilot is Captain Carlos Tabernella. Do you need any help getting there?"

Herc replied, "No sweat, we're own our way," and in reaction to the concern fairly dripping from the phone, he tried to ease the tension, "Good work Winston, we'll see you soon."

As they disconnected, Winston thought, "Sooner than you think."

The flight plan which Captain Tabernella filed would take them from Farmington, New York at 480 miles per hour to Jupiter Regional Airport, with one quick touch and go at the small executive airstrip in West End, Bahamas.

It had been decades since Winston had used his fists. He had done a little boxing in prep school, and had been on the fencing team in college, but the only thing he had battled lately were billfish. However, if his daughter was being threatened, he pledged by God, he was going to be in the fight.

6:55 a.m. Eastern Standard Time found Herc and Fiona in the semi-secret second floor apartment of a Bronx chop shop. Despite the massive flow of adrenaline over the chaotic day's events, Fiona had succumbed to her exhaustion and was sound asleep in Speedy's queen-size bed.

The Gonzales clan understood the ethical conundrum with which she was and would, for the future, grapple but, she seemed to be resting well, so the door to the bedroom was closed under the maxim. " Everything will look better in the morning."

However, though Fiona's exhaustion was nearly complete, she did not immediately find a pathway to dreamless sleep. She had been on a guilt-driven treadmill of debate and supposition for the past six hours while she was conscious, and now a new, oddly-lighted floor show threatened to upstage her subconscious as well. Her head touched down on the goose down, and almost at once she drifted away from the extraordinary situation in which she found herself. As if in a grainy 8mm film, she returned to the scenes of the day's crimes. She flinched at the deafening reports from the pistol she seemed to always hold, and she subliminally examined her provisional claim to integrity, or was that decency? With the memories of at least one, possibly two, murders insinuating themselves, Fiona's tortured mind sought a few seconds alone and undisturbed, in a secure retreat, for contemplation and a detached look at the possible consequences.

In an apparent effort to normalize her perspective and intellectualize her qualms, her mind invented a safe zone and the means to subjectively consider today's field trip. These ruminations took the form of a single resolution which was projected from a smudgy replica of the classroom of her Sarah Lawrence freshman Philosophy, Ethics and Logic class.

The contention was simply stated: ***German philosopher Immanuel***

Kant juxtaposed a constant moral imperative against the usually self-serving employment of situational ethics as the rationalization of wrong doing, i.e. Resolved: To kill is always wrong. Please take either the affirmative or negative position and defend it in 500 words or less. Use personal examples if appropriate.

She knew Professor Greco prized conciseness, but after totaling and re-checking her word count she felt certain he would want more. Despite innumerable efforts, she could not develop a cogent response containing more than eight words. "But he was trying to kill my friend!"

Hours earlier, and, after Fiona had been gently removed from the main room, Doc had given Manolo a thorough examination, he said, "I don't think there is anything particularly wrong with this kid. Let's wake him up."

He withdrew a small cloth covered vial from his case and broke it with his fingers. He waved it under the boy's nose, and Ay, Kurumba! Manny began to stir, apparently trying to get away from the invisible fumes, "Spirits of harts' horn," he said to the small, but intensely interested group of spectators, "You know, smelling salts."

For Manolo's part, he was understandably confused, and the questions seemed to be wedged like the Three Stooges in a door opening. Finally, he was able to spread out and get organized, "What happened? How did I get here?" and then he sat bolt upright, "What about the girl, is she alright?"

Marie rushed forward to embrace the young man and spoke for the group, "Fiona is fine. She is resting. She is the one who brought you home. That little girl is one tough chickadee."

Herc interrupted the celebration, "Doc, now that this kid is done lying about, do you think you could patch me up?"

With Marie's help, Doc removed Herc's bloody clothes to expose a rather neat hole in his shoulder. Marie inspected the garments and noticed and read aloud the words embroidered on the linen hand towel they had taken from Billy the Blade's kitchen: If it has tires or testicles, it's going to be trouble, and drawing on many years of dealing with both, she reacted, "You've got that right!"

Everyone, especially Herc, enjoyed a good cleansing laugh from Marie's comment. It was just what the doctor would have ordered, had he wanted a prescription to lift the pall of anxiety that had blanketed the kitchen since the blue-grey Caprice had pulled through the garage door downstairs.

Herc barely grimaced as the doctor injected the area several times with lidocaine, and, within a few moments, he felt nothing as the wound was thoroughly cleaned, abraded, medicated, and dressed in sterile surgical gauze. He tried the shoulder for flexibility and lifted the end of the heavy oak table to check himself for strength. "That's great Doc. I'm going to need a bottle or two of this stuff and a few clean syringes."

While Fiona slept, Herc had found her phone and retrieved her father's private number which was digitally stored under "Daddy." He had added it to his contacts as Winston and had then found a quiet corner of the apartment and made the SOS call.

He returned to have a confab with Speedy, "We need to get to the airfield in Farmington, on Long Island. Can you take us?"

Speedy grinned and said, "Can Batman fly?"

Herc gave him a puzzled look and replied, "I don't think so?"

Speedy, who had never been good with this sort of repartee, assured Herc that he could deliver them at speeds far faster than that "silly white bread clown-fighter" anyway. "Just say when."

Herc said, "Let me grab a shower and some fresh clothes, and then we should scoot."

After the doctor had addressed the wounds and worries of the small band of vigilantes, the small apartment had quieted down for a few hours, and everyone had found a comfortable spot to grab forty winks, but now the entire place slowly brought up the pulse. It was soon humming like a bee hive. Marie returned from retrieving Fiona's freshly cleaned school clothes, which were neatly wrapped in brown paper, and she had also picked up warm bagels and donuts. As coffee percolated in the kitchen, Fiona emerged rubbing her eyes and stretching. Marie, who had always longed for a daughter, gestured for her to take a seat at the table, and, while she wolfed down three donuts, Marie produced a brush and began working some of the knots from the girl's auburn hair. Fiona endured the grooming and politely asked if it would be okay for her to stay dressed in the coveralls for the trip.

Speedy said it was alright with him, but he would not be making that call, and with a nod he acknowledged his wife's preeminence in the arena of appropriate fashion. Marie smiled tolerantly, finished tying the freshly pressed lace ribbon around Fiona's ponytail, and firmly denied her request, "This family does not get on any plane, much less a fancy private jet, dressed like grease monkeys." She handed the girl the neat stack of dry cleaning and pronounced the first order of the day, "Go Change."

Happy to be considered one of the family, Fiona philosophically shrugged off the denial of her request, "It was worth a shot."

When she returned just a few minutes later, Marie took her hand and led her to a full-length mirror on the back on the apartment's entry door. She stood behind her fussing with the collar of her blouse, and gazing wistfully at the girl's spit and polished reflection, she said over her shoulder, "Now this is how a young lady should look. Manolo, have you finished cleaning Fiona's shoes?"

Marie had not been the only member of the Gonzalez tribe who had been engaged in wistful gazing, and the boy leaped forward to present the shoes. He had removed most of the evidence of yesterday's travail, but the blood and mud-spattered laces could not be salvaged. He had replaced them with the lanyard from his sunglasses, and rather than just placing them in her outstretched hand, he took that hand and directed her to be seated. When she compliantly followed his direction, he knelt before her, slipped the saddle oxfords over her argyle knee socks, and tied perfect, if backward, bows. He looked shyly up to meet her eyes, the bandage around his head showing a slight crimson seepage from his wound Fiona gently brushed back a lock of his jet-black hair and bent to lightly kiss his battered face.

Herc emerged from the bedroom just in time to see the end of this tender exchange and said, "Aren't you afraid you'll get cooties? There is just no telling where he's been."

The spell broken, both teenagers blushed, stammered and then busied themselves with preparations for departure. After the patch job on Herc's shoulder, Doc had departed, but not before preparing a small post-operative care package. As requested he had included several vials of the lidocaine, pain pills, a course of antibiotics, clean dressings and half a dozen new syringes. All of this was accompanied by a list of simple instructions. Herc glanced over the hand-written note, wadded it up, and discarded it. Fiona immediately uncrumpled and folded it, and put it in her pocket.

The previous night Herc had shown that he was not bullet proof, nor was he impervious to pain, and despite her unflagging devotion to him, she would be assuming the role of nursemaid and perpetual nag. She removed the cap from the amoxicillin bottle, removed a single pill and handed it to him with a glass of water. To overcome his distain Marie supplied the verbiage, which Fiona also tucked away for future use, "It's just a pill. A tough guy like you can surely swallow a little pill."

Speedy had cleaned the Caprice of the detritus of yesterday. Despite the troupe's lethal encounters, the only apparent signs were a little of Herc's blood on several more of the linen hand towels from Billy's kitchen. One of them which had caught his eye was only slightly blood stained and he had sent it to the laundry with the other soiled garments. He tucked it into it into the inside breast pocket of Herc's freshly cleaned leather jacket – his hope was that it would provide some inspiration at some point in the future.

By the time Johnny and Willis had fixed Corina's car, had a beer, and decided it was time to intervene for the girls' own protection, it was too late. The women had already donned their finery and were off to the ball. The sun was just setting, and, while it did feel a bit early to be stepping out, this was Palm Beach and things started not long after the early bird dinner specials concluded.

Sunlight slowly yielded to another evening's twilight and within a few moments the beautifully pink and purple streaked sky would slip away and night would claim another day. For a few minutes the girls rode together in silence. Katie had put the top down on the elegant sports coupe, which allowed them to appreciate the giant royal palms towering along both sides of the grand Royal Park Boulevard.

Suddenly Corina spoke, "I can't believe I let you talk me into this Dancing for Dollars, how embarrassing!"

"Three points here," Katie replied, "First, I believe your only other option for tonight was doing your laundry. Second, you are a terrific dancer and should help them raise a bunch of money for these pitiful women."

She held up her hand to stop Corina's predictable interruption in protest. She continued the enumeration of her considered arguments, "Third, we are dressed to the nines and are headed for the Breaker's Mediterranean Ballroom where gentlemen of breeding and culture will line up to pay for the honor of a dance with us."

Corina made several false starts, complete with flared nostrils and rolling eyes, in a vain attempt to defend her position, but then she let her head loll against the leather head rest. She willed her mind to go blank and reset. Her friend was right. Alright, Corina needed to engage the drives that contained her "I'm steppin' out" memories so she simulated, as best she could, a relaxed, jaunty posture, and tried to enjoy the ride along the expansive boulevard and into Palm Beach. Palm Beach where the standard of elegance was set. She accepted, with a sigh, that her friend might be right, "Actually, I didn't have anything to do tonight. I did my laundry Thursday."

"My point exactly" Katie persisted, "you stay home to do laundry to free up Saturday night to do nothing. Let's look into getting you a life."

As the midnight blue Aston Martin DB9 turned up the enormous Norfolk Pine Tree lined Breakers Boulevard, Corina thought about days in her past when her weekends were crowded with parties and fun. She thought resignedly, "I am going to open myself to the possibilities tonight might offer." Corina also vowed tonight would be different than similar resolutions she had made in the past. The Breakers was renowned for its extravagant holiday decorations, and she felt awash in the mottled moon glow that penetrated the palm fronds; it lent the storied formal gardens of the elegant seaside resort a stately aura reminiscent of days gone by. As Katie pulled the Aston Martin under the massive portico where an ever-alert team of valets awaited, she turned to Corina and said, "Tonight's mission – Let's party like we're Kennedys."

Corina enthusiastically nodded her acceptance, checked her lipstick in the passenger side mirror and then accepted the white gloved hand of the uniformed doorman as she slid her petite figure out of the car.

Katie made everyone within earshot chuckle, saying "Now this is what I'm talking about." She extended her hand to receive the valet's ticket, but rather than just accept the stub, she took his gloved hand, pushed lightly on his chest to create a little separation and deftly performed a quick little twirl under his arm. "Just loosening up – you can't go into this place cold. You could damage something."

Corina laughed over her shoulder at the antics of her friend. Katie's three inch heals clicked on the marble floor, and the fabric of her long green silk skirt popped as she hurried to close the few yards separating her from Corina.

Even though she could only catch a glimpse of the dark green and black lace garter high on Katie's tanned thigh, as she noticed the high slit in Katie's skirt, a slight smile engaged her face just as a little shiver coursed Corina's spine. Being a few inches taller than Corina, Katie took Corina's hand, and moved it to the crook of her arm. They then paused just long enough to allow another two of the staff to hold open both elegant cut crystal double doors, and usher the giggling twosome into the ornate grand promenade of Henry Flagler's opulent ocean-side hotel.

Tonight's Charity gala was among the first of the new season. It was being staged in the largest of the 1920s era hotel's lavish ballrooms. A 35-piece orchestra was in place with sheet music corresponding to the Great Gatsby gala's theme. As with all such events, there was a perpetually tipsy grand dame, whose vision of the opulence and grandeur of the golden age was being made to live again, if only until midnight. This night's matron was one Vivian Golightly, bon vivant and a member of the Palm Beach 400, a true throwback from a grander age. In her salad days, Vivian had once attended a cotillion event to raise funds for a worthy charity in which the all the members of her debutante class were persuaded to dance with eager young suitors at the staggering price of one dollar per dance. Her illusions of an enchanted evening with a mysterious stranger had been dashed by a few members of the popular crowd. These ne'er do wells had conspired to only dance with their own beaus, leaving many of the not-so-lovely girls perched on the periphery of the dance floor. She suspected it might happen again unless she took measures to prevent it. And, as is true with the most effective plans, simplicity was at the heart of her plan. This night's assemblage ranged from debutantes to dowagers, all of them looking for some escape from the hum and thrum of every day, and tonight Lady V felt up to the challenge.

Daniel Swell found himself watching the brightly colored clown fish as they darted from coral to castle in the aquarium which also served as the bar which he found himself seated. The Alcazar Lounge was the most stylish of the many theme styled restaurants within the vast layout of The Breakers. As he tugged at the over-starched collar of his formal shirt, he thought back through the conversation that had landed him in this uncomfortable predicament. Vivian Golightly, a great aunt from his mother's side of the family, had cornered him at a Thanksgiving Day meal a few weeks ago. Daniel was always astounded how quickly and quietly she could move. Despite his heightened awareness of Aunt Vivian's desire to see him properly matched and married, and his ardent desire for exactly the opposite, she had, almost silently, seated herself on the sofa next to him during a commercial break in the broadcast of the Alabama vs. Auburn Iron Bowl. She had pounced like a lithe jungle cat, and had subtly extracted his promise to attend tonight's elegant tribute to a simpler time.

He knew that his attendance would be just the beginning of this elaborate thrust and parry, but, as a result of having held many different part-time jobs at the Breakers Hotel since his sixteenth birthday, he also knew the complete layout of this hotel. His stints in the various kitchens spread over the large campus had included assisting pastry chefs and fry cooks. He had been a valet, a bellhop and a gardener. One summer he had taught crafts to the children of the wealthy guests in the Breakers Summer camp. He had used this string of menial chores to indicate his flexibility, as well as to demonstrate the lengths to which he would extend himself for the team. It never failed to generate conversation when a prospective employer reached the section of his resume entitled "Early Work Experience". This myriad of skills and know-how he had acquired while employed by Flagler

Systems, Inc. had been consolidated to just three iconic roles: butcher, baker and candlestick maker.

Should it become necessary, his knowledge of its almost six hundred rooms, ballrooms, and restaurants, including its service passages, loading docks, and elevators would give him unlimited routes of retreat and redoubt. And despite the slightly stiff nature of his patent-leather dancing shoes, Daniel reasoned, "Vivian can make me show up but, should the debutante in Vivian's scheme turn out, as he fully expected she would, to be more Miss Congeniality than the winner of the swimsuit contest – she will never see me slip away."

He recalled some of her erstwhile attempts. Shelly Commander came to mind. Shelly was a beautifully buxom blonde who had limited conversational impulses. Shelly could fit nicely into skin tight jeans and loved tequila poppers. Daniel compared her to Aunt Vivian's giant but ancient oceanfront house; Shelly was architecturally speaking, a veritable treasure trove on the lower floors but, sadly, not too much upstairs. She was perfectly fine company for the weekend, but Daniel knew the time would quickly arrive when he would actually have to talk to her.

How and where to find the correct woman for the long haul was the question that more than occasionally interrupted and overwhelmed his shorter term hedonistic urges. On his "must have list" all he wanted in a companion was a stunningly beautiful, and athletic gal who understood the value of laughter. A knowledge of Chaucer was not required, but a little Steinbeck and Twain wouldn't hurt his feelings. The music she enjoyed should be melodic and have some verve to it. Clear blue eyes, or perhaps green, and the superstructure to fill out a cashmere sweater also made the "nice to have" addendum.

Under the influence of several beers, and a heavy meal laced with Tryptophan he had let down his guard and been persuaded to begin the Waltzing for Dollars portion of the night's festivities. After the silent auction and the five-course meal, all the men were to be herded into a line and would be required to shell out ten bucks to dance with whichever girl appeared from behind curtain number one – you talk about buying a pig in a poke. Oh well, he had agreed and backing out would require some medical emergency on par with a bout of appendicitis or an encounter with a bullet, so he would do as he had been instructed: show up on time, smile, and dance with whomever came around the curtain. However, until the dancing began and his presence was required, he would be in the Alcazar Lounge watching Notre Dame's perpetually over-rated football team take it on the chin at the hands of Florida State.

For as long as Katie could remember and probably far beyond, the Breakers had set the holiday benchmark in opulent decoration. She dared anyone to find a more opulently festooned festival, or a finer feast for Christmas Eve. The elegant main promenade featured Alexander Bonanno hand painted ceilings from the 1920s more than thirty feet above the polished Travertine marble floors, massive and ancient French tapestries, Persian carpets, and live orchids in elaborate arrangements on antique occasional tables throughout the many ornate naves and vestibules. As Corina succinctly stated it, "This place is the tits."

As they approached the Mediterranean Ballroom, a small squad of lackeys saw them coming and began the scraping and bowing ritual accorded the muckedy-mucks in charge. Donald Westcott, the overtly gay event coordinator, greeted them warmly, took their wraps and offered them champagne. "Could this be a more perfect night? Did you see that moon? Ms. Montgomery you've been to see Philippe - your look is fantastic. I must say that green is your color, so elegant and sleek, and that neckline. The gentlemen will be queuing for a dance all night."

Donald could have continued his masterfully servile flattery, but Katie cut him off, "You are too kind Donald. Do you remember my colleague Corina Dare?"

He turned his critical eye on Corina and gushed, "Oh Ms. Dare, you are exquisite. This off the shoulder gown really plays to your physique. I believe the two of you may well be the loveliest belles at the ball."

Corina blushed a little at Donald's adroit fawning and whispered to Katie, "I can see why you keep this guy around."

"Yes, Donald is good for your ego," she replied and returned her attention to him, "Did we finally settle tonight's protocol to Vivian's satisfaction?"

"I think we have won her approval with this drapery." said Donald gesturing at the deep red curtain with gold brocade near the bandstand. "This is how it will work. The gentlemen will line up to purchase dances to the left for the princely sum of ten dollars, and the ladies will queue behind the curtain, this way no one will know with whom they will be paired as Lady Vivian wished. It should absolutely effervesce with mystique."

As Katie and Donald reviewed a few other details, Corina wandered over to the immense artificial tree which had been lavishly decorated and lighted; there must have been five hundred ornaments and at least ten thousand tiny twinkling lights. After thirty minutes they could hear the crowd beginning to gather in the vestibule just beyond the double-doored entrances, and, with every detail noted on the clipboard and secure in Donald's manicured hands, they repaired to the powder room to put their feet up for a few minutes as the doors were opened. They would make their debut after the crowd had assembled.

As they had another flute of champagne Katie got around to checking her cell phone for missed calls and messages. She had missed half a dozen from Johnny, one from Fiona, but the one that caught her attention was the call from Hercules Dendy. She listened to that message first, and when she heard his voice commanding her to contact Johnny, she swung into a fevered retrieval of the others. Johnny had left a series of roughly the same message, but with what she felt contained increasing urgency, "Katie, Johnny Dendy here, please call me."

Fiona's was simply, "Mom, I miss you, please call me", but because of her suddenly spooked state, Katie felt she could discern trouble even in this short note.

First, she dialed Fiona, but after just one ring, it went to voice mail. Next, she tried to return Herc's call. Again, it went to voice mail. She fumed, "Why doesn't anyone answer their flippin' phone?"

Corina could see the angst growing in her friend's face and could hear it in her voice. Katie then turned to her and asked, "Have you received any messages on your phone?"

Corina started to check, but then remembered she had left it at Willis' house that morning when she had stormed off "I have not had mine all day. I think it's somewhere in Willis' bedroom. Try calling it on your phone."

After what seemed to Johnny, an eternity, in which he had repeatedly and unsuccessfully tried to call Katie, Hercules, Fiona, and even Gaspipe Glenn with no luck, he thought, "Why doesn't anybody answer their frickin' phone?"

Suddenly his phone rang. It was Herc. His older brother retold the tale of how he had arrived in Manhattan, had tucked Fiona under his protective wing, and how he was now planning an intervention with Billy the Blade and Black Bart.

Willis had been brought in on the conversation via speaker and the three of them agreed that Katie and probably Corina should be, if not actually captured and contained for their own well-being, clandestinely watched with an eye out for the possibility of a pre-emptive strike.

The two agreed that dark suits and white shirts would be their best cover, and in case they should need to split up, they would stash the El Camino just outside the Breakers' grounds on Royal Poinciana Boulevard. Willis would transfer to Johnny's BMW, but rather than relinquish the keys to their transportation, Johnny produced a handicapped parking permit which he hung from the rearview mirror and discreetly slipped into a vacant slot near a side entrance. As they began to search the hotel for the girls, they could have passed for FBI agents or maybe members of the Secret Service.

Willis found a large flat-panel monitor in the corridor which displayed the evening's event listing and their associated ballrooms. "Here we go. They are in the Mediterranean. We can probably do a little I spy from the veranda on the east side of the hotel, or maybe go in through the kitchen on the north side."

Johnny replied, "Let's give finesse a chance. Stick to the back hallways and stay in the shadows outside. Those chicks will really get exercised if they catch us."

Katie hated public speaking, but under the influence of half a bottle of Dom, she felt at ease at the podium of the dais. She affixed a rather plastic smile as she thanked each of the women in her court. She promised this evening's festivities would rival the rapture, and would transport this elegantly gowned and gloved assemblage back in time, where style and substance comingled to produce ambiance, and then, with the addition of music, as predictably as a chemical reaction, romance would follow. She then introduced the inimitable Dame Vivian Golightly, who, despite her girth, moved swan-like across the dais and graciously accepted the microphone.

Vivian thanked Katie, her court, and all the smartly attired sophisticates, both young and not so young, for their support on this Holy night. She then explained the Dancing for Dollars fund raiser, and she excused Katie to begin the first waltz with her favorite nephew. The waltz she had chosen to begin this wonderful Winter's Night seemed obvious and a bit cliché, but she reassured herself with the thought, "When, for Pete's sake, was Johann Strauss not au courant?"

Daniel Swell had avoided the speeches and, in the nick of time, had found his way to the front of the rather lengthy line and with a smile. And a grand bow as the spot light illuminated him, he withdrew his wallet from an inside breast pocket and prepared to extract a clean $10 bill to kick off the night's premiere event. Daniel had prepared himself mentally for three minutes of three/four time with a matronly philanthropist, his standard compliment "you move like a mist" which he would follow with a, "Please save a space on your dance card for me", and then escape. But he froze and then quickly melted as he beheld the Christmas miracle before him.

From Katie's perspective, this would be her last selfless act on behalf

of Palm Beach's domestic tranquility; she could just picture the five foot –
two, two hundred forty-pound, balding video nerd who would be waiting
on the other side of the curtain, Palm Beach inbreeding on display, but
as she gazed across the transaction table at Vivian's nephew, she was cast
backward in time, to a night nineteen years before. That night she had
looked unexpectedly up to find these same eyes, and on that night, had also
granted a request for a dance, but that one had lasted all night, had greeted
the sunrise, and had hovered in her psyche ever since. When the sun finally
rose, they separated, and Katie went off to marry another man.

Daniel, with some effort, disengaged from her green eyes, looked back
into his billfold, and withdrew a $100 bill, which he handed over to the
cashier, offered Katie his hand, and to the melodic strains of the Blue
Danube, they went waltzing away.

Katie said softly, "It has been a while since I've done this. Any words
of advice?"

Daniel smiled and said, "Just this: Remember the waltz is a contact
sport."

They moved together a little tentatively at first, but within the space of
a few seconds Daniel deftly took control and they gave into the urge to fly.
Katie cast off her concerted effort to follow and just allowed her partner
to lead her, and with subtle pressure he gracefully turned and spun them
as they glided over the inlaid marble. Katie was perhaps the last person on
the island to recognize what was apparent to everyone else. Her smile had
transformed itself from synthetic to authentic, and her eyes were dancing
too.

Corina said with real admiration to the willowy blonde in line behind
her, "That girl makes friends fast!"

After half a dozen other couples, including Corina and the video
nerd of Katie's nightmare, joined the waltz. Daniel reduced the space they
covered by inducing tighter turns, and as they settled into a corner of the
dance floor, he spoke, "This sure feels familiar."

Ordinarily Katie would have deflected the statement with a wise-acre retort, but she wanted to stay in this transported state, and she gave a soft response, "I have wanted this a thousand times in the last twenty years."

The waltz ended and Katie started to take her leave when Daniel clasped her hand and said, "Where do you think you're going? According to my math I should have another nine dances coming."

"You know, I think you are right," she replied, "Hell, why don't we make it an even dozen?"

They shared the Vienna Waltz, and just a glance in Vivian's direction reassured them both that she was content with their arrangement. Between the second and third number, Daniel had a friendly but animated word with the orchestra's conductor. They shook hands in that manner used to disguise a neatly folded bill, and he quickly returned to Katie, who asked, "What was that all about?"

Daniel replied, "I accused him of having never been outside of Austria, and I asked him if he could swing. For that matter, can you?"

The conductor shuffled some sheet music, tapped his baton on the music stand, whispered a few instructions to the brass section, and the silver-gowned female soloist stepped to the microphone. He then energetically began motioning to the cornet, tenor sax, and trombone players, who all rose and began the first few iconic notes of Benny Goodman's "In the Mood." Daniel said to Katie, "I forgot to ask my dear. Do you Jitterbug at all?"

Katie faked surprise and replied, "It's been years. Hopefully it will come back to me, but first let me lighten the load a little." She caught Corina's eye a few yards away and had a quick huddle with her.

Corina gushed, "Who is he? I've never seen you dance like that! I would cut in, but I don't think I can keep up." Katie interrupted her saying, "Do me a favor – slip this into my purse." Katie discreetly removed from her green and black lace garter, a matt black .32 caliber semi-automatic pistol which she concealed in a cloth dinner napkin from a nearby table. Explaining a pistol, no matter how stylish, clattering across the floor was something she wanted to avoid. Almost everyone Katie knew would have drawn back and many would have refused the weapon, but Corina accepted the piece with excitement and the words "How cool!"

Katie eagerly returned to Daniel for what she prayed would not be a fiasco. Daniel smiled widely and began this high energy dance from days gone by. He winked at Katie, which she interpreted to mean that he could lead from a distance and just do what he did. He made the first three or four exaggerated steps, and then he paused and invited Katie to repeat or reply with her own interpretive pace and measure. Their interplay was lively and funny. Daniel made her spin like a top, and just as she felt she would surely fall, he would expertly catch her, slow her down momentarily and then send her spiraling in another direction. The crowd gave them room which Daniel used for the next two and a half minutes to swoop, sling, spin and fling Katie about, and up to the point Daniel gave his new best friend, the Maestro, the I'm all in gesture, was probably better than…just about anything.

They withdrew to wild applause onto the veranda overlooking the glassy Atlantic Ocean. A waiter brought them fresh flutes of champagne and Daniel, wheezing slightly, proposed a two-word toast, "To Yesteryear."

Katie resisted the release of a torrent of questions and touched her glass to his and repeated, "To yesteryear."

The statuesque blonde that Corina had been chatting with as they watched Katie and Daniel create sparks that threatened to burn down the house was beautiful, friendly, and, like everyone else in the Mediterranean Ballroom, completely absorbed in the interaction between the dancers. Corina felt that there was more to her than met the eye, and that was saying something, because what met the eye was overwhelming.

Even among the beautiful people who comprised the international jet-set clientele of Palm Beach and The Breakers, this gal was exceptional. Five feet nine inches of all over tan, and shoulder length hair. Her voice was soft and cool, her eyes were clear and bright, and if this were not enough, she had a smile so sweet you could pour it on your waffles. She spoke perfect English, but with a delightful Spanish accent. As Corina witnessed how effortlessly and ambidextrously this enchantress twirled men about her little fingers with a shy smile or peck on both cheeks of an acquaintance, Corina made a mental addition to the list of things which she should upgrade: Coquetry.

 The Zombies – She's not there:
https://www.youtube.com/watch?v=M8BkkFJI910

Between dances Corina, in her friendly but frank manner, extended her hand and said, "My name is Corina Dare, and I have this nagging suspicion that you're not from around here."

"Your suspicions are correct Corina Dare. I am a visitor to your lovely island. I live in Buenos Aires. My father named me, and he is among the very few to call me Anna-Sophia. To most people I am simply Anna, but to my best friends I am Sofi – Please call me Sofi."

Corina was instantly mesmerized and could have listened to her speak all night, and then she blushed a bit as she realized that she still held Sofi's elegant satin-gloved hand. Fortunately, or not, depending on one's perspective, the spell was broken by orchestra's brass section, and the two returned their attention to the dance. Like the rest of the tuxedoed gathering, they followed the two dancers, and both cheered Katie and Daniel as they finished their high energy pas de deux, and exited through the French doors to the veranda.

Scanning the crowd which lined the floor, Corina by way of recovery, asked, "Alright Sofi, you must be accompanied by a prince charming. Point him out."

Anna-Sophia laughed easily and said wistfully, "Alas, I'm unescorted, but I think your friend has already captured the heart of the only prince here tonight."

It was true that Anna-Sophia was from a well-respected family in Argentina, but unlike many of the upper tier, who could trace their South American genealogy back hundreds of years, there were no records of the Escudo dynasty before 1944. And while her parents and grandparents were mute on the subject, Anna-Sophia knew she did not have the physical characteristics of most of her Latina contemporaries. A little research led her to believe they might be Aryan immigrants, possibly refugees, but there was also a very good chance the Escudo clan's deepest secret was that they were part of the Odessa network. This secret society was comprised of high-ranking German Wehrmacht officers – you know Nazis who had stuffed their meager possessions, mostly their clothes, a few priceless paintings, some jewelry, and several suitcases filled with Swiss Marks and gold bars into a German submarine, and got the hell out of Europe just before the, suddenly temperamental, Red Army soiled their Persian carpets with its muddy boots after kicking in the front door.

In case you have not yet made the connection, Anna-Sophia Escudo is the youngest daughter of Davey "Longball" Escudo, the former steward of the Green Flash before he ran afoul of the Amatos and had to give it over all those years ago. In his youth Davey had been a promising baseball talent, maybe even, in a limited sense, a prodigy. He was just okay as a slightly slow outfielder, with an average glove and an above average, but inaccurate arm. Try as he might, he could not seem to consistently hit the cutoff man. Prodigy? Well, yes. When it was his turn at the plate, he had an innate ability to put the round bat on that speeding and spinning round ball, and a keen eye for the strike zone. And when he got his pitch, a low and inside fastball, he could really give it a ride. However, when he combined his incomplete skills package with his love of the New York nightlife, his trip to the show (he was called up from the triple A Richmond Virginians late in the season to bolster right-handed hitting) was, as the expression goes, for just a cup of coffee. In sixteen plate appearances, he had compiled two base-on-balls, five hits including a homerun, but was thrown out at second twice. Not a bad performance, and were it not for also being thrown out of several high-profile Manhattan night clubs, with one arrest for public indecency, he might have hung around the "Bigs" a bit longer.

With his family's money behind him, and the city that never sleeps laid out before him, Davey quit baseball and got into the gangster business, which was infinitely harder than standing in the batter's box and letting Sandy or Warren fire fastballs at his head. To say he was run out of town was a massive understatement, and as he was recovering at the family estate on the cliffs overlooking the sea, his missing digits and prodigious use of cocaine caused his underlings to jokingly, and behind his back, change his nickname from "Longball" to "Eightball".

As he ruthlessly grew his Peruvian marching powder empire, he demonstrated, more than once, to an ambitious lackey or would-be competitor, even with a diminished grip, he could still wield his 36-ounce signature model Louisville Slugger. One Kilogram - a weight consistent with his export business, and the increment he used to measure the growth of the family fortune.

From his well-worn leather easy chair, in his later life, he sometimes told Anna-Sophia, the only remaining jewel in his life for which he cared, of the splendid emerald, which he had once possessed, its incomparable beauty, and how its 714 carets not only equaled Babe Ruth's lifetime homerun mark, but also matched precisely the weight of a regulation, major-league horsehide. These were the thoughts that occupied her father's final, years, days and hours, and in the end, he turned away from the Green Flash and back to his love of baseball. He would sometimes travel to Cuba or the Dominican Republic to watch "Winter Ball" and would anonymously sponsor an impoverished, but talented, youngster on his way up the rickety ladder of professional baseball.

Davey Escudo was laid to rest in his family's mountaintop cemetery. Among the provisions that were lovingly placed beside him in his coffin were a small supply of bubblegum, a baseball autographed by Joe D, Casey Stengel, and Mickey Mantle, his personalized Louisville Slugger, and his Rookie Year Baseball card.

Among the items which Anna-Sophia inherited at his passing were his two obsessions. First, she found real peace in the sun-drenched bleachers of any spring-training game. She found that a hot dog and a cold beer fit her hands and frame of mind, and there was always an old timer who had seen Mickey or Joe in their prime and between innings would relate a time he had witnessed a triple play, or some base-running screw-up which had ended a rally. The other subject which was never far from her mind was the Green Flash. The closest she had come to seeing it was in a series of photographs taken decades before which, according to the wishes expressed in her father's will, had come to her.

Now, thanks to a call from the states, rumors had reached Argentina of the gem-gone-missing so many years ago, and those murmurings hinted that it might have resurfaced in Palm Beach. And although she had never seen the actual gigantic emerald, she had seen a flawed glass copy that mimicked the size and shape, but its color was streaked and unconvincing. However, the way her family's own violent history had become entwined with the stone's bloody past to her was compelling, and that allure had pulled Sofi north to investigate. Part of her travel preparations had included a phone call to a private cell phone where she had left a tantalizing message.

Dan Swell leaned against the decorative old-world concrete balustrades which lined the veranda as he sipped his champagne and caught his breath. He took in the tranquil view of the moon's reflection on the glassy Atlantic and the coconut palm lined shore. Katie did the same. They both wanted to bathe a while in the surrealistic light and just breathe the charged air. During the past two decades they had encountered each other only three times. Two of those three encounters had been at night, and those two had had sweaty finishes followed by years of secret reflection, silent longing, but zero contact. Daniel hoped tonight was not just a random collision, and that his life was not just a numbers game – stand on the same corner long enough and the entire world will walk past three or four times. His instinct warned him the first one to speak would probably be the loser, but he finally turned his gaze from the sea to Katie Callahan and asked, "Do you know many people who've been lucky in love?"

Katie, consciously slowing her roll, considered the situation, and the question, for a second or two and smiled, "No, I guess not. I feel like I've had a couple of near misses myself, but if you accept the macro-metrics, the empirical evidence does not really support happily ever-after." Then, as she reached for open-mindedness, she added optimistically, "I suppose one must allow for lightning strikes."

"Romance requires hope. Plus, lightning strikes are the number one cause of wild fire in this corner of our swamp," replied Daniel with his easy chuckle.

Just then a stray chill blew across the moonlit veranda and a shiver coursed Katie's spine. Daniel noticed her slight tremor and quickly doffed his dinner jacket and placed it upon her shoulders. She accepted the warm coat and detected his scent. It was not at all contrived or overpowering like so many of the dandies at the ball, no caustic "stinkum" as her father had disdainfully called colognes and after-shave. Daniel's aroma had a subtle combination of a mild soap, just a hint of citrus from his shaving cream and the rest of his fragrance Katie surmised was just the way he smelled – clean. As she turned she curled silently closer, leaning into him. Their silhouettes merged and they slowly swayed with the palms, Katie whispered, "Nice."

For his part Daniel allowed his chin to rest lightly on her head as he regarded this seemingly star-crossed, possibly fate-driven encounter, the needle of his contentment meter was pegged, "Yes ma'am, I'd have to say this is a high time."

Concealed within the purple shade of an adjacent seaside balcony, Johnny Dendy felt an icicle pierce his heart.

 Kacey Musgraves – High Time:
https://www.youtube.com/watch?v=wO7qC-fD97c

From Willis' perspective, which was just inside the butler's pantry of the Mediterranean Ballroom, Corina seemed safe enough, so he decided to go find Johnny who was out on one of the verandas watching over Katie from a distance. He stepped quietly up beside his friend and joined the surveillance. He offered Johnny a small set of binoculars, but at Johnny's refusal he put them to his own eyes. Focusing on Katie and some new guy he said, "Looks like everybody is having fun tonight but us. There are some pretty drunk chicks inside. You wanna go try our luck?"

Johnny reached out and with the slightest pressure forced the spy glasses down, "I don't think so, and I don't want to hear a bunch of guff from you, but I think we ought to get these girls outta here."

Resisting the urge to jab an obviously tender nerve Willis replied, "Why's that?"

"Herc just sent me some info on the goons that are stalking Fiona." Johnny continued, "This stuff is serious, and there might be real danger lurking in the shadows here."

"Even more dangerous than you? Who could be more..."

Johnny cut him short with just a look.

Willis fell silent for a second and then stated the obvious, "I'm with ya pal, but it might require a little finesse. It doesn't look like Katie is ready to call it a night, and I know Corina is gonna resist the notion."

Johnny thought for a moment and said, "Don't I know it, and I hate the thought of breaking in on them, but what if that guy is one of them?" gesturing toward Katie's apparent paramour.

Willis chuckled at the thought, "I can't feature that guy as mobbed up. Did you see him dance? Plus, it seems like they might have a history."

Johnny countered, "I know it seems far-fetched, but is it worth the risk?"

A light seemed to come on for Willis, and he replied, "Why don't we switch assignments?"

A confused look clouded Johnny's face, "What are you suggesting?"

"Well Katie might take a warning from me better than finding out you've been spying on her, and Corina might sober up a bit if you…"

Johnny quickly agreed saying, "Anything is better than this. Let's go."

As Corina stood with her new friend Sofi, she scanned the crowd, and her gaze suddenly locked with the pale blue eyes of a well-groomed man at the edge of the dance floor. His dark blue Hickey Freeman suit fit him very well, and the starched white collar of his dress shirt really accentuated his powerful neck, but for Corina, his broad shoulders were the clincher. She shuddered a bit, and then from about forty feet away she began her move with a flirtatious wink, and without breaking eye contact she said to Sofi, "Girl, I'll catch up with you later. I thought men like that were just in magazines."

Anna-Sophia watched Corina cut through the crowd to approach the man she quickly had categorized as a jock, and she took real pleasure in the forthright manner in which Corina pursued this fresh prize. Just as Corina reached her new fascination, Sofi laughed out loud as Corina laughingly mimicked her. On tip toes, she kissed first one cheek, and in the continental style, the other cheek of the rugged stranger. "This Corina Dare was a quick study."

She would have loved to have watched this encounter develop, but her attention was drawn away by the soft hum and subtle vibration of the cell phone in her Daniella Ortiz lizard skin clutch. She withdrew to a quiet alcove and accepted the call, "At last. I was beginning to think you had forgotten me, or thrown me over for another woman."

From twenty-six hundred miles away, Glenn gasped in mock anguish, "Hardly! My love, surely you must know forgetting you is not within my capacity. As far as I am concerned, you are irreplaceable." Glenn paused a moment for effect and continued, "While it is always a wonderful surprise to hear from you, I must say your proposition has me especially intrigued."

Anna-Sophia replied slyly, "Glenn, I suspect you to be a rogue, but you are just my kind of rogue. However, you have found me in a place that is not private enough, and at a time that is not convenient for this discussion. May I return your call in several hours?"

Out of his other ear Glenn could hear faint splashes coming from the shower in his suite's bathroom, and considered for a moment what he might be up to in several hours' time. He presumed his non-fraternization with Ginger would have ended by then. He answered, "Sure."

As an afterthought Anna-Sophia inquired, "From where are you calling?"

Glenn answered cutely, "I'm at a very nice resort out west. Let me tell you, the towels are so thick and fluffy I can hardly close my suitcase."

Just as Corina reached the young man she had spied from forty feet away, the orchestra began a grand rendition of "Some Enchanted Evening," and the timing of the soloist's opening lyric could not have been more precise. "You may see a stranger from across the room…"

She placed her hands confidently on his shoulders, and, waiting until she had lightly kissed him on both cheeks, she delivered her opening, "Hi, I'm Corina. You got ten bucks on you?"

The stranger responded, "Hello, my name is Diego. I'm sure I can come up with a sawbuck. Whatcha got in mind?"

"Well they've got this waltzing for dollars dealio going on here, and so far, I'm trailing the pack."

Diego quickly retrieved his sterling money clip from his pants pocket, peeled off a fifty, and placed it in her hand. "We can't have that."

Corina accepted the bill without the slightest overture of returning any change, and with a quick fold, she tucked it into her cleavage. She offered her hand and they moved smiling to the dance floor. She was surprised how well her new partner moved as they went for a twirl, and, as they moved, she probed, "So what do you do when you aren't knocking out ladies at charity dances? Please tell me you are a spy or a secret agent."

"Would that I were." Diego sighed, "Alas, I am a mere accountant and financial advisor in a small private firm."

They chatted amicably to the Rogers and Hammerstein masterpiece which dove-tailed nicely with the seaside scenario, and when the song ended Diego bowed slightly, thanked her for the dance, and asked, "Could I interest you in a drink over at Nick & Johnnies'?"

"Is that the bar where Chuck and Harold's used to be?"

Diego nodded.

Corina looked for Katie, and when she could not immediately see her, she hesitated for a second, but for just a second. "Why not? Let me grab my stuff."

She returned to the table where she and Katie had been seated, picked up her black cashmere wrap, spun it lightly about her shoulders, grabbed up her small beaded bag, and turned to go. She then glimpsed Katie's gold purse and was reminded of its contents. Not just the gun, but also the valet's ticket for the Aston Martin. She did a quick assessment based upon the simple question, should I take Katie's purse with me, or should I leave it unattended? She quickly and unknowingly reached the first codicil of the Hippocratic Oath – Do no harm. She snatched up Katie's bag and slipped her small bag inside it, and hurried to catch up with her newest friend, who was checking his Blackberry, as he made his way to the grand lobby of the gaily lighted Breakers Hotel.

True enough, Diego was engaged in digital communication via his Blackberry, but rather than the addictive "crackberry" compulsion to which many of his generation had fallen prey, he made two concise transmissions. The first to a similar device located on the sixth floor of the Palm Beach Towers, a scant four blocks away, "Proceeding as planned."

The other had an even shorter transit. This one went to the gangsters in the Breakers parking lot, "Get ready, it's about to kick-off."

Diego slipped the device into his jacket's breast pocket just as Corina caught up and took his arm, "Anything good?"

Diego smiled and replied, "Just routine business correspondence. You'll have to drive. I came by taxi."

Corina's pulse quickened a bit at the thought of the speedy Aston Martin and said, "Have I got a treat for you."

In Palm Beach, L'il Augie felt that things were finally starting to turn in his direction for a change. Getting the aging and increasingly incompetent Rocco and The Mic out of police custody was becoming an all too frequent task, but he retained several shyster criminal lawyers who specialized in overcoming "Danger to themselves and to the Public" arrest warrants. Despite being caught in a residential neighborhood under dubious circumstances, with weapons drawn, and no believable excuse, they eventually produced concealed weapons permits and were allowed to post bond.

The text he had received from Billy assured him that he had, in the form of a captured daughter, the leverage he needed to bring Winston Montgomery to heel. He was still working on grabbing the soon-to-be-ex Mrs. Montgomery but felt that this additional hostage would also be in his grasp before sunrise.

He worked the keyboard of his computer until he at last found the cell phone records of and, more importantly, the number associated with Winston's phone. He dialed the number and was mildly surprised that despite the early hour, to have it answered after just one ring, "Montgomery."

L'il Augie began, "Listen up Montgomery. I believe you've got something I want, but as in any good deal, I definitely have something you want."

A defiant voice on the other end responded, "Oh yeah, who the fuck is this?"

"I've been doing some research and it seems you got suddenly rich about the same time some guys knocked over the vault at the Palm Beach Towers about thirty years back." L'il Augie was not even mildly surprised this time at the silence coming from Winston's end of the line. He surmised the whirr of confusion going through his mind was overwhelming and allowed a full fifteen seconds to pass before he continued, "Now that I know who you are, I'll bet diamonds to lug nuts I could just grab you and beat what I want out of you, but since we are both educated, sophisticated men of the world, I thought I would give reason a shot."

"What exactly is it you want?" Winston replied meekly.

"For starters, two million in bearer bonds."

Winston seemed to be composing himself some as he replied with a snort of derision, "That's a pretty healthy start. Anything else before I tell you to go pound salt?"

L'il Augie resisted the surge of anger he felt at Winston's cockiness, knowing he held the still secret trump card. "There is one more item I would like you to include. One giant emerald."

There seemed to be a slight crack in Winston's bravado, but he replied, "Two questions. Where do you suppose I could get that kind of dough and what was that other question? Oh yeah, if I could, why would I just hand it over to you?"

L'il Augie responded calmly, "Both good questions. In order, first I don't care where you get it, just get it. Second, if you ever want to see this little girl again, you will do precisely what I ask."

At that instant Augie hit the send key to transmit Fiona's bound and blood-spattered image to Winston's phone.

An involuntary gasp of horror escaped Winston, and his attitude became predictably compliant, "It will take some time to get the money. Please don't hurt my daughter."

"What sort of man do you take me for?" L'il Augie replied, "I could never harm a single hair on her sweet little head, but the guys holding her are somewhat less civilized than we, and have certain, shall we say, disturbing proclivities. So, don't take too long. I'll be in touch in eight hours." The line disconnected.

Despite possessing the knowledge that L'il Augie was being deceived about Fiona's capture, Winston still felt a knot of angst form in his stomach. He was reasonably content that Hercules Dendy could and would protect his daughter, but he had seen some pretty gritty stuff in his life, and he had witnessed a few well-constructed plans come apart under the sort of pressure that gangsters like these could apply. He turned again to the alphabetically arranged contacts list of his cell phone, and scrolled down to the one listed as JPB, and touched the illuminated number. Within ten seconds the circuit completed and in Delray Beach, Florida, the phone in the pocket of one Jean Pierre Baptiste began to vibrate. Within a few more seconds a voice came on the line. "Yeah Mon."

Jean the Baptiste, as he was known in many Caribbean ports was, to say the very least, an interesting man. He was now "passing" as a forty-year-old Bahamian charter boat captain from Crooked Island, but he had begun life at a lower station. The alterations he had made to his identity were all driven by his need to be older and wiser. Twenty years prior, at the age of thirteen, a number he was convinced held mystic power, he had stolen a nineteen-foot day sailor in Port a Prince, Haiti, and had skillfully outrun Hurricane Andrew to Rum Cay in the southern Bahamas. He weathered the category five storm in a small concrete block building which somehow withstood the 150 mile an hour winds and mountainous waves, and when he emerged he discovered his small craft was gone. As he searched the shore line for it, he found a replacement craft which would serve his transportation needs. A Bertram 31 yacht bobbed about 50 yards off shore. Its anchor line was tangled in the shallow coral reef. The anchor was gone but the venerable fiber glass deep Vee was in perfect condition. Filled with petrol and stocked for deep sea fishing, it had half a dozen pricy rods and reels. He found

pre-rigged Ballyhoo baits in the ice chest and even the reefer was filled with
sandwiches, fruit, and beverages. JPB took every second of the next three
minutes to check out the vessel and then turned the key to start the engines.
After clearing the reef, he considered the question of where the owners of
this fine craft could be located. The paperwork he uncovered included a
few receipts from San Salvador, an island approximately fifty miles to the
east, and he reasoned that the boat had broken free and had been driven by
the wind to this beach.

As Jean Pierre skirted the reefs and wreckage surrounding the small
island of Rum Cay, he calmly sorted through his options. There was probably some sort of payday awaiting him about fifty miles to the east, on the
island of San Salvador were he to return the Bertram to the owners, but
as he ran the probable sequence of events of such an endeavor through
his mind, it occurred to him that this was not, by any means, a sure thing.
The owners, if they were even on the island, might not be easily found,
and he felt certain that eventually the Bahamian authorities would become
involved. The men who policed the seven hundred islands of the Bahamas
were notorious for their ill treatment of penniless refugees, especially
undocumented minors from Hatti. He realized his initial instinct toward
doing the right thing would, after perhaps months of confinement and
privation, ultimately end with his forced return to the impoverished island
he had risked his life to escape.

His original escape plan was to sail to Miami, ditch or sell the day sailor,
and make his way north to Delray Beach, in Palm Beach County, where a
large community of Haitian ex-patriots was rumored to exist. Since he had
no other viable plan in mind, he would use this one as the rough outline
for the next few days, and using a map of the Caribbean he found in the
chart drawer, he enjoyed a sandwich and a beer as he pointed the small
power boat north toward Nassau. Once this decision had been made, he
began a thorough search of the vessel. He felt he was golden until he ran
out of fuel, but when that happened he would find himself, once again, in
the position of poor child refugee, undocumented, unwanted, and on his
way back to Haiti.

He found some loose change in one of the galley's drawers and then he discovered a small safe built into the bulkhead of the cabin. At first Jean Pierre searched the boat for a tool he could use to pry open the door, but before he defaced the boat, a single salient thought crossed his mind. It was so crystalline a moment that he, even now, viewed it as not only as a moment of salvation, but the cornerstone of his life's philosophy. Check the key ring. He did and found that aside from the ignition there were two other keys. One was for the gas cap and the other opened the safe. The safe held the wherewithal he would need to begin his new life. At this early age, he had learned that while brawn had its place, he should always look for an easier way, and in this case, it was the most straight forward approach. At thirteen, bobbing alone in the Gulfstream, he had independently discovered a version of Occam's razor: When presented with a variety of options, first try the simplest one with the fewest variables. He had employed this pattern of reason ever since.

He had relatives in Freeport who might have taken him in if he were penniless and hungry, but coming to town in this fine craft would make him the rich uncle, and the people he might have turned to for support in his hour of need would pounce on him like a pack of feral dogs, and quickly pick him clean. He knew instinctively that, because of his relative good fortune at the hands of hurricane Andrew, he should steer clear of his kin.

A plan began to assemble itself in his mind. Jean Pierre was large for his age, and he had the beginnings of a peach fuzz beard. A scar that was partially concealed in his left eye brow, which made him look somewhat older than his lucky thirteen, and the small shock of white hair which sprouted in his left temple lent credence to his contrived age advancement. Among the simple alterations he made to his identity was his pronouncement that he was nineteen, and the captain of a small charter boat based on Crooked Island, Bahamas.

As he motored north, he rigged one of the fishing rods with a ballyhoo and began to troll. Within minutes the bait was hit by a large Bluefin tuna, which, since he was alone, he just dragged behind the boat until the fish had exhausted itself and he was able to reel it in. With some effort, he was able to boat, clean and pack the two-hundred-pound fish in ice. This was a pleasant enough pastime, so he rigged another bait, and this time he brought in a sixty-five-pound Wahoo. By the time he reached the southern tip of Andros Island, he had exhausted his bait, was low on fuel, but he had landed a nice sized sailfish and two more tuna. He found a ready market on Andros. The chef from the US Navy's officer's club happened to be on the dock when Jean Pierre arrived, and he bought his entire catch for $1200 cash, and gave him his phone number should he want to do business again. For the next year JPB was the primary supplier of fresh fish to the US Navy base on Andros, primarily because his fish were fresh and well below market price. The quartermaster saw it as a twenty percent savings, but the young captain viewed it as one hundred percent profit and the beginning of his new life. He could buy gas and was allowed to shop at the Base Exchange. His easy, almost child-like affability allowed him to make friends, and within a few months he had established a going concern and the beginnings of legitimacy.

Through his youthful energy and genuine warmth, over the next few years, he slowly converted his fantasy life into his actual identity. While earning a nice living as a charter boat captain, he was befriended by many of his wealthy clients. The comments people made about JPB fell into two narrow categories, the first of which was usually said to his face, and the second was always said behind his back. "Jean Pierre, you have the most beautiful smile I have ever seen," was typical and true of the former category. He did have a set of penetratingly white and perfect teeth.

The comments of the latter group were divided into two subsets. The first always whispered in a manner of actual awe, "That is the blackest man I have ever seen!" was typical of the straight-forward observation of the first encounter with him. The secondary subcategory was always made with an attempt at bigoted humor, and took the form of comparisons of the tone and shade of his skin to inanimate objects. "Until he smiled I thought I was looking at an eggplant," or, "That guy's skin is the color I would expect to find at an oil well point 4000 feet down!" or "The ace of spades ain't got nothing on him" or "Man, that is one black bird!"

These comments had initially caused Jean Pierre some mental anguish, and he had wasted more than a few birthday wishes hoping for a lighter complexion, but eventually he made peace with this seemingly cruel fact, and found there were advantageous aspects of his coloring. He was all but impervious to the ultraviolet rays of the sun, which, as a man who spent most of his daylight hours bobbing in the reflective cooker of the Caribbean Sea, was a real plus. He now chuckled when he overheard one of these witty barbs, knowing that by day's end his pale clients would be glowing with painful sunburns he would never have to endure. Another plus which he actively nurtured was his natural furtiveness. In this regard he had much in common with the Martin. Not just the type of dark swallow, the purple martin, but he also mimicked the qualities of the Blackbirds from the Lockheed Martin Skunkworks. At night, he was invisible.

One of these pale clients become friend was one Winston Montgomery. Within a year of encountering him, Winston had researched the maritime salvage laws and had helped JPB claim the 31' Bertram as his own. His banker friend, Michael Gaines, for a nominal fee, which Winston covered in exchange for future fishing favors, worked quietly to establish a Bahamian birth certificate and primary education transcript, immunization records, to which he insisted JPB submit, and in short order documented his Crooked Island origin. Once these official government documents had been inserted into the Bahamian citizen database, he had helped Jean Pierre to apply and acquire a Bahamian passport. With a little help from his friends, he had transformed himself from penniless refugee to expatriate, and then on to a documented citizen of the world.

He re-christened his boat the "Apocalypso" and now he was legally open for business, and business was good. As one might expect, Jean Pierre was devoted to Winston, and over the decades that followed, he had performed all manner of services for his American patron. When

Winston phoned asking him to meet him at the Biz Jet terminal of the Jupiter Regional Airport, he had a one-word response, "When?"

 Jimmy Buffet – Havana Day Dreamin':
https://www.youtube.com/watch?v=oJtVfBpMyW4

As the Cessna Citation streaked south at 38,000 feet above the glassy Atlantic Ocean, Captain Tabernella was the only one aboard who witnessed the dramatic sunrise. Herc and Fiona had melted like butter into the supple leather upholstery of the private jet and only awoke at the slight mechanical whirr of the landing gear being deployed. Both were slightly confused as they touched down on a small island's crude crushed coral landing strip. The plane quickly taxied to a stop and the pilot opened the passenger compartment door, lowered the stairs, and greeted whoever was waiting, "Ola senior`, come aboard. Do you have any luggage? Make yourself comfortable. I'll turn around and we will be gone before anyone knows we were here."

From her seat in the plane's cabin, Fiona could only see the shadow of whoever was about to board and was mildly curious to see who was being greeted with such deference. Herc had already figured it out and was not surprised to see the well-tanned face of Winston Montgomery appear from around the entry bulkhead.

"Daddy!" was Fiona's response as she sprang into her father's arms. Herc could and did appreciate the reunion, and he uncoiled slightly, releasing the handle of the Glock 9mm in his belt. He noticed the relief in Winston's face as he embraced his daughter, he also noticed a single tear course his cheek. As he spoke, he extended his arms, "Let me get a look at you – it's been three or four months since I have seen you."

There was an obvious glow of pride as he took in the sight of his daughter. Although only a few months had passed since they had last shared each other's company, there were subtle, but marked, differences in her appearance. Her hair was longer and what about this makeup? He would have to make several slight realignments to overlay the reality standing before him with the pictures in his wallet, not to mention the ones in he carried in his head and his heart. "My, have you grown?"

Fiona was the one to break the spell as she turned to acknowledge Herc, "Daddy, you remember Hercules Dendy, don't you?"

In the time it took her to say those few words, Winston composed himself and extended his hand, "Certainly. Mr. Dendy, it is a pleasure to see you again. I will never be able to thank you properly for protecting my daughter."

Herc smiled, accepted his hand, allowed himself an affectionate glance in Fiona's direction, and said, "It's been a mutual effort. She is pretty good at protecting herself."

The pilot stowed Winston's small satchel, retracted the steps and sealed the cabin door. With a nod of approval from Winston he returned to the cockpit, spun the small jet around on the shell-rock runway, and nudged the throttles forward. Ninety seconds later the altimeter read 4500 hundred feet above sea level, and he radioed the tower in Jupiter requesting an approach path and clearance to land. The plane had not been on the ground in the Bahamas for more than three minutes, and any absence from ground control radar could be easily explained by way of a client request to do a little low-level wave hopping, but thanks to Captain Tabernella's spotless record, the subject would never come up.

In the intervening fifteen minutes of flight time between West End and the Jupiter Regional Airport, Fiona gazed out the small round window. Winston and Hercules put their heads together and spoke calmly and quietly about the possible ways the next twenty-four to forty-eight hours might unfold. Like military men planning a battle they listed the strengths and weaknesses of their team versus the opponent's. Herc enumerated the members of their company, including his younger brother Johnny and his friend and law partner Willis.

Winston had always harbored an admiration for Johnny, which was tinted with a slightly green wash of jealousy over the chaste affection his soon to be former wife had always had for her friend and confidant. Then it suddenly occurred to Winston that if L'il Augie had tried to capture

Fiona to use as leverage, he might have similar designs for Katie, and he almost involuntarily blurted out, "What about Katie? That thug might go after her too."

With a quick glance in Fiona's direction, Herc responded quietly, "We think you are right about that, but Johnny is trying to keep an eye on Katie and her friend Corina."

Winston grimaced, "I hope he is drawing hazardous duty pay. Corina does not have even a nodding acquaintance with low-profile, and Katie seems to go a little nutty around her."

Herc, who had never been introduced to Corina, also grimaced, "I can't wait to meet this chick. It sounds like bedlam should be her middle name," as he tried it on, "Corina Bedlam Dare – I like it."

Fiona perked up and joined the discussion, "Corina is terrific, and, if we're going to war, I want her on our side!"

Over the years Winston had developed a self-protective pattern of playing his cards very close to the vest. Before disclosing any information, he always ran through a short interrogatory: Does this person have a need to know? What and who might be compromised through this disclosure? Is there any advantage to be had by withholding the information? As his law school professor Gerry Correll had put it in his rustic west Texas vernacular, "Boy, you can always blab a secret, but once you've blabbed, it cannot be unblabbed." Or in more genteel terms, "The more precious the confidence, the stronger should be the lock."

He opted for a partial disclosure regarding Jean Pierre Baptiste "I've contacted an associate who can move, unnoticed, in some circles where we might be conspicuous. He is smart, discreet and very well connected. He will be waiting when we touch down."

L'il Augie sent a text to Billy the Blade's phone inquiring as to the progress the two were making in their drive south from NYC to Palm Beach, "How goes the drive? Where are you?"

As far as he knew the gangsters were still warm blooded, on the job, and still on the payroll, instead of the two clotted blocks of ice they had become. Billy and Blackie were among the few people upon whom L'il Augie felt he could rely, but in situations like this, there were always variables outside of his or, for that matter, anyone's control. A few years back the two, on a similar mission, had been stopped by the New Jersey state police, and within a few minutes they had added the body of the young trooper to the one already in the trunk. The minor traffic violation could probably have been solved by accepting a $100 ticket for speeding, but once the blue lights came on, Billy pulled over and Blackie chambered a round in his .45. These guys were a little on the trigger-happy side. After expertly and cold bloodedly placing a slug just above the Kevlar vest's neckline, Blackie drove the police cruiser to an abandoned granite quarry, transferred the stiff they were out to bury, in the first place, to the police cruiser's trunk, liberated the riot gun, and moved the freshly dead cop to the front seat, dropped a brick on the accelerator, and watched the long arc of the car as it flew over the edge and into forty feet of lake water which had quickly formed once the site had been declared "Played Out", and the heavy duty sump pumps had been switched off. Both missing persons were still missing and the cases grew colder every day. To say they slept with the fishes would have been technically incorrect, as the high alkaline content of the water was not conducive to aquatic life, and thus the lake contained no fishes, but fishes or no, the two were as dead as Luca Brasi.

This shoot first approach to confrontation always left the door open for the unexpected, and after years of surprises, L'il Augie like to keep loose contact with his boys while they acted in his behest. By periodically checking with them, L'il Augie hoped to keep the psycho behavior down, as well as give himself an early warning system.

Herc had worked out an efficient chart with which he could easily project the 10-20, CB jargon for location, of the hoods on their imaginary drive south. He quickly responded, "So far – so good. We're just approaching Richmond."

According to L'il Augie's math, at this pace the boys would arrive in about fifteen hours, and then he would have everything he needed to get paid, and possibly get some revenge on the people whom he believed prematurely ended his father's reign and, ultimately, his life.

Across town Herc was performing the same time calculus. Whatever the good guys came up with, they had about half a day to solidify their plans if the good guys were going to keep the initiative.

True to his word, Jean the Baptiste was standing in the shade of a palm tree when Captain Tabernella taxied the Cessna Citation to a standstill at the executive jetport of JRA. Dressed all in black linen, he seemed to materialize from thin air as he stepped from the shadow into early morning sunshine. Winston saw him immediately, nodded and received the counter-nod. When Fiona saw him, she immediately broke rank and jogged to him. When just a few yards separated them, she stopped and he bowed deeply from the waist. Fiona curtsied and spoke, "What a delightful surprise to see you again Mr. Baptiste."

In his deep baritone he replied in his vaguely Caribbean accent, "You look as fine as mountain meadow in the springtime Miss Fiona. How can such a pretty girl just keep on gettin' prettier?"

Fiona tried to play one more hand of their private game, "As you have always advised Maestro, with a valiant heart, all things are possible."

"Ah girl, you have a wisdom far beyond your height."

The formality cracked and then broke away completely as he enfolded the comparatively small pale girl in his massive embrace. She almost disappeared, and were it not for her giggles, she would have been completely concealed and entirely undetectable.

JPB had been a summertime fixture in Fiona's life since she was a toddler. When it came to handling the series of increasing larger sailing craft her father had bought her as she grew, he had literally taught her the ropes. He had patiently showed her how to tie at least twenty-five sailor's knots, and how to recognize at least that many fish, as well as how catch, fillet and how to prepare them. Before Fiona turned twelve she could bring a fresh fish to almost any island, build a small campfire, find a coconut, key lime, or mango, and prepare a fine meal inside of forty-five minutes. He was responsible for her understanding of the wind, the waves and weather, but lest this appear a one-sided arrangement, in return Fiona had patiently helped Jean Pierre with his three R's. Because of her efforts he understood verb conjugation and could move easily between currencies, and he agreed with her and most of the planet, that the metric system was the way to go. But in his mind Fiona's most important contribution to his edification had been in the fields of music and literature. It was almost exclusively her domain to suggest to him the seafaring tales of Hemmingway, Steinbeck, Melville, and Verne. For one birthday, she had given him a recorder made of Acacia Koa, and taught him the basics of how to play it. As a result of their relationship he was a practically educated man, and considered by the residents of many seaside hamlets to be a philosophical problem-solver, as well as the jet-black Pied Piper. While Fiona had never met any of Jean Pierre's family, she knew he had several common-law wives, and according to her father, maybe as many as a dozen progeny, spread around the islands of the Bahamas. JPB had once tried to explain the island frame of mind concerning this family structure, where he was always welcome, and to whose upkeep he willingly contributed. "There are plenty of fine ladies in the Stream, (she understood his vernacular to mean the Gulfstream) and they seem to see me coming, but in a day or two I get the urge to go fishing, so I go. Just because I don't tarry or marry with dem girls don't mean I don't care about dem. And dem kids, they's mine and will be always."

To Fiona that pronouncement alone made "dem kids" very lucky to be his offspring – half of their genes and chromosomes came from him, so they would be smart and capable, and he would be nearby should they ever need a hand.

Amidst the revelry, Winston caught JPB's eye. "Well, little one, let's get you out of this sun before you turn into one big freckle."

He propelled her, giggling, toward the terminal, and then broke away to consult with her father. "I went by your office like you say, but your car is nowhere in the vicinity."

It took Winston a mere three seconds to connect the dots, "Katie."

"These wise guys have probably seen and done a lot of crime," Winston said to JPB, "so we have got to bring a thing or two they have not seen if we hope to come out on top."

"I don't think they have ever seen a Lamprey," replied the man who considered midnight his older brother.

As Winston considered the little-know assassin's tool, a smile began at the corner of Winston's eyes and slowly spread across his face, "That might just be the ticket. Do you have one handy?"

"No boss, but I can make one in a couple of hours if we got de time."

Rocco and the Mic were back to lurking in the shadows in Palm Beach, and despite their ridiculous run of luck in the past four days, when L'il Augie gave them new orders, they answered the bell. It was what they did. As they sat in their latest rental car, which was parked in the cordoned-off section of the parking lot labeled valet only, they began taking a rudimentary inventory of the injuries and injustices they had been dealt in connection with this "caper".

Rocco had been shot twice in the thigh at pretty close range by that vanishing Worth Avenue jeweler. The same guy had winged The Mic in the shoulder as he helped Rocco get up and get away before the Palm Beach cops arrived.

L'il Augie's veterinarian had been convinced to open his office at midnight and patch up the two hoodlums. He removed one .32 slug and cleaned two other bullet wounds that contained no spent rounds. Between the two of them they had received twenty-three stitches and they were sharing a double prescription of Amoxicillin. To say that Rocco had lost a step or two in this incident was a kind understatement. He could not imagine having to give chase on foot.

The very next day they had been ambushed in West Palm Beach where their first rental car had been destroyed and they had been arrested and jailed for doing nothing but driving down an alley. The Mic's neck was still sore from the whiplash caused by that rogue dumpster. They had mixed emotions over being forced to discard their favorite side-arms before the cops arrived. They could be considered lucky to not be caught with unlicensed firearms, but both felt this might represent another bead or two on the rosary they still prayed. Oddly, their catholic roots allowed them to both maintain a tentative grasp on a righteous afterlife. Sure, they might have to spend an eon or two in purgatory, but they were semi-certain the Virgin Mary would eventually intercede on their behalf, and they would spend eternity roaming the streets of gold. Hadn't they both gone to confession that very morning?

The ass-chewing that came along with losing track of both cars and both women they had been told to follow was much more painful and frightening than either of the other incidents, and they agreed, if given the choice, they would much rather face a loaded gun than their boss's rage.

The Mic had torn open his sutured shoulder when the Palm Beach Gardens police had grabbed them while they were just sitting in their car. In fact, at least to their way of thinking, they had been the victims that time – somebody had taken a couple of shots at them, but still they were hand cuffed and driven back down to the Palm Beach County jail.

They both had begun involuntary twitches every time the words Palm Beach were mentioned. They both longed for the safety of Bedford Stuy. This Palm Beach was not only dangerous, and not just unlucky, but this place had really bad juju.

The two idly discussed which of the opposing team they would most like to maim, "If I ever get that jeweler down again, he won't be getting' up. That you can take to the bank my friend," boasted Rocco.

The Mic countered, "I just wish I could get my hands on that skinny lawyer. What's left of him will fit in a shoe box."

Before the echo of The Mic's wish had left the parking lot, a nostalgic unease draped itself over him, and he recalled a childhood visit, with his grandmother, to a supposedly bewitched wishing well. It was a quaint structure with moss-coated stone walls and cedar shake roof. It was nestled in a perpetually shady glen. With different lighting, it might have appeared more welcoming, but the shadows propagated the sinister legend, or was it vice versa. A large ceramic tile with old English lettering had been inset, and some forty years later The Mic could still recite the poem entitled:

> ## "Ye Olde Wishing Well"
> ### Wishing you well
> ### As you wish at this well
> ### Wish all you wish
> ### But don't wish and tell
> ### Wish what you want
> ### But want what you do
> ### For whatever you wish
> ### Just might come true

This rhyming invitation-come-warning was signed, A Well Wisher.

The Mic silently withdrew his request to confront Johnny Dendy, but he sensed that this wish was already making its way through the system, and the metaphysics that governed wishing and wells would work against his retraction, and very soon he would have further reason to curse this island.

The Mic's phone vibrated signaling the arrival of an incoming text. The involuntary twitch convulsed the vein in his right temple, and recognizing his own paranoia, he calmed himself as best he could and read the message, "Get ready, it's about to kick off."

While Rocco and the Mic were spouting their braggadocio like teenagers huddled around a stolen candle in a treehouse, it had not even occurred to them that they were being watched, and their conversation was being overheard, and from very close range.

Dressed in customary black linen, Jean Pierre Baptist had soundlessly crept through the parking lot to within a dozen feet of their open windows, and could hear these silly men's silly talk. He thought, "These fellas got some more pain ahead of dem."

To a guy just watching it would have appeared this shadow's only weapons were a coconut and an oddly shaped stick, and these would not have been sufficient against guns and gangsters, but unless this guy was from Hatti, or a student of ancient tools, he could not have known this stick was called a Lamprey, named after an eel. Why JPB could not say.

The Lamprey, which JPB had carved that morning from a sturdy piece of carefully selected driftwood, was actually a sophisticated device used on his home island to lever an automobile's tire off the ground so a flattened tire could be changed. On the poor island, most of the cars that still operated were old and the factory jacks had long since vanished. An enterprising tandem equipped with a four-socket lug wrench, and a Lamprey could make an honest living patrolling the streets of Port O Prince in the daytime helping broke down motorists change a tire. One would use the Lamprey's specifically curved segment as a fulcrum, and the long straightish section as a lever to raise the vehicle's corner, while the other loosened the lug nuts and changed out the spare for the flat. Should the stranded motorist also require an inflated spare, they could, for a very reasonable price, provide one. In the nighttime the same duo, using the same tools, could make a dishonest living acquiring non-flattened tires for their inventory from cars parked in the shadows.

The Lamprey JPB had made had one additional feature. By using a hack saw he had removed the last four inches of a fisherman's gaff, and with an epoxy mixture he had embedded the strong, needle-sharp, stainless steel spike in the business end of the lever. He positioned the Lamprey and its spike just below the gas tank of the thug's car, and with one hand on the lever he tossed a coconut onto the truck of an adjacent car. Startled, the car's occupants involuntarily jumped, and then realizing it was just a falling coconut, they tensely laughed it off, but the distraction had worked, and the spike had almost silently penetrated the gas tank. In Haiti, this many times had been the first step of an assassination, once a large enough puddle of fuel had accumulated beneath the car, a lighted cigarette or glowing piece of charcoal would be introduced, and boom. Tonight's mischief would not include an explosion, just an empty gas tank and a racketeer, who despite being armed and alarmed for a shootout, would be unable to bring his high-caliber ordinance to the party, because he was sitting by the road hoping a cop, with similar firepower and a radio, wasn't his next opportunity for conversation.

Chuckling quietly to himself, and taking the Lamprey with him, Jean the Baptiste stole silently away.

The north wind had begun pick up a little and the design of The Breakers grand portico caught and amplified it, and under the laws of fluid dynamics as expressed by <u>Giovanni Venturi</u> in the late seventeen hundreds, the velocity of the wind trapped and compressed in this condition must increase. While they waited in this breezeway for the valet to retrieve the Aston Martin DB9, Diego observed this phenomenon and tried to explain the concept of the Venturi effect to Corina who listened politely, and then in her economical way replied, "Oh, kinda like the air scoop on a turbocharger."

Diego could not help but smile at how concisely she had grasped and applied a sophisticated scientific principal, "Precisely."

This chick had an efficient working knowledge of the world she inhabited, and although this information may have not been supported by the hard-won erudition of years of formal study, he recognized in her, a superior mind which had not been over cluttered and snobified with book-learning. If he had not already made plans, and were he not constructed without any soft places as he was, it occurred to him that she might fit into his life, but he knew with these thoughts he was just killing time until their chariot arrived, and the real killing could commence.

Just then the sleek little roadster glided to a stop at the far end of the covered lane, and in an effort at humor, Corina pranced over to the passenger's door, and opened it as she said, "Here, let me get that for you."

Diego replied, "You are too kind."

Then his right arm encircled her waist; a movement that Corina mistook for an affectionate embrace, and in the next second he swept her, along with himself into the open door, and the car roared away. Before she could properly register what was happening to her, Diego Lazette covered her mouth and nose with a neatly folded white handkerchief which had an industrial cleaner smell. She fought back as best she could and tried to apply the breath control training she had worked so hard on over the years, but Diego sensed her resistance and with his powerful left arm applied excruciating pressure to her abdomen. This pressure against her diaphragm would not allow her to ration her oxygen supply, and when she was forced to inhale, the chloroform worked to perfection, and her consciousness quickly became unconsciousness.

Rocco grinned his lopsided grin, and asked, "Where to Mr. Lazette?"

Diego, who held the dormant girl in his lap and stared straight ahead replied, "Get to I-95 and head south. We are going out to that little farm on Lantana Road."

There were just three witnesses to this stealthy abduction, but only one was capable of raising an alarm. The first who might have noticed there was something amiss was the young Breakers' valet Corina had given the claim stub, but he had been similarly surprised, drugged and laid down to rest in a bed of ruby begonias, and would not come to for another twenty minutes. The second was that old devil moon and he was not saying nuthin' to nobody.

The third witness was Johnny Dendy who, as a result of Willis' suggestion to switch surveillance subjects, had followed Corina from the ballroom, and had been keeping watch over her from the shadows of the rose garden. He could scarcely believe what had happened in the last three seconds, and as the Aston Martin sped away he reacted instantly – he gave chase on foot.

When the DB9 turned right onto South County Road, Johnny, already at his top speed of about twenty-three miles per hour, knew he was losing ground with every stride, and he chose to lessen the distance he would have to travel by cutting across the golf course. Hole # 16, a 180-yard par three, ran parallel to the path the kidnappers took, and he was able to maintain visual contact through the thin Australian pine hedge as he raced toward the El Camino. If asked which distance he hated the most when running track, Johnny would without hesitation say, "the 880", which was roughly the half-mile distance he would have to cover. To his way of thinking it was not really a distance race, but it required enormous stamina, and it was not quite a sprint, but to win the runner had to be really fast.

As Johnny broke through the sparse foliage of the hedge near his car he could see the taillights of the sports car he was pursuing cross the last intersection before the bridge. To his relief it pulled away slowly keeping pace with the light traffic. Staying low lest the thugs see him, Johnny fished the keys from his pocket, unlocked the driver's side door, and as Charlie Daniels had sung in Uneasy Rider, "He jumped in and fired that mother up."

 Charlie Daniels – Uneasy Rider:
https://www.youtube.com/watch?v=egGdseGTtII

Neither Rocco nor Diego noticed the El Camino about five hundred yards behind them. However, the driver of the rental car, which was supposed to be following, did notice and recognize the ghost-like Chevy, and that damned skinny lawyer behind the wheel. About then the rental car sputtered, lost power, and coasted to a stop just as the Mic approached the Royal Palm Bridge which crossed the intercostal waterway to the mainland from Palm Beach.

He sent a short text to Mr. Lazette, "You've picked up a tail. It's that skinny lawyer."

The response was assured and immediate, "Good."

As he sat in the dark the Mic had a sinking feeling. He interpreted this dread to mean this opulent island near the Gulfstream, to which the Mic had given evil anthropomorphic characteristics, was not yet done with him. While the island had seen a million stiffs like him, and did not really care, the Mic was right to sense a looming danger he could not describe past one word: black. He breathed a near silent sigh of relief when he saw in his rear-view mirror the flashing amber lights of a road-side assistance tow truck.

A large black man with a friendly whiter-than-white smile approached his window and said, "You got troubles Mon."

Inflection in speech can be a subtle thing, especially, as in this case, if there is an unfamiliar accent involved. What the Mic heard was a question. What Jean Pierre Baptist had pronounced was a statement.

Jean Pierre did not wait for the Mic's fat fingers to finish punching in his text to update his associates of his sudden incapacity. While the Mic was distracted with this task, JPB took the lid off a bright orange five-gallon bucket and emptied the contents over the Mic's head and into his lap. A quizzical look occupied the gangster's face for the moment it took to register the significance of this insult, but when he made the connection two or three seconds later the Mic dropped his phone and began to move, pawing and slapping at himself as if he were covered with fire ants, which, courtesy of this huge black man, he was.

He broke from the car and despite lingering tenderness from his earlier wounds he made pretty good time to the large fountain in the median nearby. Seeking relief from the thousands of angry insects he plunged into the lily-pad filled pond, splashing and thrashing. The Mic labored feverishly to drown those he could not wash away. At each wild gyration, the Mic could hear JPB laughing and mocking him, "That's it, oops, I think you missed one of dem little buggers!"

After forty-five seconds of whipping the pond into a froth, which also aroused several dozen of the resident frogs, the Mic felt sufficiently relieved of the stinging blight to seek some revenge, but just as he reached for the pistol in its shoulder holster JPB made an unfamiliar move. As the Mic watched, a translucent halo formed above him, and he was suddenly covered and constricted, and then with one quick snatch, he was cinched up tight and dragged from his feet. JPB shouted, "What's the matter Mon, ain't you never seen a cast net before?"

Jean Pierre tugged at the lines of the net, and dragged the writhing and sputtering tangle of gangster out of the pond, and before the Mic could orient himself, a potted plant disintegrated over his head causing a blinding flash of pain, and then all the lights went out.

The large dark shadow quickly released the draw strings of the cast net and rolled the unconscious thug onto the Bermuda grass lawn. He trussed his hands in front of his pot belly with a length of manila rope, hefted the Mic over one shoulder, and quickly moved him to the tow truck which idled at the side of the road.

Avoiding the thousands of still roiling mad fire ants in the front seat of the Mic's car, JPB slapped at the Mic's phone until he could isolate it from the larger and angrier clumps of venomous stingers, legs, abdomen, heads with over-sized maxillae and mandible sets, thoraxes, and antennae, each attached and intact set incensed and righteously suicidal. JPB defeated their last-ditch Lilliputian tactics, and disposed of the few remaining frenetic insects with a backhand whisk and a few puffs to retrieve The Mic's cell phone. He returned to the truck and disengaged the emergency vehicle's amber light cluster, and then before turning the tow truck and its uncon-scious client northward, he stopped and handed off the Mic's smartphone to a man at the wheel, of perhaps the most non-descript compact car he'd never been able to describe, and with the verbal counter sign, "Information is power", he paused a moment before he steered away.

To the modern-day street criminal, the advent and advancement of mobile communications had made the smart ones uncatchable, and even the C- minus students extremely elusive, but for the older generation of under achievers, these phones were the metaphorical equivalent of an atomic erector set in the tendrils of an amoeba and his idiot brother-in-law. Every call, every text whether in or out, every MapQuest, every pizza take-out, in short, everything these guys did was marked and remembered, and their reliably logged, and time-stamped records could be filtered and mined for data trends and oblique statistical outliers by a clever tenth-grader. Should pictorial proof be desired, there were the files of six megabyte photo-graphs these simpletons could not resist texting home. Once captured, this technology could provide a treasure trove of actionable intelligence, as well as the ability to freely sew disinformation through a presumably safe and secure input channel. Aside from the wide open back door into their employer's fortress, there was the sheer entertainment value this phone provided. It was better than a busty, fishnet stocking-clad, palm-reading hypnotist on the midway with a midget ventriloquist.

L'il Augie spent liberally upon the computers and communications he used within his empire. His offices, residences and automobiles were routinely swept for cameras and listening devices, and he was conscientious with passwords and access codes, but the electronic chains he used to secure the gates of his cyber-kingdom, as with most things, were dependent upon the weakest link. Just recently this crucial security had been repeatedly compromised by a pretty basic oversight. Three of the smartphones he provided his minions, and through which he received updates and issued orders were not only in the hands of his enemies, but were being systematically used to fog his view of the realm and foil his grand plans for world domination.

Winston added The Mic's schmoozer to the list of captured communicators, tabulating the percentage of the whole which would, like the stock grabs of a hostile takeover, be necessary to manipulate the opinions of investors toward a favorable outcome. He reached the target number of 70%, about the same time he reached Herc's cell, where he estimated if they could control two more cells in the same linkage, it would be essentially, game over. Deception, much like erosion, depended upon repetition. Six guys telling the same tale, which L'il Augie already wanted to trust, were almost impossible to ignore, and created headlines in his cranium which he wanted to believe true of himself. He was too light on his feet, too bright in his brain, and way too cool to school!

Herc and Winston took a few seconds to celebrate the confirmation that another of L'il Augie's starting line-up had been successfully, and, just as important to their team's success, secretly, neutralized.

Winston turned back to Jean Pierre, handed him an old leather satchel, and said. "Here is that bundle of evidence to give the cops a reason to take a hard look at this guy. Where are you going to stash him?"

"I gonna stuff him the cage below the Witch's Castle and change the lock. I figure to scare him silly before I leave."

As JPB drove away he chuckled contently, "Have I ever got a spot for you to sleep it off. It may be the last sleep you get for a while."

While en route to Benny Bigalow's Lantana farm Diego Lazette received the text from the Mic which he had hoped would be the result of his abduction of Corina. He was not a fan of selfies; how many times had he seen foolish people ignoring really interesting spectacles to snap a photo of themselves not witnessing that event, to later post, or brag, about what they had not actually seen. However, a picture of himself with the unconscious woman in Winston's stolen car was just the thing for which L'il Augie Amato was waiting in his Palm Beach Towers fortress. Aside from the satisfaction he took from a job well done, he also knew when this extortion scheme paid off he would be in line for a very healthy bonus.

He took several pictures before he was satisfied with the content and composition, and before he sent it to his boss, he attached an eleven-word caption: "One down, and the lawyer is about to buy the farm."

He then said to Rocco as he adjusted the rearview mirror, "Punch this thing a little, let's see if he wants to keep up."

As the Aston Martin zoomed past eighty-five, Diego could just detect the outline of the El Camino in the mirror as it accelerated to maintain contact. "Okay, he's still back there, slow it back down to the speed limit. The last thing we need is to attract the boys in blue."

According to Diego's calculations, Billy and Blackie should soon be arriving in town with Montgomery's daughter, and he would add the lawyer to their growing number of hostages. Once the negotiations for the ransom were completed, a deep and unmarked mass grave in a Lantana orange grove would hide all the evidence of their crimes, and they could get back to their more mundane looting and pillaging. Life was easier when there were no rules.

J ohnny kept a discreet distance from the midnight blue sports car, and, as he recovered from his run from the Breakers to his El Camino, he reached for his cell phone and punched in Willis' number. Willis answered before it could ring a second time, "Whassup?"

Johnny replied, "You are not gonna believe what just happened."

Willis answered tersely, "Try me."

That big guy that Corina was walking out with just snatched her, and stole Winston's car in the bargain. They were with one of those goons we assailed yesterday." Still breathing hard, Johnny continued, "I'm following them. They just got onto 1-95 heading south. Where's Katie?"

Willis replied, "Still on the veranda with the dandy."

"Go get her outta there," said Johnny, "I don't care if you have to knock them both out. L'il Augie is making his move!"

Willis' response was again a brief one, "Roger. I'll keep you apprised."

Willis' approach toward Katie and Daniel was a considered cross between "funny-running-into-you-here", and a more direct "I've-been-looking-for-you."

"Lovely evening, and I hate to intrude, but I need a quick word with you Katie."

Katie slowly turned away from Daniel and fixed Willis with a malevolent stare. "Is this more of Johnny's paranoia?"

"Possibly, but his paranoia has moved from speculation to reality – a couple of goons just stole your car and they also grabbed Corina. Johnny's following them." Willis paused for a half second as he passed an assayer's eye across Daniel and continued, "For all we know John Travolta here might be one of them."

"That's ridiculous," said Katie.

Daniel injected, "One of whom?"

Willis replied, "That's a longer story than we have time for Bub, but it makes sense that if L'il Augie put the snatch on Corina, he has someone watching you too Katie. We need a quick and quiet exit from here, and I mean right now."

Katie was certain Daniel was not an enemy, but she also knew Willis was not an alarmist. This stuff was really happening. She said, "Let's get after them." And she started toward the entrance to the Mediterranean Ballroom, when Daniel stopped her. "If there are people waiting to grab you, you don't want to get back into that mob. I know this place inside and out. Let me help you give them the slip."

Katie protested, "My purse."

Willis said, "Corina has it."

Daniel took Katie's hand and started down the previously unnoticed spiral staircase at the veranda's edge. Willis, acting as a rear guard for the retreat, trailed a few steps behind. When they reached ground level Daniel steered them into a service door and down a long hall lined with insulated HVAC plumbing, phone and Cat 5 cables, which ran amongst the bright red pipes of the fire suppression system. Along the way Katie made sparse introductions, "Willis, please say hello to Daniel Swell, an old friend. Daniel this is Willis."

Daniel glance over his should and said, "Pleasure to meet you Will."

"You too Dan. Where does this tunnel come up?"

"Near the rose garden at the south end of the main hotel." said Daniel.

Willis replied, "Perfect, my car is parked just around the corner."

When they finally emerged from the service tunnel, they were exactly where Daniel had said they would be, and Willis sprinted to his car parked in the handicapped space less than fifty yards away. Realizing she still wore Daniel's dinner jacket, Katie quickly removed it and handed it to him saying, "It has been lovely seeing you again, and I really, really hate to cut this short, but apparently the game is afoot, and my friend needs help. I'll let you know how it turns out."

Then she kicked off her green lizard skin stilettos, snatched them up, hiked up the skirt of her green silk gown, and ran barefoot across the Bermuda grass lawn. When she reached Willis' BMW she looked back to Daniel, smiled widely, blew him a kiss and leaped into the car.

As Daniel Swell watched the taillights grow smaller, he slipped into the coat Katie had just handed him, and it was now his turn to savor the light fragrance of her perfume. He had read somewhere that a memory anchored by a notable scent had five times more staying power than one without such an olfactory marker. He doubted this memory would require the prompting of her aroma, but conversely, he supposed there would be a moment in the future when an unexpected blast of this fragrance could easily propel his imagination toward a game of "I wonder how this night might have ended." He mused, "Love the one you whiff."

He walked a few steps into the rose garden where he spied the yellow bloom of a fragrant hybrid tea rose. Using his small silver pocketknife, he cut it, took one more sniff, and placed it in the button hole on the lapel of his white dinner jacket and thought, "You mix a full moon, a pretty girl, some champagne, and Palm Beach at Christmas time, there is just no knowing how it will turn out."

The roads of Palm Beach were laid out in a rectangular grid of similar sized blocks, but of necessity there were a few odd curves and unusually shaped estates, and to the locals, at least, the oddest was located in the deep cut through a coral outcropping on the northern end of the island. This two block stretch of Country Club Drive runs east and west and through rough-sawn coral walls, which rose thirty to forty feet on either side. It was poorly lighted, which lent the pass a spooky element, but there was also a whispered legend of a witch and the hill she supposedly haunted. High school boys played on these frightful stories to coax their dates closer as they feinted car trouble or the old out of gas routine – "You know it was about here on a night like tonight, with a moon like tonight, that they found Wanda Latsky wandering half naked and babbling sheer nonsense."

Tales like this were common on the island, and for the most part harmless, unless you count a lingering fear of ginger bread and broomsticks, but as for The Mic, at the very minimum, he was in for a long night. After using his ancient, but trusty bolt cutters to remove the pad lock on the gate to the crude cage, a three feet, by three feet, by two feet deep carve out in the witch's wall, JPB strained a little to fold the still unconscious Mic's 235 pounds into this reportedly haunted cave. He had cleared the thug's pockets of keys, knife, wallet and smokes. Jean Pierre then deposited a plastic water bottle and a book of matches from a local bar called The Pirate's Well within easy reach and then covered the Iron Gate, which covered the opening in the coral cliff, with a tough black burlap bag, which he secured with plastic ties over the bars of the ancient, but sturdy gate. Before fitting the gate with a new lock, he applied a generous basting of Karo syrup about the upper torso of the unconscious gangster, and murmured to the "no-seeums", "Come and get it."

The further south Johnny followed the Aston Martin sports car containing the two hoodlums and Corina, the more weird and wicked the scenarios grew that popped into his mind. Were they headed for a port and a tramp freighter that could steam into the boundless Caribbean Sea from which there would be no trace and no return? Maybe there was a rendezvous with a small plane at a grass landing strip in the Glades, and a long silent drop into vast Lake Okeechobee, but that seemed like a lot of trouble to lose one woman. When they exited I-95 at Lantana Road and headed west the pieces of this strange puzzle assembled themselves in his head. L'il Augie had somehow trapped and identified the bogus license plate of headless Benny Bigalow, and his little farm, west of the turnpike, was where they were headed.

As soon as Johnny put this together he pulled onto the shoulder of the road and called Willis who was about seven miles and five minutes behind him and was closing the gap quickly.

"Willis, these guys are taking Corina out to Benny's place, and I'm not certain about this, but I suspect they know I'm following them."

Willis replied, "Katie and I are just a few minutes out. How do you want to play this?"

"I think we should approach it carefully, and from a distance." Johnny replied, "Ya'll come in the back way and meet me at the back gate. Kill your lights as soon as you leave the blacktop. You can see fine by the light of the moon."

After ending this brief exchange, Johnny extinguished his lights and turned down the dirt access road which ran the along the western side of Florida's Turnpike. After six hundred yards or so he turned west and came to a stop at a galvanized pipe gate in the fence that surrounded the

Bigalow farm. As he waited for his cohorts to join him, Johnny began to assemble and inventory his meager weaponry. Two slingshots and two screw-cap mason jars filled with nuts and bolts. "Boy that didn't take long," he thought as he loosened his tie and removed his suit coat.

He found his mouth was suddenly dry, and he pulled a green bottled beer from the igloo cooler behind the driver's seat, opened it, and leaned against the fender of the El Camino to take his first swallow. This was the position in which Willis and Katie found him a few minutes later.

Willis looked at his watch as he crept close: quarter after midnight – time flies when you're having rum. He reached behind the driver's seat for his gym bag and, as an after-thought, helped himself to a beer. When Katie stepped up Willis tossed her the bag. "There're some shorts and a tee shirt in there you can wear. We might have to do some slinking and skulking to get close to the house. I don't know what we can do for shoes."

"I'll go barefoot," said Katie as she withdrew a short distance to change.

Willis and Johnny lightly clinked their beer bottles together in a fatalistic toast, took a sip, and then Johnny said, "I think we should go at them from different angles. You take the right and Katie and I will go down the left side. I'll start with a single shot through the windows, which ought to surprise them, and then, after a while, you lob one in from the other side. Keep them off balance."

Just then Willis caught a glimpse of Katie standing in the moonlight nearby, wearing just her underwear as she rummaged through the gym bag. He nudged Johnny with his elbow and gestured in her direction with slight movement of his head. The old friends smiled at each other unabashedly, and without speaking, watched the moon-drenched silhouette transform itself from curvy and erotic, to baggy and butch.

She completed her conversion by tucking her long hair up and under an Atlanta Braves ball cap as she rejoined them. "Did you guys get an eye full?"

Willis grinned at Johnny and said, "I don't know what you are talking about."

Despite the cover of the house, Johnny and Willis were able to periodically snap off a shot from the darkness which was well placed enough to keep Rocco and Diego off balance and on guard. They interspersed their rate of fire to make it seem plausible that there was only one sniper in the woods instead the factual three. At Johnny's suggestion, Katie took an occasional turn launching a nut or bolt through the kitchen window.

Diego had had enough of this crap, and he dragged Corina, who was now upright and conscious but still confused and groggy, by one arm from inside the house out onto the back deck, and despite her full resistance when she reached the door jam, he seemed to just twitch his powerful upper body, and she was snatched free of the solid hold she thought she had established. She was slung like a ragdoll in front of him and at that point he released her wrist and encircled her waist and drew her close to his body, and he slowly raised the pistol in his other hand. In case he did not already have the hidden assailants' attention, he suddenly fired two shots into the air and returned the smoking barrel of the gun to within several inches of Corina's temple. This move was deliberate and intended to send a clear signal. Like a children's game of hide and go seek when the seeker had had enough, Diego said in a strong but measured voice, "Come out, come out, wherever you are."

"It would be a shame if you made me spoil this little gal's make-up, but either you come in or I promise it will get messy."

He then twirled Corina out to the length of his arm and slapped her across her face and then reeled her back in. She gave a game effort at defiance, but she was utterly defenseless in this situation, and she, along with everyone else, knew it. A blotch appeared at the corner of her mouth, and at first it looked to be smeared lipstick, but within another second it became apparent Corina's lip was torn and the smudge was a trickle of blood. A sinister grin formed on Diego's face and he said loud enough for Johnny to hear, "Well what do you know. She aches just like a woman, but she breaks like a little girl."

 Joe Cocker – Just like a Woman:
https://www.youtube.com/watch?v=tfxLznYkpF0

Without hesitation, Johnny yelled, "Alright, don't hurt her I'm coming in."

Johnny turned and gave his slingshot and ammo to Katie and whispered, "I'll go, you stay until the light hits me, and then go find Willis. They don't know how many of us are out here."

Katie felt her courage sag and grabbed Johnny's arm, "Isn't there some other way to get Corina out of this? I think he intends to kill you both."

"I don't see one, and we are about outta time."

About the same time as Johnny raised himself from his prone position on the sandy berm, Willis slithered up behind him and whispered. "What the hell is your plan?"

"I'm gonna try and get him to fight me. He is a cocky bastard and if I can separate him from Corina maybe you two can make a difference from here."

"Look at him - his delts and traps – that guy is a wrestler. If he gets a'holt of you - It's over."

Seeing no way out of tangling with him, he grabbed his half empty St. Polli Girl beer bottle, took a sip, and poured the rest of it over his head. "Hopefully he'll think I'm drunk."

Diego stayed behind Corina and, as Johnny came into the light from the house, Johnny threw in a bit of a staged stagger, and with a slight slur he spoke, "Typical New Yorker, slapping women and then hiding behind their skirts. You've messed up your own state to where hell won't have it, and now you're down here messing up mine. And don't get me started on the way you schmucks ruined Mickey Mantle, the only great thing ever in New York."

Johnny did not look directly at Diego, but he sensed his drunken taunts were striking home. "Yes sir, you give me choice between eating breakfast with a busload of Arab terrorists with cholera, or a broke-nosed moron from Queens, damned if I wouldn't pick the ragheads."

Diego responded tersely, "I don't think you're going to be around for breakfast."

Johnny made quick eye contact with Corina, winked, and then rejoined his barrage of verbal abuse, "Why don't you pick on something your own size, you know like a hippopotamus, or a dump truck full of horseshit?"

Diego felt his face flush, and he slung Corina roughly to Rocco. He also tossed him his pistol, and then he stepped down into the barnyard saying, "Hold this floozy while I make this guy look like a Coney Island pretzel. They're pretty great."

Rocco's strong hand caught Corina's arm just above the elbow and squeezed. Then to add a little emphasis he pushed the barrel of the gun into her ribs and snarled into her ear, "This shouldn't take long cutie, and what's left of your boy won't make patch on Diego's pants."

Corina shouted, although her sentiment seemed more bluster than belief, "Come on Johnny, give him the treatment!"

Had this contest been held under the lights of a square ring, it might have been heralded using the well-worn, but still fragrant, bait of a David vs. Goliath encounter, in which the cheap seat bookies might have averaged against Johnny at thirteen to two, and amongst everyone, except the opponents they may have had in common, the spectacle would have been widely regarded as hubris meeting nemesis. Sadly, the sure money on Lazette would have had to go begging. As is the presumption of De Camptown Races. There could be no bet on the bob-tail nag if nobody bet on the bay.

Both combatants had faced their proposed/deposed selves in the mirror of a locker room before, or of an emergency room after, to conclude their win or loss had, at least, been sanctioned, even if by corrupt deciders. And the event could produce opposing points of view, of which there would be no censorship. But this scuffle was a closed set, and if the event was chronicled at all, the only version recorded would be that of the victor's.

Johnny was not the sort of pugilist who would prolong a slugfest for the sheer exhibition of his endurance. He would have his counter know his intentions right up front. If given his choice, he would retire to a neutral corner for the last minute of any round, but in this case, as his old man had advised, and Herc had reinforced, "Once it comes to fighting, get on with it, and get it over."

Diego, however had a broad streak of feline-like cruelty, and preferred to let his opponent/victim writhe in despair on the boundary of escape, before applying the kill shot. He was going to punish this obnoxious drunk, and he was going to enjoy it.

Out in the long shadows of the barnyard, Willis's cell phone vibrated in his pocket. It was Herc. Willis started the whispered conversation with, "Herc, Johnny is about to fight this big wrestler looking guy that works for L'il Augie and I don't like the odds. Plus, another thug has Corina and is holding a gun on her."

Hercules's response was immediate, "As soon as Johnny takes him out, you get the other one. Then, and this is important, get ahold of their cell phones. I gotta run now, but call me back."

Willis was mystified at Herc's confidence in his little brother, but he willingly signed on to the optimism and said to Katie, "When this gets going, it might not last very long, so while they are distracted let's move closer and get a better angle."

In the cool night air, the combatants circled each other looking for cracks in their opponent's defense Johnny circled clockwise in a boxer's attitude, his fists tightly clinched; Diego assumed a grappler's lower and more centered posture. With distain Diego slapped away Johnny's first few probative jabs, and then he made the first quick move; he lunged at Johnny's front leg, but Johnny saw it coming and danced out of reach and then delivered a hard left which split his adversary's lower lip and followed with a left uppercut, which always came to an opponent as an unwelcome surprise. This combination began a substantial blood flow. Johnny opined, "Hurts huh?"

Diego, slightly surprised, wiped his jaw, and upon finding the familiar metallic taste of his own corpuscles, projected a sinister grin. First blood did not mean jack to him – it was on!

Diego now gave Johnny a little more respect, but very little more. He felt he had absorbed what had to be at least one of his rival's best shots, and he was fine. If he had to wade through another fusillade it would be worth it to get him into the Diego comfort zone, which was on the ground.

It was a hell of a thing the way Johnny could use his fists to double up or double down. The fourteen straight lefts Johnny threw at Diego's head wasn't the modern-day record for a street fight, but it was an impressive number none-the-less, and these missiles were used mostly to block and blur his opponent's vision, and to disguise the eventual appearance of the widow-maker. Experienced and inexperienced practitioners and publicists of the pugilistic arts agreed, when you hit a guy on his ear with a hard left hook, his reflexes could, and often did, spasm, through muscle memory, to guard against the sudden arrival of the train (an over-head right coming straight down main street), but what followed Johnny's hook was something else entirely. That same punishing left was usually left unattended at the merest hint of a right, and a viewing of the fight film was often required before the phantom uppercut left could be detected, and although sensible observers could disagree which of the two lefts did the most damage, they could usually agree it was a left what undid the counter-combatant. However, this night, the very occasional blow that landed did not seem to have any noticeable effect.

For Johnny's part, this was just what he had feared. He thought he had hit him right a couple of times, and not only had he not folded, this guy seemed undamaged and enraged. He was now advancing for more. Diego came low and hard; and while Johnny landed a good left over Diego's right eye, which opened a new bloody gash, Johnny was caught. Both of his arms were pinned between their chests, and Diego began a rib-crushing bear hug against the trunk of an oak tree. Their faces were inches apart, and, splattering blood in his face, Diego snarled, "Say goodnight Johnny."

Johnny arched his back against the tree trunk, lifting both of his legs, which made Diego support not only his entire weight, but also all the additional load he could leverage from his angular frame against the tree trunk. As Diego tried to shift his grip, Johnny placed his shoes' hard leather in-soles against the wrestler's legs just below the knees. With all the force he could muster he raked them down the length of both shins, and as Diego reacted with alarm to this fresh pain, Johnny slammed his forehead into his opponent's face, re-breaking Diego's septum – more blood. As Diego staggered backward, Johnny was able to wriggle free Diego tripped over a concrete block that lay in the yard and landed hard on his back. As Johnny approached to inflict further damage, Diego moved his right leg to sweep Johnny's feet from under him and scrambled to his feet, hoisting the block over his head with the blatant plan of the sudden euthanasia of his adversary. Johnny could not react fast enough to avoid this ending, but suddenly the spotlights from house eaves went out, which served to disorient Diego and caused him to pause in his assault just long enough for Johnny to dodge the concrete missile. Then, as mysteriously as they had gone out, the lights came back on, illuminating the bloodied combatants.

If there had been a ring, the ring-side judges, particularly the judge who had the day job as a hematologist, might have credited Johnny with punching above his weight, and ahead on points, but Johnny knew this was probably not the first time this guy had had to come from behind, and he was also keenly aware that the points in this contest would never be tallied, and points would not be deciding the outcome of this match. There would also be no split decision. There would be just one man left standing, the other would be out. Out of the fight, out of the pain, and out of contention, and quite possibly out of this life.

Suddenly Diego was on Johnny and he felt himself once again caught. As he was being reeled in, Johnny turned and swung his right fist wildly and connected to his opponent's left ear, which set off an oddly traditional bell ringing within in the wrestler's skull. A discordant thrum akin to "Good King Wenceslas" entered stage left. There was a slight spray of sweat, crud, and blood, but despite all of Johnny's effort to avoid it, he was drawn inexorably into a headlock - Diego was going for the choke out.

Was this it? Johnny had a pragmatic view of the afterlife, and, through a thoughtful review of the empirical evidence he had reached his agnostic stance. He used these three candles of reason to light his path: For the fifteen billion years preceding his birth he had felt nothing, and suspected he would feel nothing for the untold eons after his death. Promises of heavenly rewards for exemplary behavior should not be a compelling component of doing good, and the silly costumes and sanctimonious rituals of supposedly revealed religious truth gave further testament that all the pious, blindfolded leaders of the superstitious masses were clueless as to the will of a creator, and that sin, no matter how original, goes largely unpunished. Finally, he believed that matter and energy were cyclical, and the only true eternal elements of his brief stay here he hoped would be his re-composition into light – his only prayer had lately become, "Lord please don't turn me into dark matter."

However, none of these thoughts were coursing the paths of Johnny's brain, and, while he had never considered himself inextinguishable or indispensable, he knew that this day he was a major weapon for the good guys, and that should he be retired from the fray, his friends, his clan, his team, could lose everything. He also felt with all of this on the line there was no way he would or could quit.

Diego had done what Johnny had anticipated, and despite his strength and all his experience, Diego was about to register his first loss in over a dozen years. The thought that did occur to Johnny was another simple axiom he had acquired from years of observation, and in that deciding moment he may have even muttered it aloud, "I never knew a wrestler who could resist going for a headlock."

Diego tried to bear down, but could not maintain the hold on Johnny's wet scalp, and Johnny was able to slip his head from the vise. Now Johnny was behind his foe and he quickly encircled and pinned Diego's arms to his side. The wrestler knew how to defeat this amateur hold and gave a derisive snort, but before he could make good his escape, Johnny lifted him off the ground and turned his torso sideways ninety degrees. He spun quickly to his left and slammed Diego's head into the trunk of a Live Oak, and at impact Diego and his consciousness parted company, and that, as they say, was all she wrote.

Willis said to Katie, "Get ready." Katie closed one eye; waiting for the sign from her partner.

As Diego's corner man, Rocco was thoroughly astounded at the outcome of the fight but had no intention of throwing in the towel. While maintaining a firm grasp on Corina's left wrist, he stepped from behind her and raised his pistol to bring this show to its inevitable conclusion.

Now someone whose ears had not absorbed all the punches and slaps that Rocco's had might have heard a voice from the night say, "Now!" Rocco, however, did not.

Before he could fire his pistol, he was suddenly shuddered by two almost silent projectiles. From just outside the halo illuminated by the halogen porch light, Willis and Katie had simultaneously released a pair of half inch galvanized nuts from their slingshots, and they arrived within a quarter of a second of each other. Willis' nut struck Rocco's forearm just above the wrist, breaking both skin and bone, and causing him to relinquish his grip on the pistol. Katie's nut grazed Rocco's temple, taking a chunk of flesh and several sprigs of comically dyed hair with it, as it continued its arc through the light, and back into the darkness.

Everyone who has been in or around pugilistic circles knows the term, but the term is also a condition, as well as a psycho-pseudo physical address. This would make the forth incident over his lifespan in which unexpected accommodations would be required for Rocco on Queer Street. The other times had pretty much been uniformly pleasant experiences, but in those frame-by-frame, dream-state recollections there were no subsequent tremors of pain; there was only the soft-focus filtered fold, and while in those instances, he had beheld anew, the starry night, which he had vaguely enjoyed as if he were strolling down a seaside path on his way to the Hukilau.

 Don Ho – The Hukilau Song:
https://www.youtube.com/watch?v=oa4YdI97-PY

Tonight, to Rocco's immense chagrin, the script called for a short reprise, in which his cognizance and his consciousness were both summoned for a brief encore. Reeling spasmodically from the impact of the Imperial gage, course-thread fastener barrage, Rocco had relaxed his hold on Corina, and now it was her turn to extract a little comeuppance. She had not noticed the hardware arriving via airmail, but she did sense an opportunity to go on the offensive, she stabbed her stiletto heel into the arch of Rocco's foot, and as she drew her diminutive fist back from a short shot to his throat, Rocco resumed his slow-motion, dull-eyed, gurgling collapse to the deck. More than slightly astonished to be looking down at the unconscious thug Corina declared, "How many times do you have to be told – Don't hit girls!"

She raised her arms and did a little shuffle on the deck and shouted at the top of her lungs, "Oh Yeah! Its Lights out, and Tits up, Bitch!"

As a jolt, pain that resulted from his skirmish with the fire ants, the fountain, and flower pot brought The Mic, groaning, and scratching his way back into the world of the conscious. A good ten seconds passed before he became vaguely aware of his cramped quarters. It only required a few more seconds to defeat the rope that bound his hands, but before he could celebrate this victory he needed to figure out where he was. He could reach and rub most of the many origins of pain that ranged from merely tender, to smarting and stinging, up to those, when touched, produced outright agony. Still he explored the coral cage with his hands and feet. His discomfort quickly transformed itself into a full-blown claustrophobic panic. Had he finally achieved his ultimate fear? Had he been buried alive? Why was he dripping wet, and what was the sticky sweet taste that leaked into his mouth? Using all the strength and leverage he could muster, he strained to break or at least enlarge his cell, but to no avail, and within half a minute he gave in to his anguish and began to petition Mother Mary in prayer. After he recited the few supplications he could recall from his boyhood catechism classes, The Mic calmed somewhat, and performed a slightly more systematic exploration of what he now believed to be his grave, and discovered the matches. His thick fingers quickly removed and struck one which illuminated the coral cutout, but then an upward draft extinguished the flame. Tamping down the panic with shaky reason, it occurred to him, that there would be no wind gusts if he were underground, but the next conclusion his overheated imagination reached was just as dire. He must have been prematurely interred in the crypt of an above-ground a mausoleum.

The Mic tried the Iron Gate, but it held fast against his exertions, and his cries for help echoed loudly within this cave, but he felt certain they were not heard in the living world. He pulled at the burlap covering, but he could not gain a solid grasp, and it would not tear away. He struck another match, now conscious of the need to ration the thirty or so remaining, and with this round of flickering light he discovered the water bottle, and as the match burned his fingers before going out, he began to contemplate its meaning. After several dead ends, he reached several rudimentary deductions; whoever entombed him left this water so he would survive, and that could only mean they would be coming back for him, which did not bring him much comfort. He twisted off the cap and took several gulps of the cool liquid, but dissolved within this cool liquid, unknown and undetected, were two additives, two twenty milligram tablets of Ambien and three tabs of Windowpane blotter acid, a potent form of LSD. Despite his tight confinement, The Mic's problems were going to expand, and so was his mind.

About eight hours would have to pass before the sun rose and The Mic could hope for rescue, but within just a few minutes his thoughts would turn inward, and far beyond his fear of prosecution or even the hope of rescue, he would soon be eager to cop a plea for his eternal salvation.

JPB lingered silently and invisibly near the coral cage until he heard, and then saw, the signs that his imprisoned hoodlum had regained consciousness. He smoked a Cuban Cohiba while listening to The Mic's profane mutterings. The only visible trace of his presence was the red glow of the cigar's tip. When the cursing lapsed into crying, and eventually into prayer, to advance the mental putrefaction Jean Pierre blew several puffs of smoke through the blackened burlap gate covering, which quickly filled the small opening in the rock. A fresh flurry of fearful noises could be heard from within. Modulating his voice to simulate an other-worldly warning wafting in the wind, he whispered and repeated a chant in Haitian Creole until it was evident, that he had caught, and was holding the terrified thug's attention. He then changed to English and hissed several times, "You are on the highway to Hades unless you change your ways and confess, you see, it's your turn to speak your evil, or you're gonna burn."

JPB switched to an extemporaneous quotation of an ancient graveyard epitaph:

This is where the Mic doth lie,
Poorly Lived
And Poorly Died
Poorly Buried
And No One Cried

The barely audible sounds that formed the Mic's response left no doubt that these wind-born threats had made contact with the tattered mind trapped inside the coral cave. "I don't know anything, I was just supposed to watch the rich guy's place to make certain he doesn't call in any helpers – I just drive the car, and now the car is… Hell, I don't even know where the car is."

JPB now knew where this watchman was supposed to be, and whom he was supposed to be watching, and with another big stream of cigar blown into the coral cave, he snarled an unearthly reply, "De car be where de master require, but de driver on de way to de lake of fire…"

"Oh Jeeze, I don't wanna burn, please save me!"

He would let this jailed bird tenderize awhile. Besides, he had other important people to see while hoping to remain unseen himself. About then a flirtatious moonbeam found and briefly illuminated his perfect teeth because JPB could not help smiling at the sheer audacity of the plan. But as he steeled himself for the grim business ahead, he felt the vibrating pulse of his cell phone. His smile disappeared, and he withdrew, leaving the moonbeam to ricochet and race, in search of any trace, of the jet-black jailer. He said quietly into the mouthpiece, "Speak to me little one."

Fiona's voice spoke in a calm tone, "L'il Augie is still alone, but he seems agitated. I wish I could hear what he was saying."

JPB replied, "Keep an eye on him girl, I am five minutes away." He then disconnected and jogged south on the Palm Beach bike trail which ran along the eastern side of the Intercostal Waterway toward the Palm Beach Towers.

 Harry Nilsson – Moonbeam Song:
https://www.youtube.com/watch?v=btyelrNYCtU

Had the moonbeam, which JPB had eluded, tried a little harder, it could have detected Fiona, holding a pair of high-tech, U.S. Navy issue binoculars, and bobbing like a cork aboard the Apocalypso in a boat slip just 150 yards from L'il Augie's penthouse apartment. Fiona, unlike the moonbeam, did see the shadow stealing down the pier and handed Jean Pierre the night vision spy glasses as he came aboard.

"He has really been working that cell, and he doesn't seem to be getting the responses he wants. Can you read lips?" said Fiona.

JPB replied with a slight chuckle, "No child, but I think it's only going to get worse for dat dere fat man."

About then, Fiona's phone vibrated with a text from Hercules Dendy. She relayed the message to JPB, "Herc says to call him if it is practical."

"Well den, let's get him on de blower."

Fiona punched the number and Herc answered immediately, "Operation Obfuscation Command HQ, please report."

"Herc, it's Fiona, I mean agent Bright Star. Midnight has joined me and we are still in position to observe the Fat Tomato."

"Well done Bright Star," came Herc's obviously amused voice over the speaker, "I think it is time to curtail your reconnoiter and consolidate our intelligence. Head west and Big Daddy will meet you at the yacht club. Over."

JPB nodded at Fiona who replied, "Roger. We'll be there as soon as we can get across the ditch. Out."

The two worked together quietly to cast off the dock lines and began the short transverse of the intercostal waterway. The Palm Beach Yacht club is actually located on the West Palm Beach side, but almost directly across from the Towers, and within a few minutes the navigation lights illuminated Winston standing ready to toss a line to his daughter as JPB expertly backed into a slip. The three of them quickly made the boat secure and hurried down the center pier to the parking lot.

When they were all in the little rental car, Fiona asked her dad, "Where do we stand with all of this?"

Winston replied, "There are a lot of moving pieces, and to tell you the truth I am a little confused, but your softball coach seems to be made for this."

Within another three minutes, Winston parked on a side street around the corner from his office, and whispered, "In case someone is watching we'll slip in the back way. Keep as quiet as possible."

A decade before, Winston, who was no stranger to misdirection himself, had carefully constructed a camouflaged rear entrance, which he had patterned on Robinson Crusoe's secret path into his cave. They squeezed past an emergency whole-house generator, and he punched in the secret entry code into an electronic keypad, which caused a thirty-inch-wide by seven feet tall service panel to spring open a few inches. Even this far into his fortress the opening appeared to be just an access pane to an oversized water heater, but a careful observer might notice that on this same wall was an in-line, on-demand tankless heater which supplied the hot water to the apartment. Winston applied slight pressure to the empty tank, and it swiveled away. No one who did not already know the route could have detected it, and soon the three stealthy figures entered the apartment through a closet in a spare bedroom.

JPB had used this exit once or twice, but even he had never entered this way. "Boss, Dr. No would be proud of this lair."

Winston tried to conceal the pride in his craftsmanship but could not help but acknowledge the thought and work he had invested through the years, "A lot of toil and trouble has gone into being able to go and come without being noticed."

They found Herc in the large windowless conference room. After a round of "hugs and howdys" he asked them to be seated around the table on which, among the dry makers, post-it notes, and legal pads, were three identical smart phones. Each of them had been labeled, "Billy, Blackie, and The Mic."

"Alright, everybody put your phones on the table. If the plan is going to work, we must know immediately, and without a doubt, whose phone is which. So, let's get them all labeled."

The clatter of communicators hitting the table was almost comical. All of them produced a least one phone and Winston and Herc had two each. Winston said, "It never hurts to have a throw-away handy."

Just then one of Herc's phones began to vibrate, and as he picked it up he announced to the three sets of eyes bulging with curiosity, "Hey, everybody hold it down, it's Willis."

Before the echo of Corina's victory cry had left the secluded grove, Katie was at Johnny's side. She tried to support him but was only able to help him reach the ground. Her eyes betrayed the horror they beheld as she looked at his blood covered face. His clothes were caked with dirt and bathed in crimson. She choked back her emotions, smiled weakly, and tried to wipe some of the grime from his battered mug.

He could not suppress an embarrassed grin, as Katie for the first time he could remember, showered him with protective affection, and as he smiled at her, she noticed a gap in his snaggle-toothed grin. One of his front teeth was missing, and when he saw her reaction to this further deterioration in his appearance, the situation reverted to normal, with him feeling the need to comfort her, "Most of this blood is his you know."

She nodded and fought through her tears to force a small false laugh and said, "I guess this makes you king of the ring."

Johnny accepted the title with a modest head bob while exploring his mouth with his tongue. He discovered the missing incisor and added sheepishly, "I think I may have swallowed my crown."

Corina was touched, and a little jealous at the macabrely tender scene which was playing out just fifteen feet away, and thirty inches below the deck where she stood over her fallen foe. Shouldn't she have a gallant attendant of her own? After all, hadn't she been drugged and kidnapped, manhandled and bitch-slapped? Where was her first aid? Where was her cut man?

Before these thoughts could resolve themselves into a specific desire, Willis appeared, and she assumed her knight had arrived, but rather than follow a novella script which centered on her, he went straight to check on Rocco. He rolled the gangster over and began exploring his pockets. He collected the two hand guns, handling them by only the trigger guards, and then he retrieved a cell phone from Rocco's windbreaker and began a close examination of the gizmo. He finally looked up at her, but the inquiry he expressed did not concern her health or well-being, nor did he applaud her bravery or check her dental work, he curtly asked, "Where is the other one's phone?"

Adjusting her pride, a little, Corina began to think about his question but not without a huff of indignation, which Willis heard, but elected to not acknowledge. He brushed past her and into the house, and there, across the back of a chair at the kitchen table he found Diego's suit coat. He patted its pockets until he felt the bulge of the smart phone he sought.

He then looked at Rocco's phone which he still held in his right hand. Corina had followed him in, and suddenly he turned to her and said, "Hold this one for a minute. It's very important that we not mix these two up. Remember the one you have is the goon you K.O.'d out there. I have the wrestler's."

Corina responded, "Oh you noticed, did you?"

Willis put aside trying to understand the recent call history of Diego's phone for a moment, and turned his strained face in her direction and said, "Yeah, I noticed. You did great, until you consider you got yourself snatched, and almost killed, and Johnny beat to a pulp, and worried me and Katie to a frazzle. All because you won't listen."

Corina let the barbs just bounce off, moved in close, and said, "Yeah, but after all that stuff, it worked out pretty cool. Did you see the way Johnny worked that monster over? Then I Hai-Karated that ape in the throat, and he went down like a power window."

Willis's mouth slowly formed a smile, and he gave her a begrudged nod. He would let her have this victory for now. One day he might tell her the rest of the tale, but why deflate her when there were still hours of danger ahead? Just then Katie helped Johnny through the screen door and got him seated at the table. She hurried to wet a dish towel at the sink and returned to begin the gruesome wipe down, but before she could make much headway, Willis stopped her and took a picture of Johnny's face covered in blood with Diego Lazette's phone. Then with just a few passes of the wet cloth it became apparent that most of the blood had indeed started the day coursing Diego's circulatory. Other than lacerated hands and badly bruised knuckles, and the missing crown, Johnny's only other traces of the fight were a few reddened patches of skin.

Willis took the seat next to Johnny at the table and confided the next steps of the plan to the rest of his gang. "Herc wants us to get ahold of these phones and call him. I think he is planning to use them against L'il Augie."

He then resumed his perusal of the past texts on Diego's captured phone. The last transmission was of an unconscious Corina situated awkwardly in Diego's lap, the wrestler wore a lewd grin, and one of his large hands cupped Corina's right breast.

The response from his boss, time stamped one minute later, read, "Good job, but that's just a lady in waiting, let me know when you capture the queen."

Johnny and Willis, to use the vernacular of the underworld, tumbled to idea at the same instant. "We need a picture of Katie."

At this statement Katie turned from her ministrations to Corina's damaged lip to protest. But before she could produce word one she realized they were correct. Willis activated the camera mode and turned it upon Katie. The resulting picture was not at all convincing. As is too often the practice in photos, Katie had reflexively smiled, ruining the dejected aspect they wanted.

Willis urged Katie into a chair at the table and then tried to impart some theatrical direction, "A lovely pose if we were at a picnic. You are supposed to be in the clutches of a sadistic killer, not on a pony ride. Let's try again, but first…"

After an informed glance from Willis Johnny smirked, and squeezed a few drops of blood from his scuffed hands and dabbed them on the front of her white tee shirt. Corina, getting into the stagecraft, contributed a smear of blood from her own lip to the corner of Katie's mouth, and roughly smudged her lipstick. She spun the ball cap to where the bill was toward the rear at an unkempt angle. Willis said, "Now we're getting some-where, but it still needs something."

Then with both hands, he grabbed Katie's bloodstained shirtfront and ripped it from the collar to about half its length. Everyone, but Katie, agreed. The resulting exposure of her cleavage and the spattering of blood conveyed the depravity they sought.

While the two men worked on the best lighting Corina snapped an unexpected picture with her own phone. "What? Did you think I wasn't gonna get one for Facebook? My Christmas Vacation."

After a cleansing laugh, Katie assumed the terrified facial expression, and the scared-stiff body language of Nell being tied to the railroad tracks by Snidely Whiplash, and the money shot was taken and sent to L'il Augie.

Willis then pulled his own phone from his pocket and hit the illumi-nated call back key. Herc answered with one word, "Yeah."

Willis said, "I've got the phones."

The response was Herculean and terse, "How fast can you get to Winston's office in West Palm?"

Willis said, "I think we could probably be there in fifteen or twenty."

"Well come on then, and don't spare the horses. Timing on this con is critical, and mark the phones so you don't confuse them." Then the phone disconnected.

Willis looked over at Johnny and said, "He wants us to meet him at Winston's place. He didn't even ask about how you fared in the fight."

Johnny laughed and said, "He figures I won. He would have had plenty to say if I had lost a fist fight to a wrestler."

Then they all took a beat to consider what must be considered, the miracles of the past few minutes. Willis was the first to speak, "Johnny, I thought you were a goner for sure when that ape came at you with the cinder block, and then the lights blinked out. How did that happen?"

They all looked toward Corina, as if she had somehow intervened. "Don't look at me. If you recall, I was being pawed by that fat grease ball I flattened on the deck."

Then a wan smile formed itself on Johnny's damaged mouth, and he asked, "What time is it?"

Willis responded, "Twenty minutes to one."

Johnny did some quick math, "The fight ended about five minutes ago, and the lights flickered about a minute before that."

He looked around the small kitchen and quietly said, "Thanks Benny."

The others looked at each other quizzically, and then back at Johnny for an explanation. "I'll tell you later. We have some cleaning up to do before we head out. Come on Wil, let's secure these goons before we head for Winston's place."

Willis and Johnny each took one of Rocco's arms and dragged him to the tree under which Diego, separated from his waking will, lay inarticulate, incoherent and unaware. With plastic tie-wraps they lashed the two unconscious gangsters wrist to elbow, elbow to wrist, and ankle to ankle – oh yeah, between their bound arms, wrists and legs, grew a live oak tree.

"How about a go-pro?"

Johnny replied, "Not necessary. We can just swivel the spy cam Benny has on the back porch. I can access it through an app on my phone."

L'il Augie had been impatiently awaiting confirmation from Diego Lazette that he had finally laid his powerful hands on Kathleen Montgomery. When the smart phone in the pocket of his father's silk smoking jacket announced its arrival, he snapped his fingers, which mimicked in his mind, the sound of a bear trap slamming shut. To him, it was the final brick in what he believed to be an immovable barrier which would protect him from any counter moves Winston Montgomery might contrive to avoid coughing up, not only the dough, but also the Green Flash.

When one has an immoveable object to stand behind, conventional wisdom maintains that one is impervious to the onslaught of an irresistible force, but L'il Augie prided himself in avoiding conventional thought, and the next step in his plan was to bring the irresistible force into play himself. He would use his rude gang of mercenaries, his ruthless cunning, and the momentum brought by the capture of his adversary's bishops, knight, and, as evidenced by his latest photo of a tattered and fearful Katie, texted from Diego's phone, his queen, to crush Winston between the anvil and the sledge.

With all of these pieces under his control, he felt it was time to contact Winston Montgomery to see what progress had been made toward the fulfillment of the demands he had made. Although he had given Montgomery eight hours to comply, Amato had intentionally let twelve hours pass. He reasoned that uncertainty made everybody a little tense, and he wanted the captured daughter's condition to spur on genuine worry. He had queued the series of shocking photos to transmit at a second's notice, if Winston required a little more encouragement. If the pictures of an unconscious Corina, a beaten bloody Johnny Dendy, and his own battered wife did not compel his cooperation, there were other, more drastic measures he could take.

He used his next move to insure all the pieces were where he thought they were, one more measure to verify his impenetrable defense had no gaps, L'il Augie fired off a text to The Mic which read, "Is the pigeon still alone in his coup."

Within one minute he received a text in response, "Yes boss, and he's still alone."

L'il Augie pressed the required keys and Winston's phone began to ring. Before the second chime was complete Winston answered in a some-what breathless and obviously agitated state, "Montgomery here."

"Well done Mr. Montgomery, I appreciate your prompt reaction. Now for the big question. Are you prepared to meet my demands?"

Winston replied, "First, I want assurances that my daughter is safe."

L'il Augie had expected this tactic and, after a derisive snort, he said, "Safe is not the adjective I would choose, but trust me, she is secure."

He went on, "In case you are not aware, I have increased my leverage exponentially." He then sent the gruesome evidence of that increased leverage.

He thought he heard Winston gasp, and then actually stop breathing, as he viewed the collection of photographs.

L'il Augie waited several seconds before saying, "Are you still with me Montgomery?"

"I don't want anything bad to happen to these people, but my main concern is for Fiona, and I am not going to give you anything unless she is returned at the same time."

To L'il Augie this demand seemed like bravado, but he would be content to make this concession for two million and the priceless emerald. He replied, "While I don't think you are in much of a position to set condi-tions, all I want are the stone and the bonds. Produce those and I will turn over your little brat. Try anything and you will get her back in pieces."

Winston said, "What about the others?"

Amato replied, "Let's not get ahead of ourselves. I will call in one hour with instructions."

L'il Augie paused a few seconds for effect and said, "In the meantime, as a sign of your earnest intent, please send me a photograph of the bonds, and the emerald. Place a recent front page of a local newspaper in the frame as a time stamp."

There was a detached click signaling this call had ended. L'il Augie felt he had them just where he wanted them. They were tired and scared, and their force had been seriously depleted. By the gangster's count, Winston had on his side, himself and one also-ran real estate lawyer, out of Stetson University. If they had called the cops, he would know because of the generous retainers he dispensed, at several levels of the local constabulary.

L'il Augie fancied himself a master at game theory. He had moved his pieces with precision against a foe, in Winston Montgomery, whom he had silently pursued for decades, and now he was on the brink of check mating Bobby Fisher – he acknowledged to himself that this analogy was too sensational and switched his rhetoric comparison from chess to poker. His hand, while not unbeatable, was very strong, a veritable full house, and he could not see an outcome in which his adversary could produce a straight flush. He would play these, but had he overlooked the possibility that his opponent held two pair, all of them queens?

A soft knock came from the front door of Winston's office/apartment. The four co-conspirators all exchanged wondering glances and then wandered out of the conference room and into the anteroom. After what seemed like a long interval, Herc squeezed past them and went to the door. With his left hand, he slowly turned the door knob and allowed the door to swing inward, but in his right hand, hidden behind his back, he clutched a matt black nine-millimeter automatic pistol. A slight smile crossed his face, and he stepped back and made a welcoming gesture. A stunning blonde in evening attire, holding her own nine, walked cautiously into the room.

The same look of wonder ping-ponged among the men in the office, and Fiona too was captivated by the leisurely pace at which this woman boldly met each of their wide-eyed stares. After several tense seconds, she slipped her gun into the purse she wore on a silver chain draped from one shoulder and spoke in an obviously cultured Spanish accent, "Hercules, it is lovely to see you again, but I think introductions are in order."

Herc extended his hand to accept hers, and lightly tapped the heels of his boots together like an officer of a European cavalry brigade from a previous century, bent from the waist, and lightly kissed her hand. "My friends, I would like to introduce my good friend Miss Anna-Sophia Gabriela Escudo."

Right before her eyes, Fiona witnessed a sudden change in the posture and manners of her father and JPB. They seemed to go metamorphic, trying to display their most alluring qualities, and to exhibit all the etiquettes they knew. All this deference was apparently contagious, because Fiona too felt she needed a mirror and a comb.

With a hint of a facial blush and a wide smile, she stepped forward and extended her hand first to Winston, who stood transfixed, and then to Jean Pierre, who grinned like the Cheshire cat. "Please call me Sofi."

Sofi then turned and advanced upon the mesmerized girl and took her by both hands and said, "You have to be Fiona. I have wanted to know you for a very long time." Using her grip of Fiona's hands, Anna-Sophia gently applied subtle pressure to turn the girl as she appraised the curves of her figure and then added, "Hercules did not warn me that you have blossomed into a beautiful woman."

Her victory was complete, a coup-de-foudre. In a slow-motion bolt of lightning, she had taken the fortress without firing a shot. After a lingering appraisal of the girl, whose own blush was in full color, Sofi turned back to Herc and lithely insinuated herself within his defenses. With her three-inch heels, she was precisely at his eye level, and with her arms she encircled his neck and pressed her lips to his and then said softly, "It has been too long old friend. Are you still a bachelor? Or have you found someone?"

Herc spoke softly in this intimate proximity, "As you know I have been alone for quite a while, and even if I say so myself, it seems to be working out okay. I may be the one for me."

More glances askew. All three of the spectators, if pressed, would probably acknowledge Hercules Dendy to be handsome, heterosexual, and, potentially, a fine catch, but to have his appeal flung so suddenly in their faces left them a bit unhinged, and more than a bit curious.

Forehead to forehead, and eye to eye, Herc savored the woman, their shared memories, and the moment for several seconds and then pulled away from Sofi's embrace with a question, "Do you have it?" Actually, two questions, "Did you bring it?"

Sofi walked slowly back toward the front door, opened it, and placing the little fingers of both hands to her lips, she pierced the night with a long shrill whistle. She turned back to the group, who seemed to be even further awe-struck by this incongruity and said, "I have brought several things that may surprise you."

After an interminable wait which was only eight seconds, the door seemed to open wider of its own volition. The corner of a rather large plastic shipping case preceded its bearer into the room, and for just an instant the case diverted the assembly's attention, all but one of the assembly that is. Fiona's quick green eyes darted to the brown eyes of the young man carrying the case, and her face flared into a quizzical smile, "Manolo. How did you get here?"

Her question was answered, but only partially as Manolo smiled shyly and replied, "Courtesy of Miss Escudo and Captain Tabernella."

She was on the verge of a series of follow-on questions when Winston stepped forward and relieved the young man of his burden. He placed it against the wall in the foyer and said, "We don't have to stand in the doorway like a pack of trick-or-treaters, please come into the conference room and take a seat. Can I offer anyone a libation?"

After the assembly had reassembled around the large conference table, each of the members glancing from face to face, but not wanting to break the mystical air of suspense, Herc spoke, "First of all, let me see your cell phones."

Without hesitation Sofi and Manolo produced their phones. Fiona quickly lettered their names on a yellow post-it note and handed them over saying, "We are on cell phone lockdown."

"I would categorize it more as a security protocol than a strict lockdown." Herc then went on to the hit the high points of his plan to use these devices to infiltrate and misinform.

Fiona, feeling confident on her home turf, wisecracked for Manolo, "Like there's a difference."

Herc clouded over slightly and said, "A simple lockdown might allow us to go unnoticed tonight, which might allow us to win the battle, and if we're lucky maybe even the war, whereas a protocol will allow us to win the battle, and the war, keep our fingerprints off this entire caper, and get away clean."

Understanding the rebuke was aimed at her and feeling somewhat chastened, Fiona said meekly, "Sorry boss."

Just then one of the eight phones on the conference table vibrated.

Herc picked it up and read the text aloud, "Willis says they will be here in one minute."

He turned to Jean Pierre and said, "Katie knows you, right? Please go out the back exit and bring them in as quietly as you can. I'll text them to park in the church lot – we have too many vehicles piling up out front."

JPB went without more than a nod to do Herc's bidding. Sofi, Herc, and Winston formed a small knot, whispering among themselves, which left Fiona and Manny a chance to catch up. "How's your head?"

"Like my aunt says, it's has the same thickness as a coconut, so I'm fine. What about you? From what I've been told, this has been a heck of a week."

"You are right about that, but it sure beats taking finals, huh?"

The two teenagers laughed quietly for a moment until Fiona stopped and said, "You haven't told me why you're here."

Manny replied, "It's a strange tale Mi Vida."

He began tracing the past few days from his perspective, but for Fiona his first few sentences were a pleasant background sound, the two words "Mi Vida" echoed in her head, "My life?"

When she tuned back in Manny was explaining, "Apparently my uncle Francisco, you know Speedy, and Hercules have known Miss Escudo for a long time. She asked him to retrieve a package from a secret panel in a third-floor apartment in Newark. Well, Francisco used to be something of an acrobat, but between you and me, he is wearing a lot of that reputation around his waist these days."

They paused to wonder what they did not know about their cohorts' past lives with Fiona summarizing, "I guess you don't pick up street smarts in the library."

"Well anyway, Unc asked me for some help. We drive that Bat-mobile of his at two hundred miles an hour to Newark, and I climb a drain pipe, pick a window lock, find a secret panel behind a medicine cabinet, and grab a small brown paper-wrapped package and toss it to Francisco. Then he drives me out to a private airport on Long Island and puts me, and my stuff on board Captain Tabernella's little jet. He gives the package to the pilot and tells me to meet Miss Escudo in Florida."

"I asked him how I would know her, and he just said I was to imagine the most beautiful woman I had ever seen, and add fifty percent. She was easy to spot."

Fiona nodded her agreement, "Where do they grow women like that?"

Manny replied, "Argentina, I think."

Just then, as Manny took a seat nearer Fiona, and looking over her shoulder he said, "Wait a minute. What have we here?"

Fiona swiveled her chair see what had caught Manny's eye to discover her father's acoustic guitar, "Oh, that's my dad's old guitar. Why, do you play?"

Manny retrieved the instrument and returned to his seat next to Fiona. As he examined it, he handled it with a care bordering on reverence. He turned the guitar subtlety to better catch the light as he peered into the sound hole and eventually he said, "I thought so. This may be your old man's ax, but it is also a Martin 45. John Mayer plays one sometimes."

Manolo strummed it a couple of times and then began to softly play, expertly and with confidence. Fiona was mesmerized and when he began to sing Mayer's hit "Daughters" she listened closely and cocked her head just like Nipper, the iconic RCA Victor smooth fox terrier.

 John Mayer – "Daughters"
https://www.youtube.com/watch?v=rZLbUIa7exE

Fiona was not the only one caught in mid-sentence when Manny began to perform. Anna-Sofia, Herc and Winston could not control the muscles of their faces, or so it seemed because half smiles appeared involuntarily and all discussion ceased. When Manny finished, closed his eyes while trying to coax every decibel of vibrato from the strings, and managed a slight bow from his seated position in response to the single word salutes: "Bravo! Outstanding! Prodigy!"

Then everyone returned to their previous concerns, everybody except Fiona, who said softly, "That was wonderful. I would love to collaborate with my keyboards. From the looks of the suitcase you brought you must be planning to stay for a while."

Before responding to Fiona's inquiry, Manolo glanced out the conference room door at the large hard plastic case in the anteroom, and leaned in conspiratorially, "I would have preferred to bring my twelve-string, but this apparently is what this situation calls for, what the team needs."

To Fiona, the suspense felt unbearable, and yet she hoped it would somehow last. As an only child, she had never really been part of a gang. Oh sure, she had been on softball, soccer, field hockey, and track teams in school, but these enterprises were all scheduled as part of her regimented day – the goal to make her well-rounded. Each of these events had been carefully slotted in her calendar, and at completion she was off to her tutor, or debate practice, or some other "activity." Unlike the past few days, there were seldom any lasting consequences to her itinerary, but she, and they were now playing for life, her own and the lives of her friends, and possibly the death of anyone who came against them.

A sudden tremor of memory took hold of Fiona. She was back at the shootout in Queens and she could feel her face grow cold and ashen. Had only three days elapsed since she had intentionally taken a life? How had she white-washed this deadly sin? Oh sure, justification was lying around in piles: Herc was under fire. It was obviously him or us. They started it. But to willfully send a half-ounce projectile screaming at some twelve hundred feet per second through the body of another human...how could she reconcile that act with her pacifist beliefs? She knew, without the need for extensive introspection, that should the same circumstances present themselves again, her response would be the same. But what the hell... it was intensely personal now. "Guns don't kill. People kill. I am a killer?"

Did these fractions of a second have to mean that hypocrisy be her new cloak? This surviving in an adult world was tricky stuff. Hopefully, she would have years to sort this out, but just then a new chorus of new voices interrupted these ruminations.

The sound of these new voices was coming from the other side of the apartment. Fiona, recognizing several of the voices, leapt from her chair, and ran through the door to meet the new arrivals. The scene she encountered just around the corner was so incongruous that her powers of reason were swallowed whole. There was her mother dressed, really more like half dressed, in torn and bloody gym clothes, Corina, sporting a fat lip, and wearing a stylish little black dress, Johnny Dendy, Herc's younger brother, covered in blood and missing some teeth, and Willis, looking fresh in an Armani suit. What the hell was going on?

With her new appreciation for intrigue, Fiona embraced these new pieces of the puzzle. All would be made clear in its time, she hoped. For now, she hurried to her mother and Corina. In her embrace, Katie was torn between laughter and tears, but Corina was so energetically on the side of laughing that she influenced the entire group in that direction as she said, "Man, what a night!" She looked at Winston and continued, "Nice digs Montgomery, where's the kitchen? I could sure use a beer."

But Winston Montgomery was not listening, he was standing slightly apart and just watching, watching his daughter and wife catch up. He had always held a fascination for the epic tales of Scotland by Stevenson and Doyle, and could now imagine these two bonnie lasses, Kathleen and Fiona as the reluctant, but undeniable heroines upon which the entire tale teetered. Either of them, he imagined could have turned the head of William Wallace or Rob Roy MacGregor. Or was this more along the lines of Longfellow's grand poem Evangeline? He suddenly realized how much they resembled each other. Unlike the two-hundred-pound waddling duos he was accustomed to seeing, here was a mother-daughter team that brought him a fresh appreciation of the term genetics. This is about the point he caught Katie's eye and any warmth within his chest quickly drained away. His heart seemed to freeze as if it had been flash frozen by a quick submersion in liquid nitrogen. He turned slightly aside to avoid any direct blow which would cause his heart to shatter like a glass Christmas ornament.

Her green eyes communicated her contempt far better than words; to the point that over the past few years of their marriage very few words had passed between them. Winston decoded the glare to read, "Look at the shit storm we are all caught up in, and this is all your fault. How could you?"

Winston was hugely relieved when Corina noticed Anna-Sophia and began grilling her about her involvement, "Lady, I love seeing you again, but what is your piece of this huckleberry pie?"

Sofi glided across the dozen feet that separated them, at least it seemed that way to Corina, and she resolved that later she would find out how this lady moved like that. But that could wait, or could it? Corina was so curious about this exotic female, it was as if she had stumbled into a freak show on the midway, but in this tent, the freaks comprised the audience. While these and another twenty questions were ricocheting around her brain, she felt Sofi's cool hand touch her face, and her mind went blank. "What has happened to you my friend? Come with me and let me tend to your wound."

Sofi took Corina's hand, glanced at Winston, who gestured in the direction of the kitchen, and led the usually fulminant woman away.

Katie, noticing the absolute silence Sofi was able to project upon Corina with just a few quiet words, "Whatever that gal has, I would like to order a couple of quarts. I've never seen Corina obey commands."

In another corner, Herc was giving his brother a once over. After assuring himself of Johnny's good health, he asked in the gruff tones of older brother speak, "What is that three times, that you've had that tooth knocked out?"

Johnny replied. "Yeah, three counting the first time when you did the honors."

Willis said, "I think we could whittle a piece of Candy Corn to use as a temporary."

Fiona said to Katie, "I don't like seeing you this way. I have some clothes upstairs you can change into if you like."

This comment caught Herc's ear and pulled him away from Johnny and Willis, and he spoke over the den of the raucous reunion, "Boys and girls, let's get back to business – there is still a psychopath trying to kill us, and we've got some work to do before the sun comes up. Come back into the conference room, and let's get organized."

Even with an impending threat of the magnitude of an old world, Sicilian crime family imminently looming just over the water, the group was mostly nonplussed. Apparently one, especially in the hardened company of friends, can become inured. Danger had been their trail mate for so long now that it was almost welcome at the campfire. So, like children being called in from recess, the ten of them took chairs around the table cluttered with phones, which with the addition of those captured and owned by the platoon from the western front, now numbered seventeen.

Hercules, Willis, and Winston conferred briefly and quickly agreed, and Winston cleared his throat to get all their attention. Then he said, "Most of these phones are what we call smart phones, which means they consume a bandwidth about twenty-four times that of a regular cell phone. In everyday life and out among the public this is no big deal, but in a concentration like this, at an early hour like this, they can be detected by someone with the proper equipment."

He now had their attention and he went on, "Mr. Dendy and I agree it is time to power down at least half of these, and then we should disperse into smaller teams."

Herc, consulting a yellow legal pad spoke up, "Manny, Fiona, Katie, and Corina turn off your phones now, but take them with you when you go."

Katie glanced at Fiona and asked out loud, "Go where? I feel like we are finally safe. Why not just use one of these damn phones to call the cops?"

Herc looked to Willis to respond, and then all the heads turned in unison like spectators at a tennis match to face him, Willis paused a moment and then said, "We have left a trail of carnage behind us, and it would be best for everyone here to stay clear of it. Me and Johnny have been looking into this for a few days, and we think the local cops may be on L'il Augie's payroll. It appears this guy is wired up and down the east coast, so we cannot afford to come out of the shadows until we really back him into a corner."

Herc quieted the room, "It is likely that all the help we can rely on is already in this room."

Corina spoke, "I would rather be with the people in this room than with the finest and fanciest people in the world!" Then, as an after-thought, she looked at Anna-Sophia, and added, "Except for Sofi here who might actually be the finest and fanciest person in the world."

Sofi smiled demurely and said, "You are too kind, but I agree. Now Hercules Quinton Dendy, if you have a plan, please roll it out."

Fiona raised her eyebrows and giggled. "Quinton?"

Hercules began running the assignments, "Manny, grab your gear and go with Jean Pierre and Fiona. Willis, you take them back to the yacht club so they can take the boat back to the dock at the Towers. I know this goes without saying, but be careful, be quiet and run dark. Let me know when you are in position."

As the three started to move, a sudden surge of panic swept over Katie at the thought of sending her little girl back into the fray, and she looked to Johnny to intervene with his brother, but Johnny wanted to stick with Herc's plan, and mixing in a measure of assurance, said as much. "Fiona will be safe with JPB, and she, out of all of us, is best suited to this assignment."

"What assignment?" Katie asked.

Fiona repeated, "Yeah, what assignment?"

Suddenly the ball was in Manolo's court and he spoke up, "That big case out there contains my other hobby. It holds all the controls, microphones, cameras, and battery packs we need to get a good look into the lion's den."

Katie, still unwilling to give her consent without more detail, reached for a cigarette, lit it, and after a short exhale, said, "I'm gonna get my gun if you people don't start telling me what's going on!"

Corina backed her friend's play, "I think you ought to get your gun anyway."

Herc smiled accommodatingly at them and said, "Manny brought his RPA with autonomous OCR and video surveillance. Fiona will help with the cell GUI, and lookout."

Katie's look of astonishment was Corina's call to action, "We may be idiots when it comes to technology, but nobody is leaving until we get some answers we can understand, and somebody is probably gonna catch a bullet if we have to wait much longer." She paused and looked at Manny, and then back to Katie, "You want me to put a pill in this kid?"

Manny put his hands up even though, from what he could tell, Corina had no weapon, "Remote Piloted Aircraft with camera and sound recording capabilities. I will show Fiona how to work the app for its cell phone GUI," Katie started to growl a little, so Manny clarified, "That stands for Graphical User Interface, which will allow us to use a custom application we will install to transmit what it sees and hears via cell phone back here to you guys. You know, a drone."

JPB rose, collected his phone, and, using his head, motioned toward the door. Willis and Manolo were next, and finally Fiona began to move, but all the while she held eye contact with her mother, who she more than half expected to veto the mission. She came to her mother's side and patted her shoulder, handed her a small vial of pills and said, "Mom, make sure Herc takes two of these wide-spectrum antibiotics for his wound. Don't take no for an answer."

She glanced over at Herc and added, "He could probably use some lidocaine too." She found a vial of the pain killer, and a couple of syringes in her bag, and handed them to her mother saying, "Just draw a couple of CCs of this and inject it subcutaneously. You know, about a half inch under the skin in three or four spots around his wound."

Katie stared with mouth agape but accepted the drugs and needles, and, rather than question her daughter about the wound, and how she knew about sub-cutaneous injections and wide-spectrum antibiotics, she let it go – she would just do as she was told.

Willis caught Corina by the arm and compelled her to join him and Herc for a few quick words, "Herc, we have this friend whom, I think, we should bring in on this. She has a set of skills that we could really use."

Herc raised one eyebrow, which meant they had his attention and to please elaborate. Willis continued, "Corina, while I'm taking the surveillance squad back to the Yacht Club please fill Herc in on what we were talking about in the car. I'll call in a few minutes."

Corina began a quiet conversation with Herc, and as he listened intently, he began to nod his approval, and both he and Corina picked up a cell phone each from the conference table and left the room.

JPB spoke softly as he passed Katie's chair, "Mrs. M. you know I ain't gonna let nothing bad happen to that little girl,"

Then they were gone.

As he walked toward the doorway, Herc turned to Winston and said, "You need to make that picture of the ransom that L'il Augie wants. Here is yesterday's newspaper. I guess this will do for a time register. Anna-Sophia can help."

Before Herc got past her, Katie took the cap off the vial Fiona had just given her, shook out two pills, and held them out to Hercules. It was now his turn to do as he was told, and he popped the small capsules into his mouth and swallowed them without anything to wash them down before Katie could offer a cup of water. He said maybe later to the lidocaine and headed toward Winston's office.

Katie, realizing that she and Johnny were the only two who had no specific task assigned to them, spoke up, "We not just gonna sit here like bumps on a log are we?"

"That's exactly what you are going to do for now," replied Herc and he left room to supervise the photography and the transmission of the evidence to the gangster. "Corina, see if you can get your friend on the horn."

Corina stood up and started moving toward the door and said to Katie, "Well, in that case I'm gonna find that beer I've been craving. You want anything?"

Katie shook her head, and Corina left the room. Katie rose from her chair wondering when she and her daughter had switched roles. She was now the one being cared for by the group, as opposed to her usual role as minder of the schedule, the pronouncer of duties, and giver and enforcer of the orders. She went to the large mirror hanging on the opposite wall and was slightly shocked at her reflection. She still wore Willis' tattered gym clothes and the Braves ball cap turned backwards.

Katie took off the cap and her auburn hair tumbled out. As she tried to untangle the unruly strands by running her fingers through them she began to choke up as she spoke to Johnny, "I guess you know that you were right about the danger we faced tonight, and Corina and I only made it worse, just like you said, and we almost got everybody killed. Hell, I should just admit it. You are always right, and it seems like every time I look up you are doing something smart to counteract something stupid I've done, and it's been going on like this for decades. Do you think I will ever learn?"

She paused in this stream of confession and self-deprecation to allow a response from Johnny, but as none seemed to be forthcoming, she said, "You know you can cut me off any time you want. How about a good old, "It will be alright, Sweetie?"

She turned to face him, but still there came no response. He had curled up on the couch facing away from her, and as she approached him a small snort escaped, which at first Katie interpreted as him making mock, but as she reached his side, she realized he was sound asleep and caught up in a dream, or was it a nightmare? She smiled down at him, and tried to cover him with a cashmere throw that lay on the back of the couch, but he suddenly jerked upright as he came awake, wide-eyed and frantic. Katie gently pushed him back down, and with soothing tones said, "Hush. It will be alright sweetie."

Johnny almost immediately relaxed and turned on his side muttering, "You are the very best." He was quickly asleep again.

Katie nudged him over a bit on the couch and made a space for herself next to him, and she covered them both as best she could with the small blanket. She thought back through the years past to times of nightly bedtime stories, and she luxuriated as if in a warm bath of the tender memories of lullabies softly sung, and of quotations and rhymes by Carroll and Seuss. After just a few contented moments of pleasant reflection, she too was soon out of sight, up the river of crystal light, and over a sea of dew, to a rendezvous long overdue, in the land of winkin', and blinkin', and nod.

Claudine Longet – Here, There, and Everywhere:
https://www.youtube.com/watch?v=Taj8TLbU6Zk

After Corina made good on her threat to find a cold beer she leaned against the dark granite counter-top, took a sip, and re-activated her cell phone. She pressed a favorites key, and after several rings, a sleepy voice answered, "Corina, is that you? I went by Katie's house last night, but there was nobody home. Are you two alright?"

The sleepy voice belonged to Lacy Walden, the soon-to-be divorced friend and skip tracer. After a couple of weeks of hiding out with Katie and Corina, she had returned to her home to find her husband Dave had vacated the premises. He had taken up residence on his fifty-five-foot sport fishing vessel, which was moored in the North Palm Beach Marina about five miles away, leaving Lacy to deal with the house, and the crime-scene looking bedroom. She still carried a few regrets over the way she had dealt with his infidelity, but they were mostly comprised of her wish that she had kicked in the locked bathroom door and snatched the badly dyed blonde hair from the head of the interloper.

Corina replied, "Yeah, it's been a hell of a night, and we are fine, but I need to ask you a favor. We need your help. You know Willis, right?"

Lacy said, "We've never been introduced, but I know what he looks like."

"Good, he is on his way to your house, so put on some clothes and some coffee. He will explain his plan, and, girl, it's a doozie!"

After disconnecting from Corina, Lacy busied herself with dressing, starting a pot of coffee, and tidying her kitchen and home office, and within twenty minutes the front door chimes announced Willis' arrival. He accepted a cup of black coffee, even though it was probably only the third cup of his life; he did not need any chemical stimulus to stay awake, but there were concessions to the etiquettes of a pre-dawn visit to the friend of a friend which must be observed.

After a few minutes of pleasantries, Willis came around to laying out his plan and the short list of very specific favors he was standing in her in kitchen to request.

As he explained the predicament he and her friends had stumbled into, Lacy's attention was rapt, but as entertaining and intricate as the past week's travails were, she could not find a role in this adventure for which, as Corina had intimated, she was uniquely qualified. The more she listened, the more her blood got up, and the more she heard of the danger Katie and Corina had already faced, the more eager she became to go to war. She thought perhaps her skills with the heavy bag might be her ticket in, but with legitimately tough guys like the Dendy Brothers on the team, this need seemed like a long shot.

Even though Willis had only been speaking for a few minutes, when he paused to let the story sink in, Lacy leaped into the silence, "Wow! That's quite a tale. What can I do to help?"

Willis replied, "Corina told me about your job and your art."

"My job?" Lacy replied, "I track down bail jumpers, and how can my doodling be of any help?"

Hercules walked from the conference room into Winston's large office as Anna-Sophia watched Winston, somewhat reverently, extract from a large and cleverly concealed safe, a pouch made of a heavy crimson colored brocade with hand-tooled brown leather. The intricate tooling seemed of Irish runes, but there were also mystical hieroglyphs which hinted at an Egyptian origin. He loosened the draw string and from the pouch's opening he withdrew a smaller, simpler, green velvet bag, and from this sack he withdrew a large, no make that an immense, emerald.

Sofi set her large Channel bag on the floor to make room on the desk, she then adjusted the desk lamp to better light the giant stone, and, with Herc, she leaned in for a closer look. Winston also stared at the gem for a moment before he said, "Mesmerizing, isn't it?"

After the three of them had, for an indefinable period, gazed respectfully, and perhaps even worshipfully, at this wondrous object, which for untold centuries had been at the root of so much bloodshed, Herc thought about the struggle he and his friends had endured in just the past few days and remarked, "I suppose every time this rock surfaces, people start dying, and it has always been that way."

Anna-Sophia added, "There were several murders associated with it when it came into my father's possession, and, although he did not often speak of the violence connected to holding on to this treasure, I am certain many more lost everything."

Then Herc pulled back from the séance-like scene and asked for Winston, "What about the bearer bonds? Do you have that kind of dough?"

Winston, with some apparent reluctance, finally turned away from the emerald and went to the open stainless-steel door of his safe. He pulled from a low shelf a sheaf of elaborately engraved papers. As he counted out the bonds and said over his shoulder, "I'm about a $160,000 short, but I don't think it will be obvious in a photograph if we set it up right."

While Anna-Sophia helped reorganize the desktop to make a clear surface for the photograph L'il Augie had demanded, she asked, "Which, of all the phones, should we use to take the picture?"

Winston replied, "It has to be mine I guess. It's on the conference room table, labeled Winston."

Herc volunteered to fetch it and, as he left the room, he stopped and watched the tantalizing Ms. Escudo through the gap created by the hinges of the half-open door. She glanced over her shoulder to confirm that Herc had left the room, and then she stooped to her purse and quickly exchanged The Green Flash for one of Gaspipe Glenn's replicas. He had been wondering when and how she was planning to capture the prize, but he had been forced to wait her out. Now he could make his own move.

Herc returned to the office with Winston's smart phone and made a few suggestions pertaining to composition, depth of field, and lighting. Winston watched while Anna-Sophia made the adjustments to make it all fit within the camera's frame. Under all she placed the front page of the freshly printed newspaper. Next came the stack of bonds, partially fanned out, to give the impression there could be two hundred, instead of just one hundred and eighty-four. Finally, she laid the emerald upon the brocade pouch in the center of the composition and pronounced it ready. "Alright Mr. Montgomery, would you do the honors?"

As soon as the photo had been taken and the three of them agreed it would serve the purpose, Winston sent it to L'il Augie Amato's phone. He then double bagged the stone and returned it and the bonds to his safe. Sofi turned, picked up her bag, and left the two men in Winston's office.

When they were alone, Winston said to Herc, "Mr. Dendy, when this is over, I suspect the authorities will become involved, and, as I see it, I am really the only one they might want to question. If I am gone they will be left talking to themselves. So, I have made plans to disappear for a while. Mr. Baptiste will know how to contact me, but if you are willing, I would like to leave a few small packages in your care, for you to distribute when you judge it to be safe."

He again visited his safe, returned with several packages wrapped in brown paper, and continued, "I would encourage the recipients to treat these gifts as confidential, and even secret, but the items are completely clean and legal, with the proper paperwork and provenance."

Herc accepted the packages and placed them on the corner of the desk he had just finished realigning, and asked, "Why me? Why not your wife or Fiona?"

Winston replied. "As long as I have known you, you have acted with intelligence and honor toward me and my family, and without any trace of self-interest. I feel you are an honest man. I guess I would like to avoid the scene with Katie, and if I had to explain it all to my daughter, I don't think I could go."

Herc replied, "It seems to me, you have been dragging this big secret around for so long that your better qualities have become secret too. I'll play Santa if you want, but don't stay away too long. Every girl needs her father."

During the short ride from Winston's back to the Yacht Club where the Apocalypso was moored, JPB and Willis occupied the front bench seat, and spoke in hushed tones and clipped sentences. Manolo and Fiona hunkered close together in the open bed in the rear of the El Camino and talked and laughed about their adventure. Fiona remembered something Manny had said about his piece of the adventure before he boarded the small jet and headed south and asked, "Do you know what was in the package you retrieved from that apartment in Newark?"

"No, I don't." replied the boy, "It was wrapped in several layers of heavy brown paper, but it was small." He gestured to her to approximate the dimensions of the package, "about the size and weight of a couple bars of soap."

"I wonder why it was so important."

Then the subject was dropped, and they quickly cast off the mooring lines and moved out across the expanse of Lake Worth.

When they reached the PB Towers pier, Jean the Baptiste finished securing the bow lines of the Apocalypso, while Fiona pointed out the obstacles against, and opportunities for, concealment surrounding The Palm Beach Towers to Manolo.

The teenagers opened the large case containing the drone and its accoutrements and within just three minutes had attached two small cameras, and two listening devices. The boy was keen to explain the nuances of the gear to the girl who hung on his every word, and JPB might have found their blossoming of young love more charming, were it not for their disregard of their proximity to that bad man, and at last he said as much, "Children, dis toy might help us defeat old fatso up dere, but you got to stay invisible."

He alternated between his obvious affection for Fiona, and his mistrust of her beau, and he chose his final words for their impact. "I gotta go check on my prisoner. Be careful! Girl, don't let dis moon and dis boy get you dead."

He slipped soundlessly off the boat, and, with a final withering glare directed at Manny, he stole out of sight, and Manny quipped, "Even if we crash dis toy, we can always just outrun old fatso up dere."

Fiona replied without a trace of humor, "Maybe, but we can't outrun a bullet. Let's stick to the shadows and stick to the plan. Are we ready to have a look in the lion's den?"

"I have to make a few adjustments. It won't take very long."

Fiona, eager to involve herself in Manolo's business, leaned in and asked questions, and Manny was perfectly content to explain each step, "This cartridge contains local GPS coordinates for navigation in this area."

He next adjusted the camber of the propellers on each of the four small electric motors which would allow him to fly and maneuver the camera platform. The last thing Manny pulled from his case was a small case containing three small printed circuit chips and explained, "These are beacons which will allow me to find this bird if it gets out of range of the controller."

"How does that work?"

The boy proudly explained, "I invented these myself. You see this little capacitor here? When I turn it on with this little switch I can track it from my phone with an app I've developed." He demonstrated the signal reception on his phone. Fiona was, to say the least, impressed.

She nodded, and he continued, "This stores enough energy to power an intermittent pulse in a specific bandwidth for up to 48 hours. It gives me a couple of days to retrieve the drone if it should get tangled in something. I made up a half-dozen of them, so I can change them out."

"What is the range?" asked Fiona.

"It depends upon obstructions like buildings and mountains, but in a flat landscape like Florida, it might be a much as fifteen or twenty miles. It is also Geo-tagged to the controller app I just installed on your phone and it will sync up with Goggle maps when I turn on this micro-switch and hit the app's refresh key. I can differentiate the different chips by the colors of the Light Emitting Diode. Green is on the bird now and these have a red and a blue signal."

He put two spare homing chips in the pocket of his jeans and started off down the pier. Before disappearing into the shade, he established a three-way conference over Free Conference.com with the drone and Fiona, Herc and Winston. Well, for that matter, anyone with the dial-in number and the correct password could connect and hear whatever the sensitive microphones of the drone could detect. Fiona would be able to describe whatever action the two cameras saw, and all of it was being recorded for future playback, plus anyone in the conference could toss in his or her two cents regarding what these sights and sounds might mean, and how best to respond.

After testing the connection, Manny gave his own warning to Fiona over the conference line, "It is very easy to pay such close attention to the stuff coming in over the phone that you are not aware of the stuff going on near you, so get out of sight and keep your voice down. A place as nice as this is bound to have a roving patrol or two. If you see one, just give me a warning over the conference line. I'll be on mute, but I'll be able to hear you."

He then flicked his miniature Maglite on and off and spoke into his Blue Tooth headset, "I'll use the light as a signal, one when I land, and two when I see."

Fiona brightened and replied into her I-phone, "Excellent, an updated version of the signal from the Old North Church."

"Come back. Please say again." Was Manny's apparently confused reply.

"The signal used by Paul Revere and his buddies, "One if by land and two if by sea.""

Manny replied, "How do you mean?"

Fiona replied, "Don't you think it's ironic that we are spying and you used that phrase which was so close to the one from the Longfellow poem? All that's missing is The British are coming."

"Are you certain that is irony? I think it may be coincidence, but I'm not sure. I have trouble with the difference."

About then Herc's voice broke into the conversation and said, "The irony here is that you two are supposed to be careful and quiet, and the coincidence: you both might be idiots. Get back on the job!"

Manny identified the target balcony and said, "Sorry. We are ready to get airborne."

Herc said, "Alright, are any of the doors and windows open?"

Manny replied, "It appeared from the boat that the sliding doors from the living room to the balcony are wide open. I can tell you more when the RPA gets up to that level."

Fiona, determined to enjoy this adventure, piped up, "Remind me again what RPA stands for – Is it anything like PTA or ADD?"

Manolo could not suppress a gasp and then a chuckle. Herc replied over the conference line, "It is becoming obvious that you were not spanked enough as a child, which you still are, and I can still remedy."

Fiona was about to make a smart-aleck comeback when, through her binoculars, she saw L'il Augie walk out onto the balcony. He seemed to be pacing aimlessly while he held his cell phone to his ear. It was apparent that the conversation held all his attention. She whispered into the con-call, "The Fat Tomato is on the balcony. No wait he is going back inside."

Herc reminded Manny to come in from the east and come in slowly. Manny did as they had planned, and, on the first pass, he was able to get a pretty good view of the apartment layout. He was able to see L'il Augie who had just seated himself at a large desk and was lighting a cigar.

On the next pass, he had the craft hover above the balcony while he searched for the optimum vantage point. Herc who was watching the video in Winston's office on the other side of the intercostal waterway asked, "Can we get any sound?"

"Not from the drone while it's in flight, but I can land and detach a bug. It's a very sensitive mic I can hang from the roof outside the open door."

"Do it, but be very careful."

A few anxious moments elapsed as Manny maneuvered the drone to within inches of the roof. He was able to skillfully suspend the bug from the copper rain gutter attached to the roof just above the balcony. The almost invisible mic had the appearance of a thin wire about two feet long. Manny pulled back about twenty feet and focused one of the cameras upon the listening device.

Herc spoke, "Good spot, but I don't hear anything."

Fiona, still joking around, tapped her phone with her finger and said, "Is this thing on?"

Manny replied, "Get ready, I'm going to switch it on."

The squeal that came across the line was shrill and piercing, but within a few seconds Manny had adjusted the gain and volume controls to eliminate the feedback. "Don't worry, he can't hear that."

Fiona replied, "Are you sure? He is up and moving toward the balcony. Get out of there."

Manny repositioned the drone out of sight above the condominium's roof. Right then the bug began transmitting the gangster's agitated voice. "If I have to do all the information gathering myself, what the hell am I paying you for Caldwell?"

There were a few seconds of static before L'il Augie replied crossly to whatever was said to him over the cell phone, "Excuse me Lieutenant that is bullshit! Bigalow has been dead for almost two years. Find out who owns that El Camino, or I'm gonna get me another inside man."

After a few more seconds L'il Augie summarized, "Listen up shithead, I want results not excuses, not promises." And then he ended the call.

Herc said, "Keep monitoring this goon. I need to make another call."

All traces of the previous tomfoolery vanished from Fiona's voice as she said, "Herc, doesn't that sound like he has a cop on his payroll?"

Herc replied, "Probably more than one, so stay alert. I'll leave the line open and check in again in a few minutes."

Herc picked up the handset of Winston's office land line and dialed Willis's number. When Willis answered, he abruptly came to the point of the call, "Tell our friend we have one more guy to add to the poster, plus we need her to see what she can turn up on a Lieutenant Caldwell. We think he is with the Palm Beach Police, and on the take."

Willis conveyed the request to Lacy, who said she knew a little bit about the good lieutenant already, but she felt she could have a pretty complete profile in just a few minutes. Herc elected to wait on the line and catch Willis up on the new developments. Willis took the opportunity to share Lacy's plan, which got both men laughing. "I think twenty-five or thirty copies ought to do the trick. We need to get them up in conspicuous spots within the next few hours, definitely before the sun comes up."

Then Willis switched the phone over to speaker mode so that Lacy could tell them both what she had turned up. "It appears that Palm Beach Police Lieutenant James Caldwell hails from Hoboken, New Jersey and moved to Florida just ahead of a major hosing of that department. Allegations of impropriety circulated but nothing stuck. It looks like he is living well beyond the means of a small-town policeman with a condo on the beach worth at least a million bucks. He also advises hotels like The Breakers and the Ritz on security – he's connected all over the place."

"That could explain how the hoods know the where and the when of our girls last night," Willis added while Lacy nodded enthusiastically.

Herc thought for a few seconds and then said, "You know that old saying about how into each life a little rain must fall? I think it's time we sent a monsoon his way. Please give him a prominent place in our rouge's gallery."

Inside the coral cage things had gotten extremely uncomfortable for the Mic. Tiny biting midges, also known as no-see-ums, are virtually invisible, but the females of the species are particularly voracious blood suckers, and their bites had left dozens of swollen welts on his ankles, neck, hands and face, which caused him to writhe and scratch. The Mic was also sweating like a trail horse in Johnathan Dickenson State Park on a three-hour tour, which was the dinner bell for the Gallinipper Mosquito, one of the largest blood-thirsty insects in the Subtropics, they were drawn, en masse, to the warm mist of carbon dioxide he exhaled.

The Mic's insect problems alone were enough to stoke his fear furnace, but now bump it an order or two of magnitude with the addition of his claustrophobic confinement. The acid-enhanced introversion was good for at least several hundred-sporadic horsepower, and his guilt-driven super-stitions had a VIP backstage pass. All these constituents were leaning on the exit doors, and the pressure gages were reading well into the red even before JPB reached the coral cave within the Witch's Wall. He heard the unhappy, but rhythmic, wail which leaked from The Mic like a low wattage storm warning siren on its last leg, and he punctuated his misery by softly striking his muddled head against the steel of the gate like a bass drum. Using his cell phone JPB sent the coded message "Neptune" via a group text to half a dozen other phones within a five-mile radius.

Jean Pierre Baptiste quietly removed the padlock from the gate, snatched the black burlap sack from it, and allowed the gate to fall tempt-ingly ajar. The Mic lunged toward freedom, and, as he tumbled to the asphalt surface of the road, he was stupefied at this sudden change in his circumstances and at first sought concealment. He felt he had to choose to fight, or he had to choose to flee, but which?

JPB supplied a little impetus by growling a cautionary note of advice from the shadows, "Mon, you git de chance you better make a run for it."

The discordant chorus of indecision inside The Mic's noggin evaporated at this common-sense advice, and the decision to flee was reached on the first ballot. As he took his initial faltering steps away from his prison, he realized that a large leather briefcase was chained to his wrist. An eighteen-hundred-pound grand piano could have been at the other end of that chain, and The Mic would have adopted the same tactics. The case went where The Mic went, and The Mic went toward the lights in the distance. He had persuaded himself that nothing good could come from staying here. He knew he had to get out of the dark. Wearing just one shoe, and propelled by fear, confusion, and pain, he scurried away, and he celebrated every yard of separation from his cage with his newly acquired mantra, "Old Mic's a 'gonna change his evil ways! Yessir! Old Mic's gotta find dat brand new day."

Corina was among the recipients of the Neptune text, and this code word signaled her next task, which was to make call to the Palm Beach Fire Department. When the fireman on duty answered, she said concisely, "Hey, you've got an old drunk wandering in traffic near the Witch's Castle. Somebody is gonna run him down."

She declined to provide her name, saying she was just informing the authorities of a dangerous situation, and then she hung up. The fireman informed the lieutenant on duty, who notified the police desk sergeant, and both agencies rolled a response vehicle.

When driving the deserted streets of pre-dawn Palm Beach, anyone can make pretty good time, but with the Palm Beach Police leading the emergency units, using lights and sirens, they covered the mile and a half distance in just over two minutes. And they found, just as reported, a deranged citizen staggering down the middle of Country Club Lane. He clutched a bottle of water, an old briefcase and babbled nonsense. He had several nasty contusions, scores of what appeared to be fresh and angry insect bites, and appeared to have no other destination than the light of a street lamp. In fact, when one of the paramedics tried to lead him out of the middle of an intersection, which coincidentally, was also into the dark-ness, he went a little berserk. Trained to de-escalate a tense situation, the paramedic backed away, and in soothing tones he tried to calm the man down a little, "Just take it easy, we are here to help you. Would you like a drink of water?"

The Mic thought this to be a good idea, and said so, "Yeah."

But before the medic could hand him a fresh bottle of water, The Mic, uncapped the half-full bottle he carried and took a long pull of its clear liquid. He calmed down somewhat until the policeman took the bottle from him. While The Mic wailed, the cop examined the bottle's contents and finding it to be just water, and at the urging of the paramedics, returned it to distressed man wearing just one shoe.

The examination of this confused and paperless vagrant, which took place in the well-lighted rear of the ambulance, went along okay until the officers tried to examine The Mic's briefcase. With a fresh surge of Window Pane stoking his anxiety, The Mic threw off the young officers with ease and began to make good his escape. The two young patrolmen looked briefly at each other, and then both reached for their gun belts, but rather than un-holster their Smith and Wesson M&P9s, they both withdrew X26P Tasers. When the first jolt turned The Mic, but did not drop him, the second patrolman hit him with another charge, and down he went. The Mic writhed and twitched on the ground for a few minutes but still maintained a death grip on his satchel, and it was at this point that a consensus was reached. This psycho had earned a free ride, with police escort, across the bridge to the Palm Beach County mental health facility at 45th Street and Congress Avenue.

JPB had been standing in the shadows of the fences surrounding the Palm Beach Tennis Club, at the corner of Country Club Lane and South County Road, which was about two blocks away from the Witch's Castle, and the cage The Mic had just escaped. Actually, The Mic had been released and, surprisingly, according to their quickly evolving plan, had done precisely as expected. He had witnessed The Mic's short-lived dash for freedom and the subsequent tasering, and when he overheard the discussion and decision to transport the babbling vagrant to 45th Street, he called Willis.

"What's happening on the enchanted isle?"

Jean Pierre replied, "I can hardly believe how well you predicted what these cops would do. Just like you say, they be taking The Mic to the crazy house in West Palm."

Willis replied, "Standard governmental agency psychology – if you get the chance to pass the buck, go ahead and pass the buck."

Willis added, "Well, I better alert Sis they are on their way. Stay safe."

After disconnecting from JPB, Willis called his younger sister, who happened to oversee the emergency department of the mental health facility where The Mic was headed. She also had considerable influence as to who got a handful of aspirin before being sent home and those who did not pass go and spent the next three days on the fourth floor, in lockdown.

Over the years, Willis had found real comfort in his baby sister. Between sports injuries and accidents in his shop, Maggie was usually the first person he contacted when he needed stitches, antibiotics, or pain killers. In fact, as a Christmas gift a few years back, she had assembled a large first aid kit for his home, and each time he dripped a fresh coating of blood to the lid, as he scrambled for a bandage, he thought affectionately of her. He also enjoyed just dropping in for an unannounced pre-dawn visit, which for him, was always therapeutic. She, like he, was an insomniac, and had reasoned it out some time back - If she was going to be awake anyway, she might as well be at work. Willis also knew that she dealt, every day, with real people who had real troubles, troubles which made his minor downturns in fortune shrink in comparison. After a thirty-minute visit he always left her company reminded and aware of the insignificant measure of his bush league problems.

Maggie answered after a few rings, "Merry Christmas. Are you up late, or are you up early?"

"A bit of both." Was his chuckling reply.

"Where are you bleeding? Oh, never mind, come on in. It's finally calming down over here. Did you notice that moon tonight? They're calling it a Blood Moon, which is pretty rare I guess." Maggie prattled on without allowing a gap for Willis to answer her questions. "Anyway, it has lived up to its billing – Bloody whack jobs have really been out tonight. Come on in – use the back door."

The back door was perhaps the best card he had up his sleeve, because it meant three things which are important to any patient of any emergency room. Maggie would meet him at the back door, appraise the situation, and lead him to the appropriate station for treatment. She would make spare introductions to her staff and get him the care he needed with just a couple of sentences, "This is my brother Willis. Please sew him up, give him drugs. I'll handle the paperwork." No fuss, no muss, no charge!

Willis put on the brakes, "It's not me this time. How're you fixed over there for truth serum? There's a whack-job headed your way from Palm Beach. He is a dangerous guy by himself, but he is working for a real slime ball who is threatening a couple of my friends."

"Oh great! What do you want me to do with him?"

"I want you to Baker Act his ass and call the Sheriff's Department."

"Is he a danger to himself or others?" Maggie replied as if reading from an admission form.

"To himself maybe, but to others - For sure. We've softened him up with a little acid and Ambien, now you give a bump of Scopolamine, and he'll sing like George Beverly Shea," referencing the powerful baritone soloist from the Billy Graham crusades they had both attended as children in the company of their parents.

"There's a briefcase chained to his arm with his ID, and enough evidence to send everybody up the river. Just get the cops to bring a tape recorder and some bolt cutters – believe me, it will be worth the price of admission."

"How do you know about Scopolamine?"

Willis said, "I read. I listen, I hear things. What do you want from me? I just know stuff."

During rare family councils, his counsels were sought. Should anyone ask why, the halting manner which bespoke, at least to the Familia, the siblings' credo, "Willis knew a little about a lot, but he also knew a whole lot about a little."

A betting man knew when Willis took a position in opposition to the majority, here was a sure thing. He did not often crawl out onto a narrow branch but, to those observant few of past predictions made in the twilight, knew an average of seven to one was the payoff. Willis could see directly to the crux of the game. The clincher was his demure follow-on, "Anyway, that's a way it could fall out."

Maggie, a believer, had skipped the stages of denial, which would require careful observation of his predictions, and bowed her neck. He had now strayed into her arena of expertise. "Just what do you know?"

Willis, who did indeed know stuff, told her, "Well it's a very effective general pain management drug, but it also knocks down contrived denial. As I understand it, if you ask the right questions of someone under its influence the answers tend to be truthful."

Maggie shook her head in disbelief and replied, "In general we only use that drug on women who are having particularly hard labor."

Willis said, "And another plus, I hear it sorta clouds the previous four or five hours in their memory. The real kicker is that he answers questions about where he's been tonight, and, come morning, he doesn't remember where he was or what he said. Perfect. Hell Sis, if it makes a mother forget she's given birth, sounds like an inside-the-park homerun to me."

"I don't think you would be able to use anything he says in court, but if that brief case is with him when he gets to us, we will open it and bag whatever is in it for security reasons – the cops can go through it, no problem."

"I'm not too worried about any of the stuff he reveals holding up in court, I'm just trying to see the sun come up." Willis paused for a quick snort of laughter, "It's gonna get interesting in the second act. Let me buy you breakfast, I'll tell you the whole dealio."

Maggie replied, "I get off at 8:30. Let me get home and wash up some. I can be ready by 9:30."

"Take your time, but we should be in line at 11:00 when it opens."

Maggie's eyelids opened wider as she swung her head around violently and gazed at the wall calendar, and correctly decoded his invitation. "The Breakers Christmas Brunch! Willis don't toy with me."

Brunch in Palm Beach is an art form, and during the season there were at least a dozen high end options available. There are trendy alternatives such as The Buccan and The Pistache French Bistro, as well as old standby's like Testa's, but as in most things Palm Beachy, The Breakers did it bigger, did it grander, and did it right. Served in the lavishly ornate Circle restaurant, which is a large circular room in the fashion of a solarium, with massive windows, and frescoed ceilings at least thirty feet tall, The Breakers Sunday Brunch defined opulence and welcomed both gourmet and gourmand alike. Officially there were two seatings, but it was not unheard of for a group to disregard an impatient Maître D and unhurriedly graze though both. And while the hotel was far too dignified to display such an epithet, the phrase commonly used in the kitchen to spur the cooks and servers on was, "If it's worth doing, it's worth over-doing. Let's give 'em a show!"

Willis also knew a thing or two about his sister, "I've got the tickets, if you've got the time."

The long night of dealing with just about every form of excessive behavior had not raised his sister's blood pressure even a tic, but the anticipation of The Breakers Christmas Brunch, Willis could tell, had Maggie excited.

"Alright. One dose of Scopolamine coming right up." Maggie said, "What's this defective's name?"

"Michael Fitzpatrick," Willis replied and then added, "The key to his brief case is in his shoe."

About then Maggie got the radio call from the Palm Beach Paramedics that they were in transit with a psychotic white male, approximately fifty years of age, with various superficial injuries, and in an agitated state.

Maggie returned to her conversation with Willis, "He should be here in a minute or two. Let me get ahold of the sheriff's office. Oh, and which shoe?"

"The only one he's wearing."

After a loud, but otherwise uneventful six-mile dash, and a cursory evaluation, The Baker Act was literally just what the doctor ordered. This 1971 Florida legislation allowed an unstable person to be committed, constrained, sedated, and held for his own welfare, in a certified psychiatric facility for seventy-two hours by an authorized medical doctor - check, check, check and check.

As the Palm Beach paramedics completed the paperwork for the transfer, The Mic begged for forgiveness, and when the supervising nurse asked if he would like to speak with a priest, his eyes went wide and he said, "Oh yes sister, you are an angel! I must confess."

While Maggie was surely an angel of mercy, and a sister, the confessor she summoned was not a priest, but plain-clothes sergeant Denny Parks, a detective with the Palm Beach County Sherriff's Organized Crime Division. Then tapping on the side of a syringe to clear it of air bubbles, she administered 2.5 cubic centimeters in an intravenous injection of truth serum, and said, "Merry Christmas Michael."

According to more than one scholarly text, dawn was scheduled for 7:29 AM EST, and predictably, dawn was on-time. It was just before dawn when telephones began to ring all around the island, and just about everyone who lifted the receiver did so less than enthusiastically, but just about everyone who got the call, warmed to the overture's opening note: Scandal.

Was this an arcane reference to the 80's punk rock band fronted by Patti Smyth? No, but this tune would surely climb the local charts as quickly as any of their white-hot hits, and it was surely destined to become a one-hit wonder. However, the sentiments of their seminal song "Goodbye to you" would be a clever choice as background for this calamity.

 Scandal, Patty Smyth – Goodbye to you:
https://www.youtube.com/watch?v=_50-gOeBilc

L'il Augie, who, up to this point, had enjoyed a semi-secret inclusion within the decaying framework of old robber baron heirs and their skittish, but cash rich in-laws, was among the second wave of interested parties to receive the alarm.

In the history of the Palm Beach 400, the semi-formal ranking of the island's society, no one has, or would ever be subjected to such a sudden and complete drop in local popularity since late October in 1929. When in just a few days' time, about one third of that illustrious group had fallen from financial and social favor, but to those poor (literally) souls at least came the comfort of company in their shame. L'il Augie would be singled out for ridicule and dismissal. To be shunned is a terrible thing!

You see, despite a resume` of shady dealings and lurid deeds, he was an accomplished Bridge player, world class in fact, and there is nothing a sedentary fat cat enjoys more than winning money from his peers, and bringing a ringer to the tournament can really shorten the odds. In recent years, dozens of this self-promoting uber-class had willingly provided personal introductions, or, when not practical, had freely given a written pedigree, a letter of introduction. These hand-written documents came in a variety of forms and sizes ranging from an email, to a note on the back of a business card, to several paragraphs on a sheet of executive size, watermarked bond stationery, which usually were addressed in the following form:

To whom it may concern,

This letter will serve as introduction to my good friend, and exceptionally fine fellow, Augustine Amato Jr. The quality of his character is unassailable, his holdings are considerable and secure, and he also plays a damn fine hand of Contract Bridge, having captained several successful campaigns in pursuit of the illustrious Bermuda Bowl.

Please make him feel welcome, and extend to him every courtesy during his visit to our Island paradise.

Cordially,
The Duchess of La-de-da or some such…

All these carefully scribed eruditions, which had the convenience of an electronic format, would be quickly and quietly recalled and deleted, but those in the more durable cursive form still lost their value as an entrée to the halls of power and culture, and this ripple on the social pond, from L'il Augie's perspective, had the appearance of a tsunami.

The bearer of this bad news, having witnessed Amato's propensity toward rage when receiving bad news, had the good sense, and survival skills, to make this notification via telephone. This practical under-world practitioner was one James Caldwell, Lieutenant, Palm Beach Police

Department, and well-paid lackey, inside informer, and secret security chief of Augustine Amato, Jr. Just thirty minutes before his call to L'il Augie, his peaceful slumber had been interrupted by a call from his night-shift desk sergeant. The call began, "Sorry to call so early Lieutenant, but some strange posters have been posted all over the island. I think you ought to take a look. I'm having one delivered to your apartment by a black and white. It should be there any minute."

Caldwell, still raking the cobwebs of deep sleep from his brain, replied, "Why don't we just get them all taken down if they are so offensive?"

The desk sergeant replied nervously, "I believe that ship has sailed sir. The switchboard could be confused as the Christmas Tree over here."

"What's it about man?" But just then his doorbell rang, and he said, "Oh, there he is now. Let me get a look at this thing, and I'll call you back."

He put down the telephone receiver and padded barefoot toward the front door, stopping just long enough at the foyer mirror to make certain his hairpiece was in place and looking natural. When he opened the door he found, standing at attention and holding a 17' x 11" piece of parchment cardstock, a patrolman who could not be a day older than the required twenty-one years, who said, "Sorry to call so early Lieutenant (hadn't he just heard that exact phrase twenty seconds ago?) Sergeant Gray thought you would want to see this straight away. Should I wait for a reply?"

He took the poster from the young officer and said, "Not necessary patrolman. I'll call if I need you," and as he noticed the reds and purples of dawn he added, "You have a nice day."

Patting the pockets of his silk robe for his glasses, he retrieved them and made his way to the kitchen and casually flipped the poster onto the table. He turned to the coffee machine and made himself a cup. As the mug filled, he thought, "Everything is always such a panic to these guys. Whatever this is will probably blow over before noon."

With his glasses resting on the bridge of his nose, and a steaming cup-o-joe in hand, the lieutenant switched on the chandelier over the table and sat down to see what this fuss was all about.

The poster in front of him had the appearance of an artifact from a previous century. Its sepia colored 72-point headline almost screamed:

WANTED

Below this sensational line there appeared an accurate pen and ink drawing of L'il Augie, and his name;

Augustine "L'IL Augie" Amato, Jr.

The artist had captured not only his likeness, but also the malevolence of his glare, and as Caldwell read further, he knew the almost compulsory valediction of, "You have a nice day" he had offered the young patrolman might never again apply to him.

Directly below L'il Augie's image were several other menacing lines of large block printing;

On suspicion of Murder, Armed Robbery, Extortion, Kidnapping and International Drug Trafficking!!!

Below these lines was the command;

If you know the whereabouts of this man or any of his known associates please call The Palm Beach Police or the FBI!

Just below these lines were four smaller likenesses, also well-rendered in pen and ink, with the names and physical characteristics of each neatly lettered below. From left to right were the images of Diego Lazette, Rocco Venducci, Michael "The Mic" Fitzpatrick, and the caricature at the far right of the page made Caldwell's already spinning head try for hyper-spin. The final rendering was of himself in uniform, and right there for all the world to see, or at least all the world that mattered to him, was the name:

Palm Beach Police Lieutenant James Caldwell.

After a short, but threatening telephone conversation with L'il Augie, Lieutenant Caldwell sat, considering his predicament, at the table in the breakfast nook. Amato had volunteered to have a couple of mouth-breathers stop over and break his legs if he could not squelch this slanderous personal attack, but as far as Caldwell could tell, the wanted poster, while not official in any way, had the basics of the story right.

His situation was pretty much untenable. He could try to discount the poster as a prank, and pure rubbish, and discredit the accusations as a cruel form of public shaming, but he knew those tactics were at best a delaying action. Palm Beach loved a scandal and the story would be at first pursued in society columns on page six, but the chances were good that real journalists would start shinning their investigative lights on him, and, within a few days or weeks he would appear on the front page above the fold. He knew his veneer of respectability was rice-paper thin, and unable to withstand close scrutiny. He also reasoned these wanted posters probably would not be the only shots fired across the bow. You don't tweak the nose of a psychopath in this fashion and expect no consequences. No, he knew there was more to come, and he also knew his window of escape was probably closing quickly.

The best he could hope for from this was the loss of his job and having to face up to several felony charges, but it could be much worse. In all probability he would be ruined, his rat-holed finances would be squandered on the small chance of uncovering a legal loophole or two by the best criminal lawyers his money could buy, but he would eventually lose everything and then go to live an unfulfilling life within the state prison in Raiford, Florida. Caldwell knew that, in general, cops don't fare well in prison, especially if L'il Augie's boys were working in the laundry every day right beside, or behind, him.

On the other hand, the Bahamas were only 45 miles away, and, from there, he could choose any number of countries in the Caribbean or South America to set up shop as an expat. Maybe Rio de Janeiro, Brazil had no extradition treaty with the states, and, as he understood it, there were beaches there where the women wore no tops. He felt certain he could engage a surrogate to represent him in an off-shore fire sale to liquidate his state-side holdings within a few days for cash, and thereby enjoy his golden years free of prison bars and broken legs. It would definitely be door number two for him.

Caldwell was packed in fifteen minutes, all the while ignoring the almost constant ring tones coming from his cell phone. His suit case contained a shaving kit and several changes of clothing, but the real heft of the bag was made up of ledgers, bank records, and cash. The last call he made before he sailed the I-phone off his balcony and into the Atlantic Ocean was to his office, saying he would be investigating these posters, and would probably not be in until after lunch, and to place a squad car conspicuously near the front entrance to the Palm Beach Towers. Please contact him via police radio, using the code phrase "the south bridge is up," if Augustine Amato Jr. went out. He then headed across the north bridge and on to the Jupiter Regional Airport. While en route, Caldwell arranged over a disposable phone to charter a small plane.

There were definite advantages to having contacts in the shadier corridors of power, and several years earlier James Caldwell, anticipating the need for a disaster recovery strategy under such a cloud as was now looming, had developed several contingency plans. He wanted nothing to do with any high-speed police pursuits, or shootouts with his back to the wall. No sir, he simply removed his toupee, donned a jaunty straw hat and tropically flowered shirt, replaced his large bifocals with a pair of prescription Maui Jim's, and was in the Bahamas before anyone knew he was gone. That Christmas afternoon he began making plans to make his way to Brazil where he could begin his virtually untraceable life under the new name of Jimmy Seay, well connected bon vivant, and citizen of the world.

 Sergio Mendes & Brazil 66 – Mas Que Nada:
https://www.youtube.com/watch?v=9U1v01SGtGE

When Palm Beach County Sheriff's Deputy Denny Parks, perhaps coincidentally, perhaps ironically, received the call from Maggie, he was seated in a booth in Lake Park's Denny's Restaurant. He recognized the caller ID immediately as a "friendly," someone with whom he had frequent encounters in the mutual pursuit of maintaining or restoring the peace, but who can also be an independent witness, and a bona fide officer of the legislated oversight process.

These two often worked together. They liked one another, and they agreed upon their roles and upon their duties on the battlement they manned between the privileged and supposedly under-privileged classes, which, as they saw it, was to keep them separated. They also knew which of these classes buttered their bread.

Maggie and Denny worked together to applaud each other's heroism and selflessness, and separately they decried the onerous regulations, and tragic fund shortages as impediments to their life-saving missions. Between them, they saw to it that whichever agencies would have to absorb the tax revenue shortfall, it would be neither his nor her'n. This job was too hard to host bake sales as supplemental funding. Their mutual goal: One hundred percent of Maggie's prolific staff's baked goods should be consumed on premises by friendlies.

As on most mornings, Denny brought the coffee, and Maggie, the coffee cake.

After their exchange of pleasantries while they rode the elevator to the secure fourth floor, Denny asked, "What do you know about Michael Fitzpatrick?"

Maggie replied, "Mr. Fitzpatrick has had a rough life, and particularly tough night. It will take weeks for the blood toxicity lab-work to come back, but he is definitely hopped up on something and eager to confess his sins."

Denny said, "It's very rare for one of these mob types to say anything other than I want my lawyer.

"Well, that's about the only thing he hasn't said."

They made a cursory stop where Deputy Sherriff Parks surrendered his sidearm and switchblade to the armed attendant, and even before they cleared this last barrier, they could hear The Mic sounding off. Maggie held up a small brass key and said, "While we were cleaning him up we found this in his shoe. I think it fits the lock on the case he still has chained to his wrist. At first, we could not get near it, but we've given him something to calm him down, and I gotta tell ya, I'm a little concerned about the contents of that bag."

Parks looked down at The Mic, who was now scrubbed and bandaged and strapped down to his gurney. The natty brief case was still attached to his wrist by what appeared to be a substantial steel bicycle security cable, sat on the floor next to the suspect. He set up his small video camera and spoke, "Initial interview with Michael Fitzpatrick, December 22nd, 5:27 AM, Officer Parks and Nurse Laird attending."

"Good morning Michael. What's in your grip?"

"Just stuff I need for my job." came his reply.

Parks donned a pair of surgical gloves, and, in one smooth movement he used his bolt cutters to sever the cable, and while Maggie and The Mic watched, he used the key to open the tattered old satchel, and emptied its contents onto a stainless-steel table.

Both Maggie and Denny were astounded by what tumbled out. Among other things, there were three hand guns, a plastic-wrapped brick of cocaine, several old prescription vails, two ledger books, and a small stack of old newspapers from the early 1980s.

Using the eraser end of a pencil, he moved the items from the case around on the tabletop. Parks asked, "Who do you work for?"

The Mic replied, "Can you keep a secret?"

"Like the grave."

This reference to his tomb made it apparent to The Mic that they already knew, and his only hope was to come clean, "L'il Augie Amato, and his father before him."

Denny asked, "Are you ready to give a statement?"

The Mic replied, "If you've got questions, go ahead and ask 'em."

Denny, not quite believing his good fortune, looked over the gurney at Maggie, who routinely met and treated every form of psychosis, and said, "I have never had one of these mob underlings spill his guts before. If they ever give up any useful information, it is after weeks of plea bargains and promises of relocation in the Federal Witness Protection Program."

Maggie replied, "This guy is reacting to some physical or mental trauma. Probably both. My guess is he is trying to make a deal for his soul. These revelations are generally short-lived."

Parks said, "So after this guy sleeps this off, he will clam up and invoke his Miranda rights?"

Maggie nodded, "Why not ask him some general, open-ended questions? He seems in the mood to cooperate."

Officer Parks jumped right in, "Mic, tell me about these guns."

The Mic looked over at the table and replied simply and truthfully, "That thirty-eight is mine and the nine looks like Rocco's. We've clipped more than a couple of guys in the boroughs with those heaters. Not sure about the Luger, could be the one L'il Augie used on Sal outside of Siro's when he tried to welch on his Saratoga tab."

The Mic's candid responses affected Deputy Sherriff Parks like he himself had been gob smacked. He walked out of the field of the camera, withdrew his cell phone and awakened his partner, "Vinny, you're not gonna believe this. Get over to the office and pull up the open case files on the Amato crime family out of Newark, and hurry. We are about to collect on a trifecta!"

Parks returned to find Maggie, who had also donned surgical gloves, looking through one of the ledger books on the table. Using just her eyes, she communicated a simple idea to him, and he asked the Mic, "What are these account books about?"

"That's the whole shopping cart from L'il Augie's old man. Now that was a guy you didn't wanna cross. One dirty look from the old man and thugs would start dropping dead all over town."

Parks replied, "Big Augie? He's been dead for decades?"

The Mic's face disclosed some confusion, which after a short interval, he was apparently able to reconcile, "Yeah, those have been missing for quite a while. I guess the boss finally found 'em."

The briefcase and all its contents were itemized, photographed, and then dusted for fingerprints. So, began the chain of custody record which would be scrupulously kept until the evidence was presented in criminal court.

Winston, who had contemplated this eventuality decades before, had assembled an almost air-tight case of circumstantial evidence. Johnny had contributed the two guns he had fished from the dumpster in West Palm Beach alley and, the rest came from the loot filched from the Palm Beach Towers safe deposit boxes. He had never developed a real plan for its use, but in the last few days he had realized the old ledger books he had kept were associated with the Amatos. However, delivering this custom frame-job through the Palm Beach paramedics directly into the hands of the organized crime division of the Palm Beach County Sheriff's Department absolutely defined serendipity, and spoke to Winston of a personal providence projected by The Green Flash. He now felt certain, at the very least, it would create a diversion, and allow him a few hours or days head start.

After his intense conversation with Lieutenant Caldwell, L'il Augie Amato paced the apartment contemplating his predicament. He then went to the secret wall safe in his bedroom, opened it and withdrew a large stack of $100 bills, a passport, a small notebook computer, and an encrypted ten gigabyte thumb drive. He fired up the notebook, and using an AirCard modem, he sent a pre-typed message to the IP address: DL1. This message took the form of a blast transmission, which lasted 1/1000th of a second. Should someone listening in even be aware of the transmission, its brevity and encoding defied that someone to make anything relevant of it. Amato spent the eight minutes between sending the message, and the confirmation of receipt, carefully filling a compact, waterproof money belt with the items he had extracted from his safe.

To say that L'il Augie was cocksure was a statement of the bleeding obvious, but unlike most arrogant men who displayed his type of presumption, he could see past his confidence to a need for contingency planning. He chose not to disturb the deep red colored aura his subordinates saw and felt, which projected his confidence and the power of his will. So, most of his alternative scenarios were contrived, constructed, and contemplated in secrecy. One such plan; perhaps the most ingenious of his portfolio of eventuality, centered around one David Lithgow.

Lithgow was seldom more than two hours away from Amato but, by design, never in the same city. The comic phrase seen on tee shirts, "I'm not saying I'm Batman, but we have never been seen together," applied.

A few years back in Lexington, Kentucky, L'il Augie had been mistaken for Lithgow who happened to be attending the same reception of potential equestrian investors. L'il Augie did not like being approached by strangers, and when it happened the danger klaxon sounded the "ah-oo-ga" in his mind. When the embarrassed stranger spied Lithgow about thirty feet away, he remarked upon their remarkable resemblance. L'il Augie saw the likeness immediately, and then he demurred and retired, but not before ascertaining Lithgow's pertinent data.

Later that week, after some preliminary Googling, he made an unaccompanied, late-night call upon his doppelganger, and with the aid of a partially concealed .45, gained entrance to Lithgow's hotel suite. A wave of confusion and fear swept over the sleepy Lithgow as he began to entreat this interloper not to harm him. When Amato took Lithgow by the nape of the neck, and forced him to stand beside him facing a full-length mirror, some of the confusion went away, but the fear never did.

L'il Augie noticed an opened bottle of Dewar's Scotch on the bar and poured himself and Lithgow three fingers' worth. After a moment of silent observation, L'il Augie placed his pistol and $10,000 on table between them and then laid out his proposal. Lithgow would receive similar payments every six months just to be on standby should his resemblance be required. Since Lithgow's lifestyle was that of a bon vivant, the influx of cash would be welcome, and the sheer intrigue also appealed to him, and while L'il Augie's offer seemed to be a generous one, it also did not appear to be an offer he had the option to refuse. So, he accepted.

From his suit pocket, Amato produced a blank finger print card, and an ink pad. He expertly took Lithgow's prints and placed the card in an unmarked envelope. He would have these prints substituted for his own in the Newark police Department's files by one of his provocateurs. As Lithgow cleaned his hands, L'il Augie assured him that should he reveal, to anyone, their arrangement, David Lithgow would, beyond any doubt, be a dead ringer.

Over the past three years, David Lithgow had subbed for L'il Augie four times. Once, as grand marshal, he had ridden in a vintage Conestoga wagon at the head of a parade of twelve hundred boy scouts, which kicked off a week-long camping Jamboree. Twice he had merely sat in the back of a court room to convince several federal witnesses that their testimony mattered to the mob, and most recently as a judge in a Newark teenage beauty contest – both the prince and the pauper had found this event to be a contradiction in terms. In each of these occasions no one questioned the authenticity of the stand-in, and L'il Augie was elsewhere doing more secret and self-satisfying stuff.

In a short conversation with Lithgow this particular Sunday morning, Amato gave Lithgow very specific instructions as to where, when, and how he was to appear next, including the location of a piece of luggage he was to retrieve and bring along.

Just because L'il Augie's usual crew was apparently within hailing distance of taking the day, it didn't mean he was content with being isolated and unprotected. From his trusty smart phone, he chose a contact repre- sented by the three initials, NJN. To NJN he texted this message, "See you at the Fourth Window at 11:15 this morning." To the uninitiated, this innocuous, and seemingly innocent, combination of letters could have meant anything, but to L'il Augie, the contact code he had just texted trans- lated to New Jersey Nick.

Next, Amato send a similar text to Diego Lazette's phone, "Implementing 4th Window protocol. BIT."

L'il Augie then glanced again at the official-looking wanted poster he had removed from the lobby door of the Palm Beach Towers, looked at his watch, and headed to his bedroom suite to shower and shave in preparation for the day.

New Jersey Nick was only diligent in a few areas of his life, and even in most of those he was only diligent intermittently, but when it came to responding quickly when L'il Augie called, he was a composite of Jack B. Nimble, and Johnny on the Spot. To the boss, this fear-based punctuality, and the sheer velocity with which Nick could respond, were high on a short list of traits which L'il Augie depended upon. Add to those few traits that Nick also represented a massive barrier between him and those who might wish him harm, and one could quickly understand their codependent relationship.

Dominick Righetti was a hyper-example of mob muscle. He stood 6'4" and weighed in at an impressive 295 pounds, his neck measured a little over 22 inches in circumference, and his hands, or more concisely his fists, resembled the meaty sledges of a blacksmith. Augmenting his mass, his girth, and his reach, Nick still retained a good deal of the quickness of the outside line-backer he had played in semi-professional football just outside of Newark. In those incredibly violent, and barely legal, games, played in due-to-be-condemned stadiums of rotting inner cities, Nick had acquired several Nicknames: The One-Man Stampede, Giblet maker, and The Coma Man. His rap sheet is all that stood between Nick and Canton, Ohio's Professional Football Hall of Fame, well his rap sheet and his inability to accept coach's criticisms, penalty flags, or league imposed fines for excessive and intentionally inflicted violence. Long before Dr. Bennet Omalu, the eminent Pittsburgh neuropathologist of recent notoriety for his discovery of chronic encephalopathy (CTE), Nick understood how a sharp blow to the head could muddle a person's reasoning, and he delivered these blows with the dispassionate detachment of an Ian Fleming super-villain's henchman.

When at last no team would have him, L'il Augie recognized his potential, and after a short, one-sided discussion, New Jersey Nick relocated to a
double wide mobile home in the Florida sea-side hamlet of Briny Breezes,
just fifteen miles south of Palm Beach. There he had established a criminal
enterprise of general high jacking and loan-sharking, and a very specific
protection racket – he kept the competition down in the lucrative local
Stone Crab fishery. His payment from this later enterprise came in the
form of 20-pound bags of Colossal Stone Crab Claws and freshly made
mustard sauce. He purchased a large residential freezer which he quickly
filled, and the bags kept coming. Upon returning from a long weekend of
ribald behavior and madcap revelry in New York – The Belmont race track
gave as good as it got – he found, to his displeasure, that this freezer had
gone off line almost as soon as he had latched his suitcase four days earlier.

The stench off 700 pounds rotting seafood was staggering. He had
to face facts. He had to admit to himself that even his voracious appetite
was no match for the tax he had imposed on the local fishermen. After
several hours of intermittent retching as he disposed of the ruined crus-
tacean appendages, his next reaction was to apply for a permit to build
a twelve feet square utility room, which after the final inspections had
been performed, he converted into a large walk-in freezer. He lined the
walls of this structure with twice the insulation most designs would have
required, and the refrigeration units could have easily maintained a zero
Fahrenheit temperature in a space four times the volume. He then installed
industrial grade stainless steel shelving where he estimated he could stack
approaching 500 twenty-pound bags.

Nick quickly discovered that he was not alone in his craving for these
delicious creatures, and, once his own consumption was satiated, he found
he had a stumbled into a commodity which could be bartered for just
about any good or service he might need. His trailer needed a little fixing
up, so three bags covered a new paint job, 2 more, new plush carpeting,
new twenty-inch rims for his pickup were a very reasonable five bags, one
bag a month covered his lawn man, and he also discovered several hookers
who forgot the meaning of the word "no" for a bag a piece.

While Nick had always physically been a large man, through this singular endeavor, had become, at least locally, a big man. When, through a series of events, he became aware of a relatively new stone crab fishing vessel whose aging captain was quietly searching for a partner, Nick stepped in with the proceeds of seventy-five 20-pound bags of jumbo and colossal claws and became the defacto owner of the "Crabby Old Man," a 39-foot, shallow draft, diesel powered Crusader. Five days a week, this boat, her captain and two mates plied the waters between Florida and the Bahamas with 2100 traps baited with pigs' feet, for those tasty treats. One day a week the same crew stayed in port to perform routine maintenance on the weakest five per cent of their traps. On Sundays, because of over-exposure to rum in the sun, the boat had traditionally sat idle while the crew was recovering, but now Nick would frequently cast off the dock lines and like Gilligan, take a three-hour tour.

On this particular Sunday, as he enjoyed the beautiful sunrise, his repose was interrupted by his cell phone which sounded "The Lion Sleeps Tonight," a specific ring tone he had exclusively associated with L'il Augie. He leaped to the bedside table and read the encoded text. He dressed and then collected a pre-packed canvas duffle from under his bed, and whistling an approximation of the song of the same name, he headed to the dock of the bay where his boat was languidly bobbing. Before he cast off the dock lines to head north, one David Lithgow collected the canvas duffle bag from him, and he went his separate way.

Over the years, and on different occasions, the couch in Winston Montgomery's conference room had been the foundation supporting as many as five grown men as they watched Monday Night Football, four children of stair-step height who sat silently listening as a parent disclosed the ruin and rubble his finances had become, two and sometimes three partially clothed adults as they writhed and groped lasciviously, but far more frequently it had supported just one person comfortably napping. The couch was just not large enough to billet two people in a deep sleep without some encroachment into each other's space. During the previous four or five hours, as Katie unconsciously, or subconsciously, had several times sought just a pinch more room, Johnny had instinctively contorted his body to accommodate her. A shift here, a nudge there, had resulted in an entwinement of trunks and limbs such as one might find in a medieval forest, or in a decorative arch in the topiary section of an ornamental horticulturalist shop.

It was in this entanglement that Katie and Johnny found themselves on Christmas morning when the vibrations of one of the cell phones on the conference room table broke through their slumber and simultaneously awakened them. Four eyes, just inches apart, opened wide and then blinked furiously trying to reconcile their surroundings and their intimate proximity. They both tried to rise, but as in the wild, what nature has labored over time to construct requires some time and thought for people to deconstruct. Within two seconds, surprise changed to confusion, and confusion to embarrassment, and then embarrassment became amusement, which quickly resolved itself into laughter. Katie gathered herself, raised her head a few inches, and kissed Johnny a lingering kiss full on the mouth, then she relaxed with Johnny's bicep under her head and said while chuckling, "Well good morning and Merry Christmas Bunkie."

Much like escaping a wrestler's hold, Johnny disengaged himself from this imbroglio while feeling his face flush. As he looked down at Katie's sleepy visage, the phone vibrated again, and, before he lost his balance, he hopped awkwardly to his left and steadied himself against the table. The phone and its post-it label danced and insisted that someone pay attention. Johnny wiped his eyes and then lunged at the aggravating device. He read aloud, "Implementing 4th Window protocol. BIT. From Amato"

Katie asked, "Whose phone?"

Johnny read the label, "Diego Lazette."

Recalling the grisly business at the farm the night before, a shiver of fear coursed Katie's spine, as she wondered aloud, "Is that psychopath on the loose again?"

"I was wondering the same thing," said Johnny as he now retrieved his own phone from the table and began to manipulate the touch screen.

He called up the application that allowed him to check the surveillance camera on the back porch of Benny Bigalow's farm. There in the pale light of morning, he could see the two thugs facing each other, and still bound hand and foot, with the substantial trunk of the live oak between them. "Well whatever role that goon is to play in "The Fourth Window Protocol" is going to be delayed. I better tell Herc."

Katie rose, stretched, and then looked for herself at the message on Diego's phone. Johnny and his brother came into the room together and Katie handed Herc the phone. They re-read the text aloud several times before Johnny, via smartphone conferenced in Willis who asked, "Does this Forth Window Protocol refer to the press? – you know the Fourth Estate?"

"What about the Fourth Column?" Anna-Sophia, who had joined the discussion interjected, "Isn't that a term for a secret insurgency?"

"The term for that is a Fifth Column – I doubt that applies here," Herc said, "and what about the BIT – is that part of the protocol. We need to sort this out quickly and reply."

Concerned that Diego's lack of response might create an opening in their fog bank of deception, the men discussed if and how they should respond to L'il Augie until Katie interrupted. Applying her years of experience in teenage text abbreviation she spoke calmly, "Gentlemen, I think this is code for an escape plan, maybe the fourth variation in a series. And as for a reply, I don't think one is expected. The BIT means he is going silent for a while – Be in Touch."

Herc keyed his phone and Fiona answered, "Fiona, watch the back of the condo for any sign of a rear exit by L'il Augie."

Fiona, sounding disappointed, replied, "What happened to Fat Tomato and Bright Star?"

Herc, a bit chagrined, replied, "Sorry Bright Star, watch the back for any escape over the balcony or out a rear exit of the Fat Tomato. And be careful."

"Roger, 10-4, and out," said Agent Bright Star, and then as she turned to apprise Manolo, who had been below with JPB getting a little sack time and had only caught the last part of the conversation.

He quickly jumped to the dock and said, "I go check it out. While I'm gone I'll see if I can scare us up some breakfast."

Her eyes were smiling as they watched him run the length of the pier and disappear behind the tennis courts. She started to go after him, but before she could tie the laces of her sneakers, JPB intercepted her, "Where do you think you are goin' little missy?"

She started to explain, but JPB said, "I can't be stumbling around this boat like a blind man."

Fiona was truly puzzled by this statement asked, "What do you mean?"

JPB replied with a wink and a grin, "I figure what's going on between you and your young man is private business, so I close my eyes when you two are kissing."

Fiona rationalized her ignorance of this courtesy he had apparently been extending, blushed and said quietly to herself as much as to Jean Pierre, "Me too."

"Forget about kissing that boy for a few minutes, and help me cast off.

We need to clear out before the harbor master catch us here. Besides your daddy wants me to get you clear of that Old Rotten Tomato up der."

Fiona made another try, "But how's he gonna get back?"

Shaking his head Jean Pierre said, "Text him to take a cab."

JPB and Agent Bright Star motored back across the intercostal waterway to the Palm Beach Yacht Club to find Winston Montgomery waiting on the pier with suitcase in hand. Willis was with him. He tossed a belaying line to Fiona, who pulled the boat tight against the boat's rubber fenders. She started to make the craft fast, but her father stopped her by saying, "No need for that. We're not staying."

He flipped his case on board before taking Fiona's hand. He helped her reach the dock, and he then exchanged places with her. "Mr. Laird will get you back to your mother. Mr. Baptiste and I have urgent business elsewhere."

Winston hugged his daughter from the boat, and then the Apocalypso pulled away and headed for the Palm Beach Inlet, and the Atlantic Ocean beyond.

Fiona was struck speechless for a moment and then quietly said to Willis, "I thought we were going to spend the holidays together."

"Apparently your dad has other plans, but Herc says he left you something at his office," said Willis, "Let's go see what it is. Where's the kid?"

Fiona gave Willis a pouty recap of their recent separation at the demand of others, and Willis punched her lightly on the shoulder and said, "Quit complaining. You're in Herc's Army now, and you have orders to report soldier!"

When they arrived at Winston's office they found that the gang was all there, and Katie handed each of them a champagne flute which was filled to the brim. After several toasts to their survival and apparent success, Hercules said. "I know that nobody expected to be exchanging gifts here this Christmas morning, but since we are all together now I think I should distribute the packages that Mr. Montgomery left, so grab a seat and let's get started."

Corina squealed, "There is no time like the present for presents."

Herc began handing out the packages and sealed envelopes and suggested that they open them one at a time so that everyone might enjoy each surprise. "Who wants to start?"

Everyone volunteered, but none of them could match the zeal with which Corina volunteered, and without any objection from the others, she began. The white linen envelope she had been given opened easily, and from it she extracted two folded pieces of paper. She read aloud, **"Ms. Dare, A little something to complement your "top down, diamonds on the backseat approach to life" – please don't change."** The second sheet was the registration of the midnight blue Aston Martin DB9, which had been signed over to her for the payment of one dollar and other good and valuable consideration.

Willis looked at the document and opined, "It looks legit."

Fiona's "Me next!" won out and she removed the lid from a medium size box of considerable weight. "It's just a bunch of old books," she said as her spirits sagged a bit. Herc looked over her shoulder and commented, "I suspect there is more to the story."

There were, in fact, six old books in the box, and as he examined them one at a time, he read the titles, "The Adventures of Tom Sawyer, by Mark Twain. The Velveteen Rabbit, by Margery Williams. These three volumes are Sense and Sensibility, by Jane Austin. And this last one is The Wonderful Wizard of Oz, by L. Frank Baum."

Fiona said, "Terrific books, but he knows I have already read them all."

"I hope you liked them, because I believe every one of these is a signed first edition. There is no telling what they are worth."

And so it went. Willis was given the title to Winston's 1930 Indian Scout motorcycle. Lacy's envelop contained the business card of the owner of a high-end art gallery on Worth Avenue, and a simple note which read, **"Ms. Walden, Thank you for all your help. I think you are a talented** artist, and when you feel ready, this man stands ready to produce a one woman show. No charge. The best of luck to you."

Johnny's envelop contained the executed title to Winston's 34-foot Intrepid twin-engine speed boat. The attached note read, **"Mr. Johnny Dendy, I think you may be a Super Hero. Just keep doing what you're doing! With the deepest admiration, Winston Montgomery".**

Katie's envelope was much larger and thicker than the rest, and she was forced to swallow hard when she saw the contents. The top sheet said, **"Katie, even though you may not believe it, I will be sorry forever. With love and best wishes. W."** The rest of the packet contained two signed copies of their divorce papers, a quit claim deed to her house and several off-shore bank books. Despite her resistance, several tears coursed her cheek.

The envelope labeled Manolo Gonzalez was given to Fiona and she opened it saying, "He won't mind if I take a quick look." The note read, **"Manny, when you get ready to record, take Fiona with you. There is a prepaid week of studio time waiting for you two in New York. Winston Montgomery.**

P.S. Behave like the gentleman I know you are and everything else will take care of itself."

The last unopened envelop was addressed to Mr. Hercules Dendy and Ms. Anna-Sophia Escudo. Herc handed it to Sofi who handed it back and said, "Hercules, you open it. I'll watch."

Herc did as he had been asked and opened the letter. It read, **"Ms. Escudo & Mr. Dendy, Your courage and intelligence saved the day. Though I will never be able to repay you, I would like to offer you this token. This airline account contains one million miles of first class accommodations. It seems to me that you two fit together nicely, and while it's true you can't go back to Constantinople, may I suggest you try the Dome of St. Sophia in Istanbul."** This letter was signed, **"Your devoted, if distant, friend, Winston."**

Within fifteen minutes of the last gift being revealed, the group began to pair off and depart. Johnny and Katie were headed home by way of

Denny's big breakfast bargain. Corina offered to take Fiona to find Manolo. Lacy grabbed a ride with Willis to pick up the car she had left outside her office, and from there he went on to meet his sister.

After the crowd left Herc and Sofi alone, they opened a fresh bottle of French bubbles, and they toasted the day. They talked in the firelight about their adventure and soothsayered their way forward and backward in time. Sofi stated the obvious in tones of admiration, "You know we still have no idea how Winston came to possess The Green Flash. I wonder if he could have masterminded the robbery."

Herc's response was a bit on the nostalgic side, "Got to admire a local boy with a little initiative I guess, and talk about playing the cards close to his vest, if he pulled that job, he never told a soul."

"Well," she said, "I don't want him for a husband, but I think he will make a reliable friend, and maybe he will let us see The Green Flash every now and then."

Herc said, "Yeah maybe. Hey now that we are alone, I have something for you."

As he disengaged from their entanglement, Sofi said, "That's very sweet of you, mi trovador."

Herc returned with two identical packages, and said, "Actually, I got these for both of us. Which one do you want?"

After a short internal struggle, she chose the one in his right hand, and began opening it, and Herc asked, "Are you sure you don't want this one?"

She continued to attack the wrapping and answered, "No senor, I am content with my first choice."

Suddenly the paper gave way and a green velvet pouch dropped into her lap. Sofi looked up and Herc tossed her the remaining package. When she tore the wrapping away she was left holding an identical green velvet pouch.

She hefted the two bags, one in each hand, and allowed the possibilities to play themselves out. Unable to detect any difference, she met his eyes straight on and finally spoke. "May I still choose the other?"

Herc replied, "Sure. You can have either of them."

Sofi asked, "Why are you ambivalent about such a treasure?"

Herc took the stones from her, and without even looking at them he placed them on the coffee table just a few feet away. He then placed her feet in his lap and began to massage her tired dogs. As her eyes rolled, a deep-throated moan escaped her, and she gave into the sheer pleasure of the sensation. Herc said, "Are you certain that stone is not more trouble than treasure?"

Without waiting for a reply from Sofi, Herc continued, "First. To hold on to this so-called treasure, because you really don't have an uncontested claim of ownership, it must be kept a total secret. If anyone finds out you have an emerald of such supposed value, suddenly everyone you see is a potential threat to not only steal it, but to take out anyone who opposes them."

"Second, you can't extract any actual money from this treasure, because your whole goal is just to possess it, and so you are forced to spend on elaborate security measures."

"Third, although this stone is a real dazzler, it's too large to wear as jewelry, so it is only useful as a paper weight or a door stop, but that would require you to take it out of the safe, and then someone steals it."

"Fourth, we know of many who have died while trying to steal or defend this green rock, and why? Because society says it is irreplaceable, invaluable, unimaginably exquisite, inestimable, blah, blah…"

Sofi could not dispute any of his points and so instead she asked, "What do suggest we do with it?"

"I think we should treat it like the curse it is. After years and years of horrible misfortune, the owner of the Hope diamond wrapped it up and sent it to the Smithsonian Institute. They just dropped it is the mail. Three days later the damn thing was somebody else's problem. We keep the fake as a souvenir."

"What about Winston?"

Herc smiled and said, "He will eventually see that he is well rid of it, plus he has a copy if he wants something to look at. Believe me, things will calm down considerably with this damn rock out of the mix."

Sofi had to admit that, without the prospect of The Green Flash to occupy her waking hours, her life suddenly became more predictable, and maybe even stable. She withdrew her feet from his lap, repositioned herself so her face was a few inches from Herc's and asked, "Do you have anything that needs rubbing?"

Herc confessed he might, and then said, "I have been thinking. It would probably be prudent for us to get out of town for a while. You know, let the smoke around this caper clear. A good friend of mine swears that Christmas Day is the best day of the year to travel – everybody is celebrating, nobody's traveling."

Sofi replied, "I guess that makes sense. I have never really given the matter any thought. What have you got in mind?"

"What say we follow Winston's suggestion and head for Istanbul?"

When L'il Augie was presented with a choice between a direct overt action on one hand, and the subterfuge of covert misdirection on the other, he was truly ambidextrous. And many times, his choice was neither fish nor fowl, but rather a combination of the two. As Snoop might have said "Foissle". This Sunday morning's activity was made up of this sort of amalgam. He saw the PBPD squad car waiting outside the entrance to the Palm Beach Towers, and rather than making any attempt at stealth to avoid being seen, he boldly drove his small Mercedes convertible right past it and doffed his NY Yankees ball cap to its occupants.

He quickly navigated the seven tenths of a mile from his condominium to the grand entrance of the Breakers Hotel. After approximately five minutes behind the wheel, he turned his car over to the watchful care of the valet staff, collected his ticket, and walked into the hotel. In another five minutes, the maître d' of the Circle restaurant recognized him, discreetly accepted the folded Andrew Jackson, and showed him to his usual table near the east windows, which overlooked the glassy Atlantic Ocean.

During this series of movements, he was under the surveillance of several law enforcement agencies for the entire time, but they had been unprepared and disorganized as to exactly what they should do. For his part, L'il Augie seemed unaware of the capture net being drawn tight, and he appeared to be enjoying the morning sunshine and the view of the tranquil sea.

Within another five minutes, Denny Parks and his partner Vinny arrived. They held a quick radio discussion with the Palm Beach Police Department's desk sergeant and Officer of the Day at the Palm Beach County Sheriff's Department and developed a simple plan. Arrest him. However, before they could initiate the mechanics of slapping the cuffs on their man, L'il Augie was on the move. Detective Parks spoke into his radio, "Hold tight. We don't want this brunch turning into a blood bath. Let's see if we can still do this without any collateral damage. Follow him but keep your distance."

Following the 1st commandment of selective consumption at the majestic Breakers Sunday Brunch, "Do not fill up on waffles and omelets!" Willis and his sister were just about to return to the Beluga caviar station, when this little ballet of cops and robbers began, and with his elbow, he drew Maggie's attention to the unfolding drama. "Holy Shit! That's Augie Amato in the pink polo and patch Madras pants."

Maggie followed his wide-eyed stare but did not comprehend the import until she spied Denny Parks behind a large potted Kentia Palm with a small radio held close to his mouth. She replied, "That's Detective Parks, and he is on his ass. Do you think there's gonna be a shootout?"

"I doubt it," said Willis, "The Breakers is against plugging the guests, but this should be interesting."

As the few informed parties looked on, L'il Augie made his way through the crowd and walked briskly to the men's room, opened the door, and disappeared behind it. Parks spoke into his radio again, "Stay cool."

This five-minute increment of time seemed to take longer than the ones that had preceded it, but eventually the bathroom door opened and Amato began ambling back to his table. Parks gave the word and three plain clothes policemen fell in step with L'il Augie, and with a minimum of commotion, captured and handcuffed him. A certain amount of "What the hell do you think you are doing?" "You've got the wrong man," and "This is going to cost you your job!" shouts were to be expected, but as long as there was no gun play, Parks felt buoyant as he helped escort their prisoner to the Paddy wagon they had waiting at a side exit and said so, "Well done everyone. Let's get this bum into lockup."

Willis and Maggie chatted excitedly about what this arrest meant as they continued to ravage the different Breakers' brunch bars, but suddenly Willis just stopped talking, and he apparently had stopped listening too. He stared out of the window beside their table at a large man in a wetsuit and

Scuba gear who jogged across the narrow expanse of beach, paused briefly in the chest deep water of the gentle shore break to adroitly slip on his fins, adjust his mask, and then he disappeared beneath the surface of the sea.

With a forkful of Crepes Suzette paused in mid-flight he said, "Well I'll be dipped!"

New Jersey Nick had a healthy fear of L'il Augie Amato, but he also held a real admiration for the man whom he regarded as fearless, a state he aspired to achieve in his own approach to life. As he motored north on the intercostal waterway he considered his part in this morning's activities. His job had essentially two sequential duties; first he was to reconnoiter the Palm Beach Towers from his boat as he passed. If he saw anything or anyone suspicious, he was to use his own initiative and judgement. The second, and by far the most important, was to be on station and on time for his eleven o'clock rendezvous with his boss and idol.

As he passed the PB Towers he did see something that made him throttle back, take out his old brass spy glass and focus on a young man who seemed to be giving the back of Amato's apartment the once over. He had cased his share of jobs, and he recognized the conspicuous loitering and intermittent glances to check if anyone had noticed him. As Nick saw it, there were two pieces of bad news here for this would-be thief. He had been detected, and he was also unaware that he had been detected.

Nick quickly docked his boat at the southern-most pier of the large PB towers marina and moved to the concealment of the hedges surrounding the complex. By the time Manolo became conscious of the large man glaring at him, Nick was only thirty feet distant. The boy did not debate the choice between fight or flight, the choice was easy. As he had said to Fiona, he would just out run this giant. He started out in an easy jog, and when he saw the big man break into a sprint, he did the same, but he noticed one problem. At his own top speed, the big man was closing.

Manny tried pulling several lawn chairs into his path as he ran, but Nick easily avoided or hurtled these obstacles. The last thought the boy had before Nick launched himself at his legs was of the Nature Channel and its warning – a Grisly Bear can outrun a horse for a short distance. Manolo hit hard and most of the air was knocked out of him.

With the boy tucked under one massive arm, Nick was headed back toward The Grumpy Old Man when a movement to his left caught his eye. Despite its faux lizard skin, presumably camouflaged, hard case, Nick noticed Manolo's smart phone on the closely mown Bermuda grass. In fact, it probably would have been spied even if the somewhat muted ring tone had not caused it to shimmy like a honey bee giving directions to the rest of the hive. Like forest colors in the desert, it was exactly the wrong pattern to mask its presence. Nick plucked the wriggling phone from the ground without breaking stride and stuffed it in his pocket. Although Manny could not catch his breath, or even spell his name, he did recognize the ring tone as Fiona's; this was not going to turn out well.

She would probably be better off without him. It was inarguable. Hadn't he just been knocked down, snatched up, rolled over, and carried away? Wasn't the need for of all these dangling prepositions being perpetrated by a guy the size of an apartment building? How embarrassing. It was like being snuck up on by Mount Rushmore. Now after he had been carried to a fishing boat and thrown aboard like sack of potatoes, he had been jammed in the on-board head like a stuffed aardvark this goon had won at the state fair for midget tossing. His gloom only darkened when he heard the engine start and felt the boat begin to move.

In order to align himself properly for his mile long, underwater swim, L'il Augie took one last look at The Breakers Hotel, checked the combination compass/ GPS he wore on his left wrist, and disappeared below the surface of the calm sea. He was headed out to meet up with the fishing vessel, The Crabby Old Man.

The coordinates which had been agreed upon were; Latitude 26 42.680' N, Longitude 080 00.980' W. The Fourth Window reef, named for its landmark of putting the black chimney in line with the 4th window on the north section of the Breaker's Hotel. The ledge is easy to find and follow in either direction. It varies in height from 5 - 10 feet with depths of 66' to the sand, about 55' on top. Lots of undercuts where nurse sharks and morays hang out. Lots of growth and plenty of fish.

On this sunny Sunday morning, there were several commercial dive boats which operated from the docks near Blue Heron Boulevard anchored just east of the reef. Each of these boats transported about twenty divers working the reef in "buddy system" pairings, and they scarcely noticed the lone diver passing through their midst. L'il Augie caught sight of the red hull paint of his escape craft, and following the decompression tables, he took about ten minutes to surface, with the boat between himself and the shore.

New Jersey Nick had caught sight of his bubbles several minutes before and had hung a folding ladder from the gunnel. He accepted Amato's fins and mask and then steadied the ladder as the boss hauled himself from the water. As soon as he was on board, Nick weighed anchor and pointed the bow due east. He kicked the throttle up to twenty-six hundred RPMs, and the two men bumped fists and laughed as they made good their get-away at twenty-one knots.

Then Nick remembered the boy he held captive in the boat's head and said, "Oh I've got a surprise for you."

He reached into his pocket and produced Manny's phone. While L'il Augie reviewed what he could from Manny's phone without a thumb print or a pin #, Nick removed the stainless-steel bolt from the hasp and dragged Manolo Gonzales into the cabin. "I caught this kid spying on the back of your place, so I ran him down. If you don't think he matters we can just pitch him overboard into the Gulfstream and wish him luck – next stop England."

L'il Augie appraised the cowering youth thoughtfully before he said, "We can always decide to use him for chum, but let's hang on to him for now and see what he knows. First thing, I will need to use his right thumb for just a second. Would you kindly assist me?"

Nick twitched, or snatched Manolo's right hand toward the phone in Amato's hand, and naturally enough the rest of his body came along for the ride. The thumb print apparently passed muster, because the screen came alive. "I see you've missed a couple of calls and texts. One Fiona seems particularly concerned. This string of texts is riveting. Nick, I believe we have encountered the blush of young love."

"Here is another missed call from an Argentine number, and several from Newark. This kid gets around."

L'il Augie thought on it for several moments. "This wouldn't be Fiona Montgomery, would it?"

The look on Manny's face eliminated the need for verbal confirmation. "I guess the next thing to do is let them know you are okay, don't you? Something short but sweet, huh?"

Using the dozen or so preceding exchanges between the two as a guide, L'il Augie crafted a believably concise text to send to Fiona.

"F, Crazy day, I got a call from my youngest brother. He's at Virginia Tech. Skiing accident - Compound fractures and punctured lung. He's stable. I'm going there to help get him home. I don't want to spook the parents, so until I see how bad it is, keep it to yourself. BIT - Miss you, M"

"I think we just got our first real break. As long as they think this kid is safe and headed home, they may drop the guard a little."

For Manolo's part, he could not believe he had been jumped twice by men at least twice his weight and age. Hell, he had to admit to himself, both times it had not even been a contest. Within seconds of being discovered by the bad guys, they had simply and easily taken him out of the game. Were these captures acts of natural selection? Was he too slow and dim-witted to exist? As they motored through the deep blue waters of the Atlantic, Nick and L'il Augie gorged themselves on stone crab claws, and as for Manny, he could not see how he could avoid joining the Dodo bird in the Forever Club -extinction.

After witnessing gluttony, he, and most people, could not have imagined, Manny watched L'il Augie shed his wet suit, don white shorts and a floral-patterned shirt, and then key the mike on the marine band radio. "Pelican, Crabby Old Man standing by."

The radio crackled and apparently in response a voice said, "Pelican here. I have a visual and will touch down about one quarter knot to your east."

L'il Augie glanced at New Jersey Nick, who nodded his understanding, and throttled the engines back to 1100 RPMs, as Amato gave a one-word acknowledgement, "Roger."

A seaplane roared overhead and glided to a landing just ahead of the boat. Nick maneuvered the Crabby Old Man within a few feet of the plane and L'il Augie took his small grip and prepared to transfer.

Nick shook hands with his boss, wished him luck, and, almost as an afterthought, asked while gesturing in Manny's direction, "What do you want me to do with this punk?"

He turned to the boy and said, "There are two ways to do this. You can tell me your PIN#, or my friend Nick, you remember him, will just remove your right hand, and I'll take that with me."

Manny gave up the code.

L'il Augie tossed his satchel to the pilot who was now standing on the starboard float, turned and gave the kid a final once over, and said, "Sweat him and find out what he was up to, and then put him on ice. He might be of some value yet."

Amato clambered over the gunnel and onto the Pelican. He climbed inside, buckled up and the engines sputtered to life. After a thirty second run, the aircraft's landing pontoons achieved a brief plane across the surface of the ocean and then lifted off. It was out of sight one minute later.

Manolo chose this moment to make his plea of mistaken identity and innocence, "Mister, I don't know who you think I am, but believe me, you've got the wrong guy."

At least that is what he had intended to say, but before the last words cleared his mouth, Nick, with practiced form and power, delivered a sudden backhand to Manny's right jaw which sent him skidding across the deck. Without even looking away from the helm, he snarled, "When I want any conversation from you I'll beat it out of you!"

Manny, after the sudden blow sent him sprawling, opened his eyes to find his own private set of stars and even a few new constellations dancing before him despite the glare of the noonday sun. He concluded the situation in which he now found himself was the result of his infatuation with a pretty girl, and he recalled JPB's warning to Fiona, "Girl, don't let dis moon and dis boy get you dead."

This Christmas had started so strong with the girl and the moon and the French lessons, but now the girl and the moon were nowhere to be seen, and he was left with this ill-tempered giant, alone to find his way home, by these new stars and on his own.

The Crabby Old Man's engines brought it to a smooth plane and Nick pointed the craft south. He activated the GPS navigation system, selected a stored set of coordinates labeled Boynton Inlet, and without a sextant or the evening star for reference, the boat's auto-piloting program began steering its computer calculated track to port.

Freed of steerage duties, Nick turned and glared at the boy crumpled at his feet, and said, "You were saying something about believing you and the wrong guy? Let me tell you a little secret. I don't believe you, and, speaking of wrong guys, you've picked the wrong guy to try this bullshit on."

 The Milk Carton Kids – The Hope of a Lifetime:
https://www.youtube.com/watch?v=mEIKrwct1jQ

Willis sat in gob smacked silence for a moment before Maggie could penetrate his stupefaction, "Big Brother, are you in there?"

Willis slowly emerged from the fog, withdrew his cell phone, and discreetly dialed Johnny. Among the rules enforced by the hotel was a total ban of cell phones within The Circle restaurant, so this etiquette, added to the secrecy which lately had permeated his every move, necessitated quick and quiet communication. "Johnny, ten minutes ago I saw the cops grab L'il Augie, and haul him out of The Breakers in handcuffs."

Johnny celebrated at his end with a series of whoops and hops, and, noticing that he still wore his slightly scuffed black dress shoes, he said, "I feel like dancing!"

Willis interrupted his revelry, "I did too, but…"

Johnny held his breath as he waited for the other shoe to fall.

Willis resumed, "That was until I looked up from my Eggs Benedict to see a guy in scuba gear, who looks just like him walking into the surf behind The Breakers. I'm afraid we've been suckered. Do you think he might have a look-alike on the payroll?"

"You don't get to be a Don by being stupid." Johnny said.

"Yeah, plus there is that text about the Fourth Window protocol. I think we missed the obvious – he was talking about the Fourth Window Reef. Willis paused a moment, and in a voice filled with dread, he said, "I'm afraid that instead of going to jail, he sent somebody else, and that gangster just left town."

EPILOGUE

O n Christmas Day and at 42,000 feet, Anna-Sophia took her IPA and joined Hercules on the piano bench in the first-class lounge of Delta's 747 service to Istanbul as he idly played, with his left hand, the base line to a composition he had been fiddling around with for years. "Well, I for one am happy this year is almost over. Are you ever going to finish that tune?"

Herc replied, "Oh I have several finishes already written in my mind, but I really enjoy having the option to take it down a path less traveled if I want."

She listened while he played a couple of the alternate melody endings, and then she switched topics, "I'm still a little worried about Manolo, but Fiona says she has had several texts from him, his little brother snuck away on a ski trip and had a bad spill. Manny wants to appraise the severity of his injuries before exciting his parents."

Herc replied, "Believe me, Fiona will monitor that situation."

Anna-Sophia smiled and said, "Young love, so sweet."

She effortlessly changed subjects again, "We have had some adventure in the last few days. You were quite the leader of our merry band. That gangster really never stood a chance against you, did he?"

"Oh, I think he made a couple of common mistakes early," Herc said, "I would phrase it more along the lines of, 'He never stood a chance against we.' He's gotten used to winning and was over-confident, and we were fortunate a couple of times, and everyone on the team delivered. How would you like to run into an angry Jean Pierre Baptiste in a dark alley, or Corina Dare? But I think the game really turned on our knowledge of the battlefield."

"That and the massive overkill. By the end Senior Amato had no place to stand, so he had to run."

Herc grinned a little and replied, "First off, I've always thought overkill was under-rated, and second I'm not sure we've seen the last of L'il Augie."

Anna-Sophia acknowledged this wisdom by touching his beer glass with hers saying, "To overkill. But why was the knowledge of the battlefield so important."

Herc, sipped his brew and said, "Like Wellington at Waterloo, or Sitting Bull at Little Bighorn, we chose the place to fight."

"Why does that matter so much?"

Herc put his glass down, turned to face her, and said, "We could run without consulting a map, we had friends and sanctuary in the vicinity. Cars and boats and planes were on standby, and, most of all, we knew the character and nuances of these neighborhoods. Every little piece of insider information worked like a semi-permeable membrane which allowed us to pass through, while repelling the bad guys, and because they didn't have this knowledge, they had to take the long way round. Don't you see, it doesn't matter all where you've played before, Palm Beach is a brand-new game."

Anna-Sophia peered out the port porthole and said laconically, "Hercules, look. The sun is setting."

As he joined her at the window he said, "This is going to happen quickly. Think about this for a second, not only is the planet spinning toward us at about a thousand miles an hour, but we are making about 600 miles an hour in the opposite direction. We are heading toward this sunset at 1600 miles an hour – That's Mach 2 at least."

At 42,000 feet the view of the dimming horizon is massively expansive, and with nothing but sea between them and the Scottish coast, the Firth of Forth, and their destination, the city of Glasgow, the view was spectacularly unobstructed by clouds or land. As the last gleam of Christmas Day grew faint, a serene green sparkle briefly lighted the tableau as through a prism, or perhaps by the glimmer from the Emerald Ilse visible just short of the vanishing point. There was a final green ray which flickered and flashed, and then it was gone.

Sofi and Herc sat silent and euphoric for a moment, and then with the slightest melancholy, they asked in unison, "Did you see that?"

 Wendy and Lisa with Seal – At the Closing of the year: https://www.youtube.com/watch?v=I9EAqDe9DMI

The End…for now…

AUTHOR'S NOTE:

You, the reader may have noticed there are several threads of this tangled tale to still left to tug. "Is L'il Augie going to let this whole thing drop? The Caribbean has suddenly gotten thick with freshly renamed criminals – are we going to hear more from them? What about The Green Flash? Oh Yeah, What about Manolo Gonzales? Does he ever develop a taste for Stone Crab?

How did dawn's early light find Rocco and Mr. Lazette? And What about Johnny Dendy and Katie Callahan – could this be the start of something…?"

After a short respite to consider the wisdom of this endeavor, it seems likely that this story will be granted a continuance…

A teaser:

In response to Deputy Sheriff Denny Park's telephonic inquiry as to whether The Mic had been cleaned up, and was presentable enough to face the grand jury, the matron of the prison section of the hospital mentally ticked off the separate hygienic procedures the grimy thug she had been presented earlier that day, had endured. He had been not just bathed, but over his loud protestations, he had been thoroughly scrubbed. His three-inch beard was gone, his greasy hair had been washed and trimmed, he had been treated to the first manicure and pedicure of his life, and, as the cherry atop this creation, his nails had been polished and covered with a clear acrylic coating. As for haberdashery, the D.A. had relied upon Brooks Brothers, who for centuries has been making the slipperiest of witnesses and, for that matter, attorneys, appear trustworthy, and they had come through again. She inspected The Mic as he inspected himself in the full-length mirror. He sported a dark blue two button suit, a dazzlingly white button-down shirt, and he wore maroon braces to match a somber maroon necktie cinched in a double Winsor knot.

She proudly summarized his appearance in alliteration, "Yes sir. He has been buffed and puffed well past presentable. He has been showered, shampooed, shaved, shorn and shellacked. His own dear departed Irish Mum could only have said, "Ah Michael, I never woulda knew ya!"

"But sir, there remains a small problem. He still only has one shoe."

Addendum A

A Flash of Green
Musical Interludes

Lani Hall – Sundown Lady:
https://www.youtube.com/watch?v=FStTzPAOn5g

Grace Potter & the Nocturnals – Goodbye Kiss:
https://www.youtube.com/watch?v=MkLjw6j_9BQ

Laura & Anton - "La Vie En Rose"
https://www.youtube.com/watch?v=-NK9zdPj-os

Harry Nilsson – Moonbeam Song:
https://www.youtube.com/watch?v=btyelrNYCtU

Lake Street Dive – "What I'm doing here"
https://www.youtube.com/watch?v=lcUeothSPyc

Blood, Sweat & Tears – God Bless the Child:
https://www.youtube.com/watch?v=04rClGsbWp4

Brewer & Shipley – Seems like a long time
https://www.youtube.com/watch?v=cdCKjfVwfzc

Slim Wittman – The Prisoner's Song
https://www.youtube.com/watch?v=ym_sYjjw4bM

Tim O'Brien – Late in the Day
https://www.youtube.com/watch?v=RtfWq_ev3RE

Leo Kottke – Corina, Corina:
https://www.youtube.com/watch?v=VCg2VMtTF9c

Claudine Longet – Here, There, and Everywhere:
https://www.youtube.com/watch?v=Taj8TLbU6Zk

Willie Nelson – There's nothing I can do about it now:
https://www.youtube.com/watch?v=vAS5sbt-8yE

Grace Potter and Daryl Hall "The Things I Never Needed"
https://www.youtube.com/watch?v=ypwcitHSEQo

Over the Rhine – I want you to be my love:
https://www.youtube.com/watch?v=xNX1NAbZKW8

Nilsen, Lind, Holm, Fuentes – Hallelujah
https://www.youtube.com/watch?v=AdyTXBT5CQE

Pentatonix – Hallelujah
https://www.youtube.com/watch?v=LRP8d7hhpoQ

Fiddle Fever – Ashokan Farewell:
https://www.youtube.com/watch?v=oDkQ4FeooLA

The Band "It Makes No Difference"
https://www.youtube.com/watch?v=uSHzODm-Ik8

Brandi Carlile – Cannonball:
https://www.youtube.com/watch?v=tBYOECquvl0

Over the Rhine – Entertaining Thoughts:
https://www.youtube.com/watch?v=VZGZS0Qly80

Kacey Musgraves – High Time
https://www.youtube.com/watch?v=wO7qC-fD97c

Jimmy Buffet – Havana Day Dreamin'
https://www.youtube.com/watch?v=oJtVfBpMyW4

Charlie Daniels – Uneasy Rider:
https://www.youtube.com/watch?v=egGdseGTtII

Don Ho – The Hukilau Song
https://www.youtube.com/watch?v=oa4YdI97-PY

Joe Cocker – Just like a Woman:
https://www.youtube.com/watch?v=tfxLznYkpF0

John Mayer – "Daughters"
https://www.youtube.com/watch?v=rZLbUIa7exE

Scandal, Patty Smyth – Goodbye to you:
https://www.youtube.com/watch?v=_50-gOeBilc

Sergio Mendes & Brazil 66 – Mas Que Nada
https://www.google.com/?gws_rd=ssl#q=sergio+mendes+brasil+66

The Milk Carton Kids – The Hope of a Lifetime:
https://www.youtube.com/watch?v=mEIKrwct1

Wendy and Lisa with Seal – At the Closing of the year:
https://www.youtube.com/watch?v=I9EAqDe9DMI

ADDENDUM B

WILLIS LAIRD'S COMPATIBILITY QUIZ

1. Who was the greatest colligate basketball player of all time?
2. The number 714 has at least four iconic associations. List as many as you can. *Career home runs hit by Babe Ruth, Bastille Day (July 14ᵗʰ), the number stamped on Methaqualone, brand name* **Quaalude**, *Dragnet's Sargent Joe Friday's badge number.*
3. Who is David Clayton Thomas?
    Lead singer for the band Blood Sweat and Tears.
4. Where did you attend college if you're a hell of an engineer? *Ga. Tech*
5. Who is the spokesman for your generation? *Dylan, John Mayer, Bruce, Another?*
6. Leonard Cohen composed the song Hallelujah in 1984, and it has since been recorded scores if not hundreds of times. Which version in your opinion is the best?
7. Please use lucky number seven to ask your own question.
8. Would you rather Love or be Loved?
9. What is the most perfect dimension in sports? *Distance from home plate to first base.*
10. If you only had one song to convince a non-believer that Country Music was worth a listen, which song would you choose? *Hank Williams - Love Sick Blues, Hank Snow – A Fool such as I? Willie Nelson _ Whiskey River…*
11. If forced to give up one of these breakfast foods, which could

you most easily live without? *Orange Juice, Toast, Bacon, Eggs, Potatoes*

12. With which of the Stooges would you say I have the most in common? Which Stooge most closely resembles you?

CPSIA information can be obtained
at www.ICGtesting.com
Printed in the USA
BVHW081227050819
555098BV00026B/2010/P